PRAISE FOR LAURA GRIFFIN AND HER NOVELS

"I love smart, sophisticated, fast-moving romantic thrillers, and Laura Griffin writes them brilliantly."
— *New York Times* bestselling author Jayne Ann Krentz

"Gritty, imaginative, sexy! You must read Laura Griffin."
— *New York Times* bestselling author Cindy Gerard

"Top-notch romantic suspense! Fast pace, tight plotting, terrific mystery, sharp dialogue, fabulous characters."
— *New York Times* bestselling author Allison Brennan

"A gripping, white-knuckle read. You won't be able to put it down." — *New York Times* bestselling author Brenda Novak

"An emotional, exciting page-turner. Griffin deftly balances the mystery and the love story." — *The Washington Post*

"Griffin never disappoints with her exciting, well-researched, fast-paced romantic thrillers."
— *Publishers Weekly* (starred review)

"A high-adrenaline thriller that will keep you on the edge of your seat. . . . Griffin is a master." — *Fresh Fiction*

Titles by Laura Griffin

Standalone Novels
FAR GONE

LAST SEEN ALONE

The Texas Murder Files Series
HIDDEN

FLIGHT

MIDNIGHT DUNES

The Tracers Series

UNTRACEABLE

UNSPEAKABLE

UNSTOPPABLE

UNFORGIVABLE

SNAPPED

TWISTED

SCORCHED

EXPOSED

BEYOND LIMITS

SHADOW FALL

DEEP DARK

AT CLOSE RANGE

TOUCH OF RED

STONE COLD HEART

The Wolfe Security Series
DESPERATE GIRLS

HER DEADLY SECRETS

The Alpha Crew Series

AT THE EDGE

EDGE OF SURRENDER

COVER OF NIGHT

TOTAL CONTROL

ALPHA CREW:
THE MISSION BEGINS

The Glass Sisters Series
THREAD OF FEAR

WHISPER OF WARNING

The Borderline Series
ONE LAST BREATH

ONE WRONG STEP

The Moreno & Hart Mysteries,
with Allison Brennan

CRASH AND BURN

HIT AND RUN

FROSTED

LOST AND FOUND

LAURA GRIFFIN

MIDNIGHT DUNES

BERKLEY
New York

BERKLEY

An imprint of Penguin Random House LLC

penguinrandomhouse.com

Copyright © 2022 by Laura Griffin

Excerpt from *Vanishing Hour* copyright © 2022 by Laura Griffin

Penguin Random House supports copyright. Copyright fuels creativity, encourages diverse voices, promotes free speech, and creates a vibrant culture. Thank you for buying an authorized edition of this book and for complying with copyright laws by not reproducing, scanning, or distributing any part of it in any form without permission. You are supporting writers and allowing Penguin Random House to continue to publish books for every reader.

BERKLEY and the BERKLEY & B colophon are registered trademarks of Penguin Random House LLC.

ISBN: 9780593197387

First Edition: May 2022

Printed in the United States of America

1   3   5   7   9   10   8   6   4   2

Book design by George Towne

For Doug

CHAPTER

ONE

MACEY BURNS DROVE through the drumming rain, gripping the wheel until her knuckles were white.

"Are you here yet?" Josh asked.

"I'm running late," she told him over the phone. "I hit traffic leaving town and then it's been pouring the last two hours. I just crossed the bridge."

"It's—"

Noise drowned out his words.

"What?" she asked.

"It's a *causeway*. No one calls it a bridge here."

"I can barely hear you. Where are you?"

"At that bar I told you about, the one with the pool tables," he said. "You're going to love it."

Macey tore her gaze away from the highway to check the clock. It was almost eleven, and what should have been a four-hour drive had taken more than five.

"Sounds good, but not tonight. I haven't even found the house yet, and I still need to unpack the car."

"That's okay. I'm about to leave anyway. Where are you, exactly?"

"I think I may have missed the turn," she told him. "I just passed a sign that said, 'White Dunes Park, five miles.'"

"No, it should be coming up on your right. You'll see it."

Josh had been on the island all week scouting locations and already knew his way around.

"You need help unpacking?" he asked.

"I'm good."

"So, hey, heads up. I just found out that Channel Six is down here."

"Channel Six from San Antonio?"

"Yeah, Rayna and her crew. They're reporting on that woman who went missing two weeks ago. She disappeared without a trace."

Macey had read an article about it online. It was the type of story that normally would have captivated her attention, but she'd managed to push it out of her mind.

"We're not here to do news," she reminded him.

"No kidding. I just thought you'd want to know. In case you see them in town."

Rayna had once been Macey's fiercest rival, but that was months ago, before Macey walked away from her job and her life and the endless slog of the twenty-four-hour news cycle.

Her tires hit a slick patch, and she clenched the wheel. She didn't want to think about her old job right now. She just wanted to get to her destination. Her shoulders were in knots from the drive, and she wanted a glass of wine and a steamy shower.

"So, are we still on for tomorrow?" she asked Josh. "Nine o'clock?"

"Assuming the weather clears. No use scouting locations in the rain."

"It's supposed to be beautiful," she said. "Let's start on the north end. We can meet at my beach house."

Beach house. She pictured the sun-drenched deck overlooking the surf. She'd been daydreaming about it since she first found the listing.

"Sure you don't need help with the equipment?" Josh asked.

"I can handle it."

"Okay, well, see you tomorrow, then."

She ended the call and squinted through the swishing wipers at the sign up ahead: **White Dunes Park, 2 Miles.**

A strobe of lightning lit the sky, revealing empty fields on either side of the two-lane highway. She was well past the tourist center of Lost Beach, past the hotels and restaurants and T-shirt shops.

She hit a bump, and the car jerked right. Her heart skipped a beat as the Honda fishtailed and skidded. She clenched the wheel and tried to get control, but it careened onto the shoulder with a jaw-rattling *thunk*. She jabbed the brakes and slammed to a halt.

Macey blinked at the windshield, shocked. Her heart raced as she tried to catch her breath. The car was tilted, and the headlights illuminated a patch of weeds and a gravelly strip of shoulder.

Macey put the gearshift in park and shoved open the door. She started to get out, but the seat belt yanked her back. Unbuckling it, she slid out. Rain pelted her as she looked around in a daze.

What the hell had happened? One second she'd been driving along and the next second it was like aliens had seized control of the car. And she'd definitely felt a bump. Had she hit something?

Glancing at the road, she saw no other traffic. She retrieved her cell phone and slammed the door. Her wet flip-flops thwacked against the gravel as she walked around the front of the Honda and checked for damage. No dents. No sign of an animal.

She stopped beside the front bumper. The right tire was flat. "Crap."

She switched on her cell phone's flashlight and aimed it at the tire. Rain streamed down her face and neck. What now? She turned off the flashlight and called Josh, but he didn't pick up, so she sent him a text:

SOS! Flat tire. Call me.

A car raced past and sprayed her with water. She yelped and whirled around, but the driver didn't even slow. Cursing, she glanced up and down the highway. This end of the island was fairly desolate—mostly campgrounds and nature parks. She'd passed a marina, but that was a ways back.

When she'd planned her trip down here, she had wanted seclusion. After weeks of scouring listings, she'd been ecstatic when a long-term rental popped up on the island's north end, just footsteps from the beach. The idea of being away from town, surrounded by sand and waves and the soundtrack of nature, had been immensely appealing. But now she wasn't sure. Maybe she should have followed Josh's advice and rented an apartment in town for the summer.

Macey shivered and rubbed her bare arms, chilled from the rain despite the warm temperature. Her tank top and jeans were already soaked through, and she was out here alone and stranded.

I can handle it.

Ha. Famous last words.

She went back around the Honda and reached inside once again, this time to pop the trunk. It was a new-to-her car, and she didn't know the spare tire situation, but surely there was something in back. Macey had helped a boyfriend change a tire in college once. Well, maybe not *helped*, but she'd watched, and it had seemed pretty straightforward.

She tromped back to the trunk and slid aside the tripod and the suitcase filled with camera equipment. After finding the corner tab, she peeled back the layer of carpet.

Score! A spare tire, along with a heavy metal tool—a lug wrench?—and what had to be a jack.

But the spare seemed . . . off. She frowned down at the anemic-looking tire. Pressing her fingers against it, she confirmed her suspicion.

The spare was flat, too.

"Crap," she said again.

Macey checked her phone. Still nothing from Josh. She hated asking a man to rescue her, but it was freaking pouring, and she was out of options.

Another lightning strobe, followed by a clap of thunder. Then a jagged white bolt zapped down from above.

She looked up at the sky, awestruck. The ferocious beauty of it reminded her of why she'd been attracted to Lost Beach in the first place. She'd been lured by the film project, of course, which would pay her bills while she got her life sorted. But beyond that, she'd been attracted by the dramatic juxtaposition of nature and people. She'd been lured by the rugged Texas coast and one of the last long stretches of untamed beach and twenty-foot dunes.

Rainwater trickled down the front of her shirt, reminding her of her plight. She stared down at the useless tire.

Her trip was off to a rocky start. She wasn't superstitious—at least not usually—and she refused to take tonight as a bad omen. She was here for the entire summer, and no matter what happened, she planned to make the best of it.

A flash of light had her turning around. A pair of head-lights approached, high and wide apart, like a pickup truck. The truck slowed, and she felt a ripple of unease.

But maybe this was just what she needed—some Good Samaritan here to help her.

The truck rolled to a stop and the driver's-side door opened.

Macey squinted into the glare. Nerves fluttered in her stomach as a man got out. Tall, wide shoulders, baseball cap. She couldn't see his face, only his towering silhouette against the light as he walked toward her.

As he got closer, she saw that he was *very* tall—six-three, at least, and he easily outweighed her by a hundred pounds. Oftentimes Macey liked being short because people under-estimated her. This was not one of those times.

"Need a hand?"

The deep voice sent a dart of alarm through her.

"I'm good, thanks."

He continued moving toward her, and she took a step back.

"Is it your tire?"

She spied something in his hand, something black and bulky, like a club or—

A flashlight. He switched it on and approached the tire.

"It's fine," she said.

"It's shredded."

"I've got it handled, actually."

He took a step toward her, and she stepped back, clutch-ing her phone and wishing it was a tube of pepper spray. She kept one in her glove box for emergencies. She'd never needed it before, but of course now that she did, it was well out of reach.

He walked around her and aimed the flashlight at her trunk.

"Spare's flat, too."

She eased away from him, and he seemed to get the hint because he lowered the flashlight and stepped back.

"You need a ride?" he asked.

She stared at him. Did he seriously think she was going to climb into a truck with a complete stranger?

"My boyfriend's coming. He's on his way now. He's a mechanic," she added inanely.

The man watched her from beneath the brim of the hat. The shadows made it hard for her to make out his features, but he seemed to have a strong jaw. Beads of rain dripped from it as he stood there, looking her up and down. He was checking her out, she realized, and the back of her neck tingled.

She disappeared without a trace.

Macey's heartbeat thrummed as they stood there in the rain. He wasn't going anywhere. She'd told him she didn't need his help, and he was just standing there, looking at her.

A distant glow caught her eye as another car approached. She held her breath, watching as the low headlights drew near. Josh's ancient hatchback came into view, and she felt a rush of relief. He slowed and rolled past her, his taillights glowing as he pulled onto the shoulder.

"That's him!" Macey slammed the trunk with maybe a bit too much force in her hurry to put some distance between them. "Thanks for stopping!"

She strode toward the Toyota as the driver's-side door opened. Josh didn't get out right away, and she quickened her pace. Why hadn't he parked closer?

She glanced over her shoulder as the stranger trudged back to his truck without a backward glance.

"What the hell happened?" Josh asked as he got out.

"I had a blowout."

"How?"

"No idea. Maybe I hit something in the road."

Relief filled her as she took in Josh's familiar appearance—the ponytail, the scruffy goatee, the green army jacket. She reached up and hugged him.

"You okay?" he asked, clearly caught off guard. She wasn't a hugger.

"Fine. Thanks for coming."

He looked over her shoulder. "Who was that?"

"Some guy." She glanced back at the pickup as it pulled onto the highway. Shuddering, she watched it speed away.

"Shit, Mace." Josh walked toward her little blue Honda. "It's completely flat."

"That's what I told you."

"We're going to drown out here trying to change this."

"We can't." She strode past him. "The spare's flat, too. Here, grab a bag. You can give me a ride."

She opened the back door and reached for one of the two black duffels.

"You're just going to leave it overnight?" he asked.

"I don't know yet, but I'm definitely not leaving ten thousand dollars' worth of equipment on the side of the road."

Together, they hauled all the luggage to his car. He popped the back hatch, and they managed to squeeze everything inside. Then she went around to the passenger seat, where she shoveled fast-food bags and empty cups onto the floor.

"This is a pigsty," she said as she got in.

"Thank you, Joshua, for coming to get me in the middle of a thunderstorm," he said.

She yanked the door shut. "Thank you." She sighed. "I owe you."

"I'll add it to your tab," he said, starting the car. The engine made a little coughing sound before coming to life.

Maccy grabbed a Dairy Queen napkin from the cup

holder and squeezed rain from the ends of her hair. Josh looked over his shoulder, but the duffels blocked the view. He used the mirrors to check for traffic as he pulled onto the highway.

"You think there's a towing place open this late?" Macey asked.

"Who knows? You could look."

She used her phone to do a search.

"You're on Primrose, right?" he asked.

She glanced up. His car's wiper blades were in worse shape than hers, but she was able to make out a street sign up ahead.

"Yes, Primrose Trail. That's it there."

He hung a right onto a narrow caliche road that wasn't nearly as picturesque as the name implied. They passed a water tank and a clump of squatty palm trees, then a leaning wooden mailbox. Macey peered out the window, searching for the house that the mailbox belonged to, but it was hard to see past the overgrown vegetation.

The Toyota bumped along as they passed another mailbox. This house was closer to the road, a weathered wooden cabin on stilts. It was dark and empty-looking—maybe someone's weekend place. Macey leaned forward, searching for anything that resembled the little white bungalow that she'd fallen in love with on the website.

"I still don't get why you wanted to be all the way out here," Josh said.

"We came here for the beach. I want to be near it."

"Um, no. We came here to film commercials for the tourism board."

"Well, when we're not working, I plan to hit the beach."

"You'll burn to a crisp."

He wasn't wrong. With her strawberry blond hair and fair skin, she'd spent her whole life slathering on sunblock.

"Not to sunbathe," she told him. "I'll take pictures. Or do yoga. Or maybe take up running."

He lifted an eyebrow but didn't comment on the likelihood of her suddenly becoming athletic.

They hit a rut, and she braced her hand on the dashboard as they passed a dilapidated house on stilts, this one with a rusted boat trailer in the driveway.

An animal darted in front of the car.

"Cat!" she yelped.

Josh slammed on the brakes. "It's a possum."

"That was a cat."

He shook his head as the cat-possum disappeared into a clump of scrub brush.

"Seriously, Macey, this is the boondocks. Wouldn't you rather be in town, near all the hotels and shops and nightlife? Not to mention *people*?"

Ignoring him, she squinted through the rain-slicked windshield. Josh needed people; she didn't. In particular, he needed women and bars and things to do after work. Macey wasn't into all that anymore. She wanted peace and quiet, and a chance to get her life together after a hellacious spring.

A mailbox came into view, and she read the number.

"This is it," she said.

"This?"

"Yes."

He pulled into the driveway and parked.

Macey stared up at the little house on stilts. Peeling paint. Sagging gutters. A rectangular gray mark under the window where a flower box had once been. The place resembled the pictures just enough for her to know that this was, in fact, the house she'd rented for three months, for an unbelievably low rate that now seemed totally believable.

"It's a dump," he said.

She shot him a look. "It lacks curb appeal. So what?"

"You really rented this place? Like, you signed a contract and everything?"

"The inside is nice."

"Right."

"It is. I saw the photos." Macey pushed open the door and gazed up at the house through the veil of rain. "How bad could it be?"

CHAPTER

TWO

OWEN BREDA SPOTTED the flutter of yellow tape as he pulled into the campground. He swung toward the sand dunes, passing tents and RVs. The normally bustling campsites looked deserted, and folks had abandoned their fishing poles and campfire coffee to go check out the action.

Owen spotted McDeere near the first row of dunes, where a crowd of people had gathered. He was setting up a series of wooden barricades, which meant he'd probably been the one to tape off the scene. Owen parked beside his patrol unit and got out. The back of McDeere's khaki uniform was already soaked with sweat, and he turned around as Owen walked over.

"Morning."

Owen nodded. "Morning. You the first one here?"

"Emmet and Nicole are on the other side, talking to the kids."

"Kids?"

"Teenagers." McDeere wiped his forehead with the back of his arm. "I think the oldest one's sixteen."

Owen looked over McDeere's shoulder to the twenty-foot dunes. Some of them were white as snow. Others were covered in leafy green vines with tentacles that stretched to the flat part of the beach.

"They're in the Bowl?" Owen asked.

"Yeah. Looked like they were dune bashing when they lost control." McDeere rested his hands on his hips and turned toward the people milling near the barricades. So far, it looked like a mix of RVers, sunburned kids, and the usual array of wade fishermen who frequented this park every weekend. Most people were just gawking and craning their necks, but a few were holding up cell phones.

"No media yet," McDeere said, frowning at the crowd. He turned to face Owen. "Anything you want me to do?"

"Expand the perimeter," Owen said. "Give it a good twenty, twenty-five more yards. We need to corral all these people away from the dunes."

"Roger that."

"Then move the LBPD Suburban in front of the gap to block the view."

McDeere gave a sharp nod. "You got it."

"I'll send Emmet down to help you."

Owen trudged across the sand. It got deeper as he neared the hills, and he felt grit invading his boots, which meant he'd be dealing with it all day. He mounted a vine-covered rise and stood for a moment to survey the scene.

Tall white dunes made a concave formation the size of a basketball arena. Known as the Bowl, the place was a favorite for snowboarders, sledders, and the occasional idiot with a pickup truck. Two summers ago, some kids had flipped a Jeep here, and one of the passengers had been crushed to death.

At the bottom of the Bowl, a black SUV lay on its side like a wounded buffalo. Sun glinted off the side mirror. About thirty yards away, Nicole stood talking to a trio of boys. None of them looked old enough to drive, and maybe they weren't.

Owen shifted his attention to the opposite dune, where the department's lone CSI crouched on a blue tarp, taking photographs. Emmet was with her and glanced over as Owen walked toward them.

Emmet was dressed the same as Owen, in khaki tactical pants, all-terrain boots, and a navy Lost Beach PD golf shirt, his weapon and his detective's shield clipped to his belt.

"I hear you're the lead on this one," Emmet said.

"Yep." Owen nodded toward Miranda. "How's it looking?"

"Bad."

Owen studied his friend's eyes, trying to get a read. He looked again at Miranda crouched on the tarp with her camera. In addition to her typical white coveralls, today she wore a face mask, which gave Owen some idea of what they were dealing with.

Emmet nodded at the teens. "They're scared shitless. The one who was driving just got his license last week. If they hadn't flipped the vehicle, I doubt they would have even reported it."

"They local?" Owen asked.

"Yep. One of them's Marty Granger's son."

"The swim coach?"

"Yeah."

Owen turned to look at Miranda.

"Chief here yet?" Emmet asked.

"He's on his way." Owen looked at his friend. Owen still wasn't used to giving orders, and Emmet wasn't used to taking them. Not from him, anyway. Hard to take orders from someone who had been your drinking buddy since high school.

"McDeere could use a hand with crowd control," Owen said.

"Sure."

Emmet walked off, and Owen picked his way over to Miranda. Her light brown hair was pulled back in a tight bun. She glanced his way and lowered her camera.

"Hey," she said, lifting her gloved hand to shield her face from the sun.

"Hey."

The wind picked up and the stench hit him. Owen stepped back.

"It's bad, I know," Miranda said.

"How long you been here?"

"I just got started." She stood up and walked over, squeezing her eyes shut. "Sorry. I need a break." She pulled her mask down and swiped her forehead with the back of her arm.

Owen looked her over with concern. Miranda had spent the first six years of her career in San Antonio. Working a major metro area, she'd seen plenty of grisly crime scenes, and the fact that she needed a break this soon put a knot of dread in his stomach.

She smiled sheepishly. "Sorry."

"No problem. How's Joel?" Owen asked, hoping to distract her with a change of subject.

"I wish I knew." She sighed. "He was gone before I got up this morning. They had an early raid somewhere."

Owen's older brother had been tapped to join a multiagency task force targeting human trafficking in the region. Owen knew Joel liked the challenge, but the new role was causing tension with Miranda, who worried every time he donned a Kevlar vest before going to work.

Owen was happy for Joel. Before the task force, he'd been the department's senior detective, and he'd been battling burnout. It was good for him to get a change. Joel's absence put pressure on Owen and the other two detectives, though, and the high season was only just beginning, which always meant a spike in crime.

Owen had been hoping to get through this summer without a major case. But that hope had been obliterated—he checked his watch—eighteen minutes ago when he got this callout.

Miranda returned to the tarp and swigged from a bottle of water. "Okay." She set the bottle down and tugged her mask up. "I'm good now. You ready?"

"Yeah."

She crouched again, and Owen knelt beside her.

A bare arm protruded from the sand. A few inches away was an unmistakable tangle of human hair. The hair was brown and sandy, and flies buzzed around it.

Owen studied the arm. The flesh was blackened and putrid, and skin near the wrist had started to slough off. His gut clenched as he eyed the swollen fingers with glittery purple nail polish.

He turned away. "Damn."

"I know." Miranda gave him a sympathetic look, and Owen felt annoyed with himself.

"Any jewelry?" he asked, thinking of the description released by the sheriff's office. Twenty-five-year-old Julia Murphy had been reported missing sixteen days ago. She was thought to have been wearing a gold shamrock necklace when she disappeared.

"Not that I can see. Of course, I haven't touched anything. And it could be a while. I have a feeling the ME's going to want to bring in help."

"To remove the body?"

She nodded. "Not just remove. You're looking at an excavation here."

Emmet mounted a nearby dune and started trekking over. Owen stood.

"The ME's van just pulled in," Emmet reported.

Owen hiked to the top of the dune, where he had a view of the beachside campground with all its tents and RVs. Sun glinted off a pair of silver Airstreams parked near the police barricades. McDeere had expanded the perimeter, as directed, and he and another uniform were now standing guard and looking intimidating as onlookers continued to gawk and point. The ME's white van slid into a space between two police units.

"Shit." Emmet shook his head. "It's going to be a bad day, I can feel it. A bad summer."

"I was just thinking that."

The ME's assistants got out of the van and started zipping into white Tyvek suits.

Owen turned to Emmet. "We need to find the head park ranger. We need a list of every vehicle that's been here in the last four weeks. They book reservations by car, and we should be able to get license plates."

Emmet frowned. "You don't think it's the missing local woman? Julia Murphy?"

"Could be, but we can't assume. The victim might have been someone who was camping here. Or maybe the killer was."

"Looks like the chief is here."

Owen turned to watch as Chief Brady's white Suburban pulled into the campground.

"You gotta be kidding me," Emmet muttered. "Already?"

Owen surveyed the scene for the problem. A second white van rolled into the campground, this one with a satellite dish on top. Owen bit back a curse.

"That's Channel Six, all the way from San Antonio," Emmet said. "How the hell'd they get this so fast?"

"I don't know. But our bad day just got worse."

AN UNGODLY NOISE roused Macey from sleep. She lifted her head from the pillow, wincing at the impossibly bright light in her face. She turned her head, but it was no use. The light was everywhere, and the chorus of screeches intensified.

She threw back the comforter and swung her legs out of bed. Stepping to the window, she parted the curtains to see a flock of seagulls next door, swooping and circling above the neighbor's deck.

Macey combed a hand through her hair as she turned and surveyed the room. A disemboweled duffel lay on the floor near the door, T-shirts and towels scattered around it. Her rental cottage came furnished, but she'd had to bring all her own linens, which meant she'd been wrestling with sheets at one in the morning.

She stopped by the cottage's cramped bathroom, where she discovered that the rust-flavored water she'd brushed her teeth with last night hadn't miraculously improved. She avoided her reflection in the mirror as much as possible because it wasn't encouraging. Her eyes were still bloodshot from the tedious drive, and her skin looked pasty. Months of crap food, no exercise, and too little sleep were starting to take a toll, and part of her plan for the summer was to turn all that around.

But first, coffee. She retrieved a water bottle from her backpack and padded into the kitchen. She'd brought only the bare minimum of groceries, intending to hit the store after she got settled. Because she was an optimist, she'd packed a selection of Keurig pods. Because she was a realist, she'd also thrown in a bag of ground coffee and a pack of filters. The rental website had been short on information about the house's appliances.

Hope for the best and plan for the worst was her motto.

Macey grabbed the grocery bag and unpacked her coffee assortment on the counter as she scanned the kitchen. Microwave. Toaster.

"No way."

With a dart of panic, she started opening cabinets. She discovered pots, pans, and a collection of mismatched dishes. She opened the cabinet under the sink and yanked out the trash can. Nothing.

She whirled around and tried the pantry. The shelves were bare, except for a salt-and-pepper set and a half-empty bottle of steak seasoning.

With a last spark of hope, she grabbed a step stool and opened the cabinet above the refrigerator. Empty.

"Un-freaking-believable."

What kitchen didn't come equipped with a coffee maker?

She closed her eyes and took a deep breath. She could survive without coffee. Today. But now that she knew she couldn't have any, she could practically smell it in the air. She eyed the array of pods on the counter, and her mouth began to water.

A faint ringtone sounded from the bedroom, and she stalked back there to grab her jeans off the floor. Digging the phone from a pocket, she saw that it was Josh.

"How's your morning going?" he asked.

She swallowed a litany of complaints. He'd advised her against the beach house from the beginning, and she didn't want an I-told-you-so.

"Peachy," she said.

"Well, I'm about to throw a wrench in our plan. We're going to need to scratch the White Dunes Park field trip. There's some brouhaha going on right now, and they've got the access road blocked off."

"Oh." She dug through her backpack and found the half-finished bottle of Diet Coke she'd picked up at a gas station yesterday. Lukewarm, but at least it was caffeinated. "I was going to call you about that anyway. I have to deal with my car this morning, so we need to change the timing."

"What happened with your car?"

"It's at the shop."

"You got them to tow it?"

"'Them' implies a company." She took a swig of cola. "This is a one-man shop, Gil's, named after the owner. Gil was kind enough to return my message at eleven fifty-five, but he informed me that anything after midnight is an extra fifty."

"Nice."

"Anyway, I'm supposed to pick it up at ten. Any chance you can give me a ride over there?"

"Sure."

"Good." She headed back to the kitchen. "So, what's the brouhaha?"

"Some law enforcement thing. I was on the highway this morning, and I saw a park ranger and a cop turning cars away."

She went into the living room and peered through the dusty miniblinds. Her windows had a clear line of sight to the park, which was less than a mile north. But a layer of brine covered the windows, making it hard to see anything. She walked over and unlocked the door. Stepping onto the deck, she gazed down the beach, which was empty except for a couple of kids flying a kite.

"I don't see anything happening," she said. "But the dunes are pretty tall over there. What's going on?"

"No idea. But I was thinking we'd try another part of the island instead. I've got some ideas for Sunset Cove on the bay side. We can scope out the park tomorrow."

"Whatever you want. You can drop me off at Gil's at ten and we can go from there."

"You're assuming Gil gets it done on time."

"Good point. Let's make it eleven. We can check out the cove and then grab some lunch."

"Okay, call me if you hit a snag."

She hung up and stepped farther out onto the deck, a bit self-conscious in only her sleep shirt. The weathered deck looked out over the beach, and sunlight glimmered off the surf. She also had a terrific view of her neighbor's deck, where a portly man in Texas-flag board shorts stood at the railing, tossing something over the side. Whatever it was had the seagulls in a frenzy.

Macey cast another glance at White Dunes Park and went inside to dress. Returning to the bedroom, she surveyed the bags strewn about the floor. She checked her watch. Eight forty-five. Now would be a great time to unpack and get organized.

Some law enforcement thing.

Curiosity gnawed at her. White Dunes Park was less than a mile away. What could be happening to make police block the access road and turn cars away? She wanted to find out.

Macey changed into the stylish new running clothes she'd just spent a fortune on—not because she had a fortune to spare but because she knew spending the money would kick her butt into gear. That was the plan, anyway. She put on her sunglasses, locked the house, and zipped the key into the inside pocket of her shorts as she went downstairs.

A rickety wooden bridge spanned the vine-covered dune separating the row of houses from the beach. The sign posted beside the stairs warned of rattlesnakes, and she cast a wary glance around as she crossed the bridge.

Nothing about the rental house lived up to its description, with the very notable exception of the view. Looking north, she could see the island's famous white sand dunes, which stretched to the barrier island's northernmost tip. Turning south, she could see the town of Lost Beach, with its colorful houses and high-rise hotels.

Straight ahead was the water, blue and sparkly in the morning sun. A quartet of pelicans glided down and settled on a wave.

Macey paused on the bridge to watch. The pelicans were beautiful, and she knew she should be dreaming up some clever way to incorporate them into the ad campaign for the tourism board. Approximately thirty percent of Lost Beach visitors came to check out the island's nature preserve, which was home to more than three hundred species of birds.

After descending the steps to the beach, she stopped to stretch her quads—which made her think about the last time she'd run. It had been so long she couldn't remember.

She took a deep breath and turned her attention to White Dunes Park. From this vantage point, she could see a distant red Suburban, which in her experience usually meant the fire department. So, police, fire, and park rangers. What was going on?

She set off down the beach, focusing on her breathing as she tried to get into a rhythm. The wind was at her back, fortunately, but that meant it was going to be tougher later. But how far was she really going to run on day one? She had all summer to get in shape. She didn't need to go crazy.

Macey's breathing fell into a rhythm. She started to feel grit in her socks and veered closer to the water, where the sand was firmer. Setting her sights on the red Suburban, she plodded toward the park, going through scenarios as she jogged. People were definitely congregating. As she caught sight of several orange police barricades, her pulse picked up and she felt the familiar stirring of adrenaline.

A brawny cop in a khaki uniform stood with his arms folded over his chest beside one of the barricades, like a bouncer at a nightclub. Texas beaches were public and therefore open to foot traffic. But they weren't letting people through.

Macey noticed a flash of yellow crime scene tape, and her pulse picked up some more. Then she saw the windowless white van with the county seal on the door.

The ME was here.

Macey stopped and looked around, picking up details as her reporter's instincts kicked into gear. Local police, local fire, plus park rangers and county officials. She scanned the crowd, which looked to be mostly people from the campground and some beachcombers who'd wandered up.

Her gaze snagged on a cap of red hair.

Rayna.

The reporter had pinned her hair up in a futile effort to keep it in place amid the wind gusting off the Gulf. She wore the TV reporter attire known as "business on top, party on the bottom," which in this case meant a white blouse and black blazer over jeans and flip-flops. She held a microphone in her hand as she read from a notepad and talked to her cameraman, Ron. They were between takes, apparently.

Macey scanned the scene again. The bouncer was at the other end of the crowd now, talking to a park ranger. Without really making a plan, Macey hurried to the end of the row of barricades. She cast a furtive glance over her shoulder and then skirted around the barrier. Nerves flitted in her stomach as she darted around a sand dune and scampered up a rise. The sand was deep here, and her sneakers instantly filled. The low hill led to a taller one, and she knew this campground marked the beginning of twenty-four miles of sugary white dunes. Most of that area was protected, and only the south end of the park was frequented by people. She spied a gap between dunes and walked through, picking her way over the carpet of leafy vines and purple morning glories. She found herself staring at a vast bowl of sand.

Macey stopped and caught her breath. The white hills surrounding her looked otherworldly. The sand bowl was empty with the bizarre exception of an overturned sport-utility vehicle. Tracing her gaze along the nearby tire marks, she deduced that the driver had essentially been skiing along the dune—which was no doubt illegal—when the vehicle flipped. Had someone been killed, hence the ME?

A flash of color caught her eye. She walked farther into the bowl. Up at the top of a dune was a blue tarp. From her low vantage point, Macey didn't have much of a view, but people in coveralls and face masks crouched together. The row of big white buckets beside them sent a chill down Macey's spine.

Buckets meant sifting. Not good.

Macey stood there in the sweltering heat, watching them. Sweat trickled down the back of her neck. She rubbed it and realized she'd forgotten sunblock.

"Hey."

She whirled around.

A tall man strode toward her. He was a cop, judging from the badge and gun at his hip, and he didn't look happy.

"This is a restricted area."

She opened her mouth to respond, but nothing came out.

He stopped in front of her, blocking out the sun with his wide shoulders. Frozen in place, she tipped her head back to look at him as he frowned down at her.

"What are you doing back here? Didn't you see the barricade?"

"I—" She didn't want to lie to a cop, so she focused on the first question. "I was just out for a run." She gestured casually toward the dune. "I noticed some people up there, and I wanted to see what the fuss was about."

Macey saw her smiling reflection in his aviator sunglasses. She couldn't tell whether the clueless-tourist act was working.

"This whole area is restricted." He peeled off the shades, giving her the full effect of his stern-cop look.

The effect was powerful. His vivid blue eyes pinned her in place, and she couldn't think of a reply.

"Are you camping here?" he asked.

"No." She cleared her throat. "I'm renting a beach house, actually."

"You run every morning?"

She blinked up at him. He was questioning her now like a witness, not someone trespassing on a crime scene.

"Whenever I can," she said.

He hooked the shades into the collar of his navy golf shirt, and she noticed the Lost Beach PD crest on the front. He also wore sand-colored tactical pants and boots—very military-looking—and she figured this was his police uniform, modified for the island's rugged terrain.

"What's your name?" he asked, pulling out a notepad.

"My name?"

"Yeah." He flipped open the pad. "We're canvassing the area, interviewing people."

"Macey Burns." She watched his eyes. If he recognized the name, he didn't show it.

"You see anything suspicious in the park lately, Ms. Burns?"

"No. What happened, exactly?"

"I can't comment on that."

"I saw the ME's van. Was there a homicide?"

He glanced up, pinning her again with those blue eyes.

"I can't comment."

"I read about that missing person's case, so I was wondering if it might be related."

His brow furrowed. "Are you a reporter?"

"No. I just thought it might be related. Is it?"

O WEN STARED DOWN at her. Macey Burns was getting on his nerves, and he was pretty sure she knew it.

The last time he'd seen her she'd been rain-soaked and skittish. Now she was flush-cheeked and pushy, asking a bunch of questions that he wasn't about to answer.

She gazed up at him with those big green eyes all wide and innocent, like he hadn't caught her snooping around an active crime scene. He could have arrested her, or at least threatened to, but he had about a thousand other things that needed his attention right now. Which made him wonder why the hell he was wasting his time standing here in the blazing sun.

"How's your tire?" he asked.

Her eyebrows arched. "My tire?"

He smiled. "You don't recognize me, do you?"

Her mouth fell open. Then her eyebrows made a V. "That was *you*?"

"Yeah."

Her cheeks got pinker and she looked offended. "You're a *cop*."

"I know."

"Why didn't you say so last night? You scared me half to death!"

His smile faded at that. He'd meant to help her, not scare her.

"Did everything work out? You seemed to have it handled."

"I did." She folded her arms over her breasts. "Gil gave me a tow, so, you know, it's fine now."

He looked her over, taking in the running shorts, the shoes. Her strawberry blond hair was pulled back in a ponytail. She was in very nice shape, but if she ran regularly, it had to be on a treadmill, because her pale shoulders hadn't seen the sun lately.

"Breda."

Owen glanced up. Emmet stood at the top of the hill, waving him over.

He tucked his notebook into his pocket and pulled out a business card.

"Where are you staying, Ms. Burns?"

"Down the beach." She watched warily as he wrote on the back of the card. "Why?"

"Where down the beach?"

"Right before the Easter egg houses."

He glanced up. "Easter eggs?"

"The pastel-colored beach mansions. I'm the neighborhood just north of that. Primrose Trail."

"In answer to your question, we're investigating a suspicious death."

She looked surprised that he'd volunteered this information, but he wasn't telling her anything that wouldn't be all over the news in about five minutes if it wasn't already.

He handed her the card. "If you remember anything you may have seen here in the area that could be suspicious, give me a call. My number's on the back there."

She glanced down at the card. "You're a detective?"

"That's correct."

She looked up at him.

"Call me if you think of anything," he said.

"I will."

"And be sure to lock your doors."

CHAPTER

THREE

The station house was typically busy on a Saturday, but today they were especially slammed. Owen made his way past the crowd of reporters milling near the flagpole, ignoring questions lobbed in his direction as he pulled open the door.

The reception area was crowded, too, with wilted-looking people occupying the line of chairs along the wall. The receptionist was on the phone, and she caught Owen's eye as he walked in. Owen glanced through the glass partition that divided the reception area from the rest of the station.

"He in?" Owen asked Denise, knowing she'd understand he meant the chief.

"Conference room," she said and buzzed him in.

Owen entered the bullpen, which was noticeably cooler than reception and a good thirty degrees colder than outside. A quick scan of the cubicles told him the team meeting had already started. Still, he took a second to swing by his desk and grab a protein bar from the drawer. He hadn't eaten since a soggy sandwich five hours ago.

McDeere was at his desk on the phone, but he looked to be on hold.

"When'd they start?" Owen asked as he walked by.

"'Bout fifteen minutes ago."

Owen chomped into the protein bar and ducked into the break room to snag a bottle of water from the fridge. He wolfed down his snack before stepping into the conference room.

Emmet, Nicole, and Miranda sat around the table with the chief. Everyone looked sunburned and tense.

Nodding at the chief, Owen pulled out an empty chair at the end.

"So, that's it," Emmet was saying. "Nothing jumps out, but I haven't run through the list and done any background checks yet. I can get started on that tonight."

Chief Brady listened silently, his arms folded over his chest. He had a white buzz cut and the leathery skin of a man who spent as much time as possible on his fishing boat.

"You get three weeks' worth of records?" the chief asked.

"Four." Emmet turned to Owen. "No white Volkswagens registered at the campground recently."

Julia Murphy drove a white Volkswagen Jetta that had been missing since her disappearance. Owen hadn't really expected to find a record of it at the campground. He'd been thinking more about the vehicle of her killer. The vehicle list was going to require some research.

"How's it going at the park?" Brady asked.

"They just finished." Owen checked his watch. "The ME's team packed it in about twenty minutes ago." As Miranda had predicted, they had taken one look at the crime scene and decided to call in help. A total of four people from the medical examiner's office had spent almost eight hours excavating the body and sifting through endless buckets of sand from in and around the grave site.

Miranda had taken photographs and helped bag evidence. Even with a tent for shade, it was a hot and tedious task. Not to mention smelly.

"What happened with the drone?" Nicole asked Owen.

Brady frowned. "What drone?"

"There was a camera drone hovering over the crime scene," Nicole told him.

"When?"

"Late this afternoon. It crashed into a sand dune."

"Don't tell me it was from one of the TV stations." Brady shot Owen a look.

"Doubtful," he said. "This thing looked pretty cheap to me."

"We were waiting to see who might come retrieve it," Nicole said. "Was it still there when you left?"

"Still there. A park ranger has got an eye on it. He'll let us know if someone comes to get it."

They still had the scene taped off and park rangers stationed there to keep the tourists out until they were certain there was nothing left to recover. It would end up being a judgment call—with a wide-open outdoor crime scene, there was no way of knowing for sure.

"Okay, anything else from the park rangers?" Brady asked Emmet.

"That's it for now."

He turned to Miranda. "Tell me about the forensic evidence."

Miranda took a deep breath. "As I mentioned earlier, no clothing on the body. There were some items recovered near the grave site—a sandal, some fabric remnants—but it's unclear whether they belong to the victim."

"What do you think?" Brady asked her.

It was a high compliment. Brady didn't ask for opinions from people he didn't respect. Miranda had come to Lost Beach PD from one of the biggest jurisdictions in the state, and her training was top-notch. Plus, she had good instincts, which she'd proven over and over in the year since she'd joined the department full-time.

"The fabric remnants look too old to me, and they were found pretty far from the body," Miranda said. "The leather sandal was closer, but it's cracked and sun bleached. However, it was sitting on top of the sand, in full sun, so that speeds up damage. There's a possibility it could be hers. We'll want to find out Julia Murphy's shoe size."

"Seven."

All eyes turned to Owen.

"It's in the file," he said.

Owen had compiled a file on Julia Murphy after her sister came to the station and filled out a missing person's report. The file included everything they had on the missing twenty-five-year-old, down to the date of her last traffic ticket. Key details, such as her vehicle and physical description, had been passed along to other nearby law enforcement agencies so they could help publicize her disappearance.

"I'll take another look at the shoe," Miranda said. "Or the photograph, rather—the shoe is at the crime lab. I used a ruler for scale, so I should be able to determine the shoe size and get back to you."

"Anyone find any jewelry?" Nicole asked. "The description of Julia Murphy included a gold necklace."

"With a shamrock pendant," Owen said.

Miranda shook her head. "I didn't see anything like that."

"What else?" Brady asked. "I saw a whole tub of evidence bags."

"Some of that stuff's junk," Miranda said. "Sun-bleached soda cans, plastic bottles, candy wrappers. But we *did* find several cigarette butts, which could be helpful."

Cigarette butts meant DNA.

"Near the body?" Brady asked.

"Under it."

"*Under* it?"

"Yes, in the sand that was sifted after the body was removed. Two cigarette butts."

Owen pictured some guy leaning on a shovel, taking a smoke break after digging a hole. It was a dumbass thing to do, but Owen was constantly amazed by the stupidity of some criminals. And the arrogance.

"What brand?" Emmet asked.

"Marlboro Lights." Miranda looked around the table. "I've got photos of everything. I plan to upload those tonight, so you'll be able to look through."

The door to the conference room opened and Denise leaned her head in. "Sorry to interrupt, Chief. There's a reporter on the phone from the *Houston Chronicle*. He said you told him you'd call him before four?"

It was almost five.

"Tell him ten minutes."

Denise ducked out.

"That brings me to the other thing," Brady said. "Anyone talk to any media?"

Emmet and Nicole shook their heads.

"Miranda?" the chief asked, probably because her sister worked for a newspaper in Austin.

"I haven't talked to anyone."

The chief shifted to him. "Owen?"

"Nope. No media."

Just some nosey tourists. He thought of Macey Burns with her flushed cheeks and her pretty green eyes.

"No talking to reporters." Brady glanced around the table. "Everyone got that? I won't tolerate leaks. The last thing we need is some reporter putting details out there about what we're doing and botching up the investigation. All media requests need to go through Denise to me."

Everyone nodded.

Brady checked his watch. "One more thing, and then I know we all have plenty more to do tonight. The autopsy is scheduled for oh nine hundred."

Owen felt a stab of irritation.

"I thought it was tonight," Nicole said. "They told us—"

"The ME wants to do it himself," Brady said. "He's on his way home from Dallas right now."

The fact that the ME wanted to do it instead of handing it off to his deputy told Owen he understood the level of scrutiny this case was likely to get, both in the media and in a courtroom someday.

"I'll go," Owen said.

"You sure?" Brady asked. "You covered the last one."

"I don't mind," he said, even though driving to and from the ME's office to observe the autopsy was going to eat up a good chunk of his day. The county seat was an hour away.

"I'd like to go, too," Nicole said. "With so little evidence at the crime scene, the body is likely to be our best bet."

"Both of you go," Brady said. "Emmet can cover things here." He checked his watch again. "Okay, that should do it. We'll reconvene here at oh seven hundred. And get some rest. Tomorrow's a big day."

M ACEY WATCHED THE hazy purple clouds as dusk fell over the beach. She checked her watch and made a mental note of the time. Over the coming days and weeks, she planned to learn the light patterns across the island, and dusk on the beach was one of the most important.

"Tomorrow morning I've got a meeting with Jim Conklin," Josh said over the phone.

Macey grabbed her half-finished beer off the railing and crossed the deck, watching for splinters because she'd already gotten one lodged in her toe.

"Remind me who that is again?"

"Town councilman," he said. "He was on that conference call with the mayor."

"He sounds like a suit."

"He is."

"That's boring," she said. "I thought we were looking for local color."

"He owns a charter boat company in town."

"Still sounds boring."

"They rent fishing boats and sailboats. That's color. And he offered to set up a free charter for us. I mean, come on. Could be great film."

"True," Macey said. And anything that didn't add to their costs was a plus. They were doing this project on a tight budget and couldn't afford to turn down freebies. "Okay, so you're meeting with Jim tomorrow. And I've got a five o'clock with the Turtle Lady, Olive Albrecht."

"Now *that* sounds boring."

"It absolutely isn't. She's been monitoring sea turtle nests for fifty years here on the island. I hear she gets out there before sunrise to shoo away poachers."

"I'm asleep already."

"She'll be colorful, trust me." Macey opened the fridge and searched for dinner options. "Anyway, it's only a pre-interview. If there's nothing good there, we'll drop it."

"I'll let you take that one. I have a surf lesson."

"Since when do you surf?"

"Since never. That's why I have a lesson."

She grabbed a low-fat salad kit and tossed it on the counter beside her full-calorie beer.

"So, hey, are we still on for later?" Josh asked. "Drinks at Finn's? It's just down the beach from you."

"Depends how my unpacking goes."

"Put it off till tomorrow and come to Finn's."

"Maybe."

"You're going to like this place. I promise. It's got a good vibe."

"In other words, it's a meat market."

"It's not a meat market. And they have three-dollar drafts tonight."

"*You* should definitely go, then. I might join you."

"What have you got against meeting people?"

"Nothing. I'll text you if I can make it."

She managed to get off the phone without further badgering and then put together her salad.

Macey took her dinner outside. The deck's furniture consisted of a trio of plastic chairs that had been stacked beside the door when she'd unlocked the house last night. She dragged one of the chairs to the edge of the deck and propped her feet on the railing. Looking out over the surf, she picked at her salad. It was almost dark, and the moon was hidden by clouds, so she couldn't really see the beach. But she liked the idea of it being there, just footsteps away from her, and she loved the sound of the waves churning against the sand.

Macey looked toward the park. Lights glowed in some of the RVs, and several campfires flickered. Were people sitting around drinking and making s'mores right now, only a stone's throw away from where just this morning a dead body had been found?

Or were they huddled around the fire, talking nervously and making plans to cut short their vacations?

Watching the campfires, Macey stifled a shudder. She'd been checking her phone all day, but the headlines hadn't been updated since late morning. Body Discovered in White Dunes Park.

That was basically the story, along with conjecture about the young woman who had gone missing more than two weeks ago. After five years in the news business, Macey was a pro at reading between the lines, and she knew that all the tittering speculation was just that. Not a single reporter had managed to nail it down. They hadn't even confirmed the sex of the victim yet.

She pictured Owen Breda, with his piercing blue eyes and his tight jaw.

I can't comment on that.

He was good at stonewalling, especially for someone on a small-town police force that probably didn't deal with the media very often. But stonewalling could only get you so far, and it was just a matter of time before some tenacious reporter cultivated a chatty source inside the department. People talked. It was human nature. And even the toughest law enforcement types weren't immune to a well-placed compliment and a flirty smile. Macey had made a career out of developing sources, and she knew all the tricks.

She cast another look up the coast. The emergency vehicles had been parked there all day. Tonight's news had shown masked-up workers loading a body bag on a stretcher into a van as sunburned tourists looked on. The contrast was jarring, as it was meant to be. Like everyone else watching, Macey was beset by grim thoughts. Had the victim been shot? Stabbed? Bludgeoned? Macey knew full well that graphic footage was meant to get her to tune in later to learn more. But even knowing she was being manipulated, she couldn't help being reeled in. With the crime scene just footsteps away, the whole thing was impossible to ignore.

Macey went inside with her empty plate. She still felt hungry, and her mind flashed back to the burger joint she'd passed in town this afternoon. Chuck's. Or was it Chip's? The place had looked like a total dive, but their deck had been packed with tourists, which had to be a good sign.

On the other hand, she hadn't busted her butt jogging this morning only to throw it all away on a greasy burger.

No, she'd spend her evening unpacking, as planned. She needed to set up her editing room. And if she got enough chores done, maybe she'd meet Josh for a drink later.

She looked under the sink for a recycle bin but didn't see one. She checked the cabinet beside the fridge.

"Eek!"

She jumped back. A rat stared up at her from the shelf.

Dead, she realized. The little gray animal was caught in a trap. And on closer inspection, it looked more like a mouse.

Shuddering, she grabbed a paper towel and picked up the trap. Holding it as far away from her body as possible, she dragged out the trash can and dropped the carcass on top. Another shudder went through her, and she grabbed the plastic drawstrings, tied the bag, and strode straight out the front door. Rusty water, she could deal with. Missing appliances, fine. But rodents were a whole other story.

She rushed down the stairs. The front yard was dark except for a square of light spilling down from her bedroom window. Overgrown bushes and a fence separated her house from both neighbors, and she paused a second to get her bearings before hurrying to the side yard where she'd seen the trash can. She lifted the lid.

A shadow moved near the bushes. She froze.

Was someone there? She pictured her shirtless neighbor with the beer gut. His house was dark, and the driveway was empty. She'd assumed he was out for the evening.

She dropped the bag into the can, cringing as it landed with a loud clatter. The shadow moved again, this time at the end of the driveway.

Maybe it was the cat from last night. Or the possum—whatever.

An animal darted across the street and into some bushes.

"Hey there."

She gasped and whirled around. A man stood in the shadows at the edge of the yard. Tall, big. Her heart lurched as he stepped closer.

"Macey Burns?"

Detective Breda.

FOUR

S HE RECOGNIZED HIM as he moved into the square of light on the driveway.

"God, you did it again."

He stepped closer. "Did what?"

"You scared me to death." She looked down and realized she was clutching the trash can lid like a shield. She dropped it on the can. "What are you doing here?"

"Canvassing your street."

"Canvassing."

He stopped in front of her, gazing down at her with concern. "Are you all right?"

"Yes." She sighed. "Just a little pest removal."

He frowned, and she looked him over. He was dressed the same as before, including the serious-looking pistol holstered at his side. A Smith & Wesson M&P40, probably. Those were standard issue with many police departments across the state.

She glanced up at him. His sunglasses and hat were

gone, and his longish brown hair looked windblown, as though he'd been outside in the heat all afternoon.

"Would you like to come up?" she asked. "I'm guessing you've had a long day. If you're thirsty I've got beer, Gatorade, Diet Coke."

"Thanks, I'm good. I just have a few questions for you."

She walked around him and led him to the stairs, self-conscious now that she realized she had company for the very first time. Josh hadn't even been here yet except to help carry her bags up the stairs and drop them inside the door. How strange that her first visitor would be a cop.

His footsteps were heavy behind her, and she thought about their size difference once again. She'd invited him into her house. The circumstances weren't much different from last night. She was alone with a perfect stranger who outweighed her by a hundred pounds. Plus, he was armed.

She paused at the door and turned to look at him.

Now that she knew he was a cop, she saw him in a different light. His forceful tone of voice, his commanding presence—all that seemed less threatening now and more protective.

"We can talk out here," he said, probably mistaking her hesitation for fear.

"Inside is fine. Or outside. Whatever." She cleared her throat. "Sure you don't want a drink? I'm getting one."

He nodded. "I'll take some water, then."

"Sure."

She went inside, and he stayed out on the deck. Macey grabbed her phone from the counter and tucked it into the pocket of her cutoff shorts. Then she retrieved a pair of water bottles from the fridge. On her way back out, she snagged a hoodie from the back of the chair—not because she was cold but because she was wearing a snug-fitting tank top, and she didn't like men staring at her boobs while she talked to them. At least, not under these particular circumstances. She zipped into the hoodie and stepped outside.

He stood at the far end of the deck now, looking out at the beach.

Macey walked over and handed him the bottle of water. "Rust-free," she said.

He smiled, and she felt it down to the soles of her feet. *Whoa*.

"I take it they didn't warn you about the tap water when you rented the place?" he asked.

"Nope. Same for the little rodent problem."

He shook his head, and she watched him. The porch light cast his face in a dramatic shadow, emphasizing his sharp cheekbones and strong jaw. With his powerful build and chiseled features, he could have been a lead actor in an action film.

"What is it?" he asked.

She'd been staring. "Nothing." She sipped from her water bottle. "So. Canvassing all the way down here, huh?"

"That's right."

"You talking to everyone?"

Something flickered in his eyes, and she wondered what she'd said.

He twisted the top off the water bottle and took a long swig, then set it on the railing.

"Just covering the bases," he said.

She watched him, trying to place why she suddenly felt uneasy. It seemed like he was being evasive about something.

Well, he was being evasive about *everything*. He'd hardly told her a damn thing this morning, other than that police were investigating a suspicious death. He hadn't even confirmed that the victim was a woman.

"So, Ms. Burns—"

"Macey."

He hesitated and nodded. "How are you liking the house?"

"It's fine." She shrugged. "A little more rustic than advertised, but I like the location. Well, except for the swarm of emergency workers today. But I'm guessing that's a pretty rare occurrence, right?"

She was trying to keep things light, but he just looked at her.

"And you rented the house when?" he asked.

"Rented it? A week ago. I've got it through the summer."

His eyebrows arched. "Through when, August?"

"I have to be out by September first."

"And you found it through the website? Sand N Surf Rentals?"

"Yep."

"Are you staying here by yourself or—"

"Yep. Just me."

He gazed down at her, and she felt uneasy again, although she wasn't sure why.

"You know, your road here is pretty isolated," he said. "You notice any cars driving down it that looked like they didn't belong?"

"No."

"Any people who seemed out of place? Anyone suspicious?"

"No. But I haven't spent much time here. I was out part of the day, and I just arrived last night."

"Last *night*?"

"Yeah, my rental started Sunday, but I couldn't get down until yesterday so"—she shrugged—"you could say I'm the new kid on the block."

She sensed his disappointment. Evidently, he'd been hoping she might have some neighborhood gossip, or at least observations to share with him.

"Sorry." She smiled. "Wish I could be more helpful."

"No, that's good."

He gazed down at her, and the look in his eyes put a warm tingle in the pit of her stomach. She tried not to squirm or shift, or do something revealing, like stare at his mouth. He was extremely attractive, and he probably knew it, too. He was a detective, after all. And even if he hadn't been, he'd have to be utterly clueless not to know the effect he had on women.

"Was there anything else you wanted to ask me?"

For a long moment, he simply looked at her.

"That covers it," he said.

She nodded.

Without a word, he picked up his water bottle and headed for the stairs. Pausing at the top, he turned and glanced over her shoulder at the house.

"Good luck with your canvassing," she said. "I hope you get some leads."

He nodded. "Stay safe, Ms. Burns."

"It's Macey," she reminded him. "And I will."

THE DRONE WAS gone.

Nicole shined her flashlight at the sand dune.

"You sure that's the right spot?"

She looked over her shoulder at the park ranger who was supposed to have been watching the crime scene overnight. Specifically this dune, where police had intentionally left the crashed drone in the hopes that its owner would come looking for it. Flying a camera drone over a scene swarming with cops showed a certain level of interest in the crime. More than that, it showed arrogance. The drone's owner might be just some curious bystander with no real link to the crime.

Or maybe not.

But now they would never know, because the park ranger, Drew, had taken his eyes off the crime scene, probably in favor of watching the trio of beach bunnies he'd been chatting with when Nicole pulled in earlier this evening, just before sunset.

Sometime between sunset and now, the drone had disappeared.

"This is the place," Nicole said, aiming her flashlight beam at the very top of the dune. "See that evidence flag? I marked it. And when I did my last loop through the park, it was still there."

"Well, I didn't see anyone in and out of here, so maybe it just flew off."

Nicole shot him a look.

"It didn't just *fly off.*" She shifted her flashlight to Drew. She'd gone to high school with him, and he'd been lazy then, too, always goofing off in class and getting other people to do his homework. "The propellor was broken. Someone came and retrieved it, and you weren't paying attention."

Ignoring the stubborn set of his jaw, she traipsed to the neighboring sand dune. From there, she could see the footprints—windswept but faint—of someone who had climbed over the hill and collected the drone. Kneeling in the sand, she studied the prints. Then she took out her cell phone. Juggling the phone in one hand and the flashlight in the other, she took some pictures to document the shoe prints, which led straight down to a patch of sand that was crisscrossed with tire marks. So, either someone had driven out here to get the drone or they had come on foot and purposely walked along the tire marks to obscure their path.

Her team would probably never know which it was. Just like they would probably never get a name or a description or even a vehicle description of the drone owner because Drew was too distracted to do his job.

She glanced at him over her shoulder. He was headed back to the gatehouse now, obviously not up for any more criticism from a woman who wasn't even his boss.

Nicole walked to the edge of the dune and scanned the quiet campground, which just a few hours ago had been a hive of police activity. Some of the vacationers had already left. She'd noticed several of the minivan families packing up as the ME's people had been loading the gurney this afternoon.

She didn't blame them. Who wanted to vacation next to a fresh crime scene? And what parent wanted to explain what was happening to their little kids? People came to this park to fish and build sandcastles and tell stories around the campfire at night. Watching police recover a corpse wasn't on the itinerary.

Nicole thought about the look on the chief's face earlier and the tension that had permeated the team meeting. Today's discovery wasn't just a matter of public safety. It had potential to be an economic issue, too. Lost Beach was already dealing with a sharp downturn in tourism following a pair of tropical storms that had hit the island with a one-two punch last August. Business owners had spent the winter rebuilding, hoping to get back on their feet by summer. The tourism board had even hired a film company to shoot commercials to help lure people back to the island. The last thing the town needed at the start of the high season was a spate of negative news coverage that would scare people away.

They needed to solve this case. Soon. Her team was under pressure from all sides, and they couldn't afford any screwups.

Nicole scanned the area. The campground had been full this morning, but of the thirty-two sites, twelve had cleared out this afternoon, and she expected more to follow. Had the drone owner been one of the ones to leave? Brimming with frustration, she hiked back to where she'd parked. The camera drone might not have even been a lead, but now it was blown due to pure incompetence.

Nicole hitched herself behind the wheel of her pickup. She was in her personal vehicle because she'd already knocked off for the night and was supposed to be on her way home to get a meal and a shower and a good night's sleep. But she hadn't been able to resist one last trip to the crime scene.

For a moment she simply sat and stared through the windshield, watching the flickering flame of a nearby campfire. A young couple lounged in chairs beside a small RV. Jack and Janelle from Austin. Nicole had interviewed them that morning and even run a background check. Something in the guy's responses had felt a little off, but he had no criminal record, so maybe it was nothing.

Go with your gut.

That was Owen's advice about how to tell when people were lying—which people did all the time when talking to cops. It was simple advice, and Nicole took it to heart because Owen had a knack for reading people. Maybe because he'd been in and out of trouble so much as a kid, he was good at spotting bullshit. He had a radar for it. And having been a hell-raiser himself, Owen knew all the tricks and evasions.

Nicole started the truck and took one last look at the dune where she'd spent the better part of the day watching people excavate the remains of Julia Murphy. No official ID yet, but Nicole felt sure it was her. So did Owen. Tomorrow's autopsy likely would confirm what everyone already knew to be true, that a twenty-five-year-old woman who had been missing for sixteen days was missing no longer.

Now they had to figure out what the hell had happened to her.

Nicole called Owen on her way out of the park.

"How'd it go?" she asked.

"Just finished the last house," he said. "No one's seen anything suspicious or out of the ordinary."

"Did you go by the woman's place?"

Owen had told her about Macey Burns, who was staying at 151 Primrose Trail.

"She told me she hasn't seen anything," Owen said. "And turns out, she just got here yesterday, so that's a dead end."

"Damn. We can't catch a break, can we?"

"I know. How'd it go at White Dunes?"

"The drone is gone."

"Gone?"

"Gone. It was here at sunset. Now it's not. The ranger on duty didn't see anything, so our crappy luck continues."

"Who's the ranger?"

"Drew."

"Drew Wharton? That's our problem."

"I know."

He went quiet.

"Owen? You there?"

"I'm thinking."

"It was a long-shot lead anyway," she said.

"That's the only kind we have right now."

Owen was right. Given the circumstances, they had far too few avenues of investigation to follow, and it was making her and everyone else edgy and short-tempered.

For sixteen days, Nicole, Owen, and Emmet had interviewed Julia Murphy's friends and co-workers, but so far they didn't have any good leads. A thorough search of her home had yielded no clues, and her white Volkswagen was still missing.

And today, despite canvassing the entire area and interviewing what seemed like every person under the scorching-hot sun, their team had turned up no useful info. No one had seen Julia Murphy, or her car, anywhere near the campground. And—probably more important—no one had seen any suspicious people or vehicles in the area where the body was recovered.

"Maybe we'll get lucky tomorrow," Nicole said hopefully.

"How's that?"

"The autopsy. That could be a treasure trove of leads."

"Maybe," he said.

But his voice told her he wasn't betting on it.

CHAPTER

FIVE

OWEN WENDED HIS way through the maze of cinder-block hallways and found Nicole already in the conference room. She looked every bit as bad as she had fifteen minutes ago.

"Here," he said, plunking a can of Sprite in front of her.

She squeezed her eyes shut. "I can't."

"Just drink it."

She opened her eyes and glared at him, then reluctantly pulled the can toward her and popped open the top. Her auburn hair was back in its usual ponytail, and a shimmer of sweat covered her forehead despite the refrigerator-like temperature of the room. Evidently, they air-conditioned the hell out of all the rooms down here, not just the autopsy suite.

Nicole took a tentative sip and made a face. "Thanks." She looked at him. "This never happened to me before."

"What? Puking up your guts during a post?"

Her cheeks flushed with either anger or embarrassment. "It's only my third postmortem."

He shrugged. "Happens to everyone at some point."

She looked away from him.

"Don't sweat it. I won't tell anyone."

She scoffed. "That's not what I'm worried about."

"What are you worried about?"

"The *ME*. What do you think?"

"Relax. He's probably used to it."

"Easy for you to say. You're not the one who hurled on his shoes."

Dr. David Bauhaus stepped into the room. He wore blue scrubs and black Nikes. His shoes made little squeaks on the floor as he walked, and Owen figured he'd rinsed them off during the break. Bauhaus took a chair at the head of the table and Nicole shot a sheepish look at his feet.

"I examined the dental records," he said, opening a file folder.

The ME was forty-two and thin, with a brown buzz cut and the ramrod-straight posture of a former Marine. He seemed a little young for his job, but he had a direct, confident way about him that Owen chalked up to his military background.

"Her left central incisor is an implant, as I noted at autopsy." Bauhaus slid a paper toward them. It was a printout of a dental X-ray. "That, and the other distinctive dental work, confirms our supposition."

Owen pulled the printout closer and studied it.

"So, it's her," Nicole stated. "Julia Jane Murphy."

"Correct."

The dental records had been provided by the sister, Claire, who had reported Julia missing.

Nicole sighed. "Well, we've got our ID, at least."

"What's wrong?"

Owen glanced up, and the doctor was watching him.

"Nothing." He rubbed his bristly chin. He'd woken up

late for this morning's team meeting and skipped shaving. He'd skipped breakfast, too, but that had been a strategic choice so he wouldn't end up like Nicole.

"Just thinking about the tooth implant," Owen said. "Isn't that unusual for someone her age?"

"It is." The doctor nodded. "But I've seen it before in someone this young. Could be a sports injury, possibly a fall. Possibly abuse."

Owen lifted an eyebrow.

"I haven't had time to study all her X-rays closely. If I find any evidence of old or unset fractures, you'll see it in my report."

It was a subtle reminder that the doctor was making time for this meeting as a favor. He could have made them wait for his final report, or even the preliminary, before sharing his insights. But Owen's team desperately needed leads, and he hadn't wanted to wait around for paperwork.

"Manner of death, homicide," Bauhaus went on. "Cause of death, manual strangulation. The hyoid bone was fractured. No ligature marks, no parry wounds. I *did* observe a broken fingernail, left pinky finger, so there's the possibility of DNA . . ." He trailed off and glanced up. "Of course, all her nail clippings will be sent to the lab."

"How long does that take?" Nicole asked.

The ME shook his head. "Depends how backed up they are. The state lab is a crapshoot. I always tell detectives, don't hold your breath."

In other words, develop other leads instead of waiting around for lab results. Which was exactly why Owen was here.

The ME flipped through the handwritten notes in the file, which had been transcribed by his autopsy assistant during the exam. "As for trace evidence, we recovered some debris from her hair—also going to the lab—and some small blue fibers in her teeth." He shot Owen a cryptic look. "I'll get back to you on that. But the main thing I wanted to mention was the glass."

A young woman stopped in the doorway. She was tall and blond, and it took Owen a second to recognize her without the surgical gown and face mask. She was the autopsy assistant.

"The printout you wanted?" She stepped into the room and handed Bauhaus a paper.

"Perfect timing. Thanks, Hailey."

The ME slid the printout in front of them. It showed two shards of glass that had been photographed on a backdrop of white paper.

Owen studied the glass chunks. The ME had removed them while the victim was facedown on the table. Bauhaus had spent time on them during the autopsy, measuring and taking notes, but Owen had been distracted. Nicole had looked pretty green by that point, and he'd been waiting to grab her if she started to fall.

"This isn't ordinary glass. It's heavier," Bauhaus said. "It looks to me like some sort of high-quality glass with lead in it. In other words, crystal."

Nicole looked at Owen. "So, maybe a crystal vase or a drinking glass or something broke during the struggle. And the pieces were on the floor underneath her when he strangled her." She looked at the ME. "That's what you're suggesting, right?"

"I'll leave the hypotheticals to you two. But I just want to point out that this material was embedded in the victim's shoulder."

"Where's this evidence now?" Owen asked.

"It's been sent to the lab. After they examine it, they can tell you more about it."

Owen had already known they were looking for a primary crime scene separate from the place where the body was buried. Now it looked as though that place might be a location with high-quality crystal instead of, say, a dumpy motel room. He had another clue to go on, a good one. He was glad he'd asked for this meeting.

"Can I keep this picture?" he asked.

"Yeah, that's for you." Bauhaus looked at his notes again. "Next thing—postmortem interval. Given the condition of the body, you're looking at two to three weeks."

"And we can narrow that down, because she was last seen alive seventeen days ago." Nicole looked at Owen. "This helps."

The doctor checked his watch. "That's about it until I do the report." He pushed his chair back. "You guys got lucky with the decomp, by the way."

Nicole's eyebrows shot up. "Lucky?"

"Yes, given your jurisdiction on the island." He looked at Owen. "The sand dune was your friend here. If she'd been dumped in a marsh, you wouldn't have any of this physical evidence. And if she'd been dumped off a boat?" He shook his head. "We wouldn't even be here."

MACEY GAVE THE tub one last scrub down and sat back on her heels. Not perfect but better. She rinsed the scrub brush and stood up, shaking out her stiff legs with a groan. Her knees hurt. Same for her thighs. She wanted to believe it was the cleaning and not yesterday's piddly two miles that was making her ache everywhere.

She grabbed her bucket and the mop and stepped into the hallway.

A flash of movement caught her eye, and she looked across the house. Josh stood at her glass front door, waving his arms.

Plucking out her earbuds, Macey strode across the living room to let him in. He looked dressed for the beach this afternoon in green swim trunks and a T-shirt.

"Hey," she said, opening the door.

"You didn't hear me knock?"

"I was listening to music. What's up?"

"Who's your visitor?"

"Visitor?"

He nodded over his shoulder. "That guy. He was coming down your stairs when I pulled onto your street."

"What guy?" She stepped onto the deck and peered down the stairs at the driveway.

"He's on the bridge now. Orange board shorts."

She turned to look at the bridge over the sand dunes, where a shirtless man was walking toward the beach.

"Huh." She stared after the man. He had shaggy dark hair and a sleeve of tattoos on his right arm. "If he knocked on my door, I didn't hear him." She tucked her earbuds into the pocket of her cutoffs. "You sure he was at *my* place?"

"Yeah."

"Maybe he had the wrong house."

Josh stepped inside, and she followed him.

"Seems different," he said, looking around. "What'd you do in here?"

"I moved some furniture so I could set up an editing room. Want to see?"

"Sure."

He took off his sunglasses and followed her to the bedroom wing. Well, *wing* was a bit of a stretch for a place this small. The back of the house consisted of two bedrooms and a bathroom off a shared hallway.

"You're mopping?" Josh frowned down at the bucket.

"I had to. The place was filthy."

He eyed the tiny bathroom and lifted an eyebrow, and

she knew his standard of cleanliness was different from hers.

"Seriously, there was dust and grime everywhere. Finger smudges. Mildew in the tile grout." She made a face. "Not to mention the rat traps."

His gaze snapped to hers. "*Rat traps?*"

"I've only seen one actual rat, but yeah. Although it may have been a mouse." She gestured across the hall. "Check out the editing room."

He stepped into the spare bedroom and looked around. Macey had set up all of her computers—two laptops and a desktop—on a long table. The room had originally contained two twin beds, but she'd moved one into the closet and spread all her camera and lighting equipment out on the other.

Josh walked over and picked up one of her tripods to examine it.

"I'm using the breakfast table for a desk," she said. "I figure, I'm not entertaining, so why not?"

"Not a bad setup," he admitted. "Better than my place, at least—only five hundred square feet. I've got all my gear jammed into the living room."

Macey dusted her hands on her shorts. "So, what are you doing here? I thought you had a surf lesson."

He turned to her with a sly smile. "New plan."

"What?"

"We've got a sunset cruise."

"*We?* I'm supposed to meet the Turtle Lady."

"Call her and move it."

"I don't want to move it."

He tipped his head to the side. "Mace, come on. We've been invited for a sunset sail on a fifty-foot catamaran. Free of charge. The boat is booked for a photo shoot, but they've got room for two extra passengers." He smiled. "You and me."

Macey watched him, weighing her response. She didn't want to call Olive and reschedule at the last minute. It felt unprofessional. She thought of Olive's raspy voice over the phone and how she'd needed to check her "datebook" to see when they'd made the appointment. And it wasn't just that she was elderly; Macey had truly been looking forward to interviewing one of the island's top conservationists.

"What kind of photo shoot?" she asked.

"I don't know. Some activewear catalog. I never heard of them."

"Activewear?"

"Yoga, I think."

"Who does yoga on a catamaran?"

He rolled his eyes. "Who cares? We're talking about a *free* sailing trip." He gestured to the sliding glass door, where the afternoon sun streamed into the room. "It's a perfect day for it. The views will be amazing."

"Don't you mean the models will be amazing?"

"Come on, we'll get some great views of the island from the bay. But we have to leave now. We're due at the marina at five, and I skipped lunch, so I need to grab something to eat first."

Macey sighed. She didn't want to move her appointment. And she didn't want to drop everything and get on a boat right this second. She looked at her cleaning supplies scattered around the hallway. "I don't know."

"Mace, seriously. Are you passing this up to *mop*?"

"No. I'm thinking about Olive."

"The Turtle Lady?"

She plunked her hand on her hip. "Yes. We've had this appointment for a week."

"She's been here eighty years. She'll be here tomorrow."

"All right, all right. Give me a minute to clean this up." She grabbed the bucket of water. She started to walk toward the sliding door but then remembered it was difficult to open.

"Let me just throw out this mop water and change my clothes."

"You look fine."

She shot him a scowl and headed for the front door.

Josh was right, but she wasn't going to admit it yet. A boat trip was a good opportunity. She glanced at the sky and then looked out at the waves. It was a breezy day, and the wispy white clouds would make for some beautiful sunset shots. She walked to the edge of the deck and dumped the dirty water over the rail into a patch of grass.

Macey glanced at her neighbor's house. She hadn't seen him all day, but she'd heard his country music coming from the garage.

She turned to look at her rental cottage, noting the sliding door that led to the bedroom she'd just converted into a workspace. She walked over and stepped into the shade of the eaves as she studied the door handle. The inside latch was flipped up, which should have meant unlocked. She pulled the handle, but the door didn't budge. She examined the doorframe, noticing the smudges on the paint. She'd seen smudges like that inside the house, too, on some of the cabinets and windowsills.

Macey's stomach tightened as realization dawned.

"Oh my God." She dropped her bucket.

"What is it?"

She turned around to see Josh leaning against the deck railing.

"I *knew* he was being evasive!"

"What? Who?"

"Owen Breda."

"Who?"

"That detective," she muttered, staring down at the smudges. "He freaking lied to me."

O WEN SPOTTED HIS brother's truck in the parking lot as he pulled into the police station. He scanned the area and spied Joel and Emmet standing on the sidewalk near the docks.

Owen parked and walked over to the boathouse where Lost Beach PD kept two patrol boats and an airboat. A sheriff's department boat was tethered to a cleat nearby, but Owen didn't see any deputies around. Maybe they were inside hitting the vending machines.

"How'd it go?" Owen asked, looking his brother up and down. Joel wore jeans and a gray T-shirt, and the sweat marks indicated he'd spent some time in a Kevlar vest recently.

"One arrest, but nothing major." Joel shook his head. "Our intel didn't pan out."

Owen lifted an eyebrow.

"New CI," Joel said.

Confidential informants were a mixed bag. They usually took time to develop. And even when they provided good information, using them came with risks.

"How about you?" Joel wiped his forehead with the back of his arm. "I hear you and Nicole went to the autopsy. Anything new?"

"We got the ID confirmed."

Joel's eyebrows arched. "Julia Murphy?"

"That's right." Owen looked at Emmet. "The chief fill you in?"

"Yeah, we just had a meeting. Nicole gave us the rundown. Where were you?"

"I went to see the sister." Owen glanced at Joel, noting the somber look in his brother's eyes. Joel had done next-of-kin notifications, and he knew it was by far the worst part of the job.

"Brady wants to do a press briefing at five," Emmet said. "All hands on deck."

Owen gritted his teeth.

"Don't bother trying to duck out of it," Emmet added. "Nicole already tried. He wants everyone there, no excuses."

Joel smiled. "What, you guys don't want to be on TV again?"

Owen ignored the gloating. One advantage to being on the task force was that Joel didn't have to show his face for press briefings anymore. In fact, task force members were supposed to *avoid* cameras and keep a low profile. It was a major perk. As much as Owen liked detective work, he hated media events. They were a waste of time, particularly during the critical early days of an investigation.

Reporters could be useful sometimes, like getting the word out about a missing person. But they could foul things up, too, and their constant hovering grated on Owen's nerves.

Emmet's phone buzzed, and he stepped away to take the call.

Joel's gaze settled on Owen. They hadn't had a private conversation in days. Not since before the body was discovered and the chief made Owen the lead detective, a job that would have gone to Joel if he hadn't been tied up.

"You doing okay with everything?" Joel asked.

Owen bristled. It was a loaded question, and Owen wasn't about to answer it out here on the sidewalk.

"Fine," he said.

His brother just looked at him.

"Yo, Breda."

Owen and Joel turned around. A sheriff's deputy was waving Joel over to the speedboat.

"My ride's leaving." Joel gave Owen a long look, then turned to Emmet, who was getting off the phone. "Later," he said.

"Later."

Owen watched Joel walk away with a familiar mixture of admiration and resentment. It was a combination that had dogged him for years. Owen respected the hell out of his older brother. Everyone did. He was a good cop. Exceptional, even. And everyone knew he'd probably step into the chief's shoes at some point. Joel had had his eye on the job for years, and he'd earned it, working his ass off to the exclusion of everything else, including a personal life—at least until recently, when he'd met Miranda. Joel was *driven*, and always had been. He set a goal and went after it with laser-sharp focus.

Owen's path to detective had been more winding, and there were still days when he had no idea whether he was cut out for this work. The fact that everyone, including his own brother, seemed to second-guess Owen's commitment only reminded him that the career he'd chosen might not be a fit.

Most days, Owen was too busy to get philosophical about it. But sometimes—like this afternoon when he'd pulled up to Claire Murphy's house to tell her that her sister was dead, and he'd sat there in his car with a ball of dread in his gut and wanted to puke—Owen wondered whether he was really meant to be a cop.

"Hey, isn't that that woman?"

His attention snapped to Emmet. "What?"

"That woman from White Dunes." Emmet nodded toward the parking lot.

Owen turned to see Macey Burns striding up the sidewalk. She had her hair in a bun on top of her head and a pissed-off look on her face. Today she wore cutoff shorts and a tight white T-shirt. The uniformed cops milling near the entrance stepped aside to let her pass, and she looked oblivious to their stares as she yanked open the door and disappeared inside.

"She looks familiar," Emmet said.

"You just saw her at the park."

"No, I mean besides that." Emmet looked at him. "You know what she's doing here?"

"No idea."

But Owen had a sneaking suspicion it had to do with him.

CHAPTER

SIX

THE INSIDE OF the police station was cool and dim, and Macey took a moment to let her eyes adjust. Her gaze settled on the reception counter, where a woman with bottle-blond hair was talking on the phone. She glanced up at Macey and smiled.

"May I help you?"

"Hi, I'm here to see Detective Breda."

"Which one?"

"Uh . . . Owen, please."

"Excuse me one moment." She adjusted her headset and held up a finger, signaling Macey to wait as she took a call.

Macey stepped back, noticing the row of chairs behind her. But she was too restless to sit. A glass partition divided the reception area from a large room filled with cubicles—which at Macey's former workplace had been called "the bullpen." But while the bullpen at the TV station had always been bustling with activity in the middle of the day, this place was nearly empty. Where was everyone? She scanned the sea of cubes but saw only one uniformed officer on the phone and someone else typing away at a computer.

"What brings you in?"

She turned around. Owen Breda stood behind her, hands on his hips.

"You're here," she said.

He lifted his eyebrows.

Another detective walked up behind him, giving Macey a curious look. He was dressed the same as Owen, right down to the military-style boots.

Macey looked at Owen. "I need to talk to you." She glanced around at all the curious gazes. "About the case," she added.

What else would it be about? But she felt the need to clarify that she wasn't here for personal reasons.

Owen glanced at the receptionist. Macey heard a faint buzz, and Owen stepped around her to push open the door. "This way," he said, holding it open.

The bullpen was even cooler than the reception area, and Macey shivered slightly. Owen led her past the rows of cubicles, and she caught the eye of the uniformed officer. He'd been manning the barricade yesterday morning, the barricade she'd slipped past without being seen. His gaze narrowed as she neared his desk, and she wondered if maybe he *had* seen her.

Owen halted, and Macey stopped just short of bumping into him. He directed her into an open conference room.

She stepped through the door and looked around. Actually, it wasn't much of a conference room. The only furniture was a small table and two chairs.

It was an interrogation room.

"Have a seat."

Macey stared down at the gray plastic chair, half expecting to find it bolted to the floor. She pulled it out and sat down.

Instead of taking the other chair, Owen propped his hip on the edge of the table and looked down at her, putting her at a clear disadvantage. She darted a look at the camera mounted on the ceiling.

"What's up?" he asked casually.

Her chest tightened with annoyance. "What's *up*?" She laughed. "Well . . . for starters, I'd like to know why you failed to tell me that I'm living in a crime scene."

Something flickered in his eyes, but he remained perfectly still.

"Excuse me?" he finally said.

"My *house*. The one I *rented*." She crossed her arms, infuriated all over again as she thought about his visit last night. "Are you going to tell me I'm *not* living in the home of a murder victim?"

"Back up." He bent closer. "Why do you say it's a crime scene?"

"Are you saying it's not?"

"I want to know why you said that." His blue eyes were intense.

"Because I found out that Julia Murphy used to live there. And because there's fingerprint powder everywhere. And the place has obviously been searched by police. And now Julia Murphy is not only missing, she's *dead*, and I want to know what the hell is going on."

He eased back, still watching her closely. He seemed to be taking note of her body language. Which probably meant he understood how angry she was.

Not to mention rattled.

"Well?" she demanded.

"Well, what?"

She rolled her eyes. "Are you going to explain what's happening?"

"What do you want to know?"

"I want to know why you didn't mention any of this last night when you showed up with all your questions." She huffed out a breath. "You gave me some BS about talking to residents on my street."

"I *was* talking to residents on your street. I told you last night, we're canvassing the area."

She shot him a look. "Don't act like it's the same. You should have given me a heads-up. As a safety precaution if nothing else."

Something flickered in his eyes. Guilt? She hoped so.

"You're right." He nodded. "I apologize."

Macey drew back, surprised. She hadn't expected an apology. He'd seemed a little too arrogant to admit to a mistake.

"What would you like to know?" he asked.

She watched him silently. The apology had taken some of the wind out of her sails, and she tried to remember all the urgent questions that had been swirling through her mind on the way over here.

"Well . . ." She cleared her throat. "Can you confirm that the police were in my house after Julia went missing?"

"That's correct."

Macey's stomach knotted. She'd known it as soon as she realized that all those smudges she'd been cleaning up were from fingerprint powder. A conversation with her neighbor in his driveway confirmed that a team of CSIs had, in fact, been to the house after Julia Murphy disappeared, and also that the missing woman had, in fact, been living there before Macey rented the place.

"So." She cleared her throat again. "The victim at the park is . . ."

"Julia Murphy. We got a positive ID this morning."

Macey bit her lip. "Was she . . ."

"We don't believe she was killed at the house on Primrose Trail. We went over every inch of the place and found no evidence to suggest a crime happened there. No blood or trace evidence, no signs of a struggle, nothing. Believe me, we looked."

"Then where—"

"She was last seen by a co-worker getting into her car behind the restaurant where she worked. Her car is still missing, along with her purse, her keys, and her cell phone. We believe she never made it home."

Macey stared at him, wanting to believe what he was saying. Julia Murphy hadn't been killed at the rental house.

Macey's rental house.

But that didn't change the horrific fact that she *had* been murdered, if not there, then somewhere—her car, or someone else's car, or maybe someone's home, or on some lonely stretch of road someplace.

Macey recalled her flat tire with a shudder.

Owen leaned closer. "Are you okay?"

"Yes."

His look told her he didn't believe that.

"I don't blame you for being upset about the house," he said.

"I'm not *upset*, I'm—"

Scared.

She was scared of staying there. And creeped out to know that the person who had lived there just before her was now dead.

Macey pictured the smiling young woman whose face had been on the news for weeks. Long dark hair, bright smile, a spark of humor in her brown eyes. She looked so vivacious, and it was disturbing to think of her life being cut short.

Owen leaned closer. "If I thought there was any chance Julia Murphy was killed at that location, I would tell you." He searched her face, as if looking for signs that she believed him. She didn't know if she did. "But the fact is, we went over it—luminol, alternative light sources, everything—and found zero evidence."

"Then why all the questions?"

"What do you mean?"

"If you're so sure, then why'd you come by last night and give me the third degree? Did you interview all my neighbors, too?"

"Yes."

She gazed up at him, feeling embarrassed as she realized she'd put a little too much emphasis on their moonlight conversation on her deck. It was routine. He'd had dozens of similar conversations with dozens of potential witnesses over the past few days, and there was nothing special about it.

But she was still ticked off. She'd sensed last night that he was being evasive, and she'd been right. And what had seemed like a wild hunch while she was standing on her deck less than an hour ago was now officially confirmed.

A knock sounded at the door, and the dark-haired detective from earlier leaned his head in. "Press conference in ten," he told Owen.

"I know."

The man darted a look at Macey and then walked away.

"I have to go." She checked her watch. She was supposed to meet Josh at the marina soon. "Thanks for your time."

"I hope I answered your questions."

"Not really." She grabbed her purse and hooked it on her shoulder. "But, hey, I get it. Ongoing investigation and all that."

"I can't discuss—"

"No, I *get* it. Really. You're a detective and I'm just some lowly member of the public." She reached for the door. "If I want to know more, I'll watch the news."

Brooke Gordon sat in her boss's desk chair with a crumpled tissue in her hand.

"I knew." She dabbed the end of her nose. "As soon as I heard about the body at the park, I *knew*. But I was hoping."

Nicole looked at Owen. She didn't want to mess up the rapport he'd established with this woman by jumping in, but she was getting impatient. They'd been holed up in this closet-size office at the back of the restaurant for twenty minutes now, and they'd learned nothing they didn't already know.

"I understand this is hard to talk about," Owen said. "And I'm sorry we have to do this here."

Actually, he wasn't sorry at all. They'd specifically approached Julia's co-worker at Waterman's Grill because it was the last location where the victim had been seen alive.

That they knew of.

And Brooke Gordon was the last person to *see* her alive.

That they knew of.

Owen had a thing about revisiting witnesses to shake loose new details that they could turn into leads. He did the same with suspects, and Nicole had seen enough leads generated by these drop-in interviews that she no longer raised objections.

"Let's go back to that Thursday," Owen said, referring to the Thursday before Memorial Day, when Julia went missing.

Brooke looked up at him with watery brown eyes. Owen had been running this interview, not just because he was lead detective but because he had a way with female witnesses.

Owen had a way with females, period. Witnesses just happened to fall under the umbrella.

"You said you and Julia took your break together?" he asked.

She nodded. "Not the dinner break, but the short one. Ten minutes." She took a deep breath and seemed to compose herself. "We both had a double, and we'd been on since eleven. This was around three, I guess. I went out to vape, and Julia came with me, just to get out of the restaurant."

"Where exactly were you?" Nicole asked.

"Right outside the kitchen door. There's a picnic table back there."

"Did anyone else join you?" Nicole asked.

"It was just us."

"Do you remember what you talked about?" Owen asked.

"Not really."

"Did Julia mention her plans after work?"

"Not that I remember."

Nicole darted a look at Owen. They'd been down this path with her already, trying to tease out Julia's plans for after she left her shift at the seafood restaurant. They hadn't tracked down a single person who knew what Julia had been planning to do after work, and the friend she had spent her day with was their best bet.

"What about you, Brooke?" Owen asked. "Can you remember what you were planning to do when your shift ended?"

"Nothing." She sighed and looked at the tissue remnants. "Well, not *nothing*. I had to swing by the gas station on my way home. I drove to work on fumes, and I remember telling Jules I hoped I didn't stall out on the way home, and she said something like, 'Call me if you get stranded.'" She looked up at Owen. "But that was it. She didn't say anything about going out that night or meeting anyone or anything."

Owen nodded. "Did you two ever go out together? Meet up with friends? Anything like that?"

She shook her head. "She didn't go out much. At least, not that I knew about. I asked her to come out with my friends a few times, but she always said she couldn't make it."

"And did she ever mention a guy?" Nicole asked, getting to the real point. She could appreciate Owen's patience, but they didn't have all night here.

Brooke's attention settled on Nicole. "No."

"Never?"

She shook her head.

Nicole watched her closely. "Are you sure, Brooke? In the ten months you worked together here she never mentioned a date? A boyfriend? A hookup?"

Owen gave Nicole a warning look. He didn't want her making the witness nervous.

"No. Never." Brooke shrugged. "But that wasn't unusual. I mean, we didn't normally talk about guys together."

"What did you normally talk about?" Owen asked.

"I don't know. Work. Customers." She darted a glance at the door. "A-hole managers." She looked at Owen. "We talked about customers a lot. The thing about Julia, she was really generous. She didn't hog all the best tables. Some people do. They'll do anything to get the hostess to seat the high rollers in their section. Julia wasn't like that. She was chill."

"How can you tell the high rollers?" Nicole asked.

"You know. Men off the charter boats, here without their wives. They order top-shelf instead of well drinks. Sometimes they're on expense accounts."

"I assume they flirt with the servers?" Nicole asked.

"Flirt?" Brooke rolled her eyes. "More like grope, but whatever. They tip well, so you learn to ignore it."

"Any of these high rollers ever flirt with Julia recently?" Owen asked.

She looked at him, seeming to consider it. "No one in particular. I can't remember anyone."

"Any of these customers ever ask you out?" Owen asked.

"Sure. But I'd never go." She made a face. "Most of them are old and married."

"What about Julia?" Nicole asked.

"I don't know. If she did, she never said anything to me." Brooke looked at the clock on the wall. "Sorry, but I really need to get back."

"One more thing," Owen said. "The a-hole manager you mentioned. Which one is that?"

She shot another look at the door. "Ryan."

"Ryan Connor?"

"Yeah. No one gets along with him." Brooke looked at the clock again. "And speaking of, I need to get back to work before he gets mad. We're really busy tonight."

"Just one last question," Owen said. "You mentioned you invited Julia out with your friends a few times, but she didn't go."

"She had her own friends."

"You know any of their names?"

"I never met them. Sorry." She bit her lip. "There was this one girl who picked her up after work one time."

"Picked up Julia?" Owen asked.

"Yeah. I don't know her name, but they had a yoga class together."

"You remember her car?"

She sighed. "I don't know. Something silver and small. Maybe a Toyota?" She stood up and tucked the shredded tissue into her black apron. "I didn't really get a look at her, sorry."

"No problem." Owen moved aside so Brooke could squeeze past him.

"Thanks for your time," Nicole told her.

"Sure."

"If you remember anything else, even something small that might be helpful, give me a call." Owen handed her a card.

"I will." She smiled and slid the card into her apron.

Nicole watched her leave the office, then turned to Owen. "Give *me* a call?"

"What?"

"You're a shameless flirt."

He shrugged. "I like to make a personal connection with witnesses."

She rolled her eyes.

"What? It works," he said.

It did work. But Nicole didn't like the idea of flirting with witnesses to get info. It wasn't her style.

Still, his methods had resulted in a lot of tips over the years. The Lost Beach PD case files were littered with the names of countless women who'd found a reason to call Detective Blue Eyes with some juicy tidbit or another.

Nicole followed him down a narrow hallway and past the bustling kitchen, where the smell of grilling steaks made Nicole's stomach growl. She realized she hadn't eaten since her ill-fated breakfast, and it had been a marathon day.

They stepped out the back door into the breezy summer night. The parking lot behind Waterman's Grill was filled with crappy employee cars, in sharp contrast to the lot in front, which was filled with sports cars, SUVs, and special-edition pickups that cost a fortune.

Owen stopped beside a pair of dumpsters and turned to

look at the building. Beside the door was the picnic table where Brooke and Julia had taken their last break together.

"What is it?" Nicole asked.

"Just thinking about camera placement."

"They don't have any cameras. Remember?"

"I'm thinking about across the street." He turned and looked at the bar across the street. Situated right on the beach, Finn's was a popular hangout for tourists, and the parking lot was crowded tonight.

"That's got to be, what, a hundred yards away?" Nicole shook her head. "And it's not directly across, it's diagonal."

"Yeah, but the parking lot exit is directly across."

He was right. But still, it was probably a long shot that a security camera at Finn's would have captured anything useful at Waterman's.

"No stone unturned," Owen said, probably reading her mind. "I'll check with the manager."

They crossed the lot to where they'd both parked. They'd come separately because this was their last stop before going home for the night.

Nicole slipped her keys from her pocket. "So, what'd you think of the interview?"

"It was okay."

"Just okay? What about the thing with Ryan Connor?"

"What about it?"

"Well, we're searching for men Julia might have had problems with. We should give him a look."

"Ryan Connor is gay."

She stopped short. "He is? How do you . . ."

Owen just looked at her.

"Well, even if he is, that doesn't mean the victim didn't have a beef with him. Sounds like he doesn't get along with people."

Owen shook his head.

"What?" she asked, annoyed. They had too few leads to be dismissing anything out of hand.

"Doesn't feel right."

"What the hell does that mean? Come on, Owen. This thing happened almost three weeks ago, and we've got *no* suspects. Not a single one."

He shot her a dark look. Owen was lead detective and acutely aware of their lack of suspects. No doubt it kept him up at night and accounted for his pissy mood lately.

He stopped beside his truck, resting his hands on his hips as he looked at the pitted parking lot that was the last known location where Julia Murphy had been seen alive.

"Don't you think we should at least take a look at him?" Nicole asked.

"We can take a look. But I don't think it fits."

She arched her eyebrows, waiting for him to elaborate.

"This feels like a sexual homicide," he said. "Not that she was raped, necessarily. But the lack of clothing, the strangling."

Nicole knew what he meant. "You think we're looking for a heterosexual male."

"Yep."

"Probably someone with rage issues. No impulse control."

"Yep."

Nicole nodded and combed her fingers through her hair. She was bone-tired. And hungry. And frustrated. "I feel like we're running in circles, interviewing the same handful of people again and again. What a waste of time."

"Not totally." He folded his arms over his chest. "We got the tip about the yoga friend. She might know what Julia was up to lately or if she was seeing someone."

"We don't even have a name. Or a description. Just that she drives something 'small and silver.' Do you know how many small silver cars we have on this island? Probably hundreds."

"Yeah, but there are only two yoga studios."

She blinked at him. "Oh. Good point."

He smiled.

Nicole sighed, feeling slow for not getting it earlier. It was a solid lead on the friends-of-the-victim front. But it wasn't something she could follow up on tonight, thank goodness. She was exhausted, which was probably why she kept missing clues.

"Okay, first thing tomorrow, I'm visiting yoga studios." She pulled open her door. "Maybe I can get Emmet to come with me. Unless you want to."

"No, you run with it. I've got some other stuff in the morning."

"You sure? It was your idea."

"I'm sure." He moved for his truck. "Go home, Nicole. Sleep. You look like you're about to pass out."

M ACEY WAS SORE and sunburned, and the last place she wanted to be right now was a crowded bar. But she tried not to look too bitchy as she nursed a watery Cape Cod.

"You want another?" Josh asked, leaning in to be heard over the noise.

"I'm good."

He gazed over her shoulder at the door. He'd been watching it since their arrival. Josh had been talking up Finn's to the models on the boat, and he was convinced at least some of them would make an appearance here tonight. Macey was playing the role of wingman. She hadn't minded at first, but her patience was waning. She checked her watch and mustered a smile.

"Hey, thanks, by the way," she said. "I'm glad you roped me into sailing. Those shots from the water are going to be key to our campaign. We needed that vantage point."

"Told you it was worth bumping the Turtle Lady."

"You were right. We may even need to make room in the budget for another trip so we can get the north end of the island. You up for it?"

"Sure, just say the word." He swigged his beer and glanced across the bar. "The pool game's about to wrap up. Want to play?"

"Nope."

"Why not? You'd probably wipe the floor with those guys."

She turned to look at the pool table in back, where two men were finishing a game. Both were tall and tan, probably late twenties. One of them leaned over the table and lined up a bank shot. He missed by a mile.

"I'm not feeling it tonight," she said.

"You sure?" Josh lifted an eyebrow and picked up his beer. "I don't see any women with them."

She shot him a look. "Not interested."

"Why not?"

"I'm on a man diet."

"What's that mean?"

"Just what it sounds like."

"What, no sex?"

"Not for the foreseeable future."

He frowned. "One shitty breakup and now you want to torture yourself?"

"It's not torture." She sipped her drink. "I see it as more of a detox." She shrugged. "A summer cleanse, if you will. I'm very much looking forward to it."

"Right."

"No, really. One of my goals for the summer is to simplify my life. Get back to basics."

"What's more basic than sex?"

She sighed. "For me? How about sleep. Exercise. Developing my craft."

Josh eyed her skeptically. "You want to know what I think?"

"No."

"I think you're letting him have too much control over you."

Her shoulders tensed. But she managed to shrug. "This is not about him; it's about me."

He shook his head.

"I've lived in Texas five years," she said. "From the moment I moved here, I've been running on a hamster wheel. Now I finally have a chance to step off, and it feels good. Gives me a chance to get perspective."

Josh watched her, looking unconvinced. He knew better than anyone what a tumultuous spring she'd had and how desperate she'd been to get away. But she didn't want to talk about that tonight.

Something over her shoulder caught his attention. Macey knew what it was without looking.

"They're here." Josh looked at her and smiled. "Don't turn around."

"Who is it?"

"Katie and Piper."

"Is Piper the blond one?"

"They're both blond. Piper's the taller one."

All eight of the models on the boat had been pushing six feet, so that didn't really clarify things, but Josh didn't seem to notice.

"They grabbed a booth," he said. "I'm going to go say hi."

"I'll stay here."

"You sure?"

"Yeah." She looked at the TV above the bar. "The Diamondbacks are about to score."

He didn't need any further encouragement to leave her alone with her ice cubes. Macey turned her attention to the game. It was top of the fifth, and the D-backs were down

4–3. Maybe she should order another drink. Or she could wait until Josh got comfortable and simply slip out. She could go call her dad, who was no doubt sitting at home in Phoenix, watching the ball game. Josh wouldn't care if she took off, now that his new friends had arrived.

She sighed and touched the bridge of her nose. She'd skipped the sunblock, thinking she'd have no problem after five, but she'd been wrong.

"Macey?"

A little jolt went through her, and she turned around at the familiar voice. Owen Breda stepped over.

"Hi," she said.

"Hey." He gazed down at her with those vivid blue eyes and rested a hand on the bar. "You got some sun since I last saw you."

"Oh. Yeah." She touched her nose. "Sunset booze cruise."

Nerves fluttered as she looked up at him. She hadn't expected to bump into him here. The last time she'd seen him she'd been in a snit.

"Are you here with your boyfriend?" Owen asked.

"My . . . ?"

"The mechanic?"

Crap. She'd told him Josh was her boyfriend.

She cleared her throat. "You mean the guy from the other night? He's not my boyfriend. Or a mechanic, actually. I made that up."

His eyebrows arched.

"I didn't know you from anybody," she said. "And you seemed kind of menacing."

The side of his mouth curved up. "Menacing?"

"Yeah, you know. Dark highway. Woman stranded alone. Some stranger pulls over in a big truck . . ." She trailed off because it sounded melodramatic now. "Anyway . . ." She motioned to the empty stool beside her. "You want to sit down and have a drink or—"

"I'm on duty."

She looked him over, registering that he was dressed the same as earlier, including the badge and holster.

The bartender sauntered over. "Hey, Owen." She gave him a flirty smile. "Can I get you a drink?"

"I'm good, thanks. Is Craig around?"

"He hasn't been in yet." She darted a look at Macey, then looked at Owen again. "Want me to text him for you?"

"I'll track him down."

Owen turned his attention back to Macey. He looked at her for a moment before resting his hand on the bar again.

"So, how'd you like the cruise?" he asked.

Was he really interested in this? Or was he just being polite?

"Fine," she said. "We did a loop around the bay. I got some good shots, actually."

"Shots?"

"Film. I'm doing commercials for the tourism board."

Interest sparked in his eyes. "I heard about that."

"They hired my production company, so we're here for the summer."

He looked much too impressed. "How big is your company?"

"Tiny." She smiled. "Just me and anyone I hire on a contract basis. Right now, that's Josh. He does most of the camerawork and sound. I prefer the editing and production end of things."

She knew without looking that Josh was watching her from his cozy little booth, and she had no doubt she'd be hearing about this conversation later.

She glanced around, noticing that the women in their vicinity had their eyes on Owen, too. Not exactly surprising.

It might have been the badge and gun, but she had a feeling he attracted plenty of attention even without them.

"Oh, before I forget." She slapped her hand on the bar. "I meant to tell you earlier. You were asking me about people and cars on my street. Some guy came by my house today."

His eyebrows tipped up. "Who was it?"

"I don't know. Josh saw him. He was on my deck."

Owen's gaze narrowed.

"I was inside cleaning and I had my earbuds in," she said. "So he probably knocked on my door, and I didn't hear him. Anyway, he walked over the bridge to the beach."

"What did he look like?"

"I only saw him from the back."

"Generally, what did he look like?"

"Caucasian. No shirt. Orange board shorts. He had brown hair and a sleeve of tattoos."

Owen nodded, but she couldn't tell what he was thinking.

"Isn't that the kind of thing you wanted?" she asked. "People or vehicles loitering around the victim's house?"

"He was loitering?"

"I don't know what he was doing, really. He came to the door. And Julia Murphy used to live there, so that makes me think maybe he was looking for her."

Owen just watched her.

"I mean, obviously if this guy was responsible for her death, then he wouldn't come knocking on her door," she said. "But I was thinking maybe he knew her or maybe they ran with the same crowd. Could be a lead."

"Could be," he said, but he didn't sound convinced.

"It's probably nothing." She stirred her ice cubes. "I'm sure you've got plenty of better leads going, but I just thought you'd want to know."

The bartender stepped over. "Hey, Craig just showed. He's in the stockroom."

"Thanks." He looked at Macey. "I need to go."

She nodded.

But he didn't move to leave, just gazed down at her. "So, are we good now?" he asked.

"Good?"

"You're not still mad about earlier?"

She looked up at him, struck once again by those blue eyes. He had a hint of a smile now, too. A very sexy combination, and she had a feeling he knew it.

She was tempted to let him off the hook, but then she thought of all that fingerprint powder and how furious she'd been that he hadn't told her what was going on.

"That depends," she said.

He lifted a brow.

"Don't hold back on me again. If something comes up having to do with my house, I want to know about it."

He nodded. "Fair enough." He held out his hand.

She shook it. His grip was firm and warm and sent a zing straight through her.

He smiled as he let go.

"See you around, Macey."

CHAPTER

SEVEN

T HE LIGHTHOUSE WAS pink and rosy in the morning sun.
Macey pulled up to the sidewalk and parked, peering
up through the windshield at the tall white tower. Her pulse
quickened as she got out of her car and surveyed her sur-
roundings.

This was it. She could feel it. The beach, the lighthouse,
the palm trees. This location had everything.

Macey glanced around the parking lot, but the only other
vehicle was a dented white pickup with the tailgate down,
and she figured it belonged to the wade fisherman who
stood in the nearby surf, casting his line. Macey checked
her watch. Her interviewee was late, which was annoying
because she'd raced through her morning routine to get here
on time. But now she was glad to have a few private moments to herself to check things out beforehand.

She strolled up the sidewalk and tipped her head back to
look at the towering white beacon. Situated atop a grassy

hill, the lighthouse loomed high above the southern tip of the island. Macey shielded her eyes from the sun as she stared up at it. This was the image she'd been searching for, the motif. The Lost Beach tourism board had told her they wanted a sea turtle as the focal point of their advertising campaign, but ever since Macey caught her first glimpse of the lighthouse, she had been determined to convince them otherwise. And now that she stood here gazing up at the majestic old building, she knew she was right.

Plenty of island travel destinations used a turtle as their logo. A lighthouse was more distinctive. Few places had one. She was already visualizing an establishing shot that closed in on the building's cupola and then turned outward, giving the viewer a sweeping aerial view of the island's southernmost point, which would encompass the white beach and the green marshes and the shimmering blue water.

It would be breathtaking. She would make sure of it. The only eyesore would be the sprawling construction site nearby, but she could minimize that with some skillful editing.

Macey circled the lighthouse, making notes in her mind as she walked. When she reached the front again, a car was parked beside hers, engine idling. A woman with long dark hair sat behind the wheel, staring down at something in her lap as she dabbed at her eyes. Was she putting on makeup? Macey watched impatiently. Every time she told someone she wanted to interview them, whether on camera or not, they fretted about their appearance.

Finally, the woman slid from her car and looked around. Macey walked over and waved.

"Siena, I take it?"

She stepped onto the sidewalk. "Sorry I'm late, I just . . ."

She trailed off as Macey approached her. Siena's eyes were pink and puffy, and she'd obviously been crying.

"Are you all right?" Macey asked.

She nodded. "I'm fine." But her blue eyes filled with tears and she shook her head. "Well, not really. I'm having a bad morning."

Macey eased closer. "Would you like to reschedule? I'm happy to—"

"No, it's okay. I'm sorry." She looked up with a watery smile. "I don't know if you've seen the news lately about the woman at the park?"

Macey's stomach tightened and she nodded.

"We were friends, and I just—sorry." She looked down and squeezed her eyes shut.

"Siena, I'm so sorry. That's awful." Macey stood there awkwardly, wishing there was something she could say to help as the woman struggled to compose herself.

Siena Lewis was strikingly pretty. Tall and slim, she had wavy dark hair and eyes that looked extra blue right now because she'd been crying. Macey felt a pang of sympathy as she watched her try to pull herself together.

"We should do this another time," Macey said.

"No, it's okay." She wiped her cheeks. "Really." She smiled. "I need to be out of the house. All I've done is watch the news, and my boyfriend's right—I need to turn the TV off and get some air." She forced another smile and looked around for the first time. "So, here I am, Lighthouse Point. Most scenic spot on the island. Or at least, the spot most Instagrammed."

Macey just watched her, not sure whether to insist on postponing. But it probably *was* good for Siena to get her mind off it. Wallowing in news coverage wasn't going to help her.

Siena turned toward the lighthouse. She took a deep breath and straightened her shoulders. "It's beautiful, isn't it?"

"It is."

She turned to Macey. "I'm glad you called me. Who gave you my name? You mentioned you talked to a councilman?"

"Jim Conklin. He said your entire family has ties to this place, and you're the expert."

"Well, I don't know about expert, but we definitely have ties. I'm a fifth-generation BOI." She smiled. "That's 'born on island.' There aren't very many of us. My great-grandfather was the last of the original lighthouse operators." She gazed up at the building. "Have you ever been to the top?"

"Not yet. Is it open?"

"Not right now, unfortunately. They're still finishing up the reno. I can probably get someone to let you in, though. The Lost Beach Historical Society is in charge of the renovation, and I know people over there."

"That would be great, thanks."

"You'll probably want to take a camera up to the top and get some shots for your commercial."

"We're doing several commercials, actually."

"Really?"

"Five in total, plus a film montage that they plan to use at the welcome center downtown."

"Sounds interesting." Siena started down the sidewalk, and Macey fell into step beside her. "So, do you like advertising?" She sent Macey a sidelong glance. "I took a class in college. It always seemed like fun, but I ended up majoring in hospitality."

"I'm new to the field, but I like it so far," Macey said. Until her company got off the ground, she wasn't eager to emphasize how green she was. "So, where do you work now?"

"The Windjammer Inn. I'm at the reception desk. During the high season, I work at the Island Beanery, too. Have you been there?"

"No, but I think I saw the sign in town. Isn't it on the beach?"

"Yeah. We've got this big bay window looking out over the water. And we have *amazing* pastries. It's a popular place. Kind of a landmark, actually. It's been here forever."

They reached the far side of the building, and Siena led her across the lawn, where the grass glistened with dew.

She turned to face the lighthouse. "So, what would you like to know about it?"

"I don't know. You tell me."

"Well, let's see. It's ninety-five feet tall. One hundred and nine steps all the way to the top."

"It looks really old. Any good ghost stories?"

She smiled. "Funny you should ask. We used to always say it was haunted."

"'We'?"

"Kids on the island. It was all boarded up for a long time, so it was kind of spooky-looking, especially at night." She lowered her voice. "People used to sneak in there and smoke pot. Or so I've heard."

"I can't imagine all those stairs in that condition."

"Yeah, I don't recommend it." She tipped her head to the side and eyed the lighthouse fondly. "It was built in 1858 to help guide ships through the pass. The original building had fifteen lamps and twenty-one reflectors." She smiled. "Do I sound like a tour guide?"

"Yes, and it's great."

"I can't tell you how many times I've heard the spiel. Let's see, it was in operation until 1910, when the land was sold to the state. The lighthouse closed down soon after that. Then during World War II, the government stationed some troops here and made it into a lookout. I guess they were worried about potential invasion from the Gulf? Hard to imagine now. After the war, they dredged the channel and had more ship traffic, so it was up and running again—that's when my great-granddad was the lighthouse keeper—until 1979, when it closed and fell into disrepair. There was some talk of tearing it down for a while, but the historical society made a big fuss, and they raised money to save it."

"And the renovation?"

"That started several years ago. New paint, new windows, new railing for the spiral staircase. But there was a fire last summer that slowed everything down."

"A *fire*?"

"Yep. Arson. A woman was trapped inside and had to be rescued."

Macey's stomach knotted as she looked up at the lighthouse and imagined the terror of being trapped up there.

"It set the timeline back, but the crew was here all winter, getting everything fixed, and now it's almost ready to reopen. They're just finishing up the gift shop in the villa there." She gestured to a white adobe cottage with a red tile roof. The little structure was surrounded by palmettos and bright pink oleanders. "That's Villa Bonita, the keeper cottage. My great-grandparents lived there when my great-grandad was working here."

"Really? How charming."

"Didn't used to be." She made a face. "After they moved, it became infested with rats and snakes."

Macey motioned to the construction zone beyond the lighthouse's gravel parking lot.

"And what's that over there?" she asked. "Looks like a big project."

"That's our newest resort," Siena said. "I'm surprised Jim Conklin didn't tell you all about it."

"Is he the developer?"

"No, that would be Miles Hancock, another local big shot. But Jim is friends with him. And Jim's always promoting something. He's so salesy. He always reminds me of a used-car dealer."

Macey remembered the guy from the conference call. Golf tan, thick hair, perfect teeth. Macey didn't really mind salesy people. In this line of work, people were always selling something—the mayor, the tourism board, the chamber of commerce. Even the Turtle Lady was promoting an ideology. Macey was used to it. After all, the purpose of her work here was to attract tourist dollars. But Macey planned to be subtle with her message, not beat people over the head with it. You could have a sales pitch wrapped in artistry.

Macey looked past the adobe villa toward the surf beyond. Then she turned back to the lighthouse. The morning sun had turned it from pink to yellow. Her initial impression was right: She'd found her motif. Now she just needed to tell Josh.

And convince the tourism board that this was better than a turtle.

"I can line up that inside tour, if you're interested," Siena said. "My great-grandmother's in the historical society, and I'm sure she'll be happy to get someone over here with a key."

"Your great-grandmother is . . ." She trailed off, trying to find a polite way to phrase it.

"Alive and kicking." Siena smiled. "She's ninety-two, and she's a pepper pot."

"I'd love to interview her."

"Oh, she'd adore that. Talk about stories. She knows every scandal that ever happened on this island."

They made their way back around to the front of the lighthouse where their cars were parked. Siena pulled her phone from the pocket of her shorts and frowned down at it.

"Hate to rush us, but I have to go soon. I've got to be at work at ten and I need to run an errand first." A somber look came over her face as she looked at Macey. "Sorry again about earlier."

"Please don't be. I understand."

"I've been a mess ever since the news." She looked down and seemed to be fighting back tears.

"I'm so sorry for your loss, Siena."

She nodded.

"I really appreciate your coming out here," Macey said. "Especially today, with everything going on."

"No, it's good. I needed to get out of the house." She took a deep breath. "Anyway, I'm off to work. Good luck with your filming." She glanced up at the lighthouse. "I hope it turns out well."

"I'm sure it will. Lost Beach is a special place."

"I know. Or at least I *did*." She turned to look at the water. "Growing up here, it seemed so idyllic. People would always tell me I lived in paradise. But now with all the growth and the traffic and the crime . . . It's very unsettling."

"I understand."

She shook her head. "Sometimes I barely recognize my hometown anymore."

OWEN PULLED INTO Macey's driveway and parked behind her little blue car. As he got out, he glanced at her new tire, which she'd probably overpaid for because Gil made a living by ripping off tourists.

He hiked up the weathered wooden steps and stopped at the top to survey the property. The shrubs were overgrown and the yard needed mowing, just like the neighbors' properties. Owen had been by here multiple times over the past three weeks searching for clues about Julia Murphy's case—first with a CSI team and then by himself to interview neighbors. So far, he'd turned up nothing useful.

Maybe this time would be different.

Owen knocked on the door and waited. The house felt empty. No lamps on, no pipes running. On the coffee table in front of the couch was a lone plate and a pair of mugs. Maybe she'd had someone over for coffee? Maybe someone had spent the night?

Maybe it was none of his damn business.

A mewing sound pulled his attention across the deck, where a mangy white cat rubbed its neck against the corner of the house. It padded over to the door and gazed up at him expectantly.

Owen turned toward the beach and spotted Macey on the bridge. She wore one of those fitted running tops and short black shorts, and even from a distance he could see exactly what had turned every cop's head back at the station house yesterday. Owen knew the second she noticed him because her brisk pace slowed and then resumed. He walked to the edge of the deck and waited for her.

She reached the top of the stairs looking flushed and sweaty, a lot like she'd looked the other morning when he'd caught her snooping around his crime scene. And he had the same gut-level reaction as he'd had then.

"Hey," she said, catching her breath. "What brings you here?" She plucked out her earbuds and walked over.

"Work," he said, although that wasn't really true. He could have asked her to come to the police station for this. Or sent Nicole out to handle it.

She eyed the folder in his hand. "Uh-oh. Am I in trouble?"

He smiled.

"Come inside," she said, wiping her forehead with the back of her hand. "I need something to drink first."

He followed her to the door.

"Are you still on duty?" she asked as they stepped into the dim house.

"Yeah. Why?"

"I was going to offer you a beer." She checked her watch. "It's after five o'clock."

"I see you aren't on island time yet."

"Island time?"

"It's always after five o'clock."

She dropped her earbuds on the breakfast bar and crossed the kitchen to the fridge. He leaned back against the counter as she took out two bottles of water and handed him one.

"Thanks."

He set down his file and twisted the top off the bottle. For a moment, they stood in her kitchen, swilling water and watching each other.

"How far'd you run?" he asked.

"I'm embarrassed to say."

"Why?"

"I'm sure to someone like you, it's nothing."

"Someone like me?"

"You know. Athletic." She grabbed a dish towel from the door of the oven and blotted her neck, then blew out a sigh. "Two miles."

"That's good."

"Right. I know I probably look like I just ran a marathon." She tossed the towel onto the counter and nodded at the file folder. "So, what's in there?"

"A six-pack."

Her eyebrows tipped up. "Mug shots?"

"Yeah."

"Of who?"

"Possibly of your visitor. You want to take a look?"

"Sure, but I seriously doubt I'll be able to help. I only saw him from behind."

"I understand."

She stepped around him and switched on a bright light in the center of the kitchen. Owen took out the first page of photographs—three rows of two—and set it on the counter.

He watched her eyes.

"Anyone look familiar?"

She shot him a worried glance. "I didn't see his face. The hair color is right, but . . ." She sighed.

"Look at the tattoos."

She focused on the page again, tracing her finger over the shoulder in one of the pictures. "It was his right arm," she murmured. "But the tattoo was, I don't know, denser than this. Almost solid black ink." She looked up at him. "I remember thinking at the time it was one of those tribal designs. You know what I mean?"

"Yeah."

"But I really couldn't see from a distance."

He took out the second sheet of paper. One of the six photographs included a tribal design like she was describing, but the man had it on both arms and stretching up to his neck.

Owen watched her eyes and tried to conceal his disappointment.

"Nope." She sighed. "Sorry."

"No problem."

"I wish I'd seen him from the front."

He slid the pages back and closed the folder.

"You know, he could have simply had the wrong house. We can't really assume he came here looking for Julia Murphy." She tipped her head to the side. "But you know that already."

He nodded.

"Which makes me think . . . your investigation is hitting some walls."

It was a simple statement of fact. No judgment in her voice. For some reason he didn't feel defensive, even though he was extremely frustrated with the status of the case. "Hitting some walls" was putting it mildly.

"We're trying to piece together how the victim spent her last days," he said. "Where she was, who she was with. But so far no one's been able to tell us what she was doing besides work."

"Did she have a boyfriend?"

He didn't answer.

"I know, I know." She waved a hand. "You can't tell me. What about her girlfriends?"

"We're working on it."

"Have you talked to Siena Lewis? I was with her this morning, and she was pretty shaken up by Julia's death."

"Siena Lewis."

"Her great-grandfather used to be the lighthouse keeper. She walked me around the grounds."

"No, I know the family. You're saying she was friends with Julia?"

"Evidently. She was really upset by the news. You should interview her."

Owen gazed down at her, not happy with the turn the conversation had taken.

"What's wrong?"

"Nothing."

She sighed. "You don't like getting advice."

That wasn't the problem. At least, not all of it. Owen didn't want her involved in his case. But not only did Macey live at the victim's house; now she was feeding tips to detectives. And the thing was, he needed them. His investigation was completely stalled, and he needed any and every lead he could get, even coming from Macey.

Which didn't sit well with him.

She folded her arms over her breasts. "Well, far be it from me to tell you how to run an investigation. But if you *do* decide to talk to her, she works at the Windjammer Inn. And also a café. The Coffee Beanery, I think."

"The Island Beanery."

"That's the one."

He smiled slightly.

"What?" she asked.

"Nothing." Owen's sister owned the place, but Macey obviously didn't know that.

His phone buzzed. He pulled it from his pocket and read a message from Nicole: CALL ME ASAP!

He tucked his phone away and looked at Macey. "I have to go."

She didn't look surprised. But Owen didn't move to leave. He just stood there, taking in her green eyes and her flushed cheeks and her skin that smelled like sunblock. He wanted to stay right here in her kitchen and take her up on that beer she'd almost offered him. And maybe dinner, too.

Which was a hell of a thing when he was juggling about ten different aspects of a murder investigation and he'd hardly had time to even sleep in three weeks.

His phone buzzed again, and Macey glanced at his pocket. Owen grabbed his file and headed for the door.

"I'll keep an eye out for tattoo guy," she said behind him. "Maybe I'll spot him on the beach."

"If you do, *don't* approach him."

"I won't."

He stepped onto the deck and turned around. "If you see him or anyone else who looks suspicious—"

"If I see anything suspicious, I'll give you a call."

CHAPTER

EIGHT

OWEN PARKED HIS pickup right beside Nicole's unmarked police unit at the edge of the row of campsites. He looked ticked off as he trudged across the sand toward her.

"Did I catch you at dinner?" Nicole asked him.

"No. Where is he?"

"Campsite number 9. White van."

"The Volkswagen?" he asked.

"Yep."

It was one of those old VW vans that was so ancient, it was cool again. The door was open, and it had a yellow tarp attached to the roof for shade. A man sat there now in a lawn chair, watching them warily as he pretended to read a book.

"What's your take?" Owen asked in a low voice.

"He's . . . I don't know. Odd."

"How?"

"You'll see. That's why I wanted you to talk to him here, in his element, so you could get a feel for him."

"How old is he?"

"Twenty-eight. San Antonio address. He's a grad student at UTSA, supposedly, working on a grant."

"'Supposedly'?"

She shrugged. "He seems a little dodgy. Until I check out his story, I'm taking everything he said with a grain of salt."

Owen glanced at the van again. "Okay, I'll talk, you observe. If he contradicts something he already told you, feel free to jump in."

"Got it."

She and Owen walked to the campsite at the far end of the row. They passed a couple lounging in camp chairs, beers in hand, feet propped on a cooler. At another campsite, a sunburned mom handed out hot dogs and juice boxes to a trio of equally burned boys under a blue canopy. The hot dogs smelled amazing, and Nicole realized she hadn't eaten all day. After striking out at the yoga studios, she'd decided to return to White Dunes Park to interview people and maybe catch a glimpse of the elusive person who'd been operating a drone over their crime scene. She hadn't found him.

But she'd found Edward Snell.

As they neared his campsite, he stood up and dropped his book on the chair behind him. *A Birder's Guide to the Texas Coast.*

Snell was tall and skinny, and his faded blue T-shirt hung loose on his lean frame. The tarp above him made his skin look yellow and jaundiced.

"Mr. Snell? Detective Breda, Lost Beach PD."

Owen stopped beside the tarp, and Snell stepped out from under it.

"Detective Lawson tells me you may have information that could be relevant to our investigation."

Snell cast a nervous look at Nicole. "I guess."

"Tell me about your last trip to White Dunes Park," Owen said. "The trip before this one. When did you first get here?"

Snell cleared his throat. "That would be May twenty-fourth. I was here Monday to Friday the week before Memorial Day."

Nicole had sketched out these details to Owen over the phone.

"You left here Friday?" Owen asked.

"That's right, Friday morning. I try to avoid holiday weekends."

"Oh yeah? Why's that?"

Snell just stared at him, like the answer was obvious. It was, but this was Owen's way of getting a read on the guy.

"The noise, the crowds—none of that's conducive to my work."

"I see." Owen rested his hands on his hips. "And what kind of work do you do?"

"I'm an ornithologist." He glanced at Nicole, probably wondering why he was having to repeat everything he'd already told her. "I'm part of a grant through UTSA. We're studying migration patterns of various bird species on the lower Texas coast."

Owen nodded. "And so you spent the holiday weekend where?"

"Back in San Antonio."

"All right. So take me through Friday morning."

Nicole tensed, wondering whether Snell's story would stay the same. If it didn't, that would be a red flag.

"I got up early," Snell told him. "Before dawn."

"What time, exactly?"

"Five forty-five." He darted a look at Nicole. "I remember because I'd set the alarm on my phone. I wanted to get in position before sunrise."

"Position for what?"

"There's a group of roseate spoonbills that nests in the marshes just across the highway from here. You can see them from the top of the dunes. I wanted to be there when they started moving."

"All right. Then what?"

"Then I grabbed my camera and my binoculars and hiked up the sand dune over there."

"Wait. Take me through it," Owen said. "Did you brush your teeth first? Make coffee? Hit the head?" He nodded at the bathroom facilities at the far end of the row.

"Yeah, well, sure. I used the restroom and then I grabbed a coffee—one of those Starbucks cans. And then I got my gear together and hiked up the dune there."

Owen waited, watching him, his arms folded over his chest.

"At the top, I found a good vantage point." He turned toward the dune, shielding his face from the evening sun. "There's a good spot there, right at the top, and you can see their nesting sites. So I spread out a beach towel, got my camera ready, and got out my binocs."

"What kind of binoculars do you use?"

He tensed at the question. Nicole caught it, and she was sure Owen did, too.

"Nikon. Why?"

"Just curious. You have them around or . . ." Owen glanced around the campsite.

Snell hesitated a moment, then ducked under the tarp and reached into the van. Nicole had gotten a fairly good glimpse of his setup during her first interview. The van was crammed with plastic milk crates filled with all kinds of stuff—flashlights, protein bars, cans of soup. Snell rummaged through a duffel and retrieved a pair of binoculars, then stepped over and handed them to Owen.

Owen whistled. "Nice."

"They're good for bird watching."

"I bet." Owen handed them back. "So, you went up to the top of the dune . . . ?"

Snell looked from Owen to Nicole, then back to Owen again.

"I was up there about ten minutes. The sky was just getting light, and I saw this person about, I don't know, maybe a hundred yards south."

Owen watched him, no doubt taking in every detail.

"He was coming down the dune to his car. It was parked in the sand there—the flat part."

"How far from the highway?"

"I don't know. Thirty feet maybe? Right at the base of the dune."

"What sort of car?"

"A white Jetta. It was facing south, but I could see it from the back."

"A Jetta."

"That's right."

"You sure?"

"I'm sure." He sounded impatient now. "I know a Volkswagen when I see one. I practically live in mine."

Owen nodded. "What did this guy look like?"

Snell sighed. "Dark hair, medium build. Like I told Detective Lawson." He looked at her, maybe hoping she'd confirm the description, but she didn't say a word.

"Race?" Owen asked.

"White."

"Any tattoos?"

He shook his head. "No idea."

"What about his clothing?"

"It was hard to tell much because I only saw him from a distance. Something dark, I think. Maybe a T-shirt and jeans or something? He just looked like a shadow, really."

"Okay. What did he do?"

"Nothing. Just walked down to his car and drove away."

Owen watched him, obviously hanging on every detail.

"Was he carrying anything with him?"

"No."

"Did he open the trunk or the back seat?"

"No." Snell shook his head. "He just got in the car and left."

"He was empty-handed?"

"Yeah, I think." He looked unsure now. "I mean, he was pretty far away, like I said. He could have had a phone in his hand or something."

"You know what time this was?" Owen asked.

Snell looked relieved by the question. "Yeah. *That* I know for sure. It was 6:25, right before the birds started moving. I know because that was when I took my first picture that day, and all my photos are time-stamped on my camera."

For the first time since he'd started the questioning, Owen darted a look at Nicole.

"Hey, you mind double-checking that with us?" Nicole asked.

"What, the time stamp?"

"Yeah. We'd love to see it, just to confirm."

"Sure." He returned to the van again, actually climbing into it this time, and they heard him rummaging around inside.

Owen stepped away. Nicole followed him.

"Well?" She kept her voice low. "See what I mean about dodgy?"

"Yeah."

"You think he's odd?"

"I think he's using his binoculars for more than bird watching." Owen turned to look at the line of campsites.

The SUV closest to them had the cargo door open and one of those hanging shower bags suspended from the roof. A woman in a white bikini stood there now rinsing off under the spray. Nicole noticed that a handful of other campsites had similar portable showers.

Okay, creepy. And this was why she needed Owen—he noticed things she missed. Snell might be inside his van right now deleting pictures before he brought out his camera.

Nicole looked at Owen. "You think he's lying about what he told us? I mean, the man on the dune, the VW. He could have gotten those details off the news."

"He could have."

She looked back at the van, feeling deflated. She'd been so excited about this lead, but maybe this guy was just an oddball. Some people had a weird compulsion to get involved in a police investigation.

"Good work, Nicole."

She turned to look at him, surprised by the compliment.

"I'm glad you found this guy. We need to bring him in for a formal statement, then vet everything he says. And it wouldn't hurt to get him on video."

"You think he's credible?" she asked.

"Either way, he's important. If his story's legit, he's our first eyewitness." Owen glanced at the van. "And if it's not, he's a suspect."

CHAPTER

NINE

THE ISLAND BEANERY occupied a prime location in the middle of the tourist strip overlooking the water. The sunflower-yellow cottage had white shutters and ginger-bread trim, and the flower boxes filled with petunias reminded Macey of what her rental house should have looked like if it had lived up to its photos.

The shop was busy with midday customers when Macey stepped inside. She waited in line and read the specials—jalapeño cheddar croissants and New York–style cheesecake. Her mouth started watering just reading the chalkboard.

"Well, hello there."

She turned to see a smiling man in a pink golf shirt. He wore mirrored sunglasses, and she couldn't see his face.

"Jim Conklin. We met on a conference call." He took off his shades.

"Oh, hi. Of course."

He was one of the councilmen who had approved funding for her film project, and she tried to think of something charming to say.

"I see you've already found our best coffeehouse," he said.

"This is my first time here. What do you recommend?"

"Everything. You can't go wrong." He lifted a pastry bag. "I always get banana bread."

"Sounds good."

"So, how's the filming going?"

She'd been prepared for the question, but it still made her nervous.

"Great!" she assured him. "We're still scouting locations, but it's going well so far."

"And I hope you enjoyed your cruise with us?"

"We did. Thank you. We caught a beautiful sunset."

"That's what we like to hear." He grinned and winked. "Be sure to include our logo in your shots, now."

"Oh. Well, we weren't actually getting shots of the boat itself. Our focus was on the bay and getting a view of the island from the water."

His smile dimmed.

"I'm sure your business will benefit from our campaign, though, like everyone else's," she said brightly. "A rising tide lifts all boats, as they say."

"Well, we can all agree on that." His smile was back, and she hoped she'd been diplomatic enough.

Conklin departed with his banana bread, and Macey gave her order to the woman at the register. No sign of Siena, so maybe she had the day off.

As she scooted around the crowd to wait for her coffee, her attention was drawn across the room to a big fireplace. She walked over to examine the whimsical masonry made of conchs, scallops, and clamshells. A collection of starfish decorated the driftwood mantel. Inside the fireplace was a row of fat pillar candles, and Macey imagined a cozy glow filling the room on chilly evenings.

Flanking the fireplace were built-in shelves crammed with books and board games—Monopoly, Sorry, Settlers of Catan. Her gaze fell on a battered box of Risk, and she felt a pang of homesickness. She hadn't played since Christmas, when she'd gone to visit her dad. Risk was their thing. Or at least, it had been. Her dad had never been much of a talker and only became more taciturn after Macey's mom died, but their marathon Risk games had given them a way to spend time together.

"Macey?"

She turned around. Owen Breda stepped over, and a swarm of butterflies filled her stomach. He was dressed as usual, with his holster and badge.

"Hey." She couldn't suppress a smile. "What's up?"

"Not much. Working. And getting some caffeine." He nodded at a table behind him that was opening up. "Want to sit?"

"Oh. I—"

"Here." He pulled out a chair for her, and she found herself sitting down without really deciding to as he took the chair across from her. "What'd you get?" he asked.

"Uh . . . latte. You?"

"Same."

"Well, *hello*." The barista appeared at their table holding a cup in each hand with little plates balanced on top. She set everything down. "I'll get some sugar. One sec." She smiled at Owen and bustled off.

Macey blinked down at all the food. Her blueberry muffin was twice as big as she'd expected. Owen's plate was piled with three croissants.

"I didn't realize they had table service here," she said.

"They don't."

The barista was back. She set a stack of sugar packets in front of Owen and pulled a chair right up to the table.

Owen sighed. "Macey, this is my sister, Leyla."

She smiled. "Lovely to meet you, Macey. Sorry to butt in on your coffee but I have to get an update." She turned to Owen. "*How are you?*"

"Fine."

She rolled her eyes. "You've been dodging my calls. What's going on?"

"Nothing."

Another eye roll as Macey watched the two of them with interest. Leyla had long dark hair and vivid blue eyes, which she accentuated with black eyeliner. Her makeup was flawless, but even without it she would have been beautiful.

"So, have you made an arrest?" Leyla asked.

"Don't you think you would have seen it on the news?"

"Well, are you close?"

His jaw tightened. "No."

"What about the white VW? Has it been recovered?"

Owen's brow furrowed. "How do you know about the VW?"

"I run a coffee shop. I hear things. This case is all anyone's talking about."

Macey sipped her latte and watched the back-and-forth, enjoying Owen's obvious annoyance.

"Then when we make an arrest, I'm sure you'll hear about it."

"I'm sure I will." Leyla shifted her attention to Macey. "Sorry, Macey. We've been a little consumed with all the news. Everyone has."

"No problem."

"Macey's a filmmaker," Owen said. "She's here making commercials for the tourism board."

Leyla lifted an eyebrow. "Is that right? How interesting."

"She's touring all our attractions—the lighthouse, the parks."

"That's one reason I stopped by, actually," Macey said. "I hear the Beanery is a something of a local landmark."

Leyla beamed. "Well, we've been here since 1951, longer than any other beachfront business. Originally, this place was an ice cream parlor."

Having successfully distracted his sister, Owen went to work on his pastry.

"But then the ice cream place shut down," Leyla continued. "Couldn't compete with Carmen's Creamery and Confectionary on Main Street. Have you been there yet?"

"No."

"Oh, you need to go. Definitely. *That* place is truly historic. They've been making saltwater taffy since 1905. They do demonstrations every day at three in the summertime."

"Hey, is Siena working today?" Owen cut in.

"She's in back doing inventory," Leyla said. "Why?"

"I need you to put her on break so I can talk to her."

"About what?"

"None of your business."

"You don't need to be rude."

"I'm not. I'm just stating a fact." He started on the second croissant and glanced at the coffee bar. "Put her on break for fifteen minutes so I can talk to her."

Leyla sighed and looked at Macey. "Do you have older brothers, by chance?"

"No."

"I've got three. And none of them has any manners."

Owen looked offended. "I have manners."

Ignoring him, Leyla stood up and smiled at Macey. "It was very nice to meet you, Macey."

"You, too. I'd love to hear more about your business sometime."

"Come by when it's slower and we'll talk over coffee." She shot a look at Owen. "You've got fifteen minutes."

She walked away, and Owen polished off his second croissant.

Macey smiled and sipped her latte. "You two look alike."

"People say that." His gaze settled on Macey. "Sorry I can't stay." He pushed back his chair. "I need to do this interview."

She nodded at his plate. "Don't you want the last one?"

"That's for you." He stood up. "Leyla's a genius with pastries. She wins awards." He glanced back at the counter, where his sister was talking to Siena now. He looked at Macey. "Would you like to have dinner tonight?"

The question caught her off guard.

"I . . ." She scrambled for a response, but she had no plans. No excuse whatsoever. "I was going to work on edits tonight."

"How about a dinner break?"

She didn't answer.

"Have you been to Chip's? Best burgers on the island."

She stared up at him, sorely tempted. If she said yes, both of her diets would be blown. Destroyed. Annihilated.

"Yes."

"Yes, you've been to Chip's? Or yes, you'll have dinner with me?"

"I'll have dinner with you."

The corner of his mouth curved in a smile, and she could have sworn he looked relieved. He probably wasn't used to women hesitating.

"Good," he said. "I'll pick you up at seven."

NICOLE STRODE INTO the bullpen, searching for Owen. Or Emmet. Or even Joel, who barely showed his face anymore.

Adam McDeere sat at his desk, looking bored as he sat on the phone, probably on hold. The sweat marks on his uniform told her he'd spent a lot of time outside this afternoon.

"Where is everyone?" Nicole asked him.

"Brady's in his office. Emmet and Miranda are working the motel burglary."

"What motel burglary?"

"Someone busted into a couple rooms over at the Sand Dollar."

"Where's Owen?"

"I dunno." He glanced over his shoulder. "He was here a minute ago."

Owen walked out of the conference room, holding a stack of papers in one hand and his phone in the other. He was scrolling through messages.

Nicole met him at his cubicle. "Guess what."

He sat down, not looking up from his phone. "What?"

"I tracked down the silver Toyota."

"What silver Toyota?"

"The one Julia Murphy's friend Brooke told us about. It belongs to a woman who had a yoga class with Julia over at Dharma Yoga. Her name is—"

"Siena Lewis."

Nicole frowned. "How'd you know?"

"I interviewed her a couple hours ago."

"You did? Why didn't you tell me?" She sat on the edge of his desk.

"I didn't know you were working on it still. Anyway, turns out she had some good info."

"Oh yeah?"

Owen tossed the stack of papers on his desk and leaned back in his chair. "It sounds like she knew Julia Murphy a lot better than her co-workers did. They did yoga together three times a week."

"Does she know what Julia was up to the day she went missing?"

"No. Evidently, Julia had been working a lot, and she'd skipped out on their classes recently. But get this, Siena told me that about six months ago, Julia started seeing some new guy."

Nicole's pulse picked up. "Who?"

"That's what I'm working on. She didn't have a name."

"Well, what does she know about him?"

"Not a lot. Just that Julia started seeing him around Christmas and she was secretive about it. Never mentioned his name. When Siena pressed her about it, she said it was no big deal and they'd stopped going out."

"Secretive as in . . . maybe he's married?"

Owen nodded. "Possibly."

"Well, what else would it be?"

"I don't know. I'm going with married. That's what makes the most sense."

"Or maybe her friend knows the guy and wouldn't approve for some reason? Maybe he's Siena's ex or something?"

"That's a possibility, too."

"We should be able to find out who it is. All the more reason we need the victim's phone records. What's the status with that?"

"They came in this morning." Owen shook his head. "There's not much there. I'm still going through numbers, but it's mostly back and forth to her workplace, her sister. Some restaurants in town, where she probably ordered take-out food. She didn't make a lot of phone calls, and we don't have her text messages."

"So, no calls to this mystery boyfriend?"

"Not on the phone number we have records for."

Nicole crossed her arms. "Hmm."

"What?"

"That reinforces the idea that he's married. Maybe he didn't want any messages back and forth that his wife might find."

"That would make sense. But listen to this." Owen grabbed a fast-food cup from the corner of his desk and took a slurp. "Siena said she never knew the guy's name, but she thought he was rich."

"Why?"

"Because around the time Julia started seeing him, she turned up with some expensive stuff. A brand-new iPhone, a designer purse, things like that."

"What kind of purse?"

"A Gucci hobo bag."

"Gucci? Seriously?"

"Yep."

"That's not the kind of thing you give a casual hookup. You have any idea how much those cost?"

Owen grabbed a spiral notebook off his desk and flipped through. "Those purses start at, like, nineteen hundred dollars."

"Could have been a knockoff. Maybe he was trying to impress her." Nicole tipped her head to the side. "On the other hand, it would be hard to pull off a fake iPhone. Do we have any proof he gave her one?"

"Just what Siena said—that she thought these gifts came from the guy Julia was seeing. So, I circled back with Julia's sister, Claire, to see if she knew anything about the gifts or the boyfriend—"

"I thought you already asked her about recent boyfriends. She said Julia didn't have any."

"Right. That's what she said, and she confirmed that again today. Claire Murphy had no idea about a designer purse, but she *did* know her sister had a new iPhone. She said she noticed it last time Julia came to visit her in Corpus Christi.

This was back around Easter. She said it was the newest model with all the bells and whistles, and she made a snarky comment about it because it was nicer than hers. But Julia didn't say anything about it being a gift from anyone."

Nicole leaned over Owen's shoulder to look at the computer screen, where he'd been researching Gucci handbags. Just like her car, the victim's purse, wallet, and cell phone remained missing.

"Well, no place on the island sells iPhones," Nicole said. "Someone would have to go to the mainland. Or else order it online."

"Maybe this guy's from out of town. He could be someone with a weekend place here."

"True. So, he could have bought it anywhere. Still, it should be easier to track down a phone purchase than a handbag."

"Breda!"

They glanced up to see the chief leaning his head out of his office. "Is Miranda back yet?"

"She's still at the Sand Dollar with Emmet."

He cursed and looked around. "I need you to head down to the shrimp docks."

Owen was already grabbing his keys. "What's going on?"

"We got a report of a white VW parked in the lot down there. Looks like it's abandoned."

CHAPTER

TEN

MACEY SLID BEHIND the wheel.

"So, what do you think?" she asked as Josh got into the passenger seat. "Am I right, or am I right?"

"You're mostly right."

"What do you mean? It's perfect." She gestured at the lighthouse through the windshield. "It's distinctive. It's iconic. It's visible from all over the island. This lighthouse is practically begging to be the center of our ad campaign."

She backed out of the space and zipped across the near-empty parking lot.

"I'm not saying it's not a good idea," he said. "I'm just saying they're attached to the turtle concept. And I don't necessarily disagree. People like animals."

"So, we'll put turtles in the ads. I'm not suggesting we ignore them. But from a visual perspective, the lighthouse is much more striking."

"Agreed. But you still have to convince the tourism board."

She turned onto the highway and glanced out the window at the sprawling construction site.

"Hey, look. We need to stop."

Josh looked at her. "Why?"

"I want to talk to them about moving those cranes out of our shot." She slowed and put on her blinker.

"Do we have time? We're supposed to be at the docks at five."

"This'll only take a minute."

She swung into the parking lot. Beside the sign for Hancock Enterprises was a giant banner showing an artist's rendering of the Playa del Rey Resort & Spa, complete with a high-rise hotel, multiple pools, and a golf course.

Macey crossed the lot to a double-wide trailer, which looked to be the construction headquarters. Several pickups were parked outside, including a souped-up Ford with oversize tires. Macey read the vanity plate.

"Check it out, Josh. He's here."

"Who's here?"

"Miles Hancock, the developer. See the plates?"

She parked alongside the shiny black truck.

"What are you going to say to him?"

"I'm going to ask him to kindly do us a favor and move his ugly cranes." She checked her reflection in the rearview mirror to make sure she didn't look too bedraggled. She'd spent the afternoon tromping around outside, so of course she did.

"My hair is a mess."

"He won't be looking at your hair in that shirt."

Macey glanced down at her scoop-neck black T-shirt. She rolled her eyes and pushed open the door. "You want to come with me?"

"No."

"I'll be right back."

"Make it quick. We're already running behind."

Macey approached the trailer, wishing she looked a bit more presentable. Jeans and sneakers weren't exactly her best business look. But everyone here was wearing hard hats and muddy boots, so she decided not to worry about it.

She reached for the door just as it opened. A bearded man in a fluorescent yellow vest stepped out. He looked her up and down with blatant curiosity as she caught the door and went inside.

The trailer was cool and dim. As her eyes adjusted, she noticed a man in the corner leaning over a set of blueprints spread out across a big table. He wore jeans and a button-down shirt with the sleeves rolled to the elbows.

"Excuse me?"

He glanced up.

"Are you Mr. Hancock?"

"No." He looked down at the plans.

"Is Mr. Hancock around somewhere?"

"No."

"Are you sure? I saw his black pickup outside."

He looked up again. "That's his son's. Miles Hancock drives a Range Rover." He frowned. "Who are you?"

She smiled and stepped forward. "Macey Burns with MMB Productions." She handed him a business card.

His frown deepened as he read it.

"We're filming commercial spots for the tourism board, and I had a question about—"

"Call our main office. The PR person can help you."

She stepped closer and glanced at the papers spread across the table. They weren't blueprints after all but some sort of schematic diagram.

"Are you the foreman?" she asked.

"The construction manager. Why?"

She smiled again. "Then this is more *your* area."

He checked his watch and started rolling up the plans. "Listen, lady—"

"It's Macey."

"I'm meeting a county inspector in five minutes. I don't have time to talk about your commercial."

"I won't keep you. I just wanted to ask about the two cranes on the property here. You see, we're doing some filming at Lighthouse Point next week, and it would be really helpful if someone could move them."

"*Move* them?"

"Just temporarily. They're smack in the middle of our shot and—"

"That's not happening."

"It would only be for a day. Two at most, while we—"

"I can't help you. Sorry. We're four months behind schedule already. Between zoning laws and tropical storms and protesters—"

"It would only be a day or two. Surely you could relocate them temporarily."

"I can't. No way." He grabbed a cardboard tube and jammed the rolled-up plans inside. "You want those cranes moved, take it up with Hancock."

"I'll be happy to." She smiled. "Where can I find him?"

He stuffed the cardboard tube under his arm and stepped around her to open the door. "This time of day? Try his home office. Or the marina where he keeps his boat." He yanked open the door, essentially kicking her out.

She exited the trailer, and he followed right behind, pulling a ring of keys from his pocket.

"Good luck," he said, turning to lock the door. "Don't tell him I sent you."

* * *

M IRANDA LIFTED HER camera and took a shot of the
license plate. She glanced at Owen. "I assume—"

"It is."

Yes, this was the vehicle they'd spent nearly three weeks
scouring the entire island—hell, the entire state—to find. It
had probably been here all along. From the instant he'd seen
it, Owen had known it was the car, even before checking the
license plate.

Owen made yet another lap around the Jetta, studying
the exterior and peering through the tinted windows. No
blood smears or any other trace evidence that he could see.
But then, he hadn't really expected anything obvious. If the
car had been dumped around the time Julia Murphy was
killed, then it had been out here for three straight weeks,
and the same thunderstorm that had shifted the sand at
White Dunes Park and uncovered the body had also likely
washed away any forensic evidence they might have recovered from outside the vehicle.

Although you never knew.

Miranda was good. Owen had once seen her lift a usable
fingerprint off a charred pool cue.

So she was definitely skilled, but she was also slow.
Owen watched as she crouched beside the front bumper,
photographing the tire. She snapped about a dozen shots.

"What is it?" he asked.

"I'm not sure. Some interesting grit in the tread."

Owen leaned over, but he didn't see anything interesting
about the gravel in the tire tread. But he wasn't a CSI.

"You mind?" Miranda looked up at him, and he stepped
back to give her room to maneuver.

He folded his arms over his chest and waited patiently,
when what he really wanted to do was yank open the door

and search every last inch of the VW for physical evidence. It had been a grueling three weeks, and he needed a break here.

He took a deep breath and waited, telling himself that Miranda's slow and methodical technique was a good thing. She was thorough.

After about a dozen more photos, she stood and returned to her evidence kit, which was a tackle box that she kept stuffed with brushes, envelopes, and about a million types of fingerprint powder. She lifted a tray and poked through a bin of glass vials.

Tamping down his impatience, Owen looked across the parking lot. The smell of diesel fuel and fish wafted over from the docks. A row of low warehouses faced the water, and a line of pelicans perched along the rooftop, waiting for scraps.

As locations went, this was a pretty good one for dumping a car. Sandwiched between an offshore drilling company and a row of commercial fishing docks, this parking lot was constantly full, with a never-ending rotation of fishermen and rig workers coming and going at all hours of the day and night. Surrounded by a sea of battered pickups and SUVs, Julia Murphy's little Jetta was hardly visible to someone not walking right past it.

Emmet pulled into the parking lot, evidently finished now with the motel burglary. He parked and walked over.

"Anything big?" he asked as he ducked under the yellow tape.

"Not yet."

Miranda returned to the tire she'd been photographing. Using a pair of tweezers, she removed a bit of gravel and dropped it into a glass vial.

Emmet looked at Owen. "You guys open the trunk yet?"

"No."

"I'm still photographing the exterior," Miranda told him. "And most of the work is going to happen at the county crime lab."

"Why?"

"We've got too much going on here." She gestured toward the sky. "Wind, weather, the helo pad. The oil company's chopper has flown over twice already, kicking up dust. The crime lab's garage is a more sterile environment. Less chance of cross contamination."

Owen gritted his teeth. Transporting the car to the crime lab had been Brady's call. Owen could see the point, but just getting it there would take an hour, and the flatbed tow truck hadn't even arrived yet.

"Shit, this is going to take all night," Emmet said.

Miranda shot him a look. "Better than losing evidence."

"Let's compromise," Owen said. "I want to at least look at the trunk here. We still don't have the victim's purse or her clothes or her cell phone. If any of that's in there, we need to get our hands on it ASAP."

"Especially the phone," Emmet said.

Miranda returned to her evidence kit. "I hear what you're saying. Let me give Brady a call and see if he'll clear it." Pulling off her gloves, she walked over to her Jeep to make the call.

Emmet looked over Owen's shoulder. "What's going on over there?"

"Where?" Owen turned around.

"Near the water."

Owen spotted Macey's friend Josh near the warehouses. The man had a camera mounted on his shoulder and appeared to be filming something. Macey stood about ten feet away, talking to a pair of men in yellow waders.

Owen checked his watch and sighed. "Shit."

"What?"

"Nothing."

Owen crossed the parking lot to Macey, feeling a pang of regret as she spotted him and walked over.

"Hey," she said.

"Hi. You're filming the docks?"

"Right now we're mostly scouting. We plan to come back tomorrow morning when they're bringing in the day's catch."

"Not one of our most scenic locations."

She smiled. "People like boats. And seafood. Believe it or not, I know what I'm doing." Her friend stepped over with the camera hoisted on his shoulder. "Have you met Josh?" she asked.

"No."

"Josh, this is Detective Breda. Detective, this is Josh Eckhardt."

The man waved with his free hand. "Good to meet you. Hey, Mace, I'm going to go check out the other side of the dock."

"I'll be there in a sec."

He walked away, and she looked up at Owen, tucking her hands into the back pockets of her jeans. She wore a black T-shirt and had a lanyard around her neck with a laminated card dangling from it.

Owen nodded at it. "What's that?"

"It's from the city," she said. "They gave them to us when they approved our film permit. Tells people we're legit so they'll talk to us."

Macey wouldn't have had any trouble getting the men around here to talk to her, even without the permit.

"Looks like you found your white Volkswagen." She looked across the parking lot and nodded. "Was it here all this time?"

"Possibly."

She raised an eyebrow, maybe picking up on his frustration.

"So, about dinner tonight—"

"You have to cancel." She smiled. "I already figured that."

"They're processing the car tonight at the county crime lab. I've got to drive up there and observe."

"No problem."

"This evidence can't wait."

"It's really no problem." She shrugged. "I'm behind on my editing, anyway."

She seemed relieved. And he had the sneaking suspicion the *yes* he'd managed to get earlier had been a fluke and the next time he tried, he was going to get a brush-off.

"So, we'll take a rain check?" he asked.

"Sure, maybe."

And there it was.

"How about tomorrow night?"

"Let's play it by ear. Seems like both of us really have our hands full with work." She looked over his shoulder and nodded. "I think someone needs you."

He turned around to see Emmet waving him over.

He looked back at Macey. "I'll call you."

"Sure, whatever."

Owen walked back to the yellow tape. Emmet stood with his arms crossed, watching him, as Miranda talked on the phone.

"That the girl from the park again?" Emmet asked. "The one living in the victim's rental house?"

"Her name's Macey Burns."

"I keep thinking I know her from somewhere."

"You don't. She just moved here."

"Yeah, but I swear I recognize her. I keep thinking she's a celebrity."

Miranda walked over. "Who's a celebrity?"

Emmet nodded. "That woman there."

Miranda turned. "Who?"

"The one with the camera guy."

"That's Macey Burns." She looked at Emmet. "The TV reporter."

Owen frowned. "TV reporter?"

"Yeah, from San Antonio," Miranda said. "She does that show *Deadline Texas*."

"I *knew* I recognized her," Emmet said. "My parents watch that show every Sunday. My mom's obsessed with it."

Owen looked across the parking lot at Macey, who was pointing at something now as she talked to her cameraman.

Macey was a reporter. *Macey*, the woman who'd been distracting him for days now with her pointed questions and her sly smile and her killer body. She was a TV reporter. Or at least she had been. Why hadn't she told him that? He'd had no idea.

Although it wasn't like he knew her that well. Or knew her at all, really. He wanted to *get* to know her. That was the whole point of tonight's dinner.

Which wasn't happening now.

"So, Brady gave the green light," Miranda said, dragging his attention away from Macey. "I'm ready if you are." She held up a slim jim.

"Let's do it."

She stepped up to the driver's side of the Jetta and slid her tool between the glass and the door panel. "First, I need to photograph the back." She swiftly popped the lock like an experienced car thief. "*Don't* touch anything yet." She set her tool down and then handed Emmet a pair of latex gloves from her kit. "Put those on. When I give the word, reach in and release the trunk. Don't touch anything else."

Owen stepped aside as she came back and lifted her

camera. She took a bunch of photographs of the trunk, then crouched down and took some more.

Would they find anything inside with fingerprints belonging to her killer? Had he been that careless?

Based on what Owen had seen so far, he didn't think they were dealing with someone careless. But that didn't keep him from holding his breath as Miranda lowered her camera and nodded at Emmet.

"Okay, you're good," she said.

Emmet leaned into the car and hit the release button. He rushed over as Miranda reached down and opened the trunk.

Owen's heart lurched as he surveyed the contents.

Emmet smiled at him. "Jackpot."

CHAPTER

ELEVEN

T HE SUN SANK low over the bay, making the clouds pink and orange as Macey drove home. After dropping off Josh, she'd rolled the windows down, and now the wind off the Gulf whipped through the car, turning her hair into a hopeless tangle.

But what did it matter? It wasn't like she had somewhere to be tonight. Her evening stretched out before her with absolutely no plans, which was bliss. Really. She could finish unpacking, or catch up on TV shows, or even get some editing done.

She'd dodged a bullet when Owen canceled, and part of her felt relieved. One of her most important goals for the summer—no, *the* most important goal for the summer— was to get her new career off the ground. She didn't want to get sidetracked. She couldn't afford to. In the three months since Macey had lost her job, she had downgraded her car, sublet her apartment, and sunk her entire not-large savings into her new business. Not to mention uprooted her life and abandoned her news contacts.

She had to make this work. She'd put everything on the line. And she'd somehow convinced Josh that she knew what she was doing. He'd left a perfectly decent job—albeit a low-paying one—at the TV station to take on this project with her, and she had to make it work out. Not just work out; she had to *nail* it. Her new business was all about referrals, and if she didn't succeed, she could forget about getting any.

Without referrals, she wouldn't land the next project. And without the next project, she couldn't pay her bills. And if she couldn't pay her bills, she'd end up right back where she'd been when she graduated five years ago: postponing her dreams to take a job she didn't want simply to pay rent.

That wasn't part of her plan. She wanted to get her production company off the ground, even if that meant starting small, with advertising work. At least she was in her chosen field. And this was her company. It had her name on it. She needed it to succeed, and not just because her bank account was on life support. Her self-esteem needed it, too. Her new endeavor demanded her full attention, which meant she didn't have time for dating and flirting and smooth-talking detectives with ocean-blue eyes.

So, we'll take a rain check?

She felt a pang in her chest as she pictured him by the boat docks. His question had sounded casual. But the intense look in his eyes had told her that her vague nonanswer wasn't going to cut it. She already knew he was persistent, which meant he was going to try again.

The sign for the Lost Beach Marina came into view. Macey slowed and glanced at the clock. On impulse, she turned onto the narrow road. As she neared the water, she saw rows of sailboat masts silhouetted against the peachy sky.

Macey pulled into the parking lot, passing a bait shack where a man stood smoking a cigarette. She turned down a row of cars and trucks parked outside a long building. The bottom level of the building was decorated with old buoys and nets, and a sign outside advertised fishing tackle. Above the store was a seafood restaurant—Rick's. At the base of the outdoor staircase was the concrete picnic table where just the other day she and Josh had gathered for their sunset cruise. The sky had been even prettier that evening, but Josh had been too distracted by all the models lounging around in yoga gear to notice.

Macey scanned the row of cars, and her gaze landed on a black Range Rover. Her pulse picked up as she pulled into an empty space beside it.

She got out and glanced around. A couple of men with white hair and sun visors were loading a cooler into the back of a Suburban. Remembering the reception she'd gotten earlier, Macey grabbed the lanyard that the tourism board had given her and looped it around her neck. It didn't have quite the magic of the press pass she used to take everywhere, but the laminated ID added a bit of legitimacy. She tucked her cell phone into her back pocket and locked up.

A sidewalk sloped down toward a long wooden dock that faced the water. Six long piers jutted from the dock, each with dozens of boat slips. The slips farthest away were occupied by motorboats, many of them sleeping securely beneath taut canvas covers. The slips closer to the shore held mostly sailboats, with tall masts jutting up some fifty feet into the air.

She started toward the water, scanning the docks for people. She didn't see anyone who looked like he belonged to the black Range Rover. But she did see a familiar young woman with a blond ponytail and a turquoise golf shirt that had the charter boat company's logo on the front. In her arms was a wicker basket filled with striped towels.

Macey approached her with a smile. "Kirsten?"

She looked up, startled.

"It's Macey. We met the other day?"

"Oh. Hi." She smiled. "I didn't recognize you without your hat."

"I'm looking for Miles Hancock. Have you seen him around?"

"Um." Kirsten glanced over her shoulder. "Not today. But we just tied up."

"Do you know where his boat slip is?"

"Which one?"

Macey arched her eyebrows.

"The Boston Whaler or the catamaran?"

"Both," Macey said.

"The Boston Whaler is on pier 5, I think. The cat's on 1."

"Got it. Thanks."

Macey headed for the dock, scanning the piers as she went. She reached the wrought iron gate and stopped short, cursing as she remembered it required a passcode. She glanced over her shoulder, but Kirsten was nowhere in sight.

Macey glanced around. The gate blocked access to the piers so random people such as herself couldn't go skulking around people's boats. The narrow gate was flanked by pointy iron bars that made it nearly impossible for someone to climb around it.

Nearly impossible. Macey was almost certain she could manage it. But if she failed, she'd do a belly flop into the water, which might attract a wee bit of suspicion.

"Excuse me." A man walked past her on the dock. He held a yellow bait bucket in one hand and used his free hand to tap in a code.

Macey hurried up behind him. "Thanks," she said breezily as she whisked through the gate and it clanged shut behind them.

The man headed for the motorboats. Not wanting to make conversation with him, Macey decided to try the sailboats first. With fake confidence, she strode down pier 1. There were only two catamarans on this pier. One of them was uncovered and the other was neatly tucked away beneath blue canvas.

Macey approached the gleaming white sailboat. It had to be thirty feet long, at least. The woodwork was polished to a high shine, and George Strait's soft drawl drifted from the cabin.

She stopped beside the bow. "Hello?"

No answer.

She spied the brown beer bottle in the drink holder beside the helm.

The boat bobbed gently in its slip. The lines were tied loosely, suggesting maybe someone had taken it out recently. She walked alongside the boat and read the black script partially hidden beneath a rubber fender: *Annabel Lee*.

Huh.

She wouldn't have expected a real estate developer to name his boat after an Edgar Allan Poe poem. But, hey, she'd never met the man. Maybe he was a literature buff.

"Hello?" She rested the toe of her shoe on the side and leaned forward to peer into the cabin. "Anyone home?"

George continued crooning about his exes in Texas, but apart from that—silence.

Macey sighed. Maybe she should try his office tomorrow.

"Stop right there."

She turned to see a man behind her.

In his hand was a gun.

WHO ARE YOU?"

Macey opened her mouth to respond, but her mind went blank. The pistol was black and clunky, and she couldn't tear her eyes from it.

He flicked the pistol at her. "Get your foot off my boat."

She snatched her foot away. Then she took a step sideways, putting some distance between herself and the sailboat.

"Who the hell are you?" he asked.

"I'm . . . Macey Burns."

"You're trespassing."

"I'm not—"

"I saw you sneak through the gate."

She dragged her gaze from the gun and looked him over for the first time. He wore a black golf shirt and visor, and she could see her distorted reflection in his Ray-Bans. He was big and bulky, like an athlete who was past his prime.

His pistol hand moved again, and her heart skipped a beat.

"You're on private property. Leave, or I'll have you charged with trespassing."

"I—" She cleared her throat. "I think we have a misunderstanding. Mr. Hancock, is it?"

His gaze narrowed. "Who sent you here? Are you a reporter?"

"No."

"Are you with one of those groups?"

"Groups? No. I'm Macey Burns, CEO of MMB Productions. I've been attempting to reach you, and your office recommended I try you here."

He just stared at her.

As her thoughts began to clear, she started to feel less scared and more outraged that they were having this conversation while he had a gun in his hand. What the hell was wrong with this guy?

Maybe he read her body language because he tucked the gun in the back of his khaki shorts.

"I'm filming commercials for the island's tourism board," she said, "and we're setting up a shoot at Lighthouse Point. I need to talk to you about your construction site."

"What about it?"

"Specifically, the cranes. They're in the middle of our shot and—"

"That's not my problem."

"Actually, it is."

His brow furrowed. She couldn't see his eyes behind the Ray-Bans, but he didn't look happy.

"Our commercial spots will be seen by millions of viewers. They'll be people's first glimpse of your new resort, and I'm sure you want to put your best foot forward."

He didn't say anything.

"If you move the cranes—"

"Do you know what all these delays are costing me?" He

took a step forward, and she stepped back. "Every week we run over schedule I'm losing money, and we're months behind already. I'm not moving anything for anybody, and that includes the tourism board."

"But—"

"You got a problem with that, talk to my lawyer." He stepped closer. "In the meantime, get off my dock."

THE GARAGE AT the county crime lab was filled to capacity, its four wide bays occupied by a car, two pickups, and a pontoon boat perched on a trailer.

Julia Murphy's white VW sat in the bay on the end, beside a white truck whose back end had been accordioned. The pickup was toast, no doubt about it. By contrast, the Volkswagen looked perfectly fine. The trunk was closed now, but every door was open, and Miranda knelt beside the front passenger side, dusting the handle with one of her brushes.

"I heard they were full," Owen said, crossing the garage. "I expected more people."

Miranda didn't look up from her work. "Everyone cleared out." She glanced up. "Oh my gosh. You didn't."

He held up the Dairy Queen bag, and the smell of French fries filled the air.

"You're evil," she said.

"Yep."

She set her tools down and walked over, smiling. She wore white coveralls and had her hair pulled up in a tight ponytail. Owen set the bag down on a metal stool near the wall.

"I'm starving." She stripped off her latex gloves and tossed them in a biohazard bin. Then she snatched up the bag and peered inside.

"Cheeseburger with fries." He handed her a cup. "And a double-chocolate shake."

She beamed. "How did you know?"

"I asked Joel."

Her gaze softened at the mention of his brother. "Thank you."

"Don't mention it. Thanks for working late."

She perched on the stool and sipped the milkshake. "I'm not supposed to eat in here."

"I won't tell anyone."

She took another slurp and closed her eyes. "That's so good. I haven't had anything since breakfast. What time is it anyway?"

"Almost eight."

She offered him some milkshake, but he shook his head. "So, did you *see* Joel, or talk to him on the phone?"

"I had an actual sighting. Passed him in the parking lot at the police station."

She sighed. "He's working too much."

"We all are."

"I know, but his is dangerous."

Owen couldn't argue with that. His brother was spending half his time conducting raids. It was exciting work, and Joel probably loved the adrenaline rush. Owen didn't bother to try to minimize the risks with Miranda, when she knew all too well what they were. Instead, he kept his mouth shut.

Owen surveyed the cavernous garage and then walked over to the Jetta. "So, what have you turned up?"

"A lot."

The knot in his chest loosened. "Finally. We're dying for a lead here."

She slid off the stool. "I hope you're not going to be disappointed."

"Tell me what you found. Any prints?"

"Tons." She joined him beside the car. "But I wouldn't be surprised if most, if not all of them, belong to the victim."

"Why do you say that?"

"Because I recovered some prints from the steering wheel, as you'd expect. But I also recovered traces of cornstarch."

"Cornstarch?"

"You know that chalky stuff you get with some latex gloves? It's a donning agent that makes them easier to put on."

"So, he wore gloves."

"That's what it looks like."

"Any hair in the car or anything like that?"

"Three hairs recovered from the driver's side. All long and brown, though, so they likely were shed by the victim."

Owen sighed. "What else?"

"I also got that gravel from the tire tread."

"What about it?"

She shrugged. "It's a little unusual. For the island, at least. Most of the unpaved roads and parking lots on the island are made with caliche. This stuff is pinkish-brown. It could be nothing, but it could be a lead."

Owen nodded. "What about the trunk contents?"

"*That* is likely your best bet."

She led him past the car to a large table made from a piece of plywood on sawhorses. She switched on a spotlight over the table. In the center of the table was a folded blue tarp.

"The tarp is interesting," she said. "Not because it's unusual—it isn't. This brand is super common. You can buy these at hardware stores everywhere."

Owen had suspected as much when he'd seen the crumpled tarp in the trunk of Julia's car.

"What's interesting is what I recovered from it: four long brown hairs and several fibers. I think this came from the original crime scene."

"So . . . sounds like he killed her, wrapped her in this thing, and loaded her into the trunk of her own car."

Miranda shuddered. "Sick, isn't it?"

Owen nodded. He'd been a cop ten years, and even to him it sounded callous.

"Then it appears he drove to White Dunes Park to dump the body," Miranda said.

"But he may not have gone through the entrance. We have an eyewitness who claims he saw someone in a white VW parked just off the highway *behind* the park around dawn on the morning after Julia went missing."

"I didn't know that."

"We haven't vetted him yet. But if this guy's story holds, then the killer didn't pass through the gate. He snuck in from the back."

"Teenagers do it all the time. Like those kids who flipped the SUV. Whoever killed her probably didn't want to be seen by a park ranger or anyone else there."

"What do you know about the fibers?" Owen asked.

"Well, I'm no expert on fibers, so I packaged them up already and took them to the trace evidence examiner here. He's got a whole database at his disposal, so he'll probably be able to tell you precisely what they are."

"What do *you* think they are?" he asked. Miranda had enough experience to at least take a stab at it.

"Two blue fibers. Probably a synthetic blend? I'd say carpet or maybe upholstery. Didn't look like clothing fibers to me."

Owen turned to the table again and settled his attention on the main piece of evidence he'd been focused on since they'd opened that trunk.

The shovel.

It had a green metal grip and a rusty metal blade. Little white granules of sand were lodged in the narrow crevice between the wood and the metal. The shovel had been left in Julia Murphy's trunk and had no doubt been used to dig her grave.

"Tell me about the shovel."

Miranda stepped over to it. "Good news and bad. Again, this looks generic to me. Several of the CSIs here looked at it, too, and they agreed. It's a cheap brand, and—again— common at hardware stores. But the good news is, it's fairly old."

"Why is that good?"

"Well, it's had a lot of wear. Even if someone wore gloves while they handled the body and dug the grave, this shovel has been used before by someone. I swabbed it thoroughly, and we'll see what comes back from the DNA lab. Maybe we'll get something useful."

"Unless the killer stole it from someplace."

Miranda frowned. "I hadn't thought of that."

Owen had. He'd thought of just about every possible way his evidence could fizzle. And so far, much of what he'd thought of had happened.

Owen raked his hand through his hair and studied the evidence before him. When they'd first opened the trunk, it had seemed like a treasure chest of evidence. But now he felt like he was pinning his hopes on a generic tarp and a cheap shovel. Oh, and some bits of gravel that could have come from anywhere.

Miranda gave him a worried smile. "Don't get discouraged. We may get lucky."

"We need to get lucky soon," he said. "Time's ticking."

MACEY MOVED HER mouse to adjust the shadows, sharpening the contrast between the lighthouse and the surrounding sky. The result was good. Actually, it was excellent considering it was one of her first efforts after arriving on the island. She'd gotten the shot from a bayside vantage point on her second morning here. The lighting was perfect, and she loved having the lighthouse in the distant background. But the boat in the foreground was a bit blurry, and she wished she'd gotten it from a different angle.

She zoomed in on the fisherman standing at the stern. Maybe he was a regular on the bay. If so, she might be able to go back and get a similar take. Not tomorrow, because she was supposed to meet Josh at the docks again. But she could go later in the week. And if he wasn't there, she might find some other guy out on his boat, casting his line against the backdrop of a fiery orange sunrise.

She closed out and clicked open another shot—this one of a great blue heron picking its way through the marsh. It had been taken the same morning as the fisherman, and she'd managed to zoom in close enough to get the distinctive black plumes on the back of the heron's head.

Beauty is in the details, one of her film professors used to say.

The bird would end up in their commercials, no question. The tourism board wanted to lure nature lovers and families to the island. One of their stated objectives was to move beyond Lost Beach's reputation as a hub for spring breakers and drunken revelers.

Macey was well aware of the inherent conflict in what she was trying to do here. Attracting people to Lost Beach was good for the island's economy but potentially detrimental to its ecology. Some members of the tourism board had voiced the same concern and had made it clear they wanted a more nuanced message than simply, "Come to Lost Beach!" Hence, one of Macey's goals was to showcase the island's natural wonders and appeal to people who would appreciate and respect the place, not trash it.

Her phone chimed. She checked the screen and saw that it was Josh.

"Hey, what's up?"

"I got your message," he said. "So, you tracked him down?"

She leaned back in her chair. "Yeah, Miles Hancock. Charming fellow, by the way. He pulled a gun on me just for looking at his sailboat."

"A *gun*? What the hell did you do?"

"What did *I* do? What kind of question is that? I didn't do anything!"

"I've seen you in action, Mace. You have boundary issues."

"What does *that* mean?"

"You've never met a gate or a gatekeeper you didn't plow right through. No Trespassing signs are invisible to you." He paused. "You want me to believe you were just looking at his boat?"

She didn't respond.

"Macey?"

"I may have put my foot on it for, like, two seconds when I was checking to see if someone was on board. But that doesn't give him the right to start waving his pistol around like he's Wyatt Earp."

Josh sighed. "This is Texas. A man's home is his castle and all that shit. Same applies to his boat. Anyway, what did he tell you?"

"When he finally put his gun away, he basically told me to get lost. I think he thought I was a protester."

"Why?"

"Well, I've been reading up on him and turns out some environmental groups have been after him over the golf course he's building. They had him tied up in red tape for months."

"That would explain why he's hostile."

"He refuses to move his cranes, and he doesn't care if his resort looks like crap in our commercials. His project is behind schedule, and he's not moving anything."

Macey swilled some cold water and plunked the bottle on the table. She'd managed to calm down since her run-in, but just talking about it got her heated up again.

Josh was silent.

"Um, hello? Do you have any reaction to me being in an armed confrontation over our filming?"

"Yeah, screw him."

"Excellent response. All our problems are solved."

"No, really. We don't need him," Josh said. "I'll work around him."

"How?"

"I'll use the drone for the lighthouse shots. I'll get everything we need and leave his property out of it. You'll never even see it."

Macey considered the idea. Drone camerawork was tricky. Josh was definitely skilled, but Lighthouse Point was going to be a crucial element of their campaign, and they couldn't afford for the shots to look amateurish.

"I'll handle it, trust me."

"I do," she said.

"Good. So, don't give this guy another thought. I'll see you tomorrow."

They got off the phone, and Macey returned her attention to her editing. Since her confrontation, she'd showered, eaten, and distracted herself with work, but still she felt anxious. She'd been in a lot of tense situations over the years. Going around with a camera crew and shoving a microphone under people's noses didn't exactly endear her to everyone. While working as an investigative reporter, she'd been flipped off, cursed out, and had doors slammed in her face. And she'd dealt with a daily wave of vitriol on social media. But no one had ever threatened her with a gun until today. She wasn't used to guns, and the experience rattled her.

Her phone chimed. She didn't recognize the number this time, and it was a local area code.

"Hello?"

"Hey, it's Owen."

She closed her eyes. His deep, warm voice had a calming effect.

"Hi." She got up from her computer and stepped over to the sliding glass door that faced the deck. "How's it going at the crime lab?"

"It's done. At least, for now."

Silence stretched out. But instead of making her feel awkward, it put a buzz of anticipation inside her.

"So, hey, do you still want to have dinner?"

She laughed. "It's ten thirty."

"I know. I was hoping maybe you're a night owl."

She smiled. "I am, actually. But I had Chip's already."

He made a pained sound. "You went there without me?"

"Someone told me they have the best burgers on the island."

"And?"

"And they were pretty good."

He gave an exaggerated sigh, and she tried to visualize where he was. Was he sitting at his desk? Driving home in his truck? Maybe walking through the door of his house or his apartment or wherever the heck he lived?

"How about a drink, then?" he asked.

She bit her lip. All night she'd been telling herself it was good that he'd canceled. He'd given her a second chance to make a smart decision. In the five hours since she'd bumped into him, she'd recommitted herself to her summer cleanse.

"I'd really like to see you."

Her heart gave a little flutter. He sounded so *polite*, and she couldn't say no. Or she could, but she didn't want to.

She cleared her throat. "Where?" If he said Finn's, she was out. She didn't want to be at a meat market tonight. And the mood there was all wrong, anyway. If she met him there, he'd probably think he could get her to go home with him. Or get her to invite *him* home with her, which she absolutely wasn't going to do.

"How about the Bitter End?" he said. "It's just down the beach from you."

"Isn't that the restaurant at the Windjammer?"

"They have a bar, too. I can meet you there in fifteen minutes."

Macey gazed up at the nearly full moon shining down on her deck. It was a beautiful night and having a cozy drink with him by the water was probably a bad idea.

"Macey?"

"I'm thinking."

"You know, you're killing my ego here."

"Ha."

"I'm serious."

"The thing is, it's already late and I have to be up early and—"

"Same," he said. "We'll keep it to one drink."

Somehow, she didn't believe he'd stick to that. Or maybe she didn't believe she would.

"Macey?"

"I'll meet you there in twenty."

THIRTEEN

I T WAS WORSE than she'd imagined.

Moonlit beach, balmy breeze, thatched-roof restaurant surrounded by flickering tiki torches. Macey spotted him right away at the far end of the bar. He wore jeans and a dark gray T-shirt that stretched over his muscular chest, and he got up from his stool as she walked over. His hair was damp, and he'd clearly been home to change. She'd changed, too, out of her SpongeBob pj's and into jeans and a gauzy white shirt. She'd even put on mascara for the first time since she'd come to the island.

"You changed," she said.

"Yep."

She took the stool beside him. She'd never seen him without his badge and gun. Although, looking him over, she realized he probably had both on him somewhere. She glanced down at his scuffed work boots and wondered if he wore an ankle holster.

A bartender walked over. "Something to drink?" he asked her.

Macey asked for a vodka cranberry and Owen ordered a beer, which told her he was officially off duty now.

"So," she said as the bartender walked away. "How's the case going?"

"Okay."

"Any leads from the car?"

"Some."

Obviously, he wasn't eager to talk about it, but she couldn't help prodding him for more. She was in the habit of fishing for information, especially when she sensed someone didn't want to talk. With Owen, she decided on the indirect approach.

"You don't look happy," she said.

His jaw tightened. "We're still waiting on lab work. It's a slow process. And patience isn't my strong suit."

"Me either."

Waiting on lab work wasn't a good sign. Eyewitness leads were much quicker to pursue, but it sounded like he didn't have a lot of those.

The bartender brought Macey's drink over and popped the top off Owen's beer. He set the bottle in front of him, along with a bill and a credit card. Owen must have slipped him his card earlier. Evidently, he'd meant it when he said they'd keep it to one drink.

"Thank you," Macey said as he signed the check and tucked the card into his wallet.

"Let's go over here," he said, picking up his beer.

She grabbed her drink and slid from the stool. Owen caught her free hand in his, putting a little tingle inside her as he led her across the patio to a long Mexican-tile railing overlooking the beach. People were gathered on bar stools along the railing in pairs and clusters. They found two empty stools on the end and set down their drinks.

A breeze wafted over them, and she caught the scent of something woodsy and masculine—his soap, probably. He hadn't shaved, though, and a thick layer of stubble darkened his jaw.

"So, how come you didn't tell me you're some hotshot TV reporter?" He tipped his beer back.

"I'm not. I'm a hotshot *filmmaker*." She squeezed lime into her drink and took a cold, tart sip. "Just kidding. I'm a complete unknown with a degree in filmmaking and a mountain of student loans."

"How'd you end up in Lost Beach? Not exactly Hollywood."

She sighed. "Long story."

He lifted his eyebrows.

"The short version is, I left my job in disgrace back in March."

"Disgrace, huh?" He shook his head. "Now I definitely want to hear the long version."

"It's really not that interesting."

"Try me."

She stirred her drink and took another sip to fortify herself.

"Well, let's see. I'll fast-forward the slow part. I grew up in Arizona, went to NYU, and graduated with plans to become a documentary filmmaker, at which point I discovered that (a) there aren't a lot of jobs for documentary filmmakers in New York, (b) there aren't a lot of jobs for documentary filmmakers anywhere, and (c) I needed to cast a wider net. So, after researching the cost of living everywhere, I moved to San Antonio and took a job at a local TV station as a production assistant."

He nodded.

"I was basically a gopher, but at least I was working in my field. My plan was to use my day job to pay the bills and use my copious free time to finish my documentary."

"What happened to the plan?"

She sighed. "I got sucked into the rat race. Long hours, crappy money, no time to look for anything else. But then I landed an associate producer job on one of their news shows."

"*Deadline Texas*," he said.

She paused. "You googled me."

"Emmet told me."

"Emmet?"

"The detective you saw at the station the other day. His family lives in San Antonio, and he recognized you."

She nodded. "Anyway, about two years ago, the lead reporter quit abruptly, leaving us totally in a panic, and they had me cover her spot for a few weeks."

He raised his eyebrows. "They just threw you in there cold?"

"It made sense at the time. I knew the show, the stories we were developing, the sources. Plus, I had the look they wanted."

"The look?"

She rolled her eyes. "You know, the hair color, the body type. I resemble the previous reporter, so I essentially stepped right into her shoes. Although they did ask me to go platinum blond, but I told them to kiss off." She shrugged. "A few weeks turned into a few months, and before I knew it, I was part of the lineup."

He sipped his beer, watching her. "None of that sounds disgraceful yet. What happened?"

She stirred her drink. "Basically, I had an affair with a source, and my boss fired me."

He lifted an eyebrow. "Ah. A sex scandal."

"Yup."

He leaned closer. "I'm not in the news business, but what's the big deal about sleeping with a source?"

"It's a conflict. A major one, in this case. It showed terrible judgment, and I deserved to get fired."

He looked at her expectantly, and she realized she was going to have to elaborate.

"You remember that news story last spring about the San Antonio ER nurse who went missing and then they found her remains and arrested her husband?" she asked.

"The doctor."

"Yes. We did this three-part series on it when it went to trial. Huge ratings. He got convicted, and now the case is on appeal."

"Okay."

"During the trial—at the very, very end of the trial—I started seeing the prosecutor."

She looked down at her glass, choosing her words carefully. She wasn't about to tell him how naïve she'd been, how stupid, how she thought she'd fallen in love. And she definitely wasn't going to tell him what a gut punch it was when she realized he'd been manipulating her.

"Aaron Burleson."

Her head jerked up. The name was like a slap.

"That was the prosecutor, right?" He was watching her with those sharp blue eyes. He remembered the story.

"Right." She cleared her throat. "The prosecution team withheld evidence. Or that's what the defense claims anyway. It's the basis for the appeal."

Which Aaron knew when he started his charm offensive. Which was why he started it. He wanted to manipulate her and control the narrative that was about to play out in the media.

It might have worked, too. But a rival network got wind

of the affair, and her bosses had no choice but to fire her. The whole thing had been humiliating.

"So, what happened with Burleson?" Owen asked. "He deep-sixed some exonerating evidence, right? Something about a witness who saw a suspicious car in the victim's driveway on the day she disappeared?"

Macey stared at him. He knew the details of the case. She shouldn't be surprised—he was a detective. It was basically a textbook example of how *not* to bring a murder case to trial. The prosecution screwed up badly, and Aaron knew it, and he used Macey as part of his damage-control effort.

Or at least he tried to. When she told him she couldn't continue covering the story and she had to disclose their relationship to her bosses, he broke up with her.

And *that* had been the biggest gut punch of all. It—very literally—knocked the wind out of her. In one awful conversation she realized not only that her supposed "relationship" was a sham but that she'd been an easy mark. It had taken pathetically little effort for him to get her to throw all her professional ethics right out the window. In no time at all, she'd become the very thing she'd always despised: a ditzy reporter with no substance, open to manipulation by some smooth-talking man.

She didn't think she'd ever forgive him for it, and she knew for certain she'd never forgive herself.

Owen was still watching her intently.

"So . . . the network decided they would cut you loose, change the subject, and hope the scandal went away," he summarized. "Which it has, right? It's been, what, two months?"

"Three. It's died down for now." She looked out over the moonlit beach, which seemed much less romantic now that they were talking about Aaron. Just thinking about him made her feel queasy.

Which was a good thing, really. She'd come here to get a fresh start and get her life back in order, and the last thing she needed was to get sucked into another romance.

"So, hey."

She shifted her attention back to Owen.

"I'm still waiting for the 'disgraced' part."

She just looked at him.

"Sounds like you made a mistake, owned up to it, and now you're moving on," he said.

"It's not quite as simple as that."

"Why not? Put it behind you. That's what I always do." He sipped his beer.

"Did you ever sleep with one of your sources, Detective? Someone who was part of a police investigation?"

He seemed to think about it. "No. But I've done plenty of other stuff I'm not proud of."

"Is that right? Do tell."

He shook his head. "That'll take way longer than one drink. We're going to have to do this again."

She smiled up at him. He had a low-key way about him that put her at ease. But was that really him or was that a technique to get her to loosen up? She didn't trust her judgment anymore. At least not when it came to men.

"What's that look?" he asked.

"I'm trying to figure you out."

"It's not too hard. What you see is what you get."

"See, I don't think so."

He seemed amused by that. "No?"

"No. If you have such a sketchy past, how'd you get into law enforcement?"

He smiled slightly. He had a nice smile, but she had a feeling he was using it to stall for time.

"You could say it runs in the family."

She remembered the receptionist at the police station asking her which Breda she was looking for.

"So . . . your dad is a cop?"

"My brother Joel." He tipped his beer back. "My dad was a game warden with Parks and Wildlife."

"Interesting. Did he retire?"

"He died."

"Oh." Guilt needled her. "I'm sorry."

His eyes turned somber. "Thank you."

Questions flooded her mind, and she searched his face for any indication that this was something he wanted to talk about.

He cleared his throat. "It's been almost six years now. Doesn't seem like it."

"My mom died when I was twelve," she said. "Sometimes it seems like it's been forever. Other times . . ." She looked out at the beach, thinking about her mother's voice and her laugh and how she used to hold her dad's free hand when he was driving. They had been in love. It was something Macey knew, deep in her bones. And now her father had spent nearly twenty years alone, while Macey had grown up and moved away and embarked on a career.

Owen was looking at her. "You still miss her."

He stated it as a fact, not a question.

"Every day. But sometimes . . ." She shook her head.

"What?"

"Sometimes I miss her more for my dad than for me, if that makes sense. It's hard watching him be by himself."

Something flickered in Owen's eyes. He didn't say anything, but she somehow knew he understood exactly how she felt. And she somehow knew that he loved his mother.

Okay, *how* had they gotten onto something so serious?

Macey sipped her drink and looked out at the surf. The

tide was out, and the beach was especially wide tonight, with moonlight glimmering off the wet sand.

"It's so beautiful," she said. "I can't believe you live here. Do you ever get used to living in a place that most people come on vacation?"

"I see a different side to it than most people."

Of course he did, given his job. She would imagine he saw a lot, and that he harbored a lot of rough images in his mind after years in law enforcement.

"Do you ever get tired of all the tourists?" she asked.

"No." He took a sip of beer and set his bottle down. "We need tourists. That's why we hired you."

"And I'm glad you did."

"So am I."

The look in his eyes when he said it made her heart do a little skip. His mouth curved in a teasing smile, sending a ripple of warmth through her. He'd turned the conversation around, and now he was being charming again. He was very good at it, and she felt slightly buzzed right now, even though they'd only had one drink.

She looked down at her glass. Every drop had disappeared. She didn't have to look at her phone to know that it was after midnight.

She pulled her phone out anyway and checked it. "I should go," she said.

"Late for your curfew?"

"Yep." She kept her voice light. "I've got to be up at five." He winced. "Why?"

"First light," she said. "It's a film thing. We plan to be set up at the docks by five thirty so we can get the sunrise over the bay and then the boats coming in."

She slid off the stool. "Thanks for the drink."

"Sure." He stood, too. "Did you park in front?"

"I walked."

"You *walked*?"

"It's not far. And the breeze is nice tonight."

"You shouldn't walk on the beach alone at night. And definitely not right now."

The sharp tone of his voice left no room for argument.

"I'll give you a ride," he said.

They walked together past the bar and the tiki torches and the tropical landscaping surrounding the Windjammer's meandering pool. They passed through the open-air lobby and came out by the valet stand at the front of the hotel. The attendant had left for the night. Owen led her to his white pickup at the edge of the lot.

He popped the locks and opened the passenger door for her, then reached around her and grabbed a baseball cap off the floor. He tossed it in the back.

She hitched herself into the big leather seat, checking out his truck as she buckled in. It smelled new. And clean. And she was surprised to realize that surprised her.

"What's that look?" he asked as he slid behind the wheel.

"Nothing. It's just really tidy, that's all."

"*Tidy?*"

"Yeah."

"No one's ever accused me of being tidy before."

The truck made a throaty growl as he started it and pulled out of the space. Macey rested her hand on the console and drummed her fingers on the faux wood. Butterflies flitted through her stomach. This was exactly why she'd walked. She'd wanted to avoid the whole awkward goodbye moment at her car door. Or at her house door if she had let him pick her up.

He reached the end of the Windjammer's palm-lined driveway and pulled onto the highway. They drove in silence, and Macey looked out the window. The moon cast a silvery glow over the trees and beach houses. Only a few homes had lights on in the windows, she noticed. In the middle of the week, the island seemed far less populated. Owen passed the spot where she'd had the blowout on that first stormy night, and she looked at him across the dark truck cab. He had a good profile. Straight nose, strong jaw. Even his Adam's apple was sexy.

He glanced at her, and she wondered if he knew what she was thinking. He was probably used to women fantasizing about him. She looked away, annoyed with herself.

He pulled onto Primrose Trail and eased down the road, gliding smoothly over the potholes that always made her teeth rattle when she drove over them in her little Honda. Her suspension was no match for his.

He pulled into her driveway behind her car and cut the engine.

"Thanks again for the drink." She pushed open her door.

"I'll walk you up."

She slid from the truck and shut the door with a soft *click*. He was busy scanning her driveway as she rounded the front.

"Your floodlight's out," he said, nodding toward the corner of the house.

"Oh. Yeah, it's been that way."

"You need to call your landlord."

"I keep meaning to." She started up the stairs. "The deck lights work, so I keep forgetting."

"Don't. It's a safety issue."

Something furry darted past her ankles, and she gave a little yelp.

"Is that your cat?" Owen asked.

"That's Possum."

"Your cat's name is Possum?"

"He's not mine." She paused on the landing. "I just call him that. He lives around here. I think someone feeds him and—"

He caught her hand as he joined her on the landing, and her heart skittered. He leaned his head down, stopping for a second, as if to give her a chance to object. When she didn't, he kissed her.

His mouth was warm and firm, and he was completely in control, which should have come as no surprise. His fingertips glided up the side of her neck, tilting her head back at just the right angle as he coaxed her lips apart. He tasted good, and she felt herself melting against him, sliding her hands over his shoulders, feeling his hard muscles beneath the soft fabric of his T-shirt. The kiss was hot and insistent, and she went up on tiptoes as his hands slid down to her waist and pulled her close.

She let herself go. She knew she shouldn't, but she did anyway, letting the moment go on and on as he changed the angle of the kiss and tangled his tongue with hers. His warm arms wrapped around her as the cool ocean breeze gusted around them. She combed her fingers into the thick softness of his hair as she flattened her breasts against his chest, and he made a low groan. The sound was like a little warning bell. She had to stop. Now. Before she did something really dumb, like invite him inside. She started to pull away, but then she changed her mind and sank into the kiss again. She didn't want it to end.

Slowly, she lowered her heels, easing back from him and blinking her eyes open.

He didn't say anything, just slid his hand to the side of her neck and stroked his thumb over her jaw as they stood there in the shadows. She could barely see him, but she felt the heat coming off him.

"Damn." His voice was low and gruff. "I've been wanting to do that for days."

A zing of excitement went through her, followed by a flurry of nerves.

He eased back, and the cool air swept in to fill the gap. He tucked a lock of hair behind her ear and dropped his hands.

"Good night, Macey."

He wasn't going to walk her the rest of the way up. She could see it in the steady way he looked at her, as though he was determined to keep his feet planted right there on the landing. Part of her was crushed. Another part of her was glad, because she didn't know if she could resist pulling him inside.

"Good night," she managed.

She turned around and walked the rest of the way, digging her keys from her purse as she struggled not to look back. But she could feel his gaze on her as she let herself inside.

CHAPTER

FOURTEEN

Nicole slipped into the conference room, where the team meeting was already well underway.

"So, that's it, unfortunately," Miranda was saying. "No prints on the tarp at all, which makes me think whoever handled it was wearing gloves. And we're still going through all the prints lifted from the car, but so far everything comes back to the victim."

It was just Miranda, Emmet, and the chief. No sign of Owen, which was weird, considering he was the lead detective.

Emmet raised an eyebrow as Nicole sat down, silently chiding her for being late.

"The tarp appears new, incidentally," Miranda added. "No wear and tear, so seems like someone took it right out of the package."

"Interesting." Brady looked at Emmet. "You try our local hardware stores? Anyone sold one of these tarps in the last four weeks?"

"None of them carry this brand," Emmet said. "But the big chains do, so we need to go to the mainland to follow up. I plan to hit the ones in Corpus today."

Brady nodded and looked at Miranda again. "What about the shovel?"

"No prints there. Again, I think our perp had gloves on. The interesting thing about the shovel is that it's old. I definitely don't think we're going to get anywhere trying to track down a purchase. But the shovel's gotten a lot of use, and I sent swabs to the DNA lab. We'll see what they come back with."

"Let's not get too hopeful. Blind DNA tests can take months to process." Brady looked at Nicole. "What about the iPhone?" he asked, thankfully ignoring the fact that she was late.

"Owen's working on that," she said. "I've been interviewing more of the victim's friends to see if anyone remembers her mentioning a guy she was seeing around the holidays, someone who may have given her a phone and a designer purse."

"Anything?"

"One of her restaurant friends remembers something."

"Are you talking about that girl Brooke?" Emmet asked.

"No, this is one of the hostesses. I talked to her last night at Waterman's. She said she remembers commenting on the new purse right around the time Julia got it, and Julia said it was a Christmas gift. She got the impression it was from a guy, but Julia didn't tell her who. She said she assumed that Julia had a sugar daddy and didn't really think much of it."

Brady's gaze narrowed. "A sugar daddy?"

"Yeah, evidently it's pretty common around here. Some of the men who have second homes come down without their wives and throw money around. I'm thinking if it turns out Julia was seeing a married man, that could help us with motive."

"It's a good angle," Brady said. "Stay on it. Talk to more of her friends."

"I will," Nicole said. "I plan to go back to her yoga place today and see who else I can find."

"We also need to follow up with the drilling company," the chief said. "They've got security cameras outside their entrance."

"I'm on it," Emmet said. "I talked to someone over there yesterday. He's going to get me the footage from the date range we need. But he already told me he thinks the car was parked too far away from the door to be captured. Their cams are primarily focused on entry points into the building."

Owen strode into the room with a Starbucks cup in one hand and a thick manila folder in the other. Since he was a loyal customer of the Beanery, Nicole figured he'd driven to the mainland this morning.

"Good news." He set his cup on the table and dropped into the chair beside Nicole. "I was just at the AT&T store in Corpus, which is the closest place that sells iPhones."

Emmet looked at his watch. "They're open already?"

"They let me in early, and I talked to the manager."

Nicole would bet the manager was a woman. And he'd gotten something big—she could tell from his body language.

"I talked her into looking up Julia's number," he said.

Nicole leaned forward. "And?"

"And they sold a phone programmed with that number to a customer on December twelfth of last year. It was purchased with a corporate credit card."

"Tell me you got a name," Nicole said.

"Yeah, of the corporation." Owen looked at Brady. "Hancock Enterprises."

Silence fell over the room.

"Hancock Enterprises," Emmet repeated. "You're talking about the developer?"

"Yep."

Brady's expression didn't change.

"He's responsible for some of the biggest projects in town," Nicole said. "The water park, the movie theater—"

"The new resort going in at Lighthouse Point," Emmet added.

"Playa del Rey," Owen said. "I know."

"Miles Hancock is married," Miranda put in. "You know that, right? His wife owns a boutique on Main Street."

"I'm aware." Owen's gaze settled on Brady. "He's at the job site right now. I drove by there on my way in."

The chief still hadn't responded. He just sat there, staring at his lead detective as the silence continued and Nicole's pulse started to thrum.

What the hell? This was the biggest break they'd had yet. Nicole was ready to go grab the guy right now and drag him in for questioning.

But Brady just sat there, drumming his fingers on the table, as if deep in thought. Maybe he was thinking about what a shitstorm it would be if one of the island's wealthiest businessmen were to be arrested for murder.

Nicole shifted her attention to Owen as he silently returned the chief's gaze. Owen looked calm, but Nicole could see the tight set of his jaw. And the intensity in his eyes told her he knew exactly what a big deal this was.

"Go talk to him," Brady said. "Take Nicole with you."

She blinked in surprise. She thought maybe she'd heard him wrong, but he turned to look at her.

"Keep it casual," Brady told her. "We don't want to spook him."

I THOUGHT YOU TOLD us he was here," Nicole said as Owen turned into the construction site.

"He was."

Owen pulled up beside the trailer at the edge of the construction zone. It was a hive of activity—workers in hard hats, dump trucks, bulldozers rumbling around. The partially finished hotel was surrounded by scaffolding, and stacks of building materials filled the lot in front. But the parking area beside the trailer was empty.

"What's he drive again?" Nicole asked.

"A black Range Rover. He's got a Jaguar and a pickup registered to him, too, but those are for his wife and teenage son."

"Doesn't his company have a storefront downtown?"

"Yeah, on Third Street. But he's never there. I talked to the receptionist earlier. When he's working, he does it from the job site or from home."

"So, let's try his house."

Owen tapped his fingers on the steering wheel as he considered it. Hancock lived in a gated beachfront subdivision only a few minutes away.

"Owen?"

"The problem is his wife. Not to mention his kids or even a housekeeper." He looked at her. "You ever met this guy?"

"No, but I hear he's an ass."

"He is. And he's already got a grudge against the department, so if we show up and try to talk to him in front of his family, he'll have his guard up for sure. Brady doesn't want us to spook him."

"Why's he got a grudge?"

"He's had a beef with us ever since last fall. Remember when they halted work here over the zoning thing? He ignored the court order, and we had to come over here and lock down the job site while the city council held hearings and finally granted the permit to build the golf course."

"I vaguely remember that. Who'd we send over?"

"Gutierrez and Dawson. I hear Hancock raised hell and nearly got himself arrested."

Nicole lifted an eyebrow. "Interesting. You said before you thought we were looking for someone with anger management problems and poor impulse control."

Owen checked his rearview mirror as a black SUV pulled into the lot. "Here we go."

"It's him?"

"Looks like."

The Range Rover halted right in front of the trailer, and Miles Hancock slid out. He peeled his shades off and scowled as he looked at their unmarked police unit, which wasn't exactly inconspicuous. Hancock wore jeans and a black golf shirt with his company logo on the front. The guy was big, but not in nearly the kind of shape he'd been in when he was an offensive tackle at UT. Hancock's football career had ended in college, and he'd taken his short-lived celebrity and segued it into a successful construction business.

Owen looked at Nicole. "You ready?"

"I'll follow your lead."

"Let's keep it low-key." Owen pushed open his door. "Mr. Hancock?"

"What?"

"Detective Breda, Lost Beach PD." Owen nodded at Nicole. "This is Detective Lawson."

"What do you want?"

"We have a few questions for you."

"About what?"

Owen removed his sunglasses. "Mind if we speak inside?"

Hancock didn't answer, but he led them up the steps to the trailer. He unlocked it with a key and flipped on the lights as he went in.

"This will have to be quick," Hancock said. "I've got a meeting in ten minutes."

Nicole shot Owen a look, and he knew she already thought this guy was an entitled jerk.

Hancock tossed his Ray-Bans on the desk. "What do you want to ask about?"

"Julia Murphy," Owen said.

"Julia Murphy." He arched his eyebrows but he didn't look surprised. "The woman who was murdered up at the park there?"

"That's right." Owen didn't bother pointing out that it wasn't clear where she'd been murdered.

Hancock walked around a drafting table and reached for a mini refrigerator. He grabbed a bottle of water for himself. "Drink?" he asked him.

"No, thanks."

He looked at Nicole, and she shook her head.

Hancock untwisted the cap on his bottle. "What do you want to know?"

"Did you know Julia Murphy?" Owen asked.

"She's a waitress over at Waterman's." He swigged his drink. "I'm there all the time."

"So, you knew her from the restaurant?" Owen asked.

"Yeah. And she's been all over the news, too."

The door opened and a man in a hard hat took a step inside, then halted. "Oh. Sorry."

"Wait outside," Hancock snapped. "I'm in the middle of something."

The man retreated and closed the door.

"What about outside the restaurant?" Owen asked. "Did you ever see Julia apart from work?"

"I don't think so."

He was hedging already. And he was starting to look antsy. His gaze shifted from Owen to Nicole and back to Owen again.

"Maybe I should get my lawyer here for this."

"That's fine," Owen said agreeably. "We're more than happy to take you down to the police station and you can give him a call."

He clenched his teeth, not happy to have his bluff called. Owen happened to know that Hancock used a Corpus Christi law firm that represented a bunch of oil companies. It would take a lawyer at least an hour to get down here while Hancock cooled his heels at the police station.

Hancock checked his watch. "Let's just hurry this up. What else you want to know?"

"So, you say you didn't see Julia outside work," Owen stated.

"I said I don't remember."

More hedging.

"Have you ever been to her house?" Owen asked.

"I don't even know where she lives."

"Is that a yes or no?"

"No." He folded his arms over his chest.

"Has she ever been to your house?"

"No. I told you. I knew her from the restaurant. She's my favorite waitress, and I do business dinners there a lot. We didn't have a personal relationship."

"No?" Nicole looked surprised.

Hancock glanced at her. "No."

"Then why did you buy her a cell phone?" she asked.

"It was a gift."

Interesting that he seemed to have that answer ready to go.

"You bought her a cell phone, but you didn't have a personal relationship," Nicole said with obvious skepticism.

"I buy gifts for lots of people." He waved his hand dismissively. "Spurs tickets, cases of wine, charter fishing trips. It's good for business."

"What about a Gucci hobo bag?" Nicole asked.

"A what?"

"A designer purse," she said. "One of Julia's friends told us you gave one to her."

"I didn't."

He was adamant about the purse, and Owen couldn't tell whether he was lying. He'd owned up to the iPhone, but that would have been easier to prove.

Hancock checked his watch again. "What else? My meeting's about to start."

Nicole looked at Owen. Owen looked at Hancock.

"That should do it for now," Owen said casually. "We'll be in touch."

Hancock hustled them to the door and pulled it open.

"Next time you want to ask questions, call ahead," he said. "I'll make sure my attorney joins us."

CHAPTER

FIFTEEN

M ACEY SCANNED THE police station parking lot but
didn't see Owen's pickup.

"Let's make this fast," Macey told Josh as she parked.
"It's already after five, and I'd like to check out Main Street
before all the stores close."

"We're good," Josh said. "Everything's open late in the
summer."

As they approached the police station, the door opened,
and several uniformed officers emerged. Macey recognized
the tall guy who'd manned the barricade at White Dunes
Park, but the other faces were new.

Owen's detective friend stepped out—Emmet. Behind
him was a female detective whom Macey had seen around
but hadn't met.

And then Owen.

Macey's heart skipped a beat, and she was glad she was
wearing sunglasses. Josh had insisted on coming with her

on this errand, and she didn't want him picking up on anything going on between her and Owen.

Owen wasn't looking in her direction, but his friend was. He said something, and Owen turned around.

"Your cop is here," Josh said.

Macey shot him a look and started to quibble with his description, but Owen peeled away from his friends and walked right over.

"Hey," he said, stopping in front of them.

Macey had always thought of Josh as tall, but Owen was even taller, and he seemed to take up much more space, probably because of the confident way he carried himself.

Command presence. She'd heard the term used by cops before, and she decided it fit him.

"Everything okay?" Owen asked, looking from Josh to Macey.

"We're just, you know, stopping in," she said, wondering why her pulse was suddenly racing.

"I'll wait inside," Josh said with a smirk.

Macey watched him walk away. So much for her effort to be casual around Owen.

"Macey?"

She looked at him, and he was watching her now with concern.

"You all right?"

"Yes. Why?"

"People don't usually stop in here unless there's a problem," he said.

"We're here about our permit."

His eyebrows arched.

"Our film permit. Actually, not the permit itself but one of the stipulations *in* the permit." She was babbling now, but she couldn't seem to help it. "It specifies that we're sup-

posed to have a police officer on location when we do our
downtown shots for traffic and crowd control."

"Just one?"

"At least. We may end up with two if there's a lot of foot
traffic."

"There will be. This is high season."

She gazed up at him. Heat flickered in those cool blue
eyes, and she couldn't believe they were talking about traffic when all she could think about was their kiss. From the
look in his eyes, she could tell he was thinking about it, too.

"Need my help?" he asked.

"Thanks, but I can handle it," she said. "It's not really a
big deal; I just like to get my ducks in a row ahead of time."

The side of his mouth curved up. "I can see that about you."

Damn. Now she was staring at his mouth. She looked at
his eyes again, remembering how his hands had felt last
night, sliding over her and pulling her against him.

She needed to go. Josh was waiting for her inside, and it
was blistering hot out here. But still, she just stood there.

"So." She cleared her throat. "How's the case coming?"

"Good."

"Really?"

He nodded. "We've had some breaks today. A local businessman suddenly looks interesting."

"You have a suspect?"

"More like a person of interest. But it's progress."

She tipped her head to the side. "Don't tell me it's Miles
Hancock."

His gaze narrowed. "Why do you say that?"

"I saw you coming out of his trailer at the construction
site."

He just looked at her.

"Josh and I were doing some scouting at Lighthouse
Point." She paused. "So, is it him?"

"I can't discuss an ongoing investigation."

She smiled. "I'm not going to *tell* anyone."

But he looked guarded now, and she could tell he regretted mentioning anything.

"Relax," she said. "I won't discuss your case with anyone. I was just curious."

He gave a brisk nod. Clearly, he was touchy about this and she'd overstepped some kind of boundary.

The flirty mood was gone now. Which was probably for the better.

"Well, Josh is waiting for me so—"

"I'll call you." Owen smiled, and this time she didn't know if it was real or fake. "You still owe me that rain check for dinner."

N ICOLE SAT ATOP her favorite sand dune, gazing out over the park. Several campfires flickered near the beach. Tents glowed, some with camping lanterns and others with the bluish light of computer screens. It always amazed her how tourists traveled all the way to Lost Beach to escape the hustle and bustle of their daily lives and then dragged all their modern conveniences with them to pass the time.

A familiar SUV rounded the bend. It pulled to a stop behind Nicole's pickup. She crushed out her cigarette in the sand as Emmet got out. He stood for a second, staring up at her, and then hiked up the dune.

"What are you doing here?" he asked.

"Probably the same thing you are."

He sat down on the sand beside her, stretching out his long legs. Unlike her, he'd changed out of his work clothes and now wore jeans and one of his faded Billabong T-shirts, the one with a reef shark on the back. He'd showered, too, which told her he was on his way out.

"So, I guess that means you're keeping an eye on things, hoping our perp returns to the scene of the crime?" He leaned back on his palms and looked at her.

"More or less."

"You really think he's that dumb?"

"You seem to." She shrugged. "We've seen stupid moves before."

"True." Emmet sighed and tipped his head back, gazing up at the moon. "Never underestimate people's capacity for stupid." He turned to her. "You gonna share your smokes?"

She dug the pack from the pocket of the LBPD jacket she was sitting on. He tapped out a cigarette as she passed him a lighter. Nicole had given up smoking years ago, and Emmet was the only one who knew she occasionally snuck cigarettes whenever she got overly stressed.

He blew out a stream of smoke. "So, what's on your mind tonight?"

"Nothing."

He watched her, waiting.

She sighed. "I'm not sure about Hancock."

"What about him?"

"Everything. Brady and everyone is so set on him being a suspect, but I don't know."

"What don't you know? It's obvious he was having an affair with her. He bought her a freaking iPhone and a purse."

"We don't know about the purse for sure."

"Whatever. The phone is enough. When was the last time some guy bought you a thousand-dollar gift?"

She scoffed. "Never."

"See?"

See . . . what exactly? Was he pointing out that she hadn't had a serious relationship in years?

"Don't get prickly," he said, obviously reading her mind.

"I'm just saying it's not the kind of thing you give your *waitress*, no matter how good she is. If he gave her the phone, he was sleeping with her."

"Fine, but that doesn't mean he killed her."

"No, it doesn't. You're right."

They looked out over the campground, where couples and families were tucking in for the night. She wondered how many of them knew a woman's body had been discovered here less than a week ago.

Emmet passed her the cigarette, and she took a drag.

"So, why don't you like Hancock for it?" he asked. "If you agree they were most likely having an affair?"

"Several reasons," she said, oddly relieved that he'd asked. He wanted her opinion. It was good to know that. Not only was she the newest detective, she was the only female one, and sometimes it felt like her input was being ignored. "First, his boats. He has two, and he keeps them down at the marina."

"What about them?"

"Well, if you have access to a boat, why bother with the hole?" She gestured to the sand dune that had been an excavation site last Saturday. "Digging a grave in the dark of night is a lot of work. And risk. Why bother if you can just load the body onto your boat and take it out to the bay?"

Emmet nodded. "Not a bad point."

It wasn't exactly effusive praise, but she'd take it. Emmet wasn't one for compliments.

"Also, this afternoon Hancock talked to Owen and me without a lawyer present," she said.

"Owen told me Hancock was in a hurry and didn't want to come all the way to the police station."

"He didn't. He was super annoyed that we had the gall to show up at his workplace with our pesky questions when he had a meeting to get to."

"So?"

"So, just think about that for a minute," she said. "If you knew that you'd murdered someone and a pair of detectives showed up, don't you think you'd be a little more worried about, say, *death by lethal injection* than getting to a meeting on time? If the guy was guilty, he never should have talked to us without a lawyer. Or he should have taken the Fifth."

"Yeah, obviously," Emmet said. "But people don't always do what they *should* do. People are stupid. Especially criminals. You just said so yourself."

Nicole sighed.

Emmet stubbed out the cigarette in the sand. "Okay, so if you don't like Hancock for it, who else do you have in mind?"

"No idea."

He made a buzzing sound. "Wrong answer. You have an idea. You just don't have a name. You've got to have a profile in mind."

He was right; she did.

"I definitely think he's local," she said.

"Me, too. Why?"

She nodded to the sand dune. "The burial site, right in the middle of the Bowl there. It's secluded. The dunes are big enough to conceal what you're doing. After you get past the top layer, the sand is the right consistency for digging. Not everyone knows that—you'd have to be local."

"Or someone who was camping here and figured that out after they arrived."

"Maybe." She paused. "Also, the back access. If you believe Edward Snell's story, then the killer pulled off the highway and accessed the park from the back. That's a longer way to haul a body, but it means someone knew the system here and didn't want the park ranger taking down their license plate or maybe remembering a face."

Emmet nodded. "Well, I *do* agree he's probably from around here. But that doesn't rule out Hancock. If anything, it makes him more of a suspect."

Nicole sighed and looked out over the campground.

"Just the fact that he's probably local is very disturbing," she muttered.

"Why?"

"Because that means whoever it is, we probably know him."

"Why is that any more disturbing than him being from out of town?"

"Because. This is my home," she said. "I care about this place. The idea that someone I grew up with could be a homicidal maniac is disturbing."

"Aren't you being a little melodramatic?"

She gaped at him. "A woman is *dead*, Emmet. But I guess since I'm female I'm getting overly emotional about it?"

"That's not what I mean, and you know it." He shot her a look. "I mean it's melodramatic calling him a 'homicidal maniac' when he could be just some prick who got pissed off at his girlfriend and went into a rage."

"How is that any better?"

"Because then we're not talking about a serial killer."

"Either way, it's disturbing. He killed a woman, drove her out to a remote park, and dug a hole." She gestured toward the dunes. "Right here at one of the most beautiful spots on the island. It shows hubris."

"Hubris," Emmet repeated.

"Yeah, pride. Brazenness. Balls. It's basically a fuck-you to police, and it pisses me off."

"Don't take it so personally," he said. "It's not about you. He just wanted a place to dump the body."

Nicole pulled her knees up and rested her arms on them. Emmet might be right about that, she had to admit.

"It still really bothers me." She sighed, looking out past the campground to the surf beyond. Way out in the Gulf, she could see the distant lights of container ships and oil tankers making their way to the Intracoastal Waterway. She'd been watching the boats all her life.

"I've always *liked* this place," she said, "ever since I was a kid and we used to come here for picnics and camp-outs. And then in high school we'd come out here for bon-fires." She rested her chin on her arms. "I lost my virginity here."

Emmet looked at her. "Oh yeah? Dillon Kucek?"

"Ew. *No.* I never slept with Dillon Kucek."

"Why not?"

"He's a pig. And he was totally full of himself."

"Who was it, then?"

"None of your business. But definitely not Dillon."

"Why not? I thought he was a big deal in high school. He was in my little sister's grade. And didn't you date him at some point?"

"Extremely briefly. He was a jerk."

"Yeah, he probably still is," Emmet said. "I hear he's a big trial lawyer up in Dallas."

"Figures," she said.

"I hear he's made some bank, too." Emmet nudged her with his elbow. "Maybe you missed out. His wife probably drives a Lexus and goes skiing every year."

She sniffed. "Money isn't everything. She still has to wake up next to Dillon."

Emmet smiled. Then he sat forward and dusted his hands. "Well, as much as I've enjoyed this trip down mem-ory lane, I'm late for Finn's."

She'd known he was headed to Finn's the second she'd

noticed his carefully mussed hair. He had to use product to get it to look that way.

"Have fun," she said.

He stood up. "You want to come?"

"Finn's is a pickup scene."

He grinned. "Exactly. You might get lucky."

She shook her head.

"You sure? Calvin's going to be there."

He still thought she had a thing for his brother, a former SEAL who now worked for the fire department. Emmet was a good detective, but sometimes he was clueless.

"I'll pass," she said.

"Oh, come on. It's better than sitting here giving yourself lung cancer and stressing about the case."

"I'll be fine. I'm just frustrated we haven't made an arrest yet."

His smile faded. "Don't get so worked up."

"I can't help it. That's how I am."

"We *will* arrest him, you know."

She looked up at him, towering over her with so much confidence in his voice. Where did he get that? Did they teach it at the police academy? If so, then she'd missed that day.

She sighed.

"I'm serious, Nik. Have some faith in us."

She looked out over the dunes. "I do."

M ACEY COULDN'T SLEEP.
Again.

She'd drifted off around midnight, and then her eyes had flown open at three forty-five. No reason, really; it was just as though her body had decided, *Hey, time to play the Insomnia Game again!*

The wind howled outside the window as she stared at the ceiling. This wake-up thing was becoming a habit. Her first night here, she'd been dead to the world, completely wiped out from driving, and hauling equipment, and stressing out over her flat tire. But every night since, she'd had trouble falling asleep. Or rather, *staying* asleep. That was the real problem. Each night, she'd managed to drift off only to wake up a few hours later with the wind whirring and whistling around the house.

She stared up at the watermark on the ceiling. When she'd first noticed it, it had looked like a wildflower. The next night, a sea anemone. Now it was a giant millipede, and she couldn't close her eyes without picturing it crawling over the ceiling and creeping down the wall.

Macey's stomach filled with dread as she braced for another night of this. The macabre thoughts in her head seemed to be on an endless loop.

Had Julia Murphy slept in this same room? It only made sense. Of the two bedrooms, this one was larger and had the bigger closet.

Had she lain awake in this same bed, staring up at this same watermark, thinking about her life and her job and her boyfriend?

Macey hadn't ever given much thought to the people who lived in a place before her, but now it seemed like she couldn't do anything without wondering whether Julia Murphy had done it, too. She was becoming so obsessed it was keeping her up at night.

Or maybe it was the other way around. Maybe lack of sleep was making her obsessed.

She flopped onto her stomach and pulled the pillow over her head, but the wind noise seeped through. She should have listened to Josh. If she had, she could be in a downtown apartment right now, surrounded by people and streetlights and the reassuring white noise of a populated area. Instead, she was on the island's desolate north end, with only the yowling wind and a handful of quirky neighbors for company.

In the daytime, she loved it here. She liked the dunes and the waves, as well as the swooping seagulls and dive-bombing pelicans. She liked jogging on the sand and watching the shrimp boats come and go. She liked that she'd learned to recognize the wade fishermen and the shell collectors who frequented this beach.

But at night it felt different, especially when the wind picked up and made that shrill, whistling noise at the corners of her house, like ghostly sound effects from some horror film. At first, she'd been fascinated by the sound and even wanted to record it to file away for some future film project. But now she found it just plain creepy.

Macey pulled the pillow tighter and tried to think about something else. Owen's voice. The deep, low-key sound that put a tingle in the pit of her stomach. She thought about his mouth and his hands, and the way her breasts had felt pressed against his chest. She sighed against the mattress.

Maybe *this* was what was really keeping her up at night.

She didn't want these complications right now. She'd been determined to avoid them—not just men in general but Owen in particular. He was too everything. Too attractive. Too confident. Too good at his job. And the understanding in his eyes when she'd opened up to him had been *much* too appealing. She'd felt tempted to trust him. She already *did* trust him. And trust was the first step down a slippery slope that she'd vowed to avoid.

One summer. That was all she was trying to do here. She just needed one distraction-free summer to get her life together and get her fledgling business off the ground. This summer was supposed to be about work—working on herself and her career. She needed to focus. But she couldn't stop thinking about Owen.

Thunk.

She bolted upright. What was that? It sounded like it had come from the driveway. She scrambled out of bed and rushed to the window.

She parted the curtains and looked down. The driveway was dark and still, and her car was a shadow.

Thunk-thunk.

The noise was definitely something downstairs. She grabbed her phone off the nightstand and padded barefoot across the house to peer through the front door. The porch light cast the deck in a yellow glow. She unlocked the door and stepped outside.

Wind buffeted her face as she surveyed the beach. Tonight the moon was hidden by clouds, and she couldn't see the water, only hear it. She slipped her feet into the sandy flip-flops she'd left by the door. Using her phone as a flashlight, she headed downstairs.

Thunk.

Macey paused on the landing. The sound was coming from the north side of the house. Scanning the yard for critters, she approached the overgrown hedge that separated her place from the neighbor's.

A gust whipped up.

Ka-thunk!

Macey whirled toward the noise. Ducking under a palm frond, she neared the fence and aimed her light at it.

Her neighbor's wooden gate stood open.

She marched over and pulled the gate closed. But then it swung open again. She shut it once more, securing the latch this time. Then she turned and looked at the dark driveway.

It's a safety issue, Owen had said.

Macey shined her light at her car. Had she remembered

to lock it? She walked over and saw that she hadn't. She opened the door and tapped the lock button, then leaned across the seat to grab the empty coffee mug off the floor. She stopped with her hand on the console. The air smelled sour and metallic, like . . . sweat?

She glanced in the back seat, making sure she hadn't left any valuables back there, but there was only an old beach towel. She slammed the door and looked around, wary now as she cast her gaze up and down the street.

Owen was right. She needed to call her landlord about changing the floodlight. She hurried up the stairs, scanning the hedges on either side of her house. At the top of the stairs, she glanced at her phone. It was 4:28.

She sighed. Should she go back to bed or just give up? In an hour, she could drive to the marshes and set up her tripod. Maybe she'd get lucky and capture a dramatic sunrise. Or maybe she'd spot another fisherman perfectly silhouetted as he cast a line from the stern of his boat. A shot like that could be a poster for the tourism board.

She glanced out over the dunes, then up at the sky as the moon peeked out from behind the clouds.

A shadow moved on the beach, and Macey's heart skittered. Was that a person? It was. The clouds shifted, and everything went dark again.

She stared out at the beach, gripping her phone. Was it him? The man from the bridge?

Was it anyone?

She squinted into the dimness, but she couldn't make out anything more than the shadowy shape of a figure. Or maybe not even that. Maybe her tired eyes were playing tricks on her.

She glanced down at her phone and bit her lip. She could call Owen. Or Josh. Or 911. But what would she say?

Yes, I'd like to report a person standing on the beach.

Macey needed to get a grip. And a good night's sleep. She reached for the door just as the sky lightened and the moon came out from the clouds. She looked back at the beach.

The shadow was gone.

SIXTEEN

OWEN NOTICED THE tension as soon as he stepped into the bullpen. Most of the cubicles were empty, but several people stood in the door to the chief's office. Owen dropped the bag containing his Italian sub on his desk and walked over to Nicole, who was leaning against the doorframe.

"What's up?" he asked in a low voice.

"Labs just came in."

Brady had his elbows on his desk and a stack of papers in front of him. Miranda sat in a chair on the opposite side, tapping her finger on the page and explaining something as Emmet peered over her shoulder.

"They couldn't get anything, even with PCR," Miranda said.

"What's PCR?" Emmet asked.

"Polymerase chain reaction," she said. "It's a process that can be used to amplify a DNA sample when there isn't much material to work with. In this case, the sample was too degraded."

"What are we talking about?" Owen asked.

The chief looked at him. "The cigarette butts found under the body. Looks like the DNA's no good."

Miranda looked at him. "It's very degraded, probably due to time and weather, which likely means the cigarette butts are too old to be from our perpetrator."

That had been a long shot, anyway. Owen hadn't been counting on it.

"We got a match with the fibers, though," she said, and he picked up on the excitement in her voice.

"The ones from the tarp?" he asked.

"The tarp from the car trunk *and* the two fibers found in the victim's teeth at autopsy. They're a poly-wool blend commonly used in upholstery fabric."

"So, what, does that mean maybe he smothered her?" Emmet asked, looking at Owen. "I thought the ME told you manual strangulation."

"He did," Nicole said. "But maybe he used the pillow or cushion first, to muffle her screams."

"Are these the labs from the autopsy or the Volkswagen?" Owen asked.

"Both," Brady said.

It was a testament to the chief's pull. He'd been rattling cages at the county crime lab for days, trying to get a rush on the physical evidence.

"What else from the autopsy?" Owen asked.

"The nail clippings," Miranda said. "We recovered DNA from beneath one of her fingernails."

Owen's pulse picked up. "Any hits?"

"None in CODIS," Brady said. "So, for now let's assume that he doesn't have a criminal record. Or at least nothing serious enough to merit a DNA sample."

"The DNA is still really useful," Miranda said. "It was recovered from beneath a torn fingernail, indicating a struggle. So, when you close in on a suspect, it's essentially a smoking gun."

As Miranda spoke, the energy in the room was palpable. They were finally starting to get some traction.

Brady looked at Owen. "Where are we on that alibi?"

Nicole turned to him, clearly surprised. "Who gave us an alibi?"

"Hancock," Owen said. "He called me up this morning to let me know he was on a business trip the week before Memorial Day, from Thursday to Sunday."

"Where?" Nicole asked.

"Cabo San Lucas, he says."

"He just called you out of the blue?" Emmet asked.

"Yep. He had his lawyer on speakerphone."

"Well, that covers our time window," Nicole said. "Julia was last seen by a co-worker after work on Thursday night, and then we've got a witness who claims to have seen a man driving what looked like her car near White Dunes Park on Friday morning, right around sunrise."

"*Claims* to have seen?" Miranda asked.

"I'm still vetting this eyewitness," Nicole said. "He seems dodgy to me."

"It'd be nice to have a DNA sample from Hancock right about now," Emmet said.

"Let's not expect to get one anytime soon," Brady said, "especially now that his lawyer's involved. Let's focus on the alibi." Brady looked at Owen. "Shouldn't be too hard to pin that down."

"I'm on it."

Actually, it was hard to pin down, but Owen didn't say so in front of the chief.

"The DNA under the victim's fingernail is a big break,"

Miranda said. "I think it's worth pursuing, even if we have to deal with his lawyer. Maybe Hancock will voluntarily give a sample just to put himself in the clear, and we can move on."

Brady didn't comment, and Owen was pretty sure it was because the guy's lawyer was a bulldog. Hancock had sicced him on Brady before when LBPD stepped in to halt his construction project over a permitting issue. He'd threatened to sue practically everyone, from the town council to the police chief.

"What about getting DNA *involuntarily*?" Nicole asked.

"I was thinking that, too," Owen said.

"What, you mean sneak a sample?" Emmet asked.

"Yeah, maybe tail him around and see if we can catch him tossing a water bottle or a coffee cup or something."

All eyes turned to Brady. He looked at Miranda, the forensic evidence expert.

"Any thoughts?" Brady asked her. "Could we get enough of a sample just from a drinking straw or something like that?"

"Absolutely," Miranda said. "But be careful about where you get it. Surreptitious DNA collection is a legal gray area. You can't just go waltzing into his yard and grab something out of his trash can. If you want to collect a sample, make sure he leaves it in a public place."

"I can tail him around some, see what I can get," Nicole suggested.

"He's more likely to notice you," Emmet said.

"Why?"

"Because you're a woman, for one. And for another, you and Owen just showed up at his office to rake him over the coals."

"We didn't—"

"Emmet's right," Brady said, cutting her off. "Someone else needs to do it."

"I'll do it," Emmet said. "I've never met the guy, so it'll be easier for me to keep a low profile."

"Let's get it done today." Brady looked from Emmet to Owen. "And nail down that alibi, too. I either want this guy crossed off our suspect list or bumped to the top."

Everyone cleared out of the chief's office, and Owen headed to the break room to grab a drink. He needed to refuel and get back to work. Hancock's alibi was bugging him. He didn't like the way it had been served up on a silver platter, with his lawyer right there on the phone making sure he said everything just right.

Could be that Hancock had been on a business trip to Mexico at the time of the murder, just like he'd claimed. Owen had already called the hotel in Cabo, and they'd had no trouble confirming his check-in and checkout dates. But that wasn't enough. With the right incentive, a hotel clerk down there could have been easily persuaded to change something in the computer. Or just lie. Owen was good at reading people face-to-face, but he was at a disadvantage when he interviewed someone over the phone. And to make things more complicated, Hancock said he'd flown to Mexico on a charter plane, and those records could be subject to manipulation, too. Owen needed something much more solid than what he had, and he needed it soon.

He fed money into the vending machine as Nicole walked in.

"That DNA lead is huge," she said.

"Yep."

"Don't you want in on it?"

His drink thudded down.

"You mean helping Emmet get a sample?"

"Yeah, I mean, it could take days to catch this guy

throwing away a coffee cup or something in a public place," she said. "I think we need a more aggressive plan."

"If we get too aggressive, we risk our evidence getting thrown out in court."

She crossed her arms. "I know, obviously. But time is of the essence here. It's been, what, five days since the body was discovered, and we still don't have a suspect?"

Owen leaned back against the counter, looking her over. "Cut to the chase, Nicole. What is it you want?"

"I want to work on this angle. Talk to Brady and see if you can get him to let me tail Hancock. He keeps sending me out to interview Julia's friends, and I think I've exhausted those leads. We need that DNA sample. If he's guilty, we'll have proof, and if he isn't, we can move on to someone else."

Owen didn't say anything.

"Plus, it wouldn't hurt to have an extra set of eyes on him in case he does anything suspicious," she added.

"If he knows we're surveilling him, he's more likely to camp out at the construction site and waste everyone's time."

"But—"

"You're better off talking to the victim's friends," Owen said. "If we could get someone on record about her boyfriend, that would be huge."

"I know, but—"

"Especially if it turns out to be Hancock, who's already denied having a personal relationship with the victim. Then we've caught him in a lie, which gives us leverage."

Nicole clamped her mouth shut. She looked mulish and frustrated, but that was too bad. As the newest detective, she was at the very bottom of the pecking order. Owen had been there once, too, and he knew how much it sucked. For him, it had sucked even more because he'd had his older brother telling him what to do all the time.

But everyone had to pay their dues.

"Fine," she said curtly. "I'll make the rounds again."

"Look, I know it's frustrating, but this isn't busywork. We have to keep trying the victim's friends. Someone might have seen something or heard about something important, and they don't even realize it. We need to be thorough."

"I know, I get it. I'm just ready for a lead here."

"Yeah, me, too."

She left the room, seeming at least somewhat placated, and Owen watched her go. He understood her impatience. Witness interviews could be tedious, but sometimes the smallest offhand comment could turn into a critical lead.

His phone beeped in his pocket as a text landed. He pulled it out. Joel.

RU watching the news?

Owen frowned at the message.

"Hey," Emmet said, stepping into the break room. "You see the news?"

"No. What is it?"

"There's a TV reporter giving a broadcast outside the station." He crossed the room and peered through the mini-blinds. "Son of a *bitch*. They're filming it right now."

Owen walked over and looked through the blinds. Sure enough, that redheaded reporter who had been everywhere the day they recovered the body was back. She was with Channel Six in San Antonio.

"*Fuck*," Emmet said.

"What's she saying?"

"She just told the entire world that we've got a suspect in the Julia Murphy homicide." Emmet looked at him.

"Who did she—"

"Miles Hancock."

* * *

MACEY GAZED UP at the sky, fighting to control the camera. As she moved the joystick, the drone swooped low over the dunes.

"Careful," Josh said.

"I'm trying."

"Use your thumbs. You'll have more control."

Macey eased her left thumb against the joystick.

"Wrong thumb. That's altitude."

She blew out a sigh and squinted into the sun. "How do you make it look so easy?"

"Practice."

"I wish I'd played more video games as a kid."

"Well, it definitely helps. But you're getting the hang of it." Josh turned away. "Looks like your cop is here."

"Huh?"

"Detective Breda."

Macey turned around, and sure enough, there was Owen walking across the beach toward her. A white police SUV was parked just off the road.

Her stomach filled with butterflies as he strode toward her. He looked like he was on a mission.

"Hey, you mind?"

She turned back to Josh. "What?"

He smiled. "That camera's worth a fortune. We probably don't want to wreck it."

She handed over the controls, and he stepped away, giving her some privacy as Owen neared her.

"Hi there," she said, peeling off her sunglasses.

He stopped in front of her, hands on hips.

"How'd you find me?" she asked.

"Your car is at your house, so I figured you were on the

beach." He tipped his head back as the drone soared overhead. "Is that your camera?"

"It's the company's, but yes. Impressive, isn't it?"

He didn't respond, just stared up at the drone. He wore sunglasses, but she noticed the tightness around his eyes.

He turned to look at her. "Was it here last Saturday?"

"What? The drone?"

"Yeah."

"You mean Saturday, while the ME was here?"

"Yeah."

She felt a prickle of unease. "No."

"Are you sure?"

"Of course. Why?" She looked at him as he gazed up at the sky. "Owen?"

He turned to face her, taking off his sunglasses. His blue eyes looked chilly.

"What's wrong?" she asked.

"You seen the news today?"

"Not since this morning. What happened?"

"A reporter gave a live broadcast outside the police station this afternoon."

He looked as though he expected her to react.

"You've had reporters there all week, haven't you?"

He nodded. "This one was from San Antonio. She announced that our department is looking at Miles Hancock as a suspect in the Julia Murphy homicide."

Her eyebrows arched. "I thought you said he was a person of interest."

"I did," he said. "She's reporting that he's a suspect."

Owen gazed down at her, and Macey's stomach tightened.

"What's with the tone?" she asked.

"Tone?"

"You said she's from San Antonio like *I* had something to do with it."

"Did you?"

She huffed out a laugh. "Yeah, right."

He just looked at her.

"Are you accusing me of *leaking* something about your investigation to a TV reporter?"

His face didn't change. Anger swelled inside her chest.

"Are you serious right now? Some reporter is from San Antonio so *I* must be feeding her news tips?" She laughed at the absurdity of it. "Oh, and that's after I specifically told you I wouldn't discuss your case with anyone?"

"Did you discuss it with anyone?"

Macey's throat tightened. She stared up at those blue eyes that were clearly searching her face for any sign that she was lying.

She crossed her arms. "No, Owen. I did not discuss your case with anyone. Not a reporter or anyone else."

Something flickered in his expression. Guilt? Or maybe it was wariness because he realized he'd pissed her off.

She slid her sunglasses back on. "Is that it? I'm busy here."

"I had to ask." He slid his sunglasses back on, too. "It's nothing personal."

Nothing personal.

"Whatever." She turned to leave.

"Macey, wait."

"No." She kept walking, looking at him over her shoulder. "If you have any more questions, call me later. I'm working."

CHAPTER

SEVENTEEN

MACEY SAT IN the booth, watching as Josh attacked an enormous platter of chicken wings. After spending three hours at her house editing, Josh had been starving. She hadn't been able to tempt him with one of her salad kits, so they'd come to Finn's.

"So who broke it?" Josh asked around a mouthful of food.

"Channel Six in San Antonio."

After hours of fuming, she'd finally calmed down enough to tell Josh about her conversation with Owen. Most likely, she'd regret telling him, but Josh knew something was wrong, and she was tired of dodging his questions.

"Rayna did a live shot in front of the police station at noon," she said, "and by five o'clock everyone was down here doing breathless updates."

"Everyone?"

"All the Corpus affiliates, plus San Antonio, and now Houston."

"Well, no wonder he's pissed."

"Are you defending him?"

"Nope." He licked his fingers and picked up another unnaturally orange wing. "But he's bound to be under a ton of pressure. You know how this goes—small department, big murder case. They're probably under-resourced, and now they've got the media spotlight shining down on them. Plus, he's the lead detective, right? That means he's under the gun. Put yourself in his shoes."

Macey slurped her margarita, giving herself a brain freeze. She didn't want to put herself in Owen's shoes. She didn't want to have sympathy for him at all. She was still too ticked off, especially considering how just the other night she'd been kissing him on her staircase.

Josh licked buffalo sauce from his thumb. "Did you tell him Rayna Jones is your nemesis and the last person in the world you'd ever leak to?"

"I wouldn't *leak* to anyone!" She stirred her margarita with a straw. "And I specifically told him I wouldn't talk about his case with anybody."

"You're talking about it with me," Josh pointed out.

"Only about what's already been on the news."

"Aha." He pointed a wing at her. "So you admit he's given you inside information. Sounds like you two have a special relationship."

"We don't."

He lifted an eyebrow.

"We don't. I barely know the man."

"Okay. So why does it bother you so much for him to ask you a simple question—were you or were you not the inside source for this story?"

"Because it's not a simple question," she said. "He's questioning my integrity."

Macey wasn't sure why that should bother her so much. She was the one who'd told him about the lapse in judgment that had gotten her fired. If she was the kind of person who would sleep with a source, maybe she was the kind of person who would leak sensitive information—like a murder suspect's name, of all things—to a TV reporter.

When she'd opened up to Owen, he'd seemed so non-judgmental. He'd made her feel as though he understood what it was like to screw up and regret it. She'd thought they had connected, but now it seemed like he was using their conversation against her.

"So, did he believe you when you told him you didn't tip off the media?" Josh asked.

"I don't know." A knot formed in her stomach as she pictured the hard look in his eyes when he'd questioned her. *It's nothing personal.* How could he say that? Of course it was personal.

"You know what? I don't want to talk about this anymore." She snagged one of his celery sticks and dunked it in ranch dip. "Let's talk about something else."

"All right." Josh picked up another wing. "How's the documentary coming?"

Macey nibbled the celery. Another not-great subject, but at least they'd moved on from Owen.

"Okay," she said.

"What's it about again?"

"The effects of climate change on lobster fishing along the eastern seaboard."

He nibbled his wing, not demonstrating a feeling about the topic one way or another. That was Macey's job—to elicit people's interest in something they didn't care about or didn't even know existed beforehand.

Josh discarded another bone onto his plate. "So, how's it coming?"

"Okay. I haven't spent as much time on it as I'd planned to." Meaning none at all. "I keep getting distracted."

"With?"

"Getting settled. The new business. Everything." She took another celery stick. "You know what's weird?"

"Um, how you said you weren't hungry but now you're eating my food?"

"What's weird is I'm kind of liking this."

"This what?"

"The work we're doing."

"What's not to like?" He sucked chicken off the bone. "We get to spend a summer at the beach getting paid to do something we're good at."

"That's the weird part. I think I *am* good at it."

"Of course you're good at it. You graduated from one of the top film schools in the world."

"I guess I was kind of a snob, though. About making commercials. But now I'm kind of liking it."

"What's wrong with commercials? They're fun to make and they pay the bills."

She shrugged. "I didn't know they'd be fun. And I like how straightforward they are. There's no mystery about what it is you're trying to say."

Josh shook his head and picked up his last wing.

"What?" she asked.

"You sound so surprised that you're enjoying what you do."

"I am."

"Do you ever miss the newsroom?"

"Nope. Well, I miss the people sometimes. But I don't miss the round-the-clock stress of it. What about you?" she asked, worried now that he'd brought it up. "Do you miss it?"

He shook his head. "I've been doing this since I graduated high school. I've had practically every grunt job you can have in this business, and I've worked for three different TV stations. Every one of those jobs was long hours and crap pay and the constant pressure of navigating office politics." He wiped his fingers on a napkin. "This is a much better gig, trust me."

She searched his expression for signs that he was being sarcastic. "This job doesn't exactly pay a fortune."

"Yeah, but we get to make our own schedule, call our own shots—literally. There's a lot to be said for autonomy."

She watched him across the table with a sudden tightness in her chest. Josh had taken a chance on her. No one else from her old job believed in what she was doing—even the ones who had politely feigned interest and wished her well. Despite what they'd said, she knew everyone thought her little startup production company was going to be a flop.

Macey cleared her throat. "You know, in case I haven't said it lately, thanks."

"For what?"

"Signing on for this. I know it's a huge risk."

"Not for me." He grinned. "You're the one who put your life savings on the line. I'm just along for the ride."

"Well, I'm glad you're along."

He pushed his plate away, clearly uncomfortable with the sentimental turn the conversation had taken. "Hey, I see a free table. You up for some pool?"

She looked over her shoulder across the bar. One of the tables in back was indeed free, but it wouldn't stay that way for long given tonight's crowd.

"Let's play." He pulled out his wallet. "You go snag the table and I'll get the bill."

"You snag the table, and I'll get the bill."

"You sure?"

"Yes," she said. "You picked up coffee this morning."

"Thanks."

He got up to grab the table. Macey looked around for

their server to ask for a check. The woman was wearing a bright yellow halter top and shouldn't be hard to spot. Scanning the room, Macey spied her at the end of the bar. She was filling a tray with drinks as people jockeyed for the bartender's attention. The guy beside her bumped her tray, and she glared at him.

Macey's pulse quickened as she looked the man over. Shaggy dark hair, medium build. He wore orange board shorts with a white T-shirt, and a sleeve of tattoos covered his right arm.

It was the *him*, the man who'd come knocking on her door, possibly looking for Julia Murphy.

Or maybe not looking for Julia. Maybe he'd simply been lost.

Macey studied his tattoos and his hair and his shorts, which were just the right shade of orange. It was him. She knew it. What she didn't know was what he'd been looking for at her house.

Only one way to find out.

O WEN WAS IN a foul mood.

He hadn't confirmed the alibi. He hadn't disproved it, either. So basically, he'd made no progress whatsoever. He'd spent half his evening on hold with a charter plane company and the other half trying to track down Hancock's personal assistant, who had supposedly booked all the travel arrangements. Owen was sure if he could just get the woman to answer some face-to-face questions, he'd know right away whether Hancock's alibi was legit. But he'd tried her at work and at home—twice—and he hadn't been able to track her down.

Now Owen crossed the crowded parking lot at Waterman's and spotted Nicole's pickup parked discreetly behind a hedge of oleanders. Crouching low, he approached the passenger side, making sure to stay clear of the side mirror. Slowly, he reached for the door handle. He yanked the door open and slid inside.

Nicole jumped about a mile. "*Damn it*, Owen! What the *hell*?"

He grinned. "What's up?"

"You gave me a heart attack!"

"Just making sure you're not asleep on the job."

She blew out a breath. "How did you know I was here?"

"Emmet told me you offered to cover for him so he could get dinner. How's it going?"

"I'm bored out of my mind."

He smiled. "You wanted stakeout duty."

"He's been in there for more than two hours." She gestured toward Waterman's front entrance, where a parking attendant stood staring at his phone. The restaurant was busy tonight, and the entire front lot was filled with expensive cars.

"Where's the Range Rover?" Owen asked.

"On the other side of that white Escalade." She looked at him in the dimness of the truck cab. "Did Emmet tell you he got fingerprints?"

"I heard."

Emmet had put flyers on everyone's windshields at the construction site. As predicted, when Hancock left work, he grabbed his flyer and tossed it on the ground. Emmet recovered it after he drove away, so they had a partial set of fingerprints, at least.

"I asked Miranda if we might be able to get touch DNA off the flyer," Nicole said. "She told me she wouldn't count on it, so we're still waiting for him to discard something else."

"We might be better off waiting until morning. Maybe

he'll stop for coffee on his way in. Leyla tells me he's a regular at the Beanery."

"I'm still hopeful about tonight," Nicole said. "I talked to the hostess earlier, and she told me Hancock and his friends sometimes smoke cigars and cigarettes on the balcony after dinner. Especially after they've spent the day fishing."

"He didn't fish today."

"I know, but I'm willing to wait." Nicole crossed her arms and stared through the windshield at the restaurant entrance. "Although the longer I sit here, the more annoyed I get."

"Why?"

"I'm tired of being in limbo. It's like Brady said, I just want to cross him off our list or bump him to the top. If the DNA matches, we'll know."

"Maybe."

She looked at him. "Maybe? What other explanation would there be for his DNA being under Julia's torn fingernail?"

He just looked at her.

"Oh." She frowned. "Rough sex?"

He nodded. "It's possible. I think this guy seems guilty, but he could be covering up an affair and not a murder. Someone else could have killed her."

She sighed. "Depressing thought."

"Yup."

"His wife and kids are at home, and meanwhile, he's in there eating surf and turf and probably playing grab-ass with the waitresses."

The mention of food made Owen's stomach growl. He hadn't eaten since lunch. Yet another reason he was in a bad mood.

"So, how's it going with Macey?"

He turned to look at her. "Who?"

She rolled her eyes. "Macey Burns, the reporter you've been seeing."

"She's not a reporter."

"Okay, former reporter. I keep seeing you talking to her."

Owen didn't comment.

"Are you two going out?" she asked.

"No."

"Really? Interesting."

"Why is that interesting?"

She shrugged. "One of my friends saw you with her at the Bitter End."

Owen sighed. He'd grown up on the island, and he'd long since gotten used to the fact that everyone knew everyone else's business. From a work perspective, it was something he used to his advantage. People shared information, the more salacious the better. But from a personal perspective, it got on his nerves.

"I'm not trying to pry," she said.

He gave her a pointed look.

"Seriously, I know it must be annoying that people are always gossiping about your love life."

"Who gossips about my love life?"

"Oh, come on. Everyone does. You and your brother are two of the most eligible men in town, and now Joel's off the market."

"People have way too much time on their hands."

"Anyway, you're missing my point here. I just wanted to suggest you be careful what you tell Macey." She paused. "You know, in case she still keeps up with her news contacts."

He shot her a dark look.

Nicole shook her head. "Forget I said anything."

Owen shifted in his seat, uncomfortable now, and it

wasn't just the pit in his grumbling stomach. He didn't feel good about how he'd left things with Macey. He kept picturing her face when he'd asked her if she was the source for that story. She'd looked angry. And hurt.

The angry part, he'd expected. He'd known the question would piss her off, but he'd had to ask. He'd figured she'd be annoyed with him, but he'd smooth it over, no big deal. But he could tell that it *was* a big deal to her.

Owen stared at the door to the restaurant, getting more and more frustrated. He hadn't meant to hurt her feelings. He hadn't even realized he could. But the look on her face was unmistakable. Owen was good at reading body language, especially women's, and there was no getting around the fact that he'd offended her.

The ironic thing was, Owen believed her. When she'd said she wasn't the source for that news story, he somehow knew that she was telling him the truth.

Basically, he'd blown it. All that effort getting her to go out with him, and then getting her to laugh and smile and let her guard down, and then getting her to let him kiss her—all that was gone. In one five-minute conversation, he'd torpedoed everything.

"Hello?" Nicole leaned forward. "You awake over there?"

"What?"

"I said, do you mind covering a minute?" she asked. "I've got to run to the gas station."

"Why?"

"I need to pee."

"Can't it wait?"

"No." She shoved open her door. "Text me if anything happens."

She left, and Owen watched in the side mirror as she jogged across the street to the gas station.

Sighing, he settled back to wait. He spied a pack of orange Tic Tacs in the cup holder and emptied half of them into his mouth. Swishing them around made him feel hungrier than ever, which only amplified his bad mood. He combed his hand through his hair and sighed. He needed a meal and a shower and a beer, and even all that probably wasn't going to make him feel better.

What he really needed was to figure out how to make things right with Macey.

His phone vibrated with a text. He pulled it from his pocket, and his pulse jumped as he saw a message from her.

Where RU?

He stared down at the text for a few seconds before responding.

Working late. Whats up?

A bubble appeared as she started to reply. Then it disappeared. He waited another minute and called her.

"Hey, what's up?" he asked.

"Hi." She paused. "Sorry to bother you."

"No problem." He caught the formal tone of her voice. And something else, too. "What's wrong, Macey?"

"I wanted to let you know, I just saw that guy."

"What guy?"

"The guy who came by my house the other day. The arm tattoos? I bumped into him at Finn's earlier."

"You bumped into him?"

"Not literally. I saw him there, and so I struck up a conversation and—"

"You talked to him?"

"Yeah. It was really casual. I just told him that I noticed

him at my beach house the other day and asked him if I knew him from someplace."

Owen gritted his teeth. Hadn't he specifically told her not to approach the guy? Why hadn't she just called him for help?

"Hello?"

"You shouldn't have talked to him," he said.

"Well, I did. We were in a crowded bar, and I felt totally safe. But then he got a little weird, so I thought I should mention it."

"How was he 'weird'?"

"He just, you know, tensed up when he realized I was renting that house. He acted squirrelly. And then he said he had no idea what I was talking about and then he left the bar right after that." She paused. "The conversation seemed odd to me, so I thought you'd want to know."

Owen glanced around for something he could write on. He popped open the glove compartment and found a stack of napkins and rummaged for a pen.

"Did you see him leave?" he asked.

"No. It was really crowded, and he just kind of slipped out. But I can tell you what he was wearing: a white Rip Curl T-shirt and orange board shorts, the same shorts he was wearing when he came to my house. Oh, and it's definitely a tribal tattoo. I saw it up close. Oh, also he's about five-eleven, medium build, brown eyes."

Owen jotted it all down.

"Oh, and he was drinking a Red Stripe."

He wrote that down, too. "You shouldn't have talked to him," he told her.

"Yeah, you said that already."

"Where are you now?" he asked, not sure he wanted to know. Maybe she'd gone home with Josh.

"I just got home. Everything's fine. I just wanted you to know in case it's relevant to your investigation."

"Thanks."

She clicked off, and Owen stared down at his phone, more frustrated than ever. Why had she approached the guy? She could have just called him up without getting near him.

And why had the guy acted squirrelly when Macey said she'd seen him at her house? Owen had no idea if the man had anything to do with Julia Murphy, but he needed to find out.

Nicole pulled open the door and slid into the truck. "Much better," she said. "What'd I miss?"

"Nothing."

She tucked her phone into the cup holder, and it immediately buzzed as a text landed. She snatched it up and read the message.

"They're coming out," she said.

"Who's texting you?"

"The hostess inside. *Damn it!*"

"What?"

"No cigars tonight, she says."

A group emerged from the restaurant. Five middle-aged men, and they looked remarkably similar. They wore Hawaiian-print shirts in different colors and baseball caps, probably from various golf courses they'd visited. The island was packed with guys like these, or at least the tourist spots were.

"Hancock's in the back," Nicole said. "Blue Hawaiian shirt. See him?"

"Yeah."

Hancock stepped around his friends, and Owen watched as he handed a ticket to the valet attendant. Then he put something in his mouth.

"What's he—"

"Toothpick," Owen said.

"No way! That's perfect."

They waited impatiently as Hancock picked his teeth and the parking attendant retrieved three cars. Two men rode away in the third one, leaving just Hancock. Finally, his Range Rover pulled around.

"Please be a litterbug," Nicole muttered.

Hancock tipped the valet and slid behind the wheel. He plucked the toothpick from his mouth and tossed it to the ground.

"And there it is." Nicole smiled at him. "Our DNA sample."

CHAPTER

EIGHTEEN

OWEN CAUGHT MACEY just as she was leaving, apparently. She loaded a big black duffel into the trunk of her car and turned around as he pulled into the driveway beside her.

"Morning," Owen said as he got out.

"Hi."

He couldn't see her eyes behind her sunglasses, but she didn't sound exactly overjoyed to see him.

She looked to be geared up for a day outside. She had on a T-shirt, jeans, and hiking boots, and her skin smelled of sunblock. Her hair was in a ponytail, and she wore a Diamondbacks baseball cap.

"Heading out?" he asked.

"I'm on my way to the nature center." She eyed the stuff in his hands. "What's that?"

"Latte and banana bread," he said, handing her the cup and pastry bag. "They're out of blueberry muffins today."

She took everything, looking flustered. "Thanks."

"It's a peace offering," he said.

"A peace offering?"

"I was a jerk yesterday. About the media thing," he added, as if she didn't remember.

"You didn't need to do that."

"Yeah, I did." He stepped closer. "You have a minute?"

"I'm running late, actually."

"This won't take long. I need to show you something."

"All right."

She stashed the food in her car, and he led her back to his truck and grabbed the brown accordion file off the passenger seat. Shuffling through, he pulled out what he needed and turned to face her.

She'd taken off her sunglasses, and he could see her eyes better now. She looked wary as he handed her a piece of paper with a photograph on it.

"That's him," she said, sounding surprised. "That's the man who came by my house."

"Are you sure?"

She nodded. "I saw him up close last night. That's definitely the guy." She handed back the paper. "Who is he?"

"Jackson Schaffer." He watched her eyes for any flicker of recognition. "Does that name ring any bells?"

"None whatsoever." She frowned. "How'd you figure out his name?"

"I went by Finn's and got them to cull through their credit card receipts for men who were drinking Red Stripe. Then I ran the names to see if anyone matched your description."

"That photograph doesn't look like a mug shot," she said.

"It's a driver's license photo."

Owen had a mug shot, too, but the driver's license picture was more recent. Jackson Schaffer had been arrested on drug charges in Austin four years ago. If the guy was still in business, and if he'd known Julia Murphy, there was the possibility that her murder might be drug related.

But Owen didn't plan to tell Macey all that. He'd wanted her confirmation on the ID, but then he was done talking to her about the case.

"So . . . I assume he's local?" she asked.

He nodded.

"Are you looking at him now instead of Hancock?"

"We're keeping our options open."

She glanced away, looking irritated. But that was too bad. He'd told her enough already.

"Thanks for the help." He folded the paper and slipped it into his back pocket. "I'm sorry you're involved in this."

"I'm not. There's a cold-blooded killer roaming around free. If there's anything I can do to help you figure out who it is, I definitely want to help."

"Well, we appreciate it."

"The sooner you arrest someone, the sooner we can all sleep at night."

He watched her closely, not sure why he was surprised to learn she was having trouble sleeping. She was living in the house of a murder victim. He'd told her that her rental house wasn't a crime scene, but he wasn't sure if she believed him. And that might not be what was keeping her up at night. Wherever the murder had happened, the killer had buried the body less than half a mile away from here. That in itself was enough to worry her, especially since she lived alone.

She watched him for a long moment, those green eyes searching his face for clues. When he didn't say anything more, she looked away.

"I need to get going, so . . . thank you for the coffee."

He nodded. But he didn't move to leave. It was on the tip

of his tongue to ask her to dinner tonight. Or drinks again. Or, hell, anything that would give him a chance to spend time with her so he could smooth things over. He wanted her smiling and talking and letting her guard down with him again. He wanted to kiss her again, but not on her stairs this time. He wanted her in a bed, where he could do everything he'd been thinking about since he'd seen her coming in from her run, all flushed and sweaty and breathing hard.

Owen knew exactly what he wanted, but he also knew his timing sucked. He was neck-deep in a homicide investigation that seemed like it could blow wide open any minute now. Maybe even today. Owen had a feel for cases, and this one felt like it was coming to a head. Which meant that even if he could get Macey to agree to see him tonight, he was probably going to be tied up with work.

"You free later?" he said anyway because, what the hell? He wanted to see her. He was *burning* to see her.

"Later?"

"Tonight. I may be able to get away for dinner."

She hesitated a moment. "I don't know if that's a good idea. I'm spending the day on the turtle boat, shadowing a marine biologist, so I'll probably be pretty wiped out tonight."

"Turtles? Really?" He smiled. "That's a new one. I've never been turned down for turtles before."

The corner of her mouth quirked.

"How about I call you? If you're tired from the turtles, we'll take a rain check," he said.

She slid her sunglasses back on, but not before he caught the look in her eyes. She was tempted to say yes. He could see it.

"Okay," she said, "but don't be surprised if it doesn't work out tonight."

At least he'd gotten her from a *no* to a *maybe*.

"I'll call you," he said, moving to leave before she could change her mind. "Thanks again for the help."

"Anytime."

N ICOLE STEPPED INTO the bullpen and took a moment to bask in the chilled air. She scanned the desks and made her way over to Emmet, who was tapping away at his computer.

"Where is everyone?" she asked.

"Not sure. I just got back from lunch."

"Who's in the interview room?" she asked, nodding toward the closed door beside the conference room.

"That would be Owen."

She arched her eyebrows. "Who's with him?"

"Jackson Schaffer."

"Who's that?"

"A friend of Julia Murphy's, supposedly."

"Really?" Nicole couldn't conceal her surprise. "Friend as in boyfriend?"

Emmet didn't stop typing. "I don't know."

She glanced at the closed door, even more intrigued now. She'd been interviewing Julia's friends for days, and she hadn't heard of the guy.

"Is 'makeup' hyphenated?" Emmet asked.

"What?"

"Makeup, the stuff you put on your face. I'm writing up the hotel burglary, and this woman is reporting three hundred dollars' worth of makeup stolen, plus a gold bracelet and two laptop computers."

She peered over his shoulder at the report on his screen. "Aren't you a little late with that?"

He shot her an annoyed look. "Hyphen or no?"

"No, I think."

"You think?"

She rolled her eyes. "Just put down 'cosmetics.'" She glanced at the door again. "How long have they been in there?"

"Almost an hour."

"Really?"

"Yeah, and I'm getting curious, too."

As if on cue, the door opened and a man stepped out. Tall, tan, nice build. He wore shorts and flip-flops and had a three-day beard. The guy looked tense as Owen ushered him through the bullpen, but that wasn't unusual. People didn't generally enjoy sitting through an hour of police questioning.

"Well, he's not under arrest," Nicole said as she watched Owen usher him out through the reception room. "Where'd we get his name?"

"Macey."

"Macey Burns?"

Owen returned to the bullpen, frowning as he scrolled through his phone. He went straight into the conference room and closed the door.

Nicole and Emmet exchanged looks. She got up and headed for the conference room, and Emmet was right behind her.

Nicole listened for a moment in case he was on the phone. When she didn't hear anything, she knocked on the door and leaned her head in.

Owen stood staring at the wall of crime scene photos. He glanced over his shoulder as she and Emmet stepped in.

"How'd it go with Jackson Schaffer?" Emmet asked.

"Good."

"*Good*, as in he's a suspect?" Nicole asked.

"I don't know yet. But listen to this." Owen stepped over to a map of the island that was taped beneath an array of crime scene photos from White Dunes Park. A red square marked the crime scene.

"Julia lived here." Owen tapped on a red dot over the victim's house on Primrose Trail. "She worked here." He tapped another dot marking Waterman's restaurant. "Schaffer lives at an apartment here, two blocks off the beach." He tapped a spot halfway between Julia's house and her workplace. "And he claims he met her at Buck's Beach Club several months ago." He tapped yet another spot between the victim's workplace and Schaffer's apartment. The beachfront bar had a huge deck and cheap drinks, and it was famous for its Jell-O shots. "Since their first meeting at the club, Schaffer told me, he's been to Julia's house four times."

Nicole perked up, and she could tell Emmet did, too. Getting someone to admit to being in the victim's home was important, and the more recent, the better.

"When?" Nicole asked.

"He said the first time was back in February. He met Julia at Buck's, and she invited him back to her place."

"His place is closer," Emmet pointed out.

"I know."

"That doesn't mean she would have felt comfortable going there," Nicole said. "Maybe she felt safer at her place."

"Then, supposedly, he bumped into her on the beach a month later, and again they went to her place," Owen said. "The third time, he said he was on the beach with some friends, and he crossed the bridge to go knock on her door, but he changed his mind when he saw a black Range Rover in her driveway and realized she had company."

Nicole pulse skittered. "A black Range Rover? He said that?"

Owen nodded.

"Hancock specifically *denied* ever being at the victim's

house," Nicole said. "He said he didn't even know where she lived."

"I know."

"When was this?" Emmet asked.

"Schaffer said this happened in April, but he couldn't remember for sure. Before Easter."

"Damn. That's good." Emmet crossed his arms and looked at the map. "Now we've got Hancock in a lie."

"Assuming this guy's telling the truth," Nicole said. "And assuming it's Hancock's black Range Rover."

"How many black Ranger Rovers do we have on the island?" Emmet asked. "I'd guess one. How many Range Rovers period?"

"Three," Owen said.

Nicole looked at him, surprised that he knew. But she shouldn't have been. Owen was thorough.

"Two of them are white," Owen informed them. "Hancock's is the only black one."

Owen stepped closer to the board and stared at one of the crime scene photos. Miranda had taken it before the excavation began, and it showed the victim's arm protruding from the sand. The photo had become stuck in Nicole's mind, and she'd even been having dreams about it. Whenever she looked at it, the stench of the crime scene came back to her. She'd started sitting with her back to the wall during team meetings so she wouldn't have to see it.

"So, assuming this Jackson kid is legit, we have Miles Hancock in a lie," Emmet said eagerly. "Is it enough for a search warrant? I'm dying to show up at his fancy house and take the place apart."

Owen shook his head. "A lie isn't enough. Brady's going to want physical evidence implicating Hancock."

"Why isn't it enough?" Emmet asked. "If he lied to investigators—"

"It's just Jackson Schaffer's word against his," Nicole said. "Maybe Schaffer did it, and he's trying to shift the blame. Anyone who watches the news knows that Miles Hancock is a suspect, so he could have just said that to implicate him."

Frustration flashed in Owen's eyes. He was still pissed about the news story. They all were. This was precisely why they tried to keep details of the investigation under wraps—to prevent potential suspects from manipulating investigators by feeding them BS.

Owen turned back to the whiteboard.

"What did you think?" Nicole asked him. "You're good at spotting liars. Did you think he was telling the truth about seeing the Range Rover?"

Owen looked at her. "Yes."

He seemed so sure of himself, and she felt a pang of envy. Maybe one day she'd have that kind of confidence, but right now she was always second-guessing her instincts.

"He was credible." Owen looked at Emmet. "And it would explain what happened with Macey."

"What happened with Macey?" Nicole asked.

"He went and knocked on her door, looking for Julia. Then later he claims he saw one of her friends, who told him Julia had been murdered, and it freaked him out."

"He hadn't seen it on the news?" Emmet asked skeptically.

"He said he hadn't." Owen shrugged. "Not everyone watches the news."

Miranda stepped into the room. "Oh good, you're here. Where's Brady?"

"Out," Owen said.

Nicole caught the excitement in Miranda's face as she shut the door behind her and looked at Owen.

"I think we've got it," she said.

"Got what?" Emmet asked.

"The physical evidence you've been waiting for."

Owen looked at her intently. "The toothpick came back already? I thought you said—"

"Not the toothpick, the fingerprint." Miranda looked at Emmet. "The one off the flyer you recovered from the parking lot."

"You're talking about Hancock's fingerprints?"

"Print," she said. "Just one, in this case. It matches a print found on the door handle of the victim's car."

Owen stepped closer. "You're sure," he said forcefully, as though he could will it into being true.

"I'm sure."

"Wait, you're talking about the Volkswagen?" Emmet asked. "I thought we already ran prints from it. You said it looked like whoever drove it had on gloves."

"I believe they did, because of the residue we found on the steering wheel. But that was probably when the killer drove the body to the burial location. This print could have come from another time. Maybe he doesn't remember leaving it."

Nicole stared at Miranda, her pulse thrumming now because it seemed too good to be true. "Let me get this straight. You're saying we have Hancock's fingerprint on the door handle of the victim's car, which the killer used to dump her body. *And* we also have a witness who saw Hancock's car in front of the victim's house—the same house he swore he'd never been to."

"Wait, his car was at her *house*?" Miranda looked at Owen. "Where'd you get this witness?"

"Macey helped find him," Emmet said.

"Macey Burns?"

"Yeah, she's living in the victim's old place," Emmet said. "This guy showed up there looking for Julia, and when we finally figured out who he was, we interviewed him. Turns out he hooked up with Julia a couple times and happened to see a black Range Rover at her house one time when he went over there, even though Hancock claims he never went to her house and didn't even know where she lived."

Nicole looked at Owen. "Can we get a search warrant?"

Owen's eyes looked intense. They were talking about a search warrant for a powerful businessman who also happened to be litigious.

Owen turned to Miranda. "Inside or out?"

"What?"

"The fingerprint on the door. Where was it?"

Nicole saw what he was thinking. It would be much harder to explain away a fingerprint on the interior of the car.

"Inside," Miranda said. "It's on the front passenger side, on the back of the door handle. And I confirmed it with the fingerprint analyst. It's Hancock's print."

NINETEEN

MILES HANCOCK LIVED in a gated beachfront neighborhood even more exclusive than Caribbean Sands. The subdivision had only twelve houses, all custom-built on half-acre lots right on the beach. Nicole had been inside the subdivision a total of three times, the first two as a food delivery driver back in high school.

The third time was today, and it was almost as intimidating. Passing Hancock's driveway, she pulled over and parked behind a pair of police department SUVs.

Nicole surveyed the house as she approached it. It was a white three-story up on stilts, with a wraparound porch and Bahamian shutters. Flanked by towering king palms, the house had a grand double staircase that led to a carved double front door on the second level. On a street of big houses, Hancock's was the tallest, and Nicole knew that was no accident. Hancock was one of the island's wealthiest residents, and he liked people to know it. Besides building numerous hotels and condos, his company was responsible for several of Lost Beach's main tourist attractions, including the water park and now the golf resort at the southern tip of the island. Hancock's influence extended to the mainland as well, where he was invested in a new subdivision of homes overlooking the bay.

Nicole got a slightly queasy feeling in her stomach as she hiked up the staircase. If they were wrong about this guy, there was going to be hell to pay.

One of the front doors opened, and Emmet stepped out. Had he been watching for her? He wore white coveralls and had paper booties over his shoes.

"Where you been?" he asked irritably.

"Whose car is that?" Nicole nodded at the dinged gray Hyundai parked in the cobblestone driveway.

"The housekeeper's."

She reached the top of the stairs. Emmet looked tense, and she sensed he'd come out here to give her bad news.

"Is she the only one home?" she asked.

"Yeah."

"What about the wife?"

"She and the kids are visiting her parents in Dallas, apparently." Emmet sighed. "Where were you?" he asked again. "We started at three."

"Brady sent me to check something." She took off her sunglasses and hooked them into her shirt collar. "What's wrong?"

"We've been at it two hours." He cast a worried look down the street. "So far, nothing."

"Who's 'we'?"

"Me, Owen, and Miranda. The county even lent us an extra CSI so Miranda could focus on photography."

Nicole tipped her head back to look up at the third floor. "This place is enormous."

"Eight thousand square feet."

"Damn." She sighed. "How much of it is left to search?"

"Miranda just finished photographing the main level, so now she's upstairs doing the bedrooms. Owen's looking through stuff now, and the CSI is dusting for prints."

"Anything interesting?"

"Yeah. What's interesting is how we've found zilch. No sign of the victim's purse, her wallet, her phone, or her keys."

"All that would be the first thing he'd toss in the bay, I'd think."

"No bloody clothes, or blood traces on anything. I checked every pair of shoes in the master closet."

"I thought you said Miranda just started upstairs?"

"She did. She started in the master suite, and I watched over her shoulder as she snapped about a million pictures. So far, nothing is even remotely suspicious." He sighed. "Oh—except for a box of latex gloves in the utility room."

Nicole arched her eyebrows. "That could be interesting. Maybe we could match the residue to what was found on Julia's steering wheel."

"The box is unopened."

"Oh."

"The good news is the maid tells us the wife goes out of town a lot and takes the kids with her. So, this house could have been a love nest."

"Which means it also could be the original crime scene."

"Right." Emmet folded his arms over his chest. "So, what did Brady have you doing that was so important?"

"Looking for Miles Hancock," she told him. "The gate attendant at the front of the neighborhood said he left here around noon and it looked like he was dressed for fishing. I checked with his assistant and turns out he's on a charter trip with some clients."

"No wonder he hasn't shown up. I've been expecting him to pull in here with his lawyer and pitch a fit. Where'd the charter go?"

"I don't know," she said. "But it's booked with Lost Beach Outfitters, and they do shark and redfish trips in the Gulf. Those can take five hours."

"Or more. It depends on when the beer runs out." Emmet checked his watch. "So, he's out with his buddies, probably getting tanked. And then maybe they'll go grab dinner somewhere and drink some more. By the time he gets back and figures out we've been here, he'll likely be shit-faced and in no shape at all to raise a stink about our search warrant. We're probably good until he manages to get a lawyer down."

"We can only hope." Nicole nodded at the door. "I want to go in and help."

Emmet opened the door and stepped aside to let her in. Compared to the blazing temperature outside, the house was cool and dim. Nicole stepped onto a long piece of butcher paper where people had left shoes, keys, and other personal items. She picked up a box and pulled out some Tyvek coveralls.

"Where's Owen?" she asked as she pulled on the suit.

"Searching the office, I think."

Nicole surveyed the living room. It had vaulted ceilings and a wall of windows facing the white-sand beach. Clear blue water sparkled in the distance.

"Nice place they've got here," she said.

"Yeah, no kidding. I'm thinking we're in the wrong line of work. I should have stayed on with my uncle's construction company."

Emmet and his brother had spent summers growing up

working for their uncle's house-framing company. It was a successful business but not exactly lucrative enough for the CEO to buy an eight-thousand-square-foot beach palace.

Nicole pulled booties over her shoes and stepped into the living room. The décor inside fit with the Caribbean-sugar-plantation feel of the home's exterior. The house had bleached wood floors, white upholstery, and nautical-themed knick-knacks on the tabletops. A giant chandelier made of shimmery abalone shells hung down over the seating area.

Nicole stepped over to one of the oversize sofas. A CSI knelt beside the coffee table dusting a mirrored coaster.

"No blue throw pillows," Emmet said, watching her. "I already checked."

"What about in the bedrooms?"

"None there, either."

"Damn."

"There's always a chance he thought to get rid of a pillow, if he used it to smoother her," Emmet said. "But wouldn't you think his wife would notice something like that missing?"

"I would," she said. "Of course, my whole apartment is about six hundred square feet, so I'd notice a dish towel missing. This place is ginormous. How many bedrooms?"

"Six," he said. "Each with its own bath."

Nicole frowned and scanned the room again. She'd never met the CSI, who was on loan from the county crime lab. The man was thin, probably late twenties, and wore wire-rimmed glasses and a plastic shield that covered his face. Beside him was a tackle box filled with all sorts of jars and brushes. He glanced up at her as she stepped over.

"Hi, I'm Nicole."

He nodded. "I'm Justin. Can't shake hands, sorry."

"No worries. How do you know what to dust?" she asked. "You can't possibly dust every surface in a place this big."

"You have to be selective. Right now I'm focused on things that might have been touched by someone who was a guest here." He made a sheepish face. "It's a lot of guesswork, unfortunately. Anything in particular you want me to hit?"

Nicole looked at Emmet. "You said you've been upstairs? I assume the master bathroom has two sinks?"

"Two everything."

Nicole looked at the CSI. "When you get up there, you might try dusting the wife's medicine cabinet."

He lifted an eyebrow.

"If our victim was up in the bedroom, she probably did some snooping," she said.

Emmet smiled. "So, you're saying women are nosey."

"Yep. If our victim was having an affair with Hancock, she'd want to know what was in his wife's medicine cabinet."

"You're here."

Nicole looked up to see Miranda peering over an upstairs balcony. She wore her typical white coveralls and held her camera in her gloved hands.

"How's it going up there?" Nicole asked.

"Slow. I'm being extra thorough so we don't overlook anything. Emmet, I'm done with the master closet if you want to take a closer look at all those shoes."

"I'll be right up." He looked at Nicole. "Want to help with the closet?"

A loud whistle sounded from the back of the house. Nicole whirled around.

"Miranda?" Owen strode from a hallway off the living room. He wore coveralls and had on latex gloves. "Where's Miranda?" he demanded.

"I'm up here."

Owen tipped his head back. "Bring your camera down, ASAP. We missed something."

"Where?"

"His office." Owen looked from Nicole to Emmet. A slow smile spread across his face. "You're not going to believe this."

CHAPTER

TWENTY

THE SUN WAS nothing more than a pink streak on the purple horizon as Macey sped down the highway. She lowered the windows and loosened her ponytail, and the breeze whipping through the car was a balm against her sunburned skin.

She inhaled a deep breath of ocean air. She couldn't remember the last time she'd felt this good. Months, probably— since before her breakup with Aaron. And definitely since before the fallout that had left her heart battered and her career in shambles.

Her phone chimed from the cup holder, and the sight of Josh's number made her smile.

"Finally," she said, picking up.

"Are you back on land, or is it going to drop again?"

"I'm back on land."

"I thought it was supposed to be a day trip. It's almost nine."

"We may have gotten a little carried away," she said.

"'We'?"

"Mark Buro and I. He's the head marine biologist at the nature center. Josh, you have to meet him. He's fascinating. The whole trip was fascinating! We rescued two injured sea turtles and released three back into the wild, and then he showed me some of the tidal flats where the shorebirds winter. You *have* to get out there and see it."

He made a noncommittal grunt.

"It's spectacular," she added. "I got some great shots."

"Tell me they're of the sea turtles and not the tidal flats."

"I got both."

"Hmm. Well, it sounds like you're in a better mood than yesterday."

"You could say that. Although I have no idea how, when I'm exhausted and famished and my nose is fried. But truly, it was an amazing day! I can't wait to show you."

When he didn't respond with her level of enthusiasm— or any, really—she gave up trying to convince him. She'd get him out on the water, and he could see for himself.

"So how'd it go here?" she asked.

"Pretty well. I went down to the wharf this morning and got some good sound. Birds and boat noises, mostly. Then I had a surf lesson this afternoon."

"I thought you already had one."

"I had two. This was my third."

"Let me guess. You have a female instructor."

"Gee, how'd you figure that out?"

"Who is she?"

He didn't respond right away, and Macey wondered what the hesitation was about.

"Her name's Rory. She teaches surfing and also works at a gift shop downtown. We're having dinner tonight after she gets off work."

"Hey, that's great!"

He paused. "Why are you all excited?"

"I don't know. I'm glad to see you zeroing in on one person."

"You sound so maternal."

"Oh, whatever. I'm not *maternal*, I'm just happy for you meeting new people."

"Thanks, Mom."

She sighed. "Okay, new topic. Are we still on for tomorrow?"

"Nine a.m. at White Dunes Park. I'll be there with the drone cam."

"Sounds good. Make sure it's fully charged," she said.

"It's charging as we speak."

They ended the call, and Macey turned onto her street.

Maternal? Since when was she maternal, with Josh or anyone else? Protective, maybe. But there was nothing wrong with that. Josh had uprooted his life to come down here with her, and she felt responsible for him. She was relieved to see him settling in. Plus, he was her only friend here, unless she counted Owen. And the situation with Owen was complicated, mainly because she was still ticked off at him.

Late this afternoon, he had called to bail on their dinner plan, which wasn't surprising. He'd said there was something big going on with the case. A *big development*, he'd called it.

She didn't mind that he'd canceled dinner. She'd been on the fence about it to begin with. It felt like another step down the slippery slope of starting a romance with someone, and that was something she wanted to avoid right now. What bothered her was him being so tight-lipped about the reason, as though he didn't trust her.

A big development. What did that mean? Had they found a new witness? Or made an arrest?

And why was he being cagey? Did he seriously think she was going to pick up the phone and tip off the media?

The whole thing irked her. This morning he'd brought her coffee and apologized for accusing her of leaking info, and he'd seemed sincere. But less than a day later, he was being evasive and treating her like a reporter.

Macey's stomach growled as she turned onto her street. She was tired and hungry and sunbaked, despite slathering on block all day. But she felt strangely happy, too.

It was the boat trip. She'd felt a buzz of excitement since the moment Mark started talking about the struggling shellfish populations in the region and the restoration efforts along the coast. The parallels between what was happening down here—the disappearing oyster reefs, the dwindling harvests—and what was happening along the upper East Coast were impossible to ignore. It was almost like she was *meant* to come down here and weave the story line into her documentary. It felt fated, somehow. All afternoon, she'd had that heady feeling she got when an issue grabbed hold of her and refused to be ignored. She hadn't felt this buzz of excitement in a long time, and she wasn't going to let Owen's phone call put a damper on her mood.

She pulled into the driveway and gathered her backpack off the floor. As she slid out and locked her car, she cast an annoyed look around the dark driveway. Her landlord had promised to send someone by today to fix the floodlight. Should she call him and give him an earful? It probably wouldn't help. On the other hand, she'd called him twice about this already, and she was sick of being nice about it. She scrolled through her phone and found his number.

In the corner of her eye a shadow moved.

A force hit her from behind, slamming her to the ground. Pain reverberated up her knees as a hand clamped around her mouth. She couldn't breathe, couldn't get air. Her heart skittered as she frantically struggled for oxygen.

A hand snaked around her, sliding over her hip, and panic zinged through her. She tried to buck and squirm and scream, but the weight wouldn't move.

No no no!

The sharp fingers dug into her pelvis.

"*Keys,*" he hissed.

She tried to turn her head, but his other hand was still clamped over her mouth. He moved it away, and she screamed.

Pain exploded at her temple as a fist connected with her face. She blinked, stunned, as sparks danced before her eyes. Then the hand was back over her mouth, smothering her.

"Give me your keys!"

The weight shifted and she tried to roll away, but his hand plunged into her front pocket. Another bolt of panic shot through her as he dug around with his sharp fingers. And then his hand slid away and the weight on her vanished.

Macey tried to scramble to her feet, but a boot landed heavily on her shoulder.

"Don't move." He leaned down, and something cold and hard pressed against the back of her neck. "Do not fucking move or I will fucking kill you. Got it?"

Her heart convulsed. She stared at the pavement in front of her, not daring to move or speak or even blink as the gun pressed against the back of her neck. She smelled sweat and dirt and felt the day's heat coming off the concrete.

"*Got it?*"

"Yes," she croaked.

The boot moved, and every muscle in her body tensed as she waited for what he might do. Pain radiated from her temple, pulsing through her head like a drumbeat as she stared at the ground.

Her car chirped, and she heard him open the door.

Don't move. Don't move. Don't move.

She forced herself to lie still, but her brain was screaming at her to run away. The fight-or-flight instinct was kicking in *hard* in favor of flight, and it was all she could do to press her palms against the pavement and remain motionless. Meanwhile, her pulse raced a million miles an hour as she sucked in gulps of hot, dusty air. Her backpack was gone. Where was her phone? It had flown from her grasp when he slammed her to the ground. Had she connected the call?

Sucking in a breath, she lifted her head slightly and strained to see in the darkness. At the edge of the grass was a bluish glow. Her phone. It had to be. But it was too far to reach for without attracting his attention.

I will fucking kill you.

Macey squeezed her eyes shut. Tears burned behind her eyelids as she thought of her dad. She couldn't die. No matter what happened, she had to stay alive, get through it. She couldn't leave him alone. She couldn't.

The footsteps moved closer, and she tensed again, pressing her cheek against the hot pavement. A car door slammed shut. Then the trunk popped open.

Was he stealing her car? Her camera? Why didn't he just take everything and *go*? Maybe he wanted cash. She felt another jolt of terror as she realized the only money she had was in a little zipper pouch with her driver's license in the back pocket of her jeans, which meant he'd have to touch her again. Her heart made a little hiccup against her ribs.

The trunk slammed shut. Macey's body went rigid as the footsteps approached. She couldn't breathe, couldn't think straight. A sour ball of fear clogged her throat.

The steely tip of the gun poked her neck again, and she closed her eyes.

Please, God. Please, please, please.

"Do not move."

Something warm and wet trickled down her temple. Was it blood? Tears? She held her breath and sent a silent prayer to her dad.

The gun went away. Then footsteps moved to the end of the driveway.

Macey sucked in air through her nose. She lifted her head and blinked into the dimness. Everything had gone dark. Her phone, her car, everything. The only light was the faint glow above the trees from her neighbor's house.

Macey listened for more footsteps, but either he'd stopped moving or he was too far away. An engine grumbled to life in the distance, and her heart lurched. Was it him? Was he leaving?

Please, please, please . . .

Macey bit her lip and strained to listen as the engine noise faded away.

SOUNDS LIKE YOUR case is coming to a head," Joel said. "I hear you had a big day."

Big was an understatement. The case had blown wide open this afternoon. And since Owen hadn't talked to his brother in days, he figured he'd heard about everything from Miranda.

"Did Miranda tell you about the necklace?" Owen asked over the phone.

"She told me you found key evidence."

"A gold shamrock pendant," Owen said. "Julia Murphy was wearing it when she went missing. I found it in the back of a desk drawer in his office."

Joel whistled. "Damn."

Owen pulled up to a stoplight and looked around. It was a clear, breezy Friday night, and the tourists were out in full force along the strip. They laughed and flirted and hopped from bar to bar, completely oblivious to the law enforcement activities going on around them. Owen had been one of them once, but now he couldn't imagine being so carefree.

"So, I assume you got the arrest warrant?" Joel asked.

"Yeah, that was no problem. But now he's AWOL. He got off a fishing charter at six, and no one's seen him since."

"We'll find him."

The pair of Mustangs in front of Owen started revving their engines. The stoplight turned green, and their tires shrieked as they lurched forward.

"He could have skipped town," Owen said when the noise died down. "The man's got access to charter planes, boats. He could be in Mexico by now."

"He's also got a wife and kids and a four-million-dollar house here. Not to mention a huge business. It's unlikely he skipped. He's probably just holed up somewhere in a panic, on the phone with his lawyer."

Owen wasn't so sure. Clearly, Hancock had gotten wind of the fact that his house was swarming with cops—probably as soon as the boat pulled into the marina, if not earlier. He'd probably freaked out. But Owen wasn't sure he was busy consulting with his lawyer, who would no doubt advise his client to turn himself in. Hancock could have easily left the country. Owen wouldn't be surprised if he had multiple passports and offshore accounts.

"There's a statewide APB on him," Owen said. "And if he doesn't turn up soon, Brady wants to involve the Marshals."

"We'll find him," Joel said again. "I'd give it twenty-four

hours, tops, before his lawyer calls and wants to work out a deal."

"I wish I had your optimism."

"Yeah, well, that's where I think this is going, but I could be wrong," Joel said.

"I hope you're not."

They ended the call, and Owen waited through another stoplight as he listened to his stomach grumble. He'd been too busy to eat or even think about food, and now it was catching up to him. He'd spent four hours at Hancock's house, with everyone shifting into high gear as soon as he'd found the necklace. The whole evening had been a blur, and he barely remembered updating Brady and writing up the warrant. And he'd called Macey to cancel dinner somewhere in there, too.

Owen sighed and combed a hand through his hair. He hadn't liked canceling plans with Macey. It was unavoidable, but still it sucked.

Every time Owen became even slightly interested in someone, his work got in the way. Joel and Miranda were lucky to have similar jobs. They both dealt with weird hours and canceled plans and having to drop everything at a moment's notice and rush to a crime scene.

The thing was, Owen wasn't just *slightly* interested in Macey. He liked her a lot, and he couldn't stop thinking about her. But he'd racked up two strikes with her in two days, and he had a feeling it wouldn't take much for him to strike out with her for good. Showing up at her house with coffee and pastries could only get him so far.

Owen spotted the neon sign for Giovanni's up ahead. The tiny restaurant had picnic tables out front and a take-out window where people were lined up for pizza by the slice. He pulled into the parking lot. The smell of fresh-baked garlic knots made his mouth start to water as he crossed the lot.

His phone buzzed, and his pulse picked up as he saw LOST BEACH PD on the screen. Maybe they'd found him.

"Breda."

"Hey, it's Nicole. I'm at the station."

"We make an arrest?"

"No. At least, I don't think so. That's not why I'm calling." She paused. "This is none of my business, but I thought you might want to know that Macey's here."

"At the station?"

"Yeah, she just walked in here to report an assault."

Owen halted in the middle of the parking lot. "What happened?"

"I don't know. I wasn't here when she first came in."

"Is she okay?"

"Her face looks pretty bad. Emmet's talking to her now."

Owen was already back at his truck. "I'll be right there."

"What are you—"

"I'm on my way."

Owen hung up and rocketed backward out of the space. He pulled onto the highway, earning a chorus of honks as he cut across traffic.

Owen's gut clenched. Where the hell had she been assaulted? She'd been on a research boat all day. It must have happened at her house. Or maybe she'd gone out tonight after he ditched their plans together. He sped across town, gripping the wheel as different scenarios flooded his mind.

He swung into the police station. The parking lot was empty except for a handful of cars, and he pulled into a front-row space beside Macey's Honda.

Nicole emerged from the building as he strode up the sidewalk.

"What happened?" he demanded.

"Don't go charging in there, okay? She's in an interview room with Emmet, giving him her statement."

"Tell me what you know."

Nicole sighed and looked at the glass door behind her. She had her backpack on her shoulder, and it looked like she was heading home for the night.

"I wasn't here when she first came in. McDeere talked to her. She was attacked at her house, evidently."

"Has she been to the hospital?"

"He tried to get her to go, but she refused. She said she just wanted to file a report."

Owen looked over Nicole's shoulder as Macey stepped into the reception room. He could see her silhouette through the glass door.

"Owen."

He glanced at Nicole.

"Calm down, all right? Don't make it worse for her."

He looked at Nicole for a long moment. Then he forced himself to take a deep breath before approaching the door as Macey walked out of the police station.

He stopped in front of her. Her right eye was swollen half-shut, and she had a gash at her temple that had scabbed over. Owen's throat tightened.

"Hey." She gave him a wobbly smile, and he felt the overwhelming urge to punch someone.

"Hi." He stepped closer. "What happened?"

"Long story. Well, not really, but I don't want to talk here." She sighed. "Can you give me a ride home?"

"Let me take you to the ER."

"I'm fine. Really. I just need some ice on it."

"Macey—"

"Just give me a ride. Please? They want me to leave my car here so someone can try to recover fingerprints from it." She turned to look at her car, and he was glad to see that the other side of her face looked all right. "I don't know what I was thinking driving it over here. I should have stayed at my house and called someone."

She looked at him.

"I'll take you anywhere you want to go."

"Thank you."

He walked her to his truck. Nicole was gone now, and the parking lot was nearly empty except for Emmet's pickup and the cars belonging to the night-shift officers. Owen opened the passenger door and stood back, careful to give her space as she climbed in.

She glanced at him, and he got that hot, suffocating feeling in his chest again.

"It looks worse than it feels," she said.

"Please let me take you to the ER."

"No. But thank you for offering."

He searched her face for any sign that he might be able to convince her. But she seemed determined to go home.

He closed the door, then walked around the front and slid behind the wheel.

"Owen?"

He looked at her.

"Let me just get through this now, because I don't want to talk about it all night, okay?"

"You don't have to talk about it at all." But he hoped she would. He was going to go crazy not knowing.

She took a deep breath. "Basically, I pulled into my driveway tonight and someone jumped me from behind. I never saw him."

He clenched his teeth, waiting for more.

"He tackled me to the ground and demanded my keys." She took another deep breath. "I was too stunned to understand what was happening, so I didn't give them over right away, and he punched me. Then he put a gun against my neck—"

"He was armed?"

"Yes. He said not to move or he'd fucking kill me, and then he rifled through my car and took all my gear—two cameras and a laptop computer—and then he left."

Owen stared at her. He was burning to know every last detail, right down to a description of the *gun* he'd fucking put against her *neck*.

"That's the short version," she said. "Emmet asked me about a million questions and got everything else—"

"How did he get there? Did you see a vehicle?"

"He drove. A pickup truck, I think. It sounded like a diesel engine." She sighed. "That's pretty much it, really. He punched me and held a gun to my neck. I don't need an ER or a rape kit or anything like that. I just want to go home and shower and decompress, all right?"

He nodded.

It wasn't nearly enough. But he could get the rest later, from Emmet. Right now he just wanted to make her comfortable.

He started the truck. "Thank you for telling me."

She nodded.

He shifted gears and backed out of the space, looking at her out of the corner of his eye. She was in the same clothes she'd been in this morning except the baseball cap was gone and her hair was loose around her shoulders.

He pulled out of the parking lot and drove a few blocks to the highway. When he reached the intersection, she put her hand on the dashboard.

"Wait. Sorry, I just—" She looked at him. "I changed my mind. I don't want to go home yet."

"Okay."

"I don't want to be there right now."

"No problem. We'll go somewhere else." He looked at her, hating the fear and confusion in her eyes. "How about we get something to eat?"

She bit her lip.

"I was on my way to pick up a pizza earlier. We could take it to the beach or my place or anywhere you want."

He figured the last place she wanted to be was a crowded restaurant where people would stare at her eye. It was all he could do to keep from staring at it, and he was making a concerted effort.

"That sounds good," she said.

"You like pepperoni? That's what I ordered, but I could call and change it."

"No, that's perfect."

He switched his blinker and turned south onto the highway instead of north. He made his way back to Giovanni's, going the back way this time instead of taking the noisy route through the bar district. She seemed to relax as they drove, and she pulled a band from her pocket and twisted her hair into a bun.

The line of people was even longer now, and he wedged his pickup between two SUVs.

"You still good with this plan?" he asked.

"Yeah."

"You want to come in with me or wait?"

"I'll wait here."

Her hand rested on her knee, and he reached over and squeezed it. "Lock the doors. I'll be right back."

CHAPTER

TWENTY-ONE

THE PIZZA BOX warmed Macey's lap, and the scent of pepperoni filled the truck.

Let's go to your place.

The words had popped out of her mouth, and now she wondered what she'd been thinking. Going to his place was a bad idea. But just the thought of pulling into her driveway made her want to throw up. And she would have felt strange about asking him to drop her off at Josh's apartment. Josh wasn't home, anyway. He was out on a date right now. With Rory, who taught surf lessons and worked in a gift shop. Shock settled over her as she realized her conversation with Josh had been less than two hours ago. *Two short hours*, and everything had turned upside down.

"You okay?"

She looked at Owen. He sounded low-key, but she knew he'd take her straight to the emergency room if she so much as hinted that she'd be willing to go.

"Yeah." She looked away, hoping he'd drop it. She gazed

out the window, watching the row of beach houses rush by as she picked at the new tear in her jeans. She'd skinned her knee when he tackled her to the ground. And she hadn't even noticed it until she was sitting in the interview room and the detective had asked about it.

Owen slowed as the sign for the Lost Beach Marina came into view.

"Where are we going?" she asked as he turned into the drive.

"My place."

He lived at the marina? She'd never asked him where he lived, she realized. She'd never asked him much of anything about himself. She'd been so caught up in her own stuff—her film project, her summer goals, her determination to avoid romantic entanglements. Now she realized she'd been totally self-absorbed.

He reached the parking lot, which was half-full. Since the fishing supply store was closed, she figured the crowd was for the seafood restaurant upstairs. Owen swung into an empty space near the building.

"Do you live on a boat?" she asked.

He smiled. "I live next to Rick's." He nodded at the building. "See those four windows? Those are loft apartments. I'm the one on the corner."

He took the pizza box off her lap, and she got out and looked up at the building. Swags of lights decorated the restaurant's covered deck, and a Jimmy Buffett song drifted down.

She joined Owen on the sidewalk. He caught her hand and held her fingers—loosely, as though he knew that her palms were scraped. Maybe he'd noticed. He was observant.

She glanced up at the busy restaurant, which overlooked the bay.

"Do you mind all the people around?" she asked as he led her past the flight of stairs with a neon sign for Rick's.

"Not really," he said. "They close at eleven, and a lot of nights I'm not even home by then. I work weird hours."

They walked to a private flight of stairs concealed behind some palm trees. At the top was a metal gate where he tapped a code into a keypad. He held the gate open, and she stepped onto a covered breezeway with four doors and four square windows.

Macey's stomach did a little dance as they walked to the last door and he shoved his key into the lock. She was nervous for some reason she couldn't pinpoint. Maybe multiple reasons. She'd never expected to be here tonight. She'd certainly never expected to be here with torn clothes and a battered face. Maybe she should have braved her dark driveway and curled up by herself at home with a hot mug of tea.

Owen opened the door and ushered her inside. He switched on a light in the hallway, and she glanced around. The first thing she noticed was that it wasn't really a hallway because the apartment was one big room.

"Wow," she said, looking at everything. It had high ceilings with exposed ducts and pipes, and industrial-looking light fixtures hanging over the living area. One side of the room had a weight bench and a rack of dumbbells and weight plates. Well, there was one mystery solved. Now she knew how he kept in peak condition.

"It's a mess," he said.

She averted her gaze from the bed in the corner and crossed the spacious living area to a row of windows facing the bay. "Nice view."

She heard the jingle of keys and coins as he emptied his pockets onto the bar that separated the kitchen and living area.

"Let me get you an ice pack."

She turned around. "Actually, do you have any rubbing alcohol?"

"Sure. It's in here."

She followed him to a bathroom that had been carved out of the open space. The room smelled like his cologne or his aftershave—something woodsy and masculine that he'd been wearing when they'd met for drinks. He switched on a light and opened the cabinet under the sink.

Macey glanced in the mirror and froze. Tears sprang into her eyes as she studied her face. It looked hideous. The bruise at her temple was even more swollen and red than it had been back at the police station, and the cut above her eyebrow was crusted with dried blood.

She glanced at Owen in the reflection, and the intense look in his eyes made her stomach hurt. She could tell how bad she looked just from his reaction.

He set a big red toolbox on the counter and unlatched the lid.

"That's quite a first-aid kit," she said.

"It's left over from my lifeguarding days."

Lifeguarding. That seemed to fit him. He removed a tray filled with bandages and handed her a stack of antiseptic wipes.

"You want me to do it?"

"I'm good," she said, tearing one open. She stepped to the sink and looked at him in the mirror. "You mind if I—"

"Sure." He scooted around her and stepped out. "Let me know if you need anything."

When he was gone, she braced herself and looked in the mirror again, trying to be more objective as she studied her injuries. The bruise was bad, but at least nothing was broken. She supposed she was lucky his fist hadn't connected with her nose. Her lungs constricted, and she felt the tip of that gun again. She'd been at his mercy. He could have done anything and left her for dead in that driveway.

Don't go there. Don't unravel.

She pressed the wipe to her cut and winced at the burn. It felt good, though. The pain told her the antiseptic was working, killing germs and cleansing the wound.

"Owen?" She cleared her throat. "Can I ask a favor?"

He came to the door with a blue ice pack in hand.

"Could I borrow your shower real quick?"

"Sure."

"I was out on the boat all day."

Plus, she had a layer of terror-induced sweat clinging to her, and she felt an urgent need to wash off. Right now. She couldn't wait another minute.

"It's no problem." He set the ice pack on the counter. "Hang on."

A few moments later he came back and put a folded green towel on the counter.

"It's a beach towel, sorry. I haven't done laundry in a while."

"Thank you. And thanks for the ice pack."

He went away, and she closed the door behind him this time. Before she could get self-conscious, she turned the shower to hot and took off her clothes, making a neat little pile on the floor atop her hiking boots. Then she stepped under the steamy spray.

She turned her back to the water and closed her eyes, taking a deep breath as it sluiced over her shoulders. She didn't want to take her hair down. She just needed to clean off, wash the day away, get rid of the sunblock and the grit and the pungent stench of fear covering her skin. She lathered up with his body wash and then made a slow turn to rinse off, pausing for a moment to let the hot water hit the back of her neck where the muzzle of the gun had touched her. A sour taste rose in the back of her throat, but she swallowed it down.

She turned off the water and stepped out. Avoiding the

mirror, she grabbed the beach towel off the counter. Beneath it was a neatly folded blue T-shirt that said *Lost Beach Annual Fun Run* across the front, and Macey's heart melted a little.

She got dressed, swapping her dirty T-shirt for Owen's clean one. It was faded and looked like it had been through the wash a few hundred times, and the softness against her skin felt heavenly. She spent several minutes with the ice pack, holding it against her bruise and hoping the swelling of her eyelid would go down. Then she poked through the first-aid kit and found a pouch of ibuprofen tablets.

When she emerged from the bathroom with a cloud of steam, Owen was in the kitchen area, leaning against the counter with his phone pressed to his ear. He glanced up, and from his grim expression, she guessed it was a work call.

She padded barefoot to the front door and set her boots and shirt in a pile on the floor. Then she crossed the living area to the sliding glass door and stepped onto the balcony.

The night air was dense and humid, but a breeze wafted up as she moved to the railing. Laguna Madre stretched out before her, vast and inky, with moonlight glimmering off the surface. The noise of the restaurant had quieted. No more Jimmy Buffett—only the clatter of plates and scrape of chairs as workers cleaned up for the night. She leaned against the railing, listening to people speak Spanish back and forth. She turned her gaze south, toward the marina, where the dark sailboat masts jutted up into the night sky. A motorboat moved away from the pier, and the white stern light grew smaller and smaller.

The door behind her opened and Owen stepped out. He'd changed from his detective clothes into jeans and a T-shirt.

He held a glass out to her. "Thirsty?"

"God. *Yes.* Thank you."

He set his beer bottle on the railing as she sniffed the drink.

"Is this a Cape Cod?"

"Yep."

She took a sip. Then another. The cold tartness was wonderful. She watched him over the glass and noticed his face looked tense.

"Everything okay at work?" she asked.

"Not really."

She set her drink on the rail. "Want to talk about it?"

"Nope."

She ignored the twinge of disappointment and turned to look at the bay again. He moved a patio chair and came to stand next to her, and she was relieved that he'd picked her good side. She could at least pretend to feel normal as long as they stayed out here in the dark.

"I might have to go in after dinner." He took a sip of beer and set the bottle on the railing.

"I figured. You probably work a lot of nights, right?"

"Yeah."

He reached out and tucked a lock of hair behind her ear. It was still up in a messy bun.

"Your hair's not wet." He lifted an eyebrow. "You didn't want to use my two-in-one, huh?"

She smiled. "I just wanted to rinse off."

"Did it help?"

"Yes."

"Good."

Something in his voice got to her, and she knew it wasn't only the work call making him tense right now. He was thinking about her attack. He probably wanted to know every detail of what had happened because that was how he was. That was *who* he was—he felt responsible for other people's safety. She got the sense that he took what had happened to her personally, as though he were somehow re-sponsible because it had happened in his jurisdiction.

But she didn't want to talk about it right now. She took another sip of her drink and set the glass beside his beer.

He reached over and touched the top of her hand, tracing his finger over her knuckles. "Can I put my arms around you?"

Her stomach fluttered. "Yes."

He slid his arms around her shoulders and eased her against him. She rested her good cheek against his chest, and he held her loosely. He pressed a soft kiss against the top of her head and sighed deeply. Macey felt something shift inside her as his intense relief permeated her.

He knew her nerves were frayed right now but he wanted to hold her, and the sweetness of it brought more tears to her eyes. She dipped her head against his shoulder and then turned in his arms to look out at the bay.

He settled his hands at her waist, and she leaned back against him, glad not to have to look into his eyes.

"It's beautiful out here," she said wistfully.

"That's why I wanted this place."

"Do you ever get out on the water?"

"Sometimes with Joel. He has a house not too far from here." He pointed south. "See that row of lights there, just past the marina? That's his neighborhood."

"Nice."

"He's got an old boat that used to belong to my dad, and we go fishing sometimes." He paused. "It's been a while. We've both been slammed with work."

She felt a twinge of envy. "You two are close."

He didn't say anything.

"Aren't you?" She turned to look at him.

"Yeah."

She sensed some tension there, but she didn't want to

pry. He was respecting her space, so she could respect his, too.

"All of us grew up in kind of a pack. The kids born here. We ran around together, played pranks on the tourists, got into trouble."

"So, you were hoodlums?"

"Mostly, we were bored. There was never much going on, especially during the off-season. All this growth here is new. We didn't even have a movie theater until about ten years ago."

He ran his hands up her arms, and she leaned her head back against his shoulder. "I always wanted a sibling. I was kind of a loner growing up."

"Oh yeah?"

"Yeah."

"You seem like an extrovert."

"Looks can be deceiving. I'd much rather spend my evening with an Alfred Hitchcock movie than hanging out in a bar." His hands felt nice on her arms, and the knot in her stomach started to loosen. "You really grew up without a movie theater?"

"Just an old dollar cinema that showed stuff that was already out on video."

"I can't even imagine that. Movies were a staple of my childhood."

"I'm telling you, it was the sticks here."

She sighed. "It's pretty, though."

She closed her eyes, enjoying the cool breeze and the warm weight of his arms around her. He held her loosely, giving her space and comfort at the same time.

"I have a question," she said.

"Shoot."

"You can't lie."

He chuckled. "What makes you think I'd lie?"

"Cops lie. It's part of the job. Interrogations, suspect interviews. I covered the crime beat, remember?"

"I wouldn't lie to *you*," he said. "What's the question?"

"Do you just happen to keep vodka and cranberry juice stocked in your kitchen?"

He didn't say anything right away, and she knew the answer.

"I might have stopped by the store the other day," he said.

A little spark ignited inside her.

"I might have been planning to invite you over."

"Interesting." She turned to look at him. "When were you planning this invitation?"

"As soon as I thought you'd say yes."

She picked her drink up and took a sip. "So, like, tonight after the dinner we never had?"

"Maybe." He paused. "Would you have said yes?"

She set the drink down. Now she'd backed herself into a corner. She hadn't been thinking too clearly about where her teasing question would lead. Her thoughts were muddled tonight, and she wasn't on her A game.

"I don't know, honestly," she said. "I've had kind of . . . mixed feelings about this."

"I know."

"It's not because of you," she felt compelled to add. "It's because of all the stuff that happened this spring."

"You don't have to explain."

But she felt like she did. He'd been nice to her. Mostly. He'd apologized for their tiff the other day, and the canceled dinners weren't his fault. Really, he'd been steadfast in his pursuit of her, and she was the one who'd been giving off mixed signals.

They stood there together, watching the moonlight glisten off the water. Or at least pretending to watch the moonlight. She was thinking about the firm wall of his chest.

And the heat of his body. And the masculine scent teasing her nostrils. She loved the way he smelled, and part of her wanted to turn and bury her face against him.

"You want to eat soon?" he asked quietly.

"In a minute."

So, maybe he wasn't quite as distracted by her as she was by him. She decided to test the hypothesis. She turned in his arms and tipped her head back to look at his face in the dimness.

She went up on tiptoes and kissed him—just a soft brush of her lips. She opened her eyes, and he was watching her warily.

"Owen?" she whispered.

"Yeah?"

"Kiss me."

She went up on tiptoes again, and he met her halfway this time. It was sweet but brief, and she lowered her heels to the ground.

"What's wrong?" she asked.

"Nothing."

Ha. Everything was wrong. But she was determined to ignore it. She needed a distraction right now, and she'd been trying for days—and failing—to tamp down this growing ache inside her.

She slid her arms over his shoulders and laced her fingers behind his neck, settling her breasts against his chest.

"Macey . . ." His voice held a warning.

"Hmm?" She kissed him, lingering this time. When she eased back to look at him, she saw the conflict in his eyes.

"You've had a bad night."

"I know. Make it better."

She kissed him again. And this time he responded, sliding his hands around her waist. She licked into his mouth and she could feel his resolve slipping, and just the knowledge that it was happening—that she was making it happen—sent a flood of desire through her. His hand slid over her bottom, and she rocked her hips against him.

"Macey."

The word was tortured this time, and she did it again, leaving no doubt about what she wanted.

He pulled back. "You don't want to do this now. Trust me, you'll regret it tomorrow."

She searched his face in the moonlight for any hint that what he really meant was *he* didn't want to do this. But all she saw was raw male desire and tightly leashed control.

She stepped back. She pulled her T-shirt over her head and dropped it on the chair.

His eyes went hot, and he reached for her arms, as if he didn't know whether to push her away or drag her closer. She wore a black sports bra, and his gaze dropped to the tops of her breasts and he made a low sound in his throat as she eased closer. She slid her hands over his shoulders and laced her fingers together.

She looked up at his eyes and saw the exact moment when he caved.

He kissed her, pulling her against him and molding her body against his, and she could feel the undeniable evidence of his desire pressed against her stomach.

"I swear to God, Macey—"

She kissed him, and whatever he'd planned to say was lost as his hand slid up to cup her breast and he made a low moan. He loved her breasts. She'd known it from the start by the way he looked at her, and she knew it now by the way he touched her, filling his hands with her curves. She arched into his touch, kissing him and tasting him and delving her tongue into his mouth as his thumb stroked her nipple through the fabric.

The warm buzz of excitement inside her grew and spread until her entire body was humming with energy. He wanted to resist her tonight. He thought she was traumatized and that she didn't know what she was doing or what she wanted, but she knew *exactly*, with every fiber of her being. She wanted *him*. Not just some guy who happened to be there but *him*. Owen Breda. The man who'd pulled over to fix her tire and brought her coffee and kissed her until she was dizzy on her stairs. He was strong and kind and protective as all get-out, and she wanted his hands on her right now, stroking over her skin and making her feel completely consumed with need.

She pulled back. "Let's go inside," she said breathlessly.

He stared at her, and the conflict was back in his eyes. But then he slid the door open and took her hand, pulling her in behind him.

The apartment was dark except for a lone light dangling over the kitchen island, and she was grateful because as determined as she was to do this, she was still self-conscious about her face. She tugged the band from her hair and ran her fingers through it, combing some over her injured eye so she'd feel less like a freak.

He pulled her across the room to his bed, and her nerves fluttered as he lifted her hand and pressed a kiss to the back of her knuckles.

"I can't believe I'm saying this, but are you sure you want to do this now?"

"Owen—"

"We can wait."

She laughed, dropping her gaze to the front of his jeans.

"I'm serious, Macey."

The earnestness in his voice made her heart squeeze. She stepped closer and reached up to touch the side of his face. "So am I. This is what I want." She stroked her fingertips over the prickly stubble along his jaw. "I'm okay, really. We can go slow."

He made a pained sound, and she kissed him, mostly to shut him up but also to keep him from talking her out of this. She knew what he was worried about—that she just wanted a distraction from everything that had happened tonight. But what was wrong with that? What was wrong with wanting to feel sexy and desired and anything besides stunned and terrified?

Owen kissed her, and she let herself get lost in it. She ran her hands over his shoulders and pressed herself against the hard warmth of his body. She wanted to feel his skin, so she dropped her hands to the edge of his T-shirt and tugged it up, tracing her fingertips along his lean waist. He pulled the shirt off and tossed it away, and she felt a rush of relief that he seemed done pretending he didn't want this.

He slid his arms around her, dipping his fingertips into the back of her jeans, and she rocked against him, loving the hard feel of his body. He eased her back onto the bed, and the mattress creaked as he leaned over her. She propped herself on her elbows, and he glided his hands around her back and slid his fingertips under her sports bra, expertly unhooking the clasp. He slid it from her arms and tossed it aside, then dipped his head down and kissed her collarbone.

"Tell me if anything hurts," he said.

"It won't hurt."

He looked up. "I mean it, Macey."

His sharp voice put a hot tingle inside her.

"Fine."

He settled next to her, resting his weight on his elbow, as one of his hands slid down over her body and settled on the front of her jeans. Then it glided back to her breast to tease and play with the tip as he kissed her deeply.

She reached for his zipper, but he caught her hand and set it on the bed beside her. Okay, so he was a bit controlling. But that excited her, too, and she decided to lie back and enjoy it. She moved her hands to his hair, tangling her fingers in it as he kissed his way down her throat. His hot mouth closed over her nipple and she arched against him.

"Owen." She wrapped her leg around him, bringing him closer. He looked up, watching her as he licked and sucked.

He moved down, making her shiver with anticipation. She closed her eyes and tipped her head back as she heard the soft rasp of her zipper and felt her jeans sliding down her legs. Cool air wafted over her, and then his breath was hot against her stomach. He kissed her, lingering over her belly button until she bucked and laughed.

"That *tickles*."

He smiled and moved over her, resting his weight on his elbow as he settled beside her. He was still being cautious, so she dipped her hand into the front of his jeans and wrapped her fingers around him, and his breath caught. He was hot and hard, and she stroked her fingers over him and reached for the button.

He kissed her deeply, and she felt the desire start to take over everything, until all she could think of was the unrelenting ache deep inside her body.

She tugged at the waist of his jeans. "Take these off."

He pulled away and got off the bed, and she sat up to watch as he stripped off the rest of his clothes.

Macey's chest tightened as she saw the contours of his body for the first time. This was really happening. Now. She scooted into the middle of the bed. He stretched out beside her, and she turned to face him, sliding her thigh between his.

He kissed her, pulling her against his body as his hand stroked over her. He hooked his fingers into her panties, and soon they were gone, too.

Macey got to her knees beside him and ran her fingers over his chest, loving the heated look in his eyes as his gaze roamed over her body. He slid his hand around her waist.

"Come here," he whispered, nudging her hips forward until she was straddling his lap, and he sat up to kiss her. His hands moved over her, one sliding over her breast while the other settled on her hip, urging her closer. And then there was the hot, delicious friction of her body sliding against his and then his mouth on her nipples, first one side and then the other, and all she could think about was how so amazingly *good* it felt, and how she wanted him inside her.

"Mace."

She moaned and pressed against him.

"Macey." He stilled her hips. "Hang on, babe."

He reached over and jerked open the nightstand drawer, and she waited impatiently as he tore open a condom with his teeth and put it on. And then she kissed him and lowered herself onto him, gasping into his mouth at the spear of pain. But then she leaned forward and there was no pain at all, only heat and need as she moved against him. He grasped her hips, and they created a rhythm together as he pushed into her again and again and again, and pleasure reverberated through her body with every surge.

"Owen." She guided his hands to her breasts. "*Owen.*"

He bucked hard beneath her and something shattered inside her, and her world dissolved into a glittery pool of light. He held her through the aftershocks as she nuzzled his neck and caught her breath.

He shifted her onto her side and searched her face. She smiled. Then he rolled her flat onto her back, and she blinked up at him as she realized he wasn't finished. She wrapped her legs around him, pulling him in tight, even as her body felt lax and boneless. The intent look in his eyes set another fire inside her, and soon she was burning again, moving and clasping and straining to keep up as his powerful body drove into her again and again.

He closed his eyes, and the muscles in his neck tightened. "Macey."

It was a groan and a plea and an apology all at once, and she knew he was trying to hold back and be careful, but she clenched her legs tighter and dug her fingernails into his shoulders.

"Yes," she gasped, and he moved faster and faster until the world started to spin and she felt herself coming apart all over again. And finally he gave a mighty thrust and collapsed on his elbows.

She closed her eyes, gasping for air as he rolled onto his back next to her. Everything was spinning. Her pulse thrummed and her limbs felt like Jell-O. She felt the mattress shift and heard him cross the room. Then she heard water running in the bathroom. She kept her eyes closed as her breath returned and her mind seemed to come back to earth.

Back to reality.

The bed shifted again, and she turned to face him as he stretched out beside her.

She couldn't describe the look on his face. It was too dim to read his eyes or to know what he was thinking. But he reached up and brushed his fingertip over her jaw.

"Too rough?" he asked.

"No." She scooted closer and nestled her head against his chest.

He stroked his finger over her hip, back and forth and back again as the silence continued.

"I knew that would happen." He rolled onto his back.

"What?"

He turned to look at her.

"What?" she asked again.

"Are you really okay?"

"Yes." She turned onto her side and scooted back, pressing her back to his front. She didn't want him to see her face right now, even in the dimness, and be reminded of her bruises.

He kissed the back of her shoulder softly, and the tenderness of it made her heart squeeze.

She closed her eyes. Reality was coming back, slowly but surely. Her head throbbed. The cut above her eye burned. And she really wanted the ice pack, but she didn't want to ask for it just now. It would only confirm his opinion that they should have waited.

Well, she had followed her heart. And she didn't want to think of being wrong about that, on top of everything else tonight.

Macey sighed heavily. She just needed to rest her eyes a minute. And her mind. Just a minute, and then she'd deal with reality.

TWENTY-TWO

S HE AWOKE TO the smell of pepperoni. Squinting, she looked around and spied a T-shirt on the floor. She grabbed it and sat up, pulling it over her head.

Owen was in the kitchen in jeans, bare-chested, pulling the pizza from the oven. He glanced at her across the bar.

"Ready to eat?"

"I'm starving."

She ran her fingers through her hair, combing some over her eye as she crossed the room. The only light was the one over the sink now, but still she felt self-conscious.

He took some plates from the cabinet and loaded a slice onto each. The muscles in his back rippled as he moved around the kitchen, and she felt a sharp tug of longing watching him. His hair was mussed, so he must have fallen asleep, too, but not for long. According to the clock on the microwave, it was 12:20.

She sat on a bar stool, and he slid a plate in front of her.

The cheese was gooey and glistening with oil, and she folded the slice in half as she picked it up.

Owen watched her as she took the first bite.

"What?" She snipped a string of cheese with her fingers and put the slice down.

Rather than answer, he turned around and opened the freezer. He retrieved the blue ice pack and set it beside her plate.

"That bad, huh?"

He still didn't answer. Instead, he took a bottle of cranberry juice from the fridge. He filled a glass with ice and juice and added a splash of Tito's. Then he came around the bar and took the stool beside her. His body was tan and muscular, and she envied his metabolism as she watched him chomp into his pizza with gusto.

"'Scuse the manners." He set the slice down. "I'm about to pass out."

"Manners?"

"My mom never let us eat without a shirt on."

She smiled. "Well, I'm *only* wearing a shirt. What would she think of that?"

His eyes heated, and he looked at her legs. His shirt barely covered the tops of her thighs. But then the lust faded, and he met her gaze.

"Macey, I need to ask you some things."

"Uh-oh." She took another bite, nearly burning her mouth this time on a scorching pocket of tomato sauce. She dropped the slice onto her plate and fanned her mouth.

"It's about tonight," he said.

"I know." She sipped her drink to brace herself. "Go ahead."

"I talked to Emmet. He interviewed several neighbors on your street."

"Oh God. Did he tell them what happened?"

"He told them there was a car burglary. No one else reported anything missing along your street, or any suspicious people or vehicles around."

She nodded.

"Why didn't you tell me about the noise in your driveway the other night?" he asked.

She'd told Emmet about the swinging gate that had awakened her and the pungent smell of sweat in her car. It was possible someone had searched her Honda that night, too, but she hadn't had any valuables in it at the time.

"I guess I didn't think to mention it."

His eyebrows arched. "Why not?"

"I thought it was just a noise at the time." She searched his face for clues about what he was thinking. "Do you think someone was at my house that night?"

"I don't know. But someone unscrewed the floodlight out on your driveway at some point. It wasn't burned out—it had been tampered with."

A chill snaked down her spine.

"So . . . you think he was waiting for me? Not just targeting random cars?"

"It's possible. I'm not trying to scare you, but you need to be aware."

"No, of course." She cleared her throat. "Don't shield me from information."

He just looked at her, and the intensity in his eyes sent a ripple of fear through her.

"You think what happened has something to do with Julia Murphy living in that house, don't you?"

"I don't know. But we can't ignore the possibility."

Her stomach knotted, and she pushed her plate away.

He covered her hand again. "We'll find him."

"Who? The guy who attacked me or Julia?" *Or maybe it's the same person.*

"Both. I promise we'll get to the bottom of this."

She turned away, frustrated now.

"What was the big development?" she asked.

He didn't respond.

"Earlier, you said something big happened today." She watched him, daring him to give her some nonanswer that would tell her he didn't trust her. *Still.* Even after tonight.

He watched her for a long moment, and she saw the debate going on in his head.

"You know how I told you we were looking at Hancock?"

She nodded.

"We have an arrest warrant out for him."

Her mouth dropped open. "You think he—"

"Yes."

"Why? What happened?"

He shook his head. "That's all I can say right now." He looked at her sharply. "Don't give me that look. You shouldn't be involved. I shouldn't have told you anything in the first place."

"You didn't. Well, hardly anything. I'm *involved* because I'm living in the victim's house."

"We don't know that for sure."

"I do." She sighed and stared across the kitchen. "So, has someone arrested him?"

"Not yet."

"When?"

"Soon. We've got the US Marshals involved, so it won't be long."

She swallowed the lump in her throat. "You know, I had a little run-in with him the other day."

Owen frowned. "With who?"

"Miles Hancock." She cleared her throat. "I went to see him at the marina, and he confronted me with a gun."

"*What?* Why didn't you tell me?"

She shrugged.

"Macey, look at me."

She looked.

"Tell me exactly what happened."

"It wasn't a big thing, really. He saw me snooping around his boat at the marina, and he strutted over with a pistol and told me I was trespassing."

"When?"

"Three days ago. Nights, I guess. This was around sunset."

"What were you doing snooping around his boat?"

"I was looking for him. We're filming at Lighthouse Point, and I needed to ask him to move his cranes out of our shot. Which he declined to do because he's a pretentious jerk."

Owen's jaw twitched, and she could see him struggling for control.

"You should have told me," he said.

"I get that *now*. But at that point, I didn't know he was a suspect in a murder case. And later, all you told me was that he was a person of interest."

He shot her a look. They both knew that was the same thing.

"What kind of gun was it?" he asked.

"I don't know. Something black and clunky."

He closed his eyes and pinched the bridge of his nose.

"Did Julia's killer use a gun?" she asked.

"I can't answer that." He got up and nodded at her plate. "You want more?"

"No."

He took their plates to the sink and turned around and leaned against the counter.

"I hate that you're involved in this," he said.

"It's not your fault I randomly picked a rental house off a website."

But the look on his face told her he thought it was more than that. Somehow, he felt responsible for her involvement. Was it because he'd interviewed her as a potential witness? Or because she'd given him the tip about the tattoo guy? Or because she'd crossed paths with Miles Hancock?

He folded his arms over his chest and looked at her. His arms and shoulders were tense, and his stress was palpable.

She got up and walked over to him, compelled to make it go away. There was no way she could, but she could at least distract him.

"So . . . when are you going back in?" she asked.

"I don't know."

She stopped in front of him and ran her finger over his arm. She glanced up, and the simmering look in his eyes told her he knew exactly what she was thinking.

"You need to ice your eye," he said.

She tipped her head to the side.

"I'm serious, Macey."

"I know." She leaned against him and slid her hands over his shoulders. "Sometimes you're *too* serious."

His jaw tightened, and she stroked her finger over the dark stubble. He wanted her. She could feel it. And knowing she had that effect on him gave her a giddy rush.

He wrapped his arm around her, resting his hand on her hip. His fingertips slid under her T-shirt and he closed his eyes.

"Macey . . ." He sighed, and the regret in the sound put a little pinch in her chest.

"Let's go to bed," she whispered.

"That's not going to fix this."

"I know." She kissed him. "Let's do it anyway."

* * *

OWEN'S PHONE DRAGGED him from a sound, sated sleep. He knew something was wrong before he even checked the clock.

He grabbed the phone from the nightstand and read the text just as a second message landed with a *chirp*. Carefully, he disentangled Macey's legs from his and slid away from her lush body.

As he got up and crossed the room, he sent a quick text to Nicole. Then he took a two-minute shower and dressed. The first gray bands of daylight were seeping through the blinds as he sat on the edge of the bed.

"Macey." He touched her shoulder. "Macey, babe, wake up."

She jerked away, then bolted upright.

"It's okay."

She blinked at him.

"You can keep sleeping. I just wanted to tell you I have to go in."

She stared at him, awareness dawning as she looked around. She touched her fingers to her eye and winced. Her swelling was down, but the bruise had turned a dark purple. "What—"

"I'm getting a ride, so you can take my truck to the police station. They're done processing your car, so it's ready whenever."

"Your truck?" Her voice was raspy.

"Keys are on the bar. Just leave them with Denise at the front desk and she'll give you yours."

Macey seemed to notice she was naked. She tugged the sheet up to cover her perfect breasts.

He leaned forward and pressed a soft kiss against her forehead. "I'll call you," he said.

She looked so sleepy and warm, and he would have given anything to spend a lazy morning with her.

His phone chirped with another message, and he stood. "Lock up when you leave."

She nodded.

He grabbed his phone and wallet off the bar.

"Owen?"

He turned around.

"Be safe."

"I will."

He slipped out, feeling a stab of guilt as he rushed downstairs. Being *safe* wasn't in his job description, and he couldn't promise that to anyone. Neither could Joel or Emmet or Nicole, and it was a source of tension in every relationship of everyone he knew who carried a badge. He could be *careful*, but that was it, and there were some people who never managed to accept that.

Anyway, he was getting way ahead of himself. He wasn't in a relationship with Macey. She didn't want one—she'd as good as told him that last night. And he was pretty sure that when the sleep wore off, and the sex hangover, she was going to have regrets. She'd just been through what had to be one of the scariest experiences of her life, and she'd jumped into bed with him only a few hours later, and anyone who knew a damn thing about trauma knew she hadn't been thinking clearly.

He should have resisted her. He should have convinced her to wait. But he'd never been much good at resisting temptation. Or waiting—for anything he wanted. And he'd wanted Macey since the moment he'd met her.

A layer of fog hung over the parking lot as he slid into Nicole's truck. It smelled like coffee, which was why he'd asked her for a ride instead of Emmet.

"Thanks for the lift."

She acknowledged him with a curt nod. Nicole was a bear in the morning before she got her caffeine fix.

Owen reached for one of the two travel mugs. "This for me?"

She shot him a glare. "Isn't that why you asked me to pick you up instead of Emmet?"

"I asked you because I'm on your way."

"And Emmet's, too."

He blew on the coffee and took a sip. It was strong and hot, and he was going to need about a gallon if he was going to function this morning after being up half the night.

"So." He replaced the mug in the cup holder as Nicole pulled out of the parking lot. His apartment was still dark, so hopefully Macey had gone back to sleep. "What do we know so far?"

"Not much. I got the same message you did."

"You didn't talk to Brady?"

"No."

The chief had sent all of his detectives—even Joel—a 911 message to come to Causeway Road, along with a directive to stay off the radio.

"He wants it quiet," Nicole said.

"Yeah, but why?"

She shot him a tired look and pulled onto the highway. "I've been awake for precisely eighteen minutes. I don't know jack about what this is. I got the same text you did."

"You talk to Emmet?"

"No."

If anyone knew what was going on, it would be Emmet, who constantly flirted with the dispatchers in an effort to vacuum up news tidbits no one else had.

"He would have called me, though, if he knew," she said.

Owen took another swig of coffee, trying hard to wake up.

"So." Nicole sighed. "How's Macey?"

He looked at her. Did Nicole know Macey was asleep in his bed right now? Maybe Nicole was asking because she'd seen him talking to Macey last night.

"Shaken," he said.

"I figured. You get her to go to the ER?"

"No." Guilt needled him. He'd given up on that, probably too soon. Instead, he'd given her sex therapy, which was what she thought she wanted from him. But she'd probably be second-guessing that today once the shock wore off and she reflected on what had happened to her.

"You should put her in contact with a victims' counselor. Or I will." Nicole looked at him. "She should talk to somebody."

He nodded, feeling guilty again. Counseling assault victims wasn't his strong suit, and he'd probably said all the wrong things last night. "I'll get her in touch with someone."

They sped down the highway, which was nearly empty. She was going too fast, given the fog, but Owen kept his mouth shut and checked his phone for updates.

Nothing.

They neared the causeway, where signs depicted the evacuation route in the event of a hurricane. It was too foggy to even see the water, and the sun was just a dim white orb in the gray haze.

Nicole made the last possible turn before the intersection and picked up Causeway Road, which sloped down beneath the bridge. The narrow street curved through the sand and petered out at an orange barricade. Behind it was a red SUV and a ladder truck, along with Brady's white Suburban. No sign of Joel.

"What's fire doing here?" Owen muttered.

"I don't know. Think we had a jumper?"

"Maybe."

Nicole passed the emergency vehicles and pulled over beside the Suburban. Several uniformed officers stood behind the barricade, and they looked over as Owen and Nicole got out. Traffic noise echoed down from the eight-lane bridge overhead as they trudged across the sand to the uniforms.

"Where's the chief?" Nicole asked over the din.

"Behind the dunes." One of the officers pointed toward a pair of sand dunes near the closest concrete column beneath the bridge.

"What's going on?" she asked.

"Brady's over there with the fire chief." He gave a stiff nod. "He can explain."

Owen's gut filled with dread, and grit seeped into his boots as he trekked across the sand.

"What the hell is this?" Nicole said, clearly annoyed by all the secrecy.

Owen wasn't annoyed so much as worried. And he was feeling a distinct sense of déjà vu as he neared the sand dune.

"Hey."

They turned around and stopped as Emmet jogged up to them. "You guys just get here?"

"Yeah," Nicole said. "What's going on?"

"I don't know. One of the uniforms overheard something about a DOA and a nine."

She frowned. "A nine?"

"A nine-mil."

They rounded the sand dune and spied Brady and the fire chief huddled near a black SUV.

"Ah shit," Emmet said. "Is that a Range Rover?"

Owen halted in his tracks.

Brady looked up. He said something to the fire chief and strode over.

"It's Hancock," the chief said without preamble.

"What happened?" Owen asked.

"I don't know. The ME's not here yet." He looked back over his shoulder. "But it looks to me like a self-inflicted shot to the head."

CHAPTER

TWENTY-THREE

MACEY TOOK HER latte to a shaded picnic table at the Beanery and sat down facing the beach, even though she couldn't see it. She needed to wake up, but all morning she'd felt like she was walking through a fog. And it *was* foggy—the mist was just starting to burn off—but it was this thick mental fog that she desperately needed to shake.

She took a sip of her drink and checked her watch. Josh was late, as usual, and the coffee she'd bought him was getting cold.

"Hey, there."

She glanced up to see Leyla standing at the table in her black apron. Macey hadn't even noticed her walk up. *Fog.*

She forced a smile. "Good morning."

Leyla sat down across from her and slid a plate with a muffin in front of her. "Coconut chocolate chip," she said.

"Oh. Thanks."

Leyla leaned forward, peering past Macey's sunglasses

with those blue eyes that looked so much like Owen's. "Macey, are you all right?"

Tears sprang into her eyes. Damn it, she didn't want to do this right now. She tried to keep her voice even.

"I was mugged last night."

"Oh my God." Leyla pressed her hand to her chest. "That's awful."

Macey nodded.

"Where did this happen?"

"In my driveway."

"Here on the *island*? That's so bizarre."

"I know, isn't it? I lived in New York City for four years, never had a single problem, then I moved here and . . ." She shuddered.

Leyla's forehead creased with concern. "Does Owen know?"

"Yes. Emmet is handling my case, though."

Leyla lifted an eyebrow, and Macey somehow knew what her look meant. Owen would be involved, no matter what. She had no doubt of that.

Macey checked her watch again and glanced at the parking lot. Still no Josh. It must have been a big night with Rory.

Leyla continued to watch her with that worried look. Macey broke off a piece of muffin and nibbled it.

"So, New York, huh? I used to live there, too," Leyla said.

"Really? Whereabouts?"

"I was in culinary school in Manhattan and shared an apartment in Brooklyn." She paused. "One night someone attacked me when I was walking home from the subway."

Macey's stomach clenched. "Oh God. I'm so sorry."

Leyla nodded. Her face was guarded, and Macey could tell this wasn't something she liked to talk about. She glanced down and twisted a silver ring on her finger. "It took a long time to process everything. For me, at least." She looked up, and those piercing blue eyes reminded her of Owen. "You should talk to someone. A professional. It helps."

Macey's stomach did a little flip. She didn't know what to say. She wasn't ready to commit to talking to anyone. She hadn't even told her dad what had happened, and just the thought of calling him about it made her queasy.

Leyla covered Macey's hand with hers. "I'm sorry for what you're going through. If you ever want to talk, or just hang out or anything, I'm here." She glanced up and stood as Josh approached the table. "I'll let you get back to your breakfast."

"Thank you," Macey said. "Not just for the muffin but—"

"Don't mention it." She smiled and walked away, and Josh turned to watch as she disappeared into the coffee shop.

"Who was that?" he asked.

"My friend Leyla."

Josh frowned. "So, why'd you want to meet here? I thought we were at White Dunes." He leaned forward. "Holy *crap*. What happened to your face?"

Several heads turned at the other tables.

"Sit down, would you?"

Josh's eyes never left hers as he sat on the bench across from her.

"I got mugged last night. That's what I wanted to meet with you about. Some equipment was stolen and—"

"Mace. Stop talking." He leaned forward. "Let me see it."

She sighed and removed her sunglasses. The muscle in Josh's jaw twitched, and the look in his eyes was pure fury.

"Did *he* do that?"

"Who?"

"Owen Breda."

"What? *No.* I told you, I was mugged."

Josh watched her with a skeptical look.

"Would you please just listen instead of getting all worked up? Here." She pushed a lidded coffee cup in front of him and a pile of sugar packets. "That's for you."

Josh took off his baseball cap and set it on the table. His long hair was down today, and he ran a hand through it.

"Okay, I'm listening."

She took a deep breath and recounted the story, focusing less on her stark terror and more on the equipment that was taken. Josh was already upset enough, and she didn't want more drama right now.

"I called the insurance company this morning," she said. "We're covered on the two cameras and the laptop computer, so that's the good news, but I still have to get everything replaced, which will take time."

"We're fine. We can use mine." He tore open a sugar packet and dumped it into his coffee.

"I've still got two computers in the office," she said. "And our files are stored in the cloud, so we haven't lost any work."

"I've got a laptop, plus my camera, plus the drone. We're good."

"Are you sure?"

He dumped another sugar in and took a sip. "I'm sure. Take your time on replacing stuff." He watched her as he downed the coffee. He studied her injury as she tore off another hunk of muffin.

"So, seeing as this happened in your driveway, are you freaking out about your house?" he asked.

"A little."

"I wish you'd get a place in town instead of staying in the boonies."

"I signed a lease."

"You can stay at my apartment if you want. The sofa pulls out."

"Thanks, but I'm fine."

"Really, it's no problem. I'll probably be at Rory's anyway."

She smiled. "Hey, hey. Sounds like things are going well with you two."

"They are, but you're changing the subject." He leaned forward. "Where did you stay last night?"

She hesitated a beat. "With Owen. And before you give me crap about my failed man diet—"

"You seriously think I'd do that? I'm not an ass, you know."

"I know."

"I'm really sorry you're hurt, Mace. Feel free to use my apartment. It's small, but the building's got decent security."

Macey didn't want to intrude on Josh. Or Owen, either. She hated depending on other people for things. At some point, she was going to have to suck it up and go home.

"Here." Josh pulled his keys from his pocket and started removing one from the ring. "You can have my spare key. They gave me two when I moved in."

"You don't need to do that."

"Just keep it. Crash there whenever you want if you're not staying with Owen."

"I'm not. That was a onetime thing."

He gave her a look that said he didn't believe her, and Macey didn't blame him. She didn't know if she believed it herself.

*   *   *

"WE'VE GOT A gunshot wound to the right temple."
Brady looked at everyone assembled around the conference table. "It appears to be self-inflicted. That's based
on the fact that he was holding the nine-millimeter pistol,
and also based on the gunshot residue on his right hand."

Nicole glanced around the room, trying to read people's
expressions. The chief looked more anxious than she'd ever
seen him. Emmet looked drained. And Owen's expression
was carefully blank.

It was Owen she was worried about. Underneath that mask
of calm, she got the feeling he was seething. Between the murder case and everything else that had happened over the last
twenty-four hours, he was a cauldron of stress about to boil
over.

"Are we sure about the GSR test?" Nicole asked.

"I watched the CSI swab his hands at the scene," Owen
said. "The test came back positive for gunshot residue."

Nicole jotted a note on her pad about the GSR. She was
keeping a list of all the forensic evidence they'd amassed in
both cases.

"So, the working theory here is that Hancock knew we
were closing in on him," Emmet said. "He heard we'd uncovered his affair and found the victim's necklace at his
house, and he knew we had an arrest warrant out for him,
so he decided to end it?"

Brady nodded.

"That's the theory," Owen said.

Nicole tossed down her pencil. "So, that's it? Case closed?"

Owen looked at her. "What's on your mind, Nicole?"

Everyone's gazes turned to her. Every person in here was
exhausted and stressed and under tremendous pressure to
wrap up the investigation.

"I think we're rushing this," she said.

"Rushing?" Emmet tipped his head back, clearly exasperated. "We've been developing this suspect for days. You yourself interviewed him, and he lied to your face."

"I know."

"We've got the gifts, the eyewitness who saw his car at her house—"

"I *know*," Nicole said, cutting him off. "But all that points to an affair, not necessarily a murder."

"She's right."

Nicole looked at Owen across the table with his arms folded across his chest, and she felt a flood of gratitude toward him for backing her up.

"None of that necessarily means Hancock killed her," Owen said. "He could have been covering up an extramarital affair." Owen paused. "But what about the necklace?"

Nicole's shoulders sagged. He was right about the necklace. It was a neon sign pointing to Hancock's guilt. Julia Murphy had been wearing the pendant the night she disappeared, and it had been found in Hancock's home office. It was like a smoking gun—even more so than the DNA under the victim's torn fingernail.

Which still hadn't come back from the lab yet.

Emmet leaned forward. "So, what are you saying, then? You think the necklace was planted in this guy's desk? And then he conveniently offed himself before he could tell us that?"

When Emmet said it that way, it sounded absurd.

"I didn't say that." She crossed her arms. "I'm just pointing out that we shouldn't rush to conclusions about anything. That's all. There are still some key things that don't add up for me."

"What in particular?" Brady asked.

Nerves flitted in her stomach as the chief's gaze settled

on her. He looked like he was listening, which was good. But clearly she was in the minority here, and everyone else was ready to call this case closed.

"I'm still bothered by the boats," she said. "He has two of them."

"You mean Hancock?"

"Yes."

"He keeps his boats at the marina," Owen said.

"I'm aware of that," she replied. "My point is, why go to the trouble of digging a hole and hauling a body to the top of a sand dune if you could just take it out in the bay and be done with it?"

"The marina is a public place with a lot of traffic," Brady said. "The burial site is much more isolated."

Nicole clenched her teeth. Even the chief didn't see the logic of what she was saying.

"Getting a body onto a boat isn't easy either," Owen said. "That marina has a shit ton of security. I know. I live there. They've got eight different security cams, one for each pier and two for the parking lot. Plus, they've got a coded gate to get on the docks."

"Why so much security?" Emmet asked. "I remember you used to be able to just go down there and launch a kayak."

"One of the charter boats was stolen in the fall," Owen said. "Some of the boat owners raised a stink and demanded a system upgrade."

"Okay, so there's your answer." Emmet looked at Nicole. "Maybe Hancock didn't want to risk having himself re-corded on video hauling a woman-size bundle—in a duffel bag or whatever—onto one of his boats. Then if he ever became a suspect, the police could review the security foot-age. So, instead, he buried her."

Nicole didn't say anything. She had to admit, it made

sense. She didn't know why she was all hung up on this. But this case had seemed so perplexing for weeks, and she was having a hard time accepting everything falling into place suddenly. Their prime suspect was dead now. They didn't even need to arrest him or have a trial or prove their case in court.

"Owen?" Brady asked. "What are your thoughts?"

Owen scrubbed his hands over his face. He looked dog-tired, and if Nicole guessed right, he'd been up all night with Macey.

Who was likely the true source of much of his stress right now.

"It makes sense," Owen replied. "Like I said, the marina has a lot of cameras. If Hancock did it, he could have decided burying the body was less risky."

"'If'?" Emmet asked. "Why are we still saying 'if'? To believe that, you have to believe the gold necklace was a plant. And that someone murdered Hancock and then staged it to look like a suicide." He looked from Owen to Nicole. "Do you two really believe that?"

Brady held up his hand. "So far, everything we have indicates suicide. If the ME comes back with something else after autopsy, then we'll look into conspiracy theories. Until then, let's take it at face value." He turned to Owen. "Speaking of, when's the autopsy scheduled for?"

"Three o'clock," Owen said, checking his watch. "I plan to leave in an hour."

"Who else is going?" Brady asked.

Emmet sighed. "I will."

"You've got your hands full with the Macey Burns case," Owen said pointedly.

"I'll go," Nicole said.

"You were at the last one," Emmet said.

"I don't mind," she said, even though she *did* mind. But

she wanted to redeem herself and prove to Dr. David Bauhaus that she wasn't a lightweight. And she wanted to do a favor for Owen, who clearly didn't want Emmet distracted from finding the person who'd attacked Macey.

"Okay, Owen and Nicole, you two go," Brady said. "Don't leave there without getting the ME's take on manner of death, even if he isn't ready to put it in writing. Everyone clear?"

"Yes," Owen said.

"Yes," Nicole echoed.

Everyone stood up and filed out, and Owen looked at her.

"Be ready to leave at two sharp," he told her. "And I'd recommend you skip lunch."

TWENTY-FOUR

J OSH TURNED DOWN the music on his laptop computer
and looked at Macey.

"You expecting someone?" he asked.

"What?"

"Someone's knocking."

Macey leaned her head back to peer through the door of
the workroom. Her heart skittered as she spotted the tall
silhouette at her glass door.

"Who is it?" Josh asked as she stood up.

"Owen."

"Oh. Should I take off?"

"No."

She padded barefoot across the house, smoothing her
hair as she went. She looked a little windblown after spending the evening outside getting shots of the shrimp boats
coming in from the bay.

Owen wore the same clothes he'd had on this morning

when he woke her up before dawn. It was dark again now, and it looked like he hadn't been home yet.

She unlocked the door and opened it.

"Hi," she said, stepping back to let him inside.

He glanced around the house, then looked down at her. An awkward moment ticked by as she wondered whether he'd kiss her.

"Just checking in," he said matter-of-factly. "How's your eye feeling?"

"Better. My headache's gone, too."

His brows arched, and she realized she hadn't mentioned the headache.

"And you made it home all right?" he asked.

"Yeah, finally. After procrastinating all morning, I finally just sucked it up and came home." She shrugged. "It wasn't that bad in the daylight. I don't know why I was being such a wimp last night."

"You weren't being a wimp."

"Anyway, Josh offered to come over to hang out and do some editing. He knows I'm a little jumpy."

Owen looked over her head, where light from the editing room spilled into the hallway. He gazed down at her again, his expression grim.

"Are *you* okay?" she asked. "You look like you've had a long day."

"I have."

She took his hand and pulled him outside, closing the door behind them. It was a breezy evening, and she led him to the edge of the deck. The sound of the waves had a soothing effect. For her they did, at least.

She leaned against the wooden rail and faced him. "I saw the news about Miles Hancock."

He nodded. "I was at the autopsy this afternoon."

She winced.

"Sorry," he said, as though the mere word would upset her.

"No, *I'm* sorry. His poor family. I heard it was a suicide?"

He looked out over the surf. "That's undetermined."

"Really?"

"We're still investigating."

The tight set of his jaw told her he didn't want to talk about it, and she figured this latest case was part of the reason he looked like he had the weight of the world on his shoulders.

"So . . ." She wasn't sure what to say. "He had a wife and kids?"

"Two teenagers. I just interviewed his wife." He raked his hand through his hair.

"That must have been awful."

He nodded. Then he glanced at the house, where several lamps inside gave it a cozy glow. In the dusky twilight you couldn't see the peeling paint and grimy windowpanes, and the place looked charming.

"Your driveway light's working again," he said.

"My landlord sent his handyman out to check all the fixtures."

"Good."

He gazed down at her, and she resisted the urge to touch him. The tense set of his shoulders didn't invite contact.

"So, what are you doing tonight?" she asked.

"I have a meeting to update the team on where we are." He looked at his watch. "Then I've got to wade through a bunch of paperwork."

"Would you like something to eat? We picked up sandwiches."

"No, I ate."

She gazed up at him, wishing she could smooth the worry lines from his forehead. Instead, she went up on tiptoes and kissed him.

He slid his hands around her waist and pulled her against him. In no time, it was like they were back on his balcony in the dark. His kiss was hot and hungry, and she immediately melded to his body. She ran her fingers through his hair, pulling his head down so she could get a better angle, and her blood heated as she remembered the feel of him last night, when they were skin to skin. She could tell he remembered, too, as he ran his hands over her hips and pulled her snugly against him.

All day she'd been thinking about last night, wondering if it was a onetime thing—some kind of emotional storm brought on by a traumatic experience. But it wasn't. She didn't know what last night was, but it wasn't a one-off.

She could almost taste his frustration as he ended the kiss and leaned his forehead against hers.

"I have to go back," he said.

"I know."

She felt the tension emanating from his body. She pulled away and looked up at him, wishing he would tell her everything that had happened to put him in such a dark mood.

He looked over her head, and something flickered in his eyes. She turned to see Josh in the kitchen opening the fridge.

Owen slid his hands to her shoulders and searched her face. "Are you okay here tonight? I can try to come back when I finish work."

"I'm fine."

He kissed her forehead, then glanced at the house again.

"If you need anything, call me," he said.

"I will."

"And lock up when he leaves."

* * *

OWEN STARED DOWN at the crime scene photos until the images started to blur. Then he moved them aside and reread the report. He'd been over it so many times that he'd lost count now, and snippets of medical jargon swirled through his head.

He picked up his beer from the coffee table and took a sip. Then he pulled the photographs back and looked at them again. The evidence wasn't coming together, and he felt like there was something important that he wasn't seeing yet. The nagging feeling that he was missing some piece of the puzzle had him questioning all his assumptions about the case.

A sharp knock pulled his attention to the door. Just by the sound, he knew who it was. He got up and crossed the apartment.

"Hey," he said as Joel stepped inside.

"I saw your light on. You just get home?"

"About half an hour ago. Want a beer?"

"Sure."

Joel stepped over and opened the fridge. He wore jeans, an LBPD jacket, and work boots. He hadn't been in a raid today. At least, Owen didn't think so. He was no longer clued in on his brother's every move.

Joel closed the fridge and popped the top off his beer. "So, how was the autopsy?"

Owen resumed his seat on the couch and heaved a sigh. "Manner of death: homicide."

Joel stopped with the beer halfway to his mouth. "You're shitting me."

"I'm not shitting you."

He took a sip and walked over, sinking into an armchair. "Did a deputy ME do the post?"

"Nope. Bauhaus did it himself."

"Damn. Bauhaus is good."

"I know." Owen watched his brother, reading the look on his face. Joel had dealt with the ME before and knew he was much too smart to make a mistake of such magnitude, especially on a high-profile case.

Joel blew out a sigh. "Shit."

"I know."

"I thought the GSR test came back positive."

"It did. He had residue on his hand from holding the gun." Owen set his beer down. "But the ME doesn't think he fired it."

"Why not?"

"Couple of reasons. Something about the stippling pattern and the shape of the wound indicate the gun was fired from at least eighteen inches away."

"Not impossible," Joel said.

"True, but the main problem is he was holding the gun in his right hand. And he's left-handed."

"You're kidding."

"Nope."

"Was it his gun?"

"We don't know. He had a big collection of pistols, so it could have been one he picked up at a gun show or someplace. Or it could have been someone else's."

Joel looked at him for a long moment. Then he looked at the paperwork spread out all over the table.

"Is that the autopsy report?" he asked.

"No. It's not done yet. I just basically cornered him in a break room afterward and got him to give me his top-line conclusions. He hasn't put it in writing yet."

Joel tipped his head to the side. "Maybe you can use that to your advantage."

"How?"

"If nothing official has been released yet, you've got

time to investigate more freely. At least you won't have the press hounding you as bad."

"They're the least of my concerns right now."

Joel leaned back in the armchair, eyeing him with interest. "So . . . this means your prime suspect in the Julia Murphy case was murdered, and it was staged to look like a suicide." He paused. "I assume you're thinking—"

"Whoever did it killed Julia," Owen finished for him.

"That's what I'd assume, too."

Owen pulled his laptop in front of him and clicked open a file. It showed a grainy black-and-white image of a parking lot filled with trucks and SUVs. He turned the computer to face Joel.

"What's this?" Joel asked.

"Surveillance footage from the lot where we found Julia's car. I got this today."

"You can see someone dumping the car?"

"No. That parking space isn't within view, just the end of the row through a gap in the cars. But look." Owen pressed play on the video. "At around 6:25 a.m. this car comes into view." He hit pause as a white car drove past the gap between vehicles. "That's Julia's Volkswagen. It's only visible for a second."

Joel leaned forward. "Can you zoom in and enhance it?"

"We tried. This is as good as it gets because the lighting is bad and it's from a distance. All you see is a shadow behind the wheel."

"Okay."

"But we know this is him dumping her vehicle. Now watch." He hit play again. "I'm going to fast-forward this. But about two minutes later, here's someone leaving."

The video showed a black pickup truck moving through the gap between vehicles. Owen played it again and hit pause. "See?"

"So he drives a black truck."

"Maybe. I think he either left it there so he'd have a ride after he dumped the VW, or he had an accomplice waiting to pick him up."

"An accomplice?"

"It's possible, but I think he did this on his own. Why pull in an accomplice if he doesn't need to? That just puts him more at risk of exposure. I think this is *his* vehicle, a black Dodge pickup."

"Could be someone else leaving the parking lot right around the same time."

"Possibly, but I don't think so. I went through all the footage from the two cams that show a piece of the parking lot, and these are the only two vehicles in and out for twenty-six minutes. If he's dumping a murder victim's car, he's going to want to be in and out of there fast. I think this is him."

"What does Hancock drive?" Joel asked.

"A Range Rover."

"That all?" Joel looked at him.

"His teenage son has a black pickup."

"And?"

"Not a match. It's a Ford, plus it's got a lift kit and a roll bar in back. Looks nothing like this."

Joel watched him for a moment. "I thought you had mounting evidence that Hancock and the victim were having an affair."

Owen was beginning to question that assumption, too.

"We know he gave her expensive gifts," Owen said. "And we know he saw her outside of the restaurant and lied to us about it. We know he was in the passenger seat of her car at some point. We'd assumed he was having sex with her, but it could have been something else."

"Like what?"

"Not sure. Maybe he was her drug hookup? Or she was his? I don't know."

Joel frowned.

"At any rate, even if they were having an affair, she could have been sleeping with someone else, too."

"Someone who has a black truck, maybe?"

"Maybe," Owen said.

"And his motive was what, jealousy?"

Owen shook his head, exasperated. "I don't know."

"Walk me through what you're working on."

Owen tipped back his beer and sorted through the scenario he'd been putting together. He set the bottle down.

"So, let's say this guy killed her. Not Hancock. We don't know the motive yet—but say he killed her at his house or somewhere," Owen said. "Shards of crystal embedded in her back make us think there was a struggle, and something got broken. We think it was spur-of-the-moment, because he used his bare hands and not a weapon."

"Manual strangulation."

"Yeah. And he may have also put a pillow over her face to muffle the sound. We found upholstery fibers in her teeth and on the tarp she was wrapped in."

Joel nodded.

"So, now he has to dispose of the body. So he goes out to dig the hole, which takes time. And maybe he doesn't want to take his own vehicle to dump the body—especially a pickup with an open truck bed—so he moves the victim to the trunk of her car and drives it to the burial site. We have an eyewitness who says he saw a man walking down a sand dune and getting into a white Volkswagen."

"So, what, he had just buried her and he was leaving the scene?"

"Yeah, and then he drives her car to the parking lot near the boat docks, parks it in a sea of big trucks and SUVs, leaves the shovel and the tarp in the trunk, and drives away. And the VW goes unnoticed for weeks until we find it and recover all the evidence."

Joel seemed to be running through it in his mind, looking for holes. Owen had been doing the same thing for days.

"The scenario works," Joel said.

"I know."

"But why kill Hancock? The police were closing in on him, and he was about to take the fall."

"Maybe he knew Hancock could wiggle out of it. If he's dead—from suicide—he never gets a chance to defend himself and put a counterargument together. And to top it off, suicide makes him look guilty."

Joel leaned back in the armchair. For a long moment they just stared at each other, and it was like so many other times—older brother and younger. Experienced and not. All his life, Joel seemed to have all the answers figured out while Owen was just waking up to the question.

"You've got a problem."

Owen's stomach knotted. "I know."

"The necklace."

"I haven't worked that out yet."

"You're thinking it was planted?"

"I don't know how else it would be there if Julia was wearing it on the night she disappeared."

"How would he plant something inside Hancock's house?"

"Who knows? Maybe pay a workman or someone? Or sneak inside himself? He could have done a lot of things if he was desperate."

Joel shook his head. "Damn. Hell of a case."

"Yeah."

"You'll figure it out."

Owen made a noncommittal sound.

"You will."

Owen's shoulders tightened with frustration, and a long silence stretched out.

"Sometimes I don't know about this," Owen said.

"This what?"

"This job."

Joel frowned. "What do you mean?"

"I'm not cut out for it."

"Of course you are."

"No, of course *you* are," Owen said. "You're a natural at this. I'm over here missing clues and fucking everything up, and meanwhile . . ."

Joel arched his eyebrows. "Meanwhile?"

"Meanwhile, some dirtbag is out there preying on people while I waste time with team meetings and press briefings and paperwork and shit."

"I know it's frustrating. But that's how this goes. Investigations take patience."

"Yeah, which is why I'm not cut out for this. I hate sitting around analyzing everything. I feel like I'm spinning my wheels and nothing's coming together."

"You haven't even got all the lab work back yet," Joel reminded him. "Something will turn up. And if it doesn't, people talk. You can count on it. Someone is bound to know something about what really happened here. Not to mention, you've got a talent for dealing with people. Keep working your sources."

Joel took a long sip of beer and leaned forward, setting his bottle on the table. "So. How's Macey?"

Owen looked at him, caught off guard by the change of subject.

"Miranda told me about her."

Owen got up and went to the kitchen. "Want another beer?"

"No."

How was Macey? Owen didn't know, and the not knowing was driving him crazy. He'd gone by her house again at 11:45 and Josh's car was still there.

Darts of jealousy had pelted his chest. It was a new feeling, and Owen didn't like it. Not that he thought there was something going on between the two of them—he didn't. Not really. But he was jealous of their casual friendship and the way the guy swooped in when she needed him and made himself at home in her house. Owen wanted to do that. Macey was rattled, and he wanted to wrap his arms around her and comfort her and make her forget everything that had happened.

"Bro?"

Owen looked up. "I don't know, to be honest." He got another beer and popped the top off. "I can't really get a read on her."

Joel got up and walked over. He leaned back against the counter and waited patiently.

"She's a little gun-shy about getting involved right now," Owen said.

"I heard about what happened to her last night."

"She was gun-shy before that."

Joel just looked at him.

"I like her a lot," Owen said. It felt good to admit it. "You will, too," he added, deciding right then that he wanted to convince Macey to spend more time with him. Much more.

"I want to meet her," Joel said.

Owen nodded, even though he had no idea when that would happen. It seemed like he'd never get out from under these two cases. Every time he felt like he was making progress, something screwy happened to set him back.

Joel reached into his pocket and put something on the kitchen counter. A black velvet box.

Owen's gaze snapped to his. "Is that—"

"That's why I came by so late. I wanted to show you."

Joel opened the box and slid it to the middle of the counter. The simple diamond ring sparkled under the kitchen light.

"Wow." Owen looked at his brother. "Does she know?"

"No one does. You're the first person."

His chest tightened. "Damn."

"I'm nervous." Joel rubbed the back of his neck. "She hasn't been too happy with me lately. I've been working so much."

"Don't be nervous. She'll say yes."

Owen watched him stare at the ring, and the vulnerable look on his face got to him. Joel's last serious girlfriend had married his best friend, and for a while Owen had thought his brother would never get past it. But then he'd met Miranda, and Owen stopped worrying. Joel was head over heels for her. And she was for him, too. She was bound to say yes.

"When are you going to ask her?"

Joel smiled. "No idea. I've barely been home in a week. I just picked this up at the jeweler today." He paused. "I was thinking we might take a few days off soon and go somewhere, get away from everything."

Owen smiled. "I'm happy for you, man."

"Thanks." Joel grabbed the ring box and slipped it into his pocket. "I'd better go. With any luck she'll still be awake when I get home."

Owen stepped over and slapped him on the back, but Joel pulled him into a hug.

"Congratulations," Owen said. "Thanks for telling me first."

"Yeah."

"Keep me posted."

"I will." Joel stepped over to the door. "And, hey, I'm glad about this thing with you and Macey."

"I'm not sure it's a thing yet," Owen said. "She's just here temporarily."

"Oh yeah?"

"She moved here for work, but she's only down for the summer."

"Just the summer, huh?" Joel smiled and shook his head.

"What?"

He reached for the door. "That's what Miranda said, too."

TWENTY-FIVE

OWEN WALKED INTO the Beanery and looked around. No sign of Macey this time, but the woman at the register gave him a sunny smile.

"Hi, Owen. Your phone order is ready at the pickup bar."

"Thanks." He offered Siena a credit card, but she waved him off.

"You're all set. Leyla took care of it."

"Oh. Tell her thanks for me."

"I will."

He put some money in the tip jar and stepped over to grab the paper bag with his sandwich in it.

"Is that Owen?" Leyla leaned her head out of the kitchen. She spotted him and stepped out, dusting her hands on her apron. "Hey, you got a minute?"

"Not really, but since you paid for my lunch—"

"I need your help with something."

Owen went behind the counter and followed her into the humid kitchen where a dishwasher stood at the sink. She led him down a long hallway to a tower of big cardboard boxes stacked by the back door.

"I need you to carry these into the stockroom for me."

"Sure." He set his bag on a counter and picked up the top two boxes.

"Put them by the shelf."

He scooted past her and into a tiny storage room that smelled like a shot of espresso. He set the boxes next to a metal shelving unit half-filled with giant bags of flour, sugar, and coffee.

"I'm glad I caught you," Leyla said. She was slouched against the doorframe now, watching him. He stepped past her into the hallway. "Macey was here earlier."

"Oh yeah?" He grabbed another two boxes and looked his sister over. She always had a sixth sense when it came to relationships, and usually it got on his nerves. Not today, though. He was hungry for any news about Macey. He'd been busy with work all morning, and they'd only traded a few text messages.

Leyla stepped over to the shelf, and he stacked more boxes at her feet.

"How was she?" he asked.

"Her face still looks terrible." She pulled a utility knife from her apron pocket and sliced open the top box. "How's her case coming?" She glanced up at him. "I can't believe it happened in her driveway. That's really disturbing."

"She told you about it?"

"We talked about it yesterday. Today she was just in for coffee." With brisk efficiency, she unloaded bags of Island Beanery House Blend and Sea Salt Caramel onto the shelf. "I didn't think we got a lot of crime like that here."

"We don't."

Most of their assaults were concentrated in the tourist hot spots, such as bar parking lots and motels. And a good number involved drunken idiots. It was rare for someone to be accosted in a private driveway. And the firearm ramped things up to a whole new level.

Leyla unloaded more coffee. "She needs to talk to someone." She gave him a pointed look.

"I know. I called social services to get a referral, but I haven't heard back yet."

"I gave her the name of a trauma counselor I was going to for a while."

"You did?"

"Yeah."

Owen's blood chilled as her words sank in. "Why were you going to a trauma counselor?"

She unloaded more bags. "It happened to me. I was assaulted."

"When?"

"Back in New York when I was walking home one night."

He just stared at her. She glanced up.

"Why didn't you tell me, Ley?"

She shrugged. "You were two thousand miles away."

Dread filled his stomach. He and Leyla had always been close. He'd thought she told him the major stuff in her life. The fact that she'd kept this to herself made him think the details were bad.

"Leyla. . . ." He didn't know what to say. "Are you all right?"

"Now, yeah." She sliced open another box. "It took a while." She set her knife down and unloaded some bags onto the shelf. "For a while I felt really . . ." She stopped and pressed her lips together. "Unmoored. Like . . . detached from everything." She looked him directly in the eyes. "It's a hard feeling to get used to."

Owen watched her, at a loss for words. Brash, confident

Leyla feeling unmoored—it didn't compute. She was always so bossy and in charge of her life.

"Be kind to her, Owen."

He pulled back, offended. "I will."

"I know you will." She set her hand on his shoulder. "I didn't mean it like that. Just . . . try to be sensitive to her feelings. They might be a little all over the map."

She went back to her unboxing, and he watched her. She'd been carrying this around for years, and he'd had no idea.

"I wish you'd told me."

"Well, I'm telling you now."

"Why?"

She grabbed the last two bags and plunked them on the shelf. "I can tell you like her. She's different from the women you usually date." She rolled her eyes. "I don't want you to screw it up." She sighed and looked at her watch. "Now go. We're slammed out there, and I need to help Siena."

She was done talking about it, and he was being dismissed. Owen gave her an awkward hug, and she literally pushed him out the door.

He drove back to the police station with a sour combination of frustration and guilt churning through his stomach, his thoughts going back and forth between Macey and what Leyla had just told him.

It's a hard feeling to get used to.

He should have gone back by Macey's house last night to check on her. He'd wanted to, but he hadn't. He didn't know how he would have felt if Josh's car had still been parked there after midnight, so he'd stayed away.

But really, he did know. He would have felt like shit. He felt like shit now. He'd spent the morning on the phone with pawnshops on the off chance that he could find someone trying to unload her stolen equipment, but the odds weren't good. More likely, everything would be sold online, which would be nearly impossible to trace.

And that assumed that whoever took her stuff wanted to sell it. He could have been looking for cash or drugs or something else of value when he grabbed the bags.

Or the real target could have been Macey and the property was secondary. Owen didn't know, and his efforts to get to the bottom of it hadn't yielded results. Same for Emmet, who was officially in charge of Macey's case but like everyone else right now was distracted with the two homicides. And what if Macey's attack had something to do with those homicides? Owen didn't know how it might be connected, but Leyla was right—Macey's attack was totally out of the ordinary for Lost Beach.

By the time Owen pulled into a parking space, his jaw was sore from clenching his teeth. He grabbed his lunch off the seat as a black Jeep pulled in beside him. Miranda got out.

Owen waited on the sidewalk as his future sister-in-law locked her Jeep and strode up to him.

"Hey," she said, and he saw the excitement in her eyes. "Did you hear the news?"

He glanced down at her hand. No ring. And something told him she wasn't talking about personal news.

"No. What?"

"The crime lab called," she said as they walked up the sidewalk together. "Brady didn't tell you?"

"No."

He held the door for her, and they stepped into the reception room. It was filled with the typical weekend crowd of tourists reporting thefts and lost property, and Owen tamped down his impatience as he waited for Denise to buzz them through to the bullpen.

"What is it?" Owen asked when they were alone again.

"So, they're going through all the evidence from Hancock's house the other day," she said as they walked through the cubicles. "Remember the envelope in his computer bag? The envelope from the Windjammer Inn?"

"Yeah, it had a thumb drive in it."

"Well, get this. They lifted fingerprints off it belonging to *Julia Murphy*."

Owen's pulse picked up. "The envelope or the thumb drive?"

"Both."

He halted beside his desk. "That's big."

When Owen had first spotted the envelope in Hancock's computer bag, he'd thought maybe the Windjammer was a rendezvous spot for him and a girlfriend. Why else go there when you had a perfectly nice beach mansion barely a mile away?

"What's on the thumb drive?" Owen asked.

"I don't know. And neither do they. Turns out it's password protected."

Emmet walked up and looked from Miranda to Owen. "She tell you about the envelope?"

"Yeah."

"Brady called up someone he knows in the FBI's cybercrimes unit in San Antonio," Emmet said. "He sent McDeere up there with the thumb drive to see if they can crack the password."

"When did he leave?" Owen asked.

"Thirty minutes ago. The question is, how long will it take them to get around to it?"

Owen looked across the bullpen to the chief's office. The door was open. Brady was on the phone, and the scowl on his face told Owen he didn't like what somebody was telling him.

"This could be a huge break," Emmet said.

"Let's hope," Miranda said.

"That's assuming the feds don't sit on it for weeks," Owen said.

"They won't," Emmet said. "Brady knows someone up there. He put in a call."

Owen glanced at the chief again, skeptical. Brady had a lot of law enforcement connections, but most of them were old-school. He wasn't aware of the chief having pull with any of the cybercrimes people in the San Antonio field office.

"I wouldn't think much of a business guy having a password-protected thumb drive in his computer bag," Emmet said. "But the fact that Julia Murphy's prints were on it *and* on the envelope it was in tells me it's relevant to our case. What do you think is on it?"

Owen looked at Emmet. "What?"

"The thumb drive. Julia Murphy handled it, so what do you think is on there?"

"If I had to guess? Something to do with sex or money," Owen said. "Two of the most common motives for murder."

TWENTY-SIX

NICOLE EYED THE clouds off the coast as she drove down the highway. It was one of those fronts that could go either way. They would get either a drenching rain or a gorgeous sunset with cotton candy clouds streaking across the sky.

Her phone chimed and she picked it up.

"Where are you?" Owen demanded.

"I just got done tracking down Jackson Schaffer. He doesn't drive a black pickup. It's a white—"

"We need you back at the station."

"Okay. What's up?"

"They cracked the passcode and they're sending the files."

"Already? How?"

"I don't know. But they accessed the drive and they're sending everything over."

"I'm on my way."

Nicole hung up and hit the gas. So much for the pickup truck lead that Owen had been so fixated on earlier. She'd spent the last hour not just tracking down Jackson Schaffer at his workplace but subtly asking around until she found out which vehicle in the parking lot belonged to him. It wasn't a black Dodge pickup but a white sedan.

Nicole ran a yellow light and checked the clock. Mc-Deere had dropped off the evidence in San Antonio less than two hours ago and wasn't even back on the island yet, so Brady's contact really must have come through. Good for him. Or for *them*, really. Maybe this was the break their team had been desperate for. Owen had sounded excited, and he'd said the FBI was sending "everything" over, which implied a lot of files. Or maybe a few big files. Video or photographic evidence would fit the bill.

The parking lot was busy with the typical weekend influx of tourists, so she pulled around to the back and swiped her ID to get through the employee entrance. Brady's office was empty. She found him, Owen, and Emmet in the conference room. Owen sat at the end of the table with a laptop in front of him, while Emmet and the chief stood behind him.

"What'd they find?" she asked as she strode into the room.

Owen didn't look up. "It's downloading now."

"What is it, exactly?"

"Three video files."

Tension hung in the air. Nicole crossed her arms and stared at the screen, and Emmet muttered impatiently.

Owen clicked the mouse and the first file opened.

A woman appeared on the screen. She was filmed from the back walking down a wooden pier. She wore a black bikini, and her long brown ponytail instantly put Nicole on alert.

"That's her," Owen said.

"It's Julia?" Nicole looked at him. "How can you be sure?"

"Flower tattoo on her left shoulder."

The woman turned around and smiled at the camera, and sure enough, it was Julia Murphy. She held up an insulated cooler bag and said something.

"We have audio?" Owen tapped at the keyboard. "Guess not."

Emmet shook his head.

Julia stopped beside a white boat and struck a sassy pose. Then she blew a kiss at whoever was filming her.

The video cut out.

"Go back," Nicole said. "I want to see it again."

Owen went back to the beginning. Nicole's pulse thrummed as she watched the video once more. The last time she'd seen this woman was on an autopsy table, and it felt surreal to see her so vibrant and flirty and full of life.

"Looks like a Boston Whaler," Owen said. "Thirty feet, give or take. Hard to tell from this angle."

"Is this pier at the marina?" Emmet asked.

"Too close up to tell," Owen said. "Maybe."

"Pause it," Brady said. "What's it say on the side of the boat?"

Everyone leaned forward. Owen zoomed in on some blurry black script on the side of the boat.

"*Reel Macoy*?" Brady leaned closer.

"*Reel Magic*," Nicole said. "Anyone know who has a boat by that name?"

Emmet shook his head. "No."

"No idea," Owen said.

"What about Miles Hancock?" she asked.

"I don't know," Owen said. "But we can find out."

She sighed, frustrated.

"What's on the other files?" Emmet asked.

Owen switched to another file and clicked it open.

The next video clip was dimmer and fuzzier. The light

wasn't nearly as good, and it looked like an indoor space with wood paneling, possibly the cabin of a boat.

"That's a bed," Emmet said.

A pair of bodies moved into view. The camera angle didn't show faces, but the black bikini bottoms were the same as before. She untied the string at her hip and tossed the bikini away, and the bodies moved onto the bed.

"Can't see his *face*," Emmet said.

"It doesn't look like Hancock," Owen commented.

Nicole looked at him. "You don't think?"

"Hancock has like forty pounds on this guy. And he's taller."

Nicole shifted her attention back to the video, getting uncomfortable now that they were really going at it on the bed and she was watching this with three men, including her boss. She kept her attention trained on the screen, and her blood ran cold as she thought about where this might lead. Had he filmed himself killing her? Nicole held her breath.

"Tell me we're not watching a snuff video," Emmet said.

Owen muttered a curse.

The video cut off. Nicole stared at the black screen, still holding her breath, afraid to even move.

"That's it?" Brady looked at him.

"That's it for that one," Owen said. "There's one more file."

CHAPTER

TWENTY-SEVEN

MACEY REACHED THE lighthouse and was surprised to find the parking lot empty. It was after five, and she was already late for her appointment.

She scanned the surrounding area. No one was here except for a lone wade fisherman standing in the water off Lighthouse Point. Nerves flitted through Macey's stomach as she looked around the empty parking lot. She'd been anxious for days, checking over her shoulder and jumping at shadows, always feeling like she was being followed. She felt constantly on edge, and she hoped the feeling would wear off soon. She'd never been this high-strung, and she didn't like it.

Her phone chimed in the seat beside her, and she checked the number.

"Hi, Siena."

"Macey, hi. My great-grandma wanted me to call you. I'm sure she mentioned that she doesn't have a cell phone?"

"She did, yeah. Is everything okay?"

"Everything's fine, but she's running late for your meeting."

"Do we need to reschedule?"

"No, she'll be there. My mom is driving her. But she's still at the beauty shop, and they had a mix-up about her appointment. She wanted to get her hair done before your interview."

"Oh, that's sweet. Are you sure she doesn't want to postpone? I don't want to rush her."

"No, it's fine. Really. Nana's finishing up now and she should be there by five thirty. She had the appointment time confused. I think she's getting a little forgetful, to tell you the truth."

"Well, I'm getting forgetful, too, and your nana's about sixty years older than me. I'm happy to wait for her."

"Thanks for understanding."

"No worries at all."

Macey hung up the phone and checked her watch. She had twenty minutes to kill. Siena's great-grandmother was bringing the historical society's key to open the lighthouse for her. Obviously, she wouldn't be taking Macey on a guided tour up all those stairs, but she was going to let Macey look around and she'd also offered Macey a tour of the now-restored villa where she and her husband had raised their family while they'd operated the lighthouse.

"Boy howdy, do I have some stories to tell *you*," she'd said when they set up the meeting.

Something about the old lady's voice and the promise of stories had kept Macey from canceling the interview even though she looked like hell today.

Macey adjusted the rearview mirror and surveyed her face. She'd spent half an hour on her makeup, using every trick she'd picked up from the makeup artists at the TV station to conceal her bruise and downplay the cut above her eye. It didn't look too hideous as long as she kept her sunglasses on.

Macey reapplied lipstick and noticed the tall cranes in the rearview mirror. She checked her watch. She still had some time, so she backed out of the parking space and headed across the highway to check out Playa del Rey.

She parked in front of the giant picture of the resort that covered the fence near the construction site. According to the artist's rendering, the resort would include a six-story hotel overlooking the bay, as well as ten casitas and an eighteen-hole golf course. Besides golf, the property offered two swimming pools, three restaurants, and a full-service spa.

Macey got out of her car and picked her way across the gravel in her white sandals. She'd decided to dress up a bit for the interview, so she was wearing dark jeans and a white eyelet blouse. Her hair whipped around her face, and she took a band from her wrist and pulled it into a ponytail as she gazed through the chain-link fence.

No landscaping yet. Or golf course. The entire plot of land in front of the hotel was a giant dirt pit with big concrete pipes and bulldozers scattered about. Unlike the last time she'd been here, the site was eerily quiet and there wasn't a hard hat in sight. Was work at a standstill because it was Sunday evening? Or because the developer was dead?

Her gaze went to the two cranes that Hancock had refused to move. They were perfectly still now, with the exception of a Texas flag fluttering at the end of one of the giant arms.

Macey surveyed the mess, trying to envision the grand hotel completed and surrounded by lush tropical landscaping. She couldn't. She made her way down the fence line and tried to get a view of the main entrance, but it was blocked by a stack of steel beams.

Her phone chimed, and she pulled it from her purse. Owen.

"Hey," she said.

"Are you at home right now?"

The sharp tone of his voice put her on alert.

"I'm at Lighthouse Point for an interview. Why?"

"Can you step away? I've got a question for you. It's about Miles Hancock."

"Sure, what is it? My interview isn't here yet, so I'm waiting around."

"You said you had a run-in with Hancock when you were snooping around one of his boats."

"Yeah? What about it?"

"Did the boat have a name, that you noticed? Maybe something painted on the side?"

"It was called *Annabel Lee*," she said. "I remember because it reminded me of the poem."

"The what?"

"The poem. It's by Edgar Allan Poe."

"Okay, was this the fishing boat or the sailboat?"

"The sailboat."

"Did you see the fishing boat?"

"No. Why?"

Silence.

"Owen?"

Still he didn't answer, and she felt a surge of annoyance. Clearly, this was something important, and he didn't trust her enough to give her even the slightest indication of what it was about.

"Owen, what—"

"We found a thumb drive at Hancock's house that contains a video clip. Julia Murphy is on the clip."

Macey didn't respond, hoping he'd keep going.

"The video shows her getting on a boat called *Reel*

Magic. And later it shows her having sex with someone on what looks like the same boat."

"Is it Hancock?"

"It's hard to tell. You can't exactly see his face in the footage. Whoever it is, we need to identify him."

Macey didn't comment. She was surprised by the information and the fact that he was sharing it. Maybe he did trust her.

"Sorry to bother you with this," he said.

"No, don't be. It sounds important to your case."

"It is. We need to identify him ASAP."

"Well, I never saw Hancock's motorboat, only the catamaran. You said the boat's called *Reel Magic*?"

"Yeah."

"That name rings a bell."

"It does?"

"Maybe I saw it at the marina or somewhere. If I figure it out, I'll call you."

"Don't stress about it. Just let me know if you think of something."

"I will."

She got off the phone and stared through the chain-link fence, but she wasn't thinking about the resort anymore.

Reel Magic. She'd seen that name somewhere, but she couldn't place it. She was a visual person, but for the life of her she couldn't come up with an image to go with the name.

Sighing, she checked her watch and then turned around to look across the highway at the lighthouse. Still no cars in the parking lot. Her attention was drawn to the lone wade fisherman. The late-day sun shimmered off the water as he cast his line.

And then her thoughts snapped into focus. She took out her phone and called Josh.

"Hey, it's me," she said. "Are you near your computer?"

"Yeah. Why?"

"I need you to look something up for me."

"I was about to go meet Rory—"

"This won't take long. It's for the investigation."

"Okay." His tone changed completely. "What do you need?"

O WEN WHIPPED INTO the crowded parking lot and created a made-up space at the end of a row. He jumped from his pickup and looked around the marina. A cluster of people stood at the base of the steps to Rick's, and reggae music drifted down from the deck.

Owen rushed to the docks, then halted when he saw the gate.

"*Shit.*"

What had he been thinking? He looked around again, searching for anyone who looked like they might be a boat owner and not a restaurant patron.

He spied a blond woman in a turquoise golf shirt. She worked for one of the charter companies. What was her name? Katie? Kristen?

"Hey, Kirsten!"

She turned around and smiled as he jogged up the sidewalk.

"Hi. It's Owen, right?"

"Right." He flashed what he hoped was a charming smile. "Hey, I need a favor. I'm looking for something on the docks, and I need the gate code."

"Oh. Sure." She frowned. "I can just let you in." She started down the sidewalk toward it.

"Don't bother. You can just tell me."

She stopped on the sidewalk and made a pained face.

"We're really not supposed to give the code out. They've been really strict lately."

"It's police business."

"Oh. Well, in that case . . ." She started walking toward the docks again. "What are you looking for?"

"I'm looking for a boat called *Reel Magic*. You know it?"

"Sure. It's on pier 4 with the Conklin charters."

"It's a charter boat?"

"No, it's his personal boat."

Owen halted. "Jim Conklin's?"

"Yeah."

Owen stared down at her. Jim Conklin was the man in the video. The city councilman, not Hancock, was the one having sex with Julia Murphy.

The puzzle piece he'd been missing suddenly slid into place.

"Are you all right?" Kirsten asked.

"Yeah." Owen looked around, scanning the piers and sidewalks. "Is he here, do you know?"

"Mr. Conklin? I don't think so. I haven't seen him in a few days, actually."

"Thanks. You know what? Forget the gate code. Thanks for your help."

He left her looking confused as he ran back to his truck. He jumped behind the wheel and started to call the chief, but his phone buzzed with an incoming call from Macey.

"Mace, I need to call you back."

"I figured it out! *Reel Magic*."

His stomach knotted. "Figured what out?"

"Where I saw that boat. It was in the bay. One morning when I was filming, I saw it out there in the water, and some guy was fishing off the back. Josh sent me the footage and I'm almost certain—"

"Drop it." Owen started his truck and shot backward

from the space. "I need you to drop the whole thing. We've identified our suspect and—"

"But you need to hear this. Owen, I'm telling you I have the boat on film. It's from a distance, but with some work we can enhance the image and—"

"Macey, listen to me. I need you to leave it alone, all right? This whole thing is about to blow up, and I don't want you near it, okay?"

No response.

"Macey?"

"I have to go." Her voice sounded flat.

Damn it, he'd hurt her feelings. He gunned the gas and raced down the road to the highway.

"Macey, sorry to be abrupt, but I need to talk to the chief and—"

"I have to go. My mom's calling me. I have to take her call."

She hung up, and Owen blinked down at the phone in his hand.

He reached the highway and slammed on the brakes. Her *mom* was calling? Her mother was dead. She'd died when Macey was twelve. Why would she say—

It hit him like a thunderbolt.

CHAPTER

TWENTY-EIGHT

M ACEY STARED AT the gun pointed at her chest.

"Get off the phone," he repeated quietly. His voice was calm, but his eyes were wild. "*Now*."

Macey's heart skittered. "I did. See?" She held up the phone.

Jim Conklin walked toward her, scowling, and snatched the phone from her hand. She lurched backward, desperate to get away from that gun.

Conklin shoved her cell into the pocket of his jeans and pointed the pistol at her again. Her stomach did a flip-flop.

"Move," he ordered.

The man's cheeks were flushed, and his too-tan skin was a ruddy brown. The armpits of his turquoise golf shirt were drenched with sweat, and he looked either manic or on drugs or both. That big silver gun glinted in the sunlight.

She tried not to look at it. "What's going on?"

"Shut up and *move*." He thrust the pistol toward her, and she scurried ahead of him. Where were they going?

She spied a big black pickup truck parked about fifty yards away, near the unfinished hotel. Her throat went dry, and she stumbled to a halt.

"I said *move!*"

She started moving again. Her legs felt like lead as she plodded toward the truck.

Never go to a secondary location.

Where had she heard that? She didn't know. But she knew that she had to get away. She couldn't get into that truck. She couldn't let him take her somewhere else, no matter what happened.

Owen knew where she was. Right now he did, at least. Had he figured out her coded SOS?

My mom's calling me. I have to take her call.

Maybe he hadn't been listening. He was distracted with his investigation, and her words might have slipped by.

Macey's heart hammered. The truck loomed closer, and acid sloshed around in her stomach. She had to get out of this.

"What's going on?" she asked, and her voice was raspy now.

No response behind her, just the crunch of his boots on gravel. The boots were brown with chunky rubber soles, like for hiking. She tried to picture the other details about him as she tromped toward the truck.

He was on something. She pictured his bloodshot eyes, which darted everywhere. And he was sweating profusely. He seemed to be under extreme duress, which wasn't good considering he had a gun pointed at her back.

He must have followed her here. All day, she'd had that niggling feeling that she was being watched, and she should have paid attention to it.

How much of her conversation had he overheard? She'd told Owen she had footage of the boat, *Reel Magic*, and a man she now realized was Conklin casting a line. But she hadn't told Owen the rest yet. She had told him that the man on the boat had been fishing, yes, but he'd also tossed something over the side. And a few minutes later when he turned toward land, he froze, probably as he spotted Macey and her tripod on the marshy shore. She'd been there with her camera, capturing the sunrise, and instead she'd captured someone tossing something—maybe evidence or a murder weapon—into the bay.

"Go around," he ordered.

She looked back. "You want me to—"

"Driver's side! Go!"

She walked around the back of the truck.

"It's unlocked," he said.

She glanced around. Could anyone see them? There was no one. Not a soul. They were well off the highway, and there was nobody to notice her being marched at gunpoint to this man's truck.

Panic zinged through her as she reached the door.

"I don't think—"

"Get in." He reached around her and yanked open the door, then prodded her shoulder with the gun.

She climbed into the truck cab, searching for anything she could grab to defend herself. She scooted over the console and snatched a pen from the cup holder. Gripping it in her fingers, she tried to sit on it as she slid clumsily into the seat.

Something on the floor caught her eye. *Her laptop.*

The realization hit her like an icy spray of water. *He* was the one. Jim Conklin had slammed her to the ground and knocked the wind out of her and punched her face with vicious force. Tears filled her eyes as all of it came flooding back. Her chest constricted, and she couldn't breathe. She reached for the door handle just as the locks made an ominous *click*.

Panic spurted through her. She looked at Conklin, and he was watching her, his beady brown eyes intent now.

His pistol was still pointed at her chest, a target he couldn't miss, no matter how bad a shot he was. Could she wrestle the gun away? She remembered the impossible weight of him on top of her on the driveway. He was stronger than he looked, and stronger than she was, certainly. Her only chance was to distract him and unlock the door so she could jump out.

He nodded at the laptop at her feet. "Log in."

She stared at him.

"Let's go!" He motioned with the gun. "Make it fast."

She reached for the laptop, and her sluggish brain started to click into gear. Her film. Of course. That's what all this was about.

She opened the laptop and stared at the dead screen. She powered the computer up. A nature scene appeared—a happy field of sunflowers—and she swallowed a hysterical giggle.

"Come on, let's go."

The passcode box appeared, and Macey's mind went blank. She stared at the box, heart thundering.

"Don't pretend you don't know the code, bitch. You think I'm stupid?"

"No."

Sweat was trickling down his cheeks now, and little drops clung to his chin. The truck cab was hot, yes, but he seemed to be unraveling, too, losing his grip minute by minute. And he still had that big silver gun pointed at her.

"Enter the fucking code."

She took a deep breath and rubbed her sweaty palm on her jeans. Her right hand was still gripping the pen under her leg, and she prayed he wouldn't notice. She used her left hand to enter the passcode.

"Now, here's what's going to happen. You're going to delete all your video files. Every last one. You got that? And

I'm going to sit here and watch you, and if you miss even one of them, I'm going to put a bullet in your brain."

Her stomach clenched.

"Got it?"

She nodded.

Got it? Just like on the driveway. And the acidy, panicked feeling was back as she watched the screen and little icons popped up all over the desktop.

He was going to kill her after she did this. He wouldn't need her. He didn't even need her now, really. She'd already entered the code, and he could delete things himself, but maybe he wasn't thinking clearly.

Her phone chimed, and he pulled it out and frowned down at the screen—just for a moment, but it was enough.

She jabbed the lock button and shoved open the door. He lunged over the console to grab her and she stabbed his hand with the pen.

A howl erupted near her ear as she leaped from the truck and landed hard on her hands and knees. She heard him behind her.

Pop!

She scrambled to her feet and ran.

Owen sped down the highway, swiping at his phone. Macey wasn't answering, and with every second that ticked by he grew more and more certain that something was wrong.

He waited through a series of rings. Emmet wasn't picking up either. He called Nicole.

"Hey, what's—"

"Meet me at the lighthouse," he told her. "Bring backup."

"What?"

"Macey's there, and something's wrong with her. We

were on the phone and she said something weird and the call ended—"

"What, you mean like she's *hurt* or—"

"I don't know! I just know she's in distress! She said her mother was calling her and her mother's been dead for years, and I think she was trying to signal me."

"All right, all right. I'm on my way."

"Bring Emmet."

"He's on a phone call with the FBI guy who sent us the file—"

"Bring Gutierrez, McDeere, whoever's around. Just meet me over there and look for Macey's car. It's a blue Honda."

"Oh shit."

His gut clenched. "What?"

"Are you in a police unit?"

"I'm in my truck. Why?"

"Something just went out over the radio. Something about Lighthouse Point."

"What—"

"Shush! I'm listening."

Owen raced down the highway, gripping the wheel as he held his breath. Over the phone he heard the faint voice of the police dispatcher.

"Nicole?"

"Okay, yeah, it's Lighthouse Point. A report of multiple shots fired."

MACEY RAN FOR the nearest cover—a dump truck. It was parked near a gap in the fence surrounding the job site. She ducked around it, crouching low as she imagined bullets whizzing over her head.

He's shooting he's shooting he's shooting.

The words ricocheted through her brain, confirming all

her worst fears. He was totally losing it. Macey knew his secret, and he thought he could save himself by deleting computer files and then killing her. It was a reckless, crazy plan—not even a plan, but a fantasy—and he was determined to carry it out.

Ping!

Her heart lurched as a bullet hit metal near her head. *Oh my God he's crazy.*

His boots crunched across the gravel as she frantically darted around the dump truck. He could probably see her feet under it, and she crept behind the giant tire. She peered beneath the muddy carriage and spied his boots on the opposite side.

Her heart galloped. Her breath came in short gasps, and she tried to be silent as she looked around. She had to get away from here, but her car was much too far away, maybe fifty yards. A row of big concrete pipes sat just inside the fence. Slowly, trying not to make a sound, she crept to the very back of the dump truck and made a dash for the first big pipe.

She dove inside and crawled to the other end, cringing as she waited for another gunshot. But all was quiet. Had he seen her? Was he following? She hunched inside the cool concrete cylinder and held her breath as she strained to listen.

CHAPTER

TWENTY-NINE

"COME OUT, COME OUT. You can't hide."

Macey's chest clenched as the singsong voice got closer. She inched forward and peered out of the concrete tube at the construction zone. Heavy equipment was everywhere—bulldozers, dump trucks, backhoes. Good hiding places, but between herself and everything was a long trench. She bit her lip and looked around.

She inched toward the opening and spied a pile of steel beams. She could hide behind them. They were bulletproof. And they were closer to her car than her current hiding spot, so if she got the chance, she could make a run for it.

"Macey?"

Her heart jumped. He'd moved farther away. Now was her moment.

She crouched on the balls of her feet and took a deep breath.

She sprinted for the steel beams, staying low and expecting to hear a gunshot at any second. But there was nothing.

She lunged around the beams and tripped to her knees, gasping for breath.

She knelt beside the pile of steel. The knees of her jeans were muddy, and she'd skinned her palms on the concrete. Her hands were shaking, too, and she closed her eyes for a moment and took a deep breath.

Owen, where are you?

She duckwalked to the end of the pile and peered around the beams. The sight of her car gave her a surge of hope. Not too far away from it, there was a narrow gap in the fence. If she could just make it over there without being spotted—"

"Oh Maaaa-ceeeey. Come out, come out!"

Terror shot through her. He was batshit crazy. But he was farther away now, based on his voice. She couldn't wait for Owen, who might not even be coming. She needed to make a run for it now.

A trio of big wooden spools sat between her and her car. The spools were wrapped in some kind of yellow cable. Not as bulletproof as steel, but they'd offer visual cover at least. Macey shifted her weight to the balls of her feet. She took a deep breath and ran.

Pop!

O WEN SET HIS sights on the lighthouse. He floored the gas as he neared the turnoff. Passing the construction site, he glimpsed Macey's car.

"*Shit!*"

He swerved onto the shoulder and slammed on the brakes. Cars whizzed by him on the highway as he shoved his truck into reverse and hit the hazard lights. He sped backward down the gravel shoulder as passing cars honked.

She was at the construction site. What was she doing

there? He reached the turnoff and spotted a black Dodge pickup truck. Owen's blood ran cold.

It was Conklin. Had to be.

Owen reached the gravel road and jabbed the brakes. He shifted into drive and jerked the wheel right as he stomped the gas. At Macey's car he hit the brakes. No one was in it. But the passenger door of the black pickup stood open, and Owen's stomach clenched as he tried to imagine what had happened there.

He scanned the construction zone but didn't see anyone. Cursing, he skidded to a halt by the pickup and pulled out his gun as he jumped out. He did a quick circle of the vehicle and yanked out his phone to call Nicole.

"She's at Playa del Rey, not the lighthouse," he said.

"You have her?"

"No, her car's here."

"I'm almost there."

"Call for backup. I'm going to look for them."

"Them?"

"There's a black pickup here, too. I think it's Conklin's."

"Conklin who?"

"Jim Conklin. *He's* the one in the sex tape with Julia. I'll explain later."

He shoved the phone in his pocket and moved for the construction site, scanning the area for any sign of movement. He walked through an opening in the chain-link fence, his pulse racing now as he looked around. The entire place seemed deserted, and a ball of dread settled in his stomach.

He spotted a flash of white at the far end of the construction zone.

Macey.

She was crouched at the base of a bulldozer that was a football field away, at least. And she didn't see him. He wanted to yell out, but clearly she was hiding from someone, cowering, and he scanned the construction site, searching for the source of her fear.

Movement caught his eye as a figure in blue darted behind a crane. Was it Conklin? The man was a hell of a lot closer to Macey than he was, maybe only thirty yards.

The man emerged from behind the crane. He was holding a gun and making a beeline across the dirt toward Macey. He'd figured out her hiding place.

Owen ran, desperate to close the distance. He wasn't in pistol range yet. He leaped over a trench and darted around a pile of PVC pipe. Conklin was stalking toward Macey with single-minded determination.

Owen still wasn't in range, but he had to distract him. He took cover beside a dump truck.

"Police! Drop your weapon!"

Conklin spun around and lifted his gun.

Pop! Pop!

The windshield shattered and glass stung his face. Owen had gotten off a shot, too, but Conklin ducked behind a pile of steel beams.

Had Owen hit him? Doubtful. He was so far away.

He glanced at Macey's hiding place. She was gone.

Owen ran toward the beams. When he got within range, he took cover behind a concrete pipe and rested his arms on the top.

"Drop your weapon and come out, Conklin! We've got backup coming."

Where the hell were they? They should have been here by now.

Owen scanned the area for any sign of movement. Sweat streamed down his back. Where was Conklin? Was he wounded? Ready to give up? Or was he crouched behind all that steel, waiting for his moment to take another shot?

A flash of white caught his eye, and he darted a look at

Macey's hiding spot. *Stay down!* He wanted to yell it, but he didn't want to draw attention to her. He needed to draw attention to himself.

In the distance, sirens.

"Hear that, Conklin? The police are coming. Put down your weapon *now* or this is going to get worse for you!"

No movement. Nothing. Owen's heart jackhammered. Sweat stung his eyes but he didn't move or blink, just kept his gaze trained on that pile of steel.

A shadow shifted. Owen pivoted as something smashed into him, slamming him to the ground. He tried to get his gun up, but Conklin clamped his hand around his wrist, squeezing with excruciating force and trying to tear the gun away. Owen held it in a death grip. Conklin's face was beet red, his eyes bulging as he struggled for the weapon. Owen held on tight and shifted under him, trying to dislodge the weight while keeping the gun pointed away from his own face.

The sirens grew louder and louder, and Conklin's bulging eyes seemed to get more frantic.

Owen kicked a leg out, struggling to throw the weight off and gain leverage.

A shadow fell over them. A blur of white, and Conklin suddenly tipped sideways onto the ground.

"Police!" someone yelled. "Hands where we can see them!"

Owen seized the moment and leaped on top of Conklin, flipping him onto his stomach. He jammed his knee into his back and pressed the gun between his shoulders.

Nicole swooped down with handcuffs, and Owen held his gun against Conklin's back as she wrestled the cuffs on.

Owen glanced up and did a double take. Macey stood there, wide-eyed, holding a sledgehammer with both hands.

"Did I kill him?" she gasped.

Owen looked down at Conklin. His arms were cuffed behind him, and he winced and grunted as Nicole held down his ankles. Several uniforms rushed over and knelt beside him.

Nicole nodded at Owen. "We've got him."

Owen climbed to his feet, still catching his breath. He tucked his weapon into his holster and stepped over to Macey. She held the sledgehammer so tightly her knuckles were white.

"Did I kill him?" she asked again.

"No." He took the hammer from her and set it on the ground a few yards away. It was evidence now. "Is he alone? Is anyone else with him?"

She blinked up at him, looking dazed.

"Is he alone, Macey?"

"Yes. Just him." She reached for Owen's face. "Oh my God, you're *bleeding*." She touched his forehead, and her fingers came away red. "Did he shoot you?"

"I caught some glass," he said.

She blinked up at him, her face contorted with shock and confusion. Chaos swirled around them as sirens wailed and more police units arrived on the scene. Nicole barked out orders as the uniforms pulled Conklin to his feet and took him to a patrol unit.

Owen looked at Macey. "Are you okay?"

She nodded.

"Are you sure?"

She nodded again, but she didn't look sure at all. He pulled her into his arms, and relief flooded him as he felt her sink against him. Her entire body was shaking.

"It's okay, Macey."

"No, it's *not*."

He squeezed her tightly. "Tell me what happened."

CHAPTER

THIRTY

MACEY SAT IN the plastic chair and stared down at her dirt-caked sandals. The knees of her jeans were muddy, but she rested her elbows on them anyway and buried her face in her hands.

How long had she been sitting here? It felt like hours. It *had* been hours since Owen had driven her to the police station and left her in an interview room with a uniformed officer and a can of Sprite to settle her stomach. Since that moment, Macey had given her statement three separate times to three separate people, including the police chief.

After the second interview, someone had led her to the bathroom to clean herself up and she'd gotten a glimpse of Owen. He'd been in a windowed office that Macey thought belonged to Chief Brady, and several men in suits had been talking to him.

She pinched the bridge of her nose. She felt a headache coming, and the thought of sitting through another minute of questioning made her want to puke.

"Macey?"

She glanced up. A tall man stared down at her with piercing blue eyes. He had a badge and gun on his hip.

"I'm Joel Breda."

She stood. "Where's Owen?"

"Sit down. Please."

She sat reluctantly, and he took the chair beside her.

"How're you doing out here?"

"Fine. Is Owen still back there?"

He nodded. "He's going through some interviews right now."

"Did he get medical treatment? His face was bleeding."

"The paramedic got him fixed up."

Macey stared at the man beside her who looked so much like Owen it was almost unnerving. He talked like him, too, with a deep, low-key voice.

"Owen wanted me to update you."

She nodded.

"Jim Conklin has been arrested and charged with attempted murder."

Macey's stomach churned.

"We're working on a boatload of other charges, and the FBI is involved."

"Why?" she asked.

"He's an elected official. It's looking like a public corruption case."

Macey tried to digest that idea. Had someone been bribing him? Extorting him? She tried to work through it, but her brain felt like mush.

"Owen's talking to some federal agents now," Joel said, "and it's liable to take a while. I know you've been out here an hour already."

It felt like much longer.

"Owen asked me to take you back to our house to wait for him. My girlfriend, Miranda, has some dinner going. I think you met her earlier, back at the crime scene?"

Miranda was the CSI, the woman in the white coveralls who'd been photographing everything. They'd met while Macey was standing near the back of the ambulance answering questions from a paramedic who seemed to think she had a concussion—probably because she was acting so spacey.

Joel was watching her now with a look of concern.

"Miranda, yes." She cleared her throat. "I met her."

"Owen's going to be tied up for at least a few more hours. So, can we give you a ride?"

Her car was still back at the construction zone, which she'd been informed was an active crime scene, probably until tomorrow.

She checked her watch. "Thank you, yes. I'd appreciate a ride. But I'd like to go home."

His brow furrowed. "Are you sure?"

"Yes. I need to clean up and take something for my headache."

Clearly, this wasn't the answer he wanted, but he nodded and stood up. Macey grabbed her purse and cast a glance through the glass into the bullpen. Cops were everywhere— Lost Beach officers, sheriff's deputies, FBI agents—but she saw no sign of Owen.

Joel held the door for her as she stepped from the station house into the sticky night air. Reporters milled on the sidewalk, and Macey hurried to put on sunglasses before anyone recognized her. She stayed close to Joel as they walked toward the parking lot, and no one seemed to notice her.

A black Jeep sat off by itself on an empty row. Miranda stood beside it with a skinny brown dog at her feet. The dog got up and wagged its tail as they approached.

Miranda smiled. "Hi, Macey. I'm so glad you finally got out of there. Long day, huh?"

"Yes."

The dog trotted over and licked her hand.

"Benji, no."

"It's okay." Macey held her fingers under his nose and then patted his head.

"Macey wants to go back to her house," Joel said.

"Oh?" Miranda shot him a worried look, then turned to Macey. "Are you sure you wouldn't like to have dinner with us? I've got a pot of chili going. You must be starving after being stuck in there all night."

"I'm fine, actually. All I really want to do is clean up and crash."

A look passed between Joel and Miranda. But they didn't argue, much to her relief.

Joel opened the Jeep's passenger door and pulled the seat forward. The dog jumped in, and he started to follow.

"Oh, I'll take the back. I'd love to sit with Benji."

"You sure?"

She climbed inside before he could object and settled into the seat beside the dog. Benji put his paws on the console and looked excited for the ride.

Macey cast a last look back at the police station and realized she still had her sunglasses on and it was ten at night. She took them off and shoved them in her purse.

They passed a row of news trucks, and Macey's stomach knotted as she saw the one for her former employer. Her television job seemed like ages ago, but it had only been a few months.

They turned onto the highway. Macey stroked Benji's head and stared out the window blearily as the neighborhoods whisked by. The Jeep was loud, and the noise saved her from having to make conversation. She was tired of questions and timelines and racking her brain for details she couldn't recall.

She couldn't stop thinking of the sledgehammer and the sickening *thud* as it made impact with Conklin's shoulder.

If she'd connected with his head, he'd probably be dead now.

"Why didn't he shoot him?" Macey blurted.

Joel turned in his seat to look at her. "Come again?"

Macey's cheeks flushed. She hadn't meant to ask that. But the question had been running through her mind for hours, and it just sort of jumped out.

"Jim Conklin. He tackled Owen to the ground and tried to get his gun away." She glanced in the rearview mirror at Miranda. "I keep wondering, why didn't he shoot him?"

Joel glanced at Miranda before settling his gaze on Macey. She could tell he knew the answer to her question but didn't want to tell her.

"Conklin was armed with a Kimber 1911 Stainless. Are you familiar with that pistol?"

Macey shook her head.

"It holds seven rounds in the magazine and one in the chamber. Near as we can tell, he fired eight shots. Miranda collected the shell casings." Joel paused. "He was out of bullets."

He was out of bullets.

That was the reason Owen wasn't dead right now. And Macey, too. The psycho who'd attacked her in her driveway, marched her at gunpoint to his truck, and stalked her through that muddy construction zone had been out of bullets.

Macey suddenly felt cold all over. She ran her hands over her arms and looked out the window. Tears welled in her eyes, and she forced them back. She didn't want to cry. Not here, not in front of these people. Owen had almost died today trying to save her life, and the only thing that had stopped that from happening was that Jim Conklin had run out of bullets.

They pulled onto Primrose Trail, and Macey braced her hand against the seat as the Jeep bumped along the pitted road.

"It's the white one, just after the boat trailer," she said.

Miranda pulled into the driveway, and Joel hopped out.

"Are you sure you'll be okay here?" Miranda asked.

"Yes, thank you."

She gave her a worried look. "I'm glad to meet you, Macey, but I'm sorry about the circumstances."

Macey rubbed Benji's head and forced a smile. "Glad to meet you, too. Thanks for the ride."

Joel offered a hand to help her out.

"I'll walk you up," he said.

"Oh, you don't need to do that."

"Lead the way."

She didn't bother trying to argue, as he was obviously just as stubborn as Owen. She dug her keys from her purse and unlocked the front door.

"Why don't you wait outside while I do a quick once-over?" Joel asked.

It wasn't really a question, so she stepped aside as he walked in and did a brief check of her house. After everything that had happened today, Owen probably would have done the same.

"All good." He stepped out and pulled a card from his pocket. "My cell number is on the back there. Call if you need anything, okay? We're just down the road."

"Thanks." She took the card, but he seemed hesitant to leave.

"Sure you're okay here alone, Macey?"

"Absolutely. I'm fine."

OWEN'S HEADLIGHTS SWEPT over the ramshackle houses. The sight of Macey's place made his stomach clench. The floodlight shone down on the driveway, but the rest of the house was dark. All of it. The bedroom windows, the side windows, the deck. Not a glimmer of light upstairs anywhere.

He checked his watch. It was 3:23, so why was he surprised? Joel had said she'd been dead on her feet earlier.

Owen drove past her house and turned around at the end of the block. Then he killed his lights and rolled to a stop by her mailbox. He looked up at the dark bedroom window, and that hot, suffocating feeling was back. He couldn't shake loose of it. When he'd seen Macey's abandoned car at that construction site it was like someone gripped his heart in a tight fist.

Owen wiped his forehead with the back of his arm. He was sweating again. He'd been sweating all night, even in the air-conditioned police station. He smelled rank and he looked like shit. His hair was filthy, his jeans were streaked with mud, and he needed a shower.

He checked his watch again, then looked at Macey's window and thought about waking her up. He tried to rationalize it. But she'd been through two back-to-back traumas and she had to sleep. The last thing she needed was him showing up dirty, smelly, and desperate for sex.

In the seat beside him, his phone glowed as a text silently landed.

RU coming up?

He glanced up at the window and thought he saw the curtain shift.

Owen cut the engine and got out before he could talk himself into doing the right thing. His pulse thrummed with a strange combination of nerves and giddiness as he trekked up the stairs. She was on the deck—just a shadow in the dark—and his heart turned over.

"Hey," she whispered.

"Hi."

She slid her arms about his waist, but he stepped back.

"You don't want to get near me," he said, taking her hand instead.

"Why were you sitting there?"

"I thought you were asleep."

"I tried, but I couldn't."

The door stood open, and she tugged him toward it. He crouched down to untie his boots. He left them outside and stepped over the threshold into the darkened living room. The only light came from the faint glow of a small TV on the wall opposite the couch.

"I've been watching Alfred Hitchcock movies," she said, pulling him toward the sofa. "Have you seen *Vertigo*?"

"No."

He went back to lock the door and wondered if she was in the habit of forgetting stuff like that. Something else for him to worry about.

He raked his hand through his hair. It had dirt and debris in it from wrestling on the ground with Conklin.

"I need a shower," he said.

"You're fine." She sat on the couch and patted the cushion beside her. "Come watch. It's the last scene."

He glanced around, then grabbed the bunched-up blanket next to her and moved it to a chair. He sat down and looked at her in the dim blue light of the TV.

She wore a silky white robe, and her hair was loose around her shoulders.

He reached for the glass on the table and took a gulp of whatever it was. Watered-down cranberry juice. It cooled his throat but didn't settle his nerves.

Why was he nervous? This was Macey.

Which was why he was nervous.

The past few hours had been an emotional roller coaster unlike anything in his life, and he still felt waves of panic hitting him at odd intervals.

She scooted over and rested her head on his shoulder, and he got a nose full of her floral shampoo.

He should ask to use her shower. But her body was warm and soft, and he slid his arm under her legs and pulled them into his lap.

She looked at him in the dim blue glow. The swelling of her eye had gone down, but the bruise was darker, and looking at it put a smoldering rage inside him. He'd never truly wanted to kill a man. Until today. Owen's chest got tight, and he felt sweat breaking out on the back of his neck.

"What?" she whispered.

He shook his head.

"What?"

He reached out and traced his finger down the side of her face. "I hate that he did this to you."

"Stop looking at it."

"I can't help it."

She sighed, resting her head on his shoulder. "It's almost over."

She meant the movie. But he wasn't watching. He was staring down at her slender arm draped over his stomach. He wouldn't have thought she could lift that sledgehammer, much less swing it solidly into a man's shoulder. She'd done that for *him*. She could have fled to safety. She'd had her chance, but instead she'd jumped into the middle of an armed struggle.

The room went dark as the movie ended.

She shifted around so she was facing him. He held her loosely in his arms, and she pressed a kiss against his neck. She eased back to look up at him, and he wished he could see her eyes better. He ran his finger over the side of her face, taking care to avoid the bruise.

"It's too dark. I can't see you."

She sighed. "That's the idea."

He kissed her forehead softly, and she seemed to sense his hesitation. He knew it bugged her, and she wanted to gloss over everything that had happened and pretend nothing was wrong. It had been the same the other night when he'd tried—and failed—to resist her.

The thing was, she did it for him. Her body, her touch, her smile. Part of him wanted to drag her off to bed and lose his mind with her. And another part of him wanted to kiss her on the forehead and then leave her alone. She needed a friend tonight, but all he could think about was pinning her under him and pounding out this burning frustration that had taken over his life.

She shifted to her knees on the sofa.

"What is it?" she whispered.

He shook his head.

She eased onto his lap, and he rested his hands on her hips. Her robe felt cool and slippery under his fingers. She kissed the side of his neck, making her way from his ear to his throat.

"I'm dirty."

She licked him. "Salty."

"Seriously, Macey, my clothes are filthy."

"So take them off."

He kissed her and slid his hands over her hips, pulling her close. Her body was warm and lush, and just kissing her opened up this bottomless pit of need inside him.

He eased back to look at her. He didn't like to talk about his feelings. But he felt compelled to try. He needed her to know.

"Today scared me," he said.

It was the most honest thing he'd ever said to her. To anyone.

"Me, too."

She leaned down and kissed him. Her mouth was hot and

sweet, and she tangled her fingers in his hair. He slid his hands up to cup her breasts through the fabric, and her soft moan completely did him in. He scooped her under him and shifted on top of her, settling his weight between her thighs.

"*Finally.*" She smiled up at him. "I've been waiting for hours."

She was trying to make things light, but he couldn't play along. He had too much crazy shit swirling through his head. He gazed down at her, and the sight of her beneath him made it hard for him to breathe.

"Are we ever going to talk about this?" he asked.

She reached up and stroked her finger over his cheek.

"Not now. I can't. Right now I just want to be with you."

CHAPTER

THIRTY-ONE

Six weeks later

N ICOLE STRODE INTO the bullpen and spied Owen standing at his desk. She changed course and walked over.
"Good, I caught you," she said. "You have a minute?"

"I'm heading out."

"This will just take a sec. Let's grab a conference room."
He frowned at his watch but then followed her.

It would take longer than a "sec," but she needed to update him in private. According to her FBI contact, the case
was at a turning point.

In the days after Conklin's rampage at Playa del Rey, his
motives started to become clear. Conklin had been one of
the key council members who opposed Miles Hancock's
waterfront golf course, and the delay over permits had cost
the developer hundreds of thousands of dollars. While Hancock was bleeding money over the stalled project, he'd gotten wind of the married councilman's affair with Julia
Murphy and come up with a scheme to force Conklin to
change his vote. The FBI believed that Hancock used

expensive gifts and cash payments to get Julia to pass along video evidence of the affair so Hancock could blackmail Conklin into switching his vote. Conklin did, and construction resumed at Playa del Rey.

The extortion scheme worked at first, but then Hancock lost control of it because he underestimated the young woman at the center of everything.

Julia Murphy decided to work both sides. When Conklin tried to end their relationship, she hit him with more money demands. With the ongoing threat of exposure hanging over his marriage and his political career, Conklin snapped. He killed Julia and set Hancock up to take the blame before killing Hancock, too.

Nicole closed the door to the conference room and sat on the end of the long table. Owen crossed his arms and looked at her.

"What's wrong?" she asked.

"Nothing."

"You've been in a shitty mood since lunch. What happened?"

"Nothing happened. I want to get out of here. I've been here since four a.m. because of the gas station holdup."

It was more than that, but Nicole let it drop. If Owen didn't want to talk about what was wrong, he wasn't going to.

"I heard from my FBI contact," she said. "They got another break."

Owen looked even more annoyed now—possibly because he hadn't wanted to turn over weeks' worth of backbreaking work to the feds. Of course, they'd promised to keep LBPD in the loop, but the reality was that Owen's team had been cut out. For weeks, Nicole had had to scrounge for tidbits from her FBI contact.

"They got an interview with Conklin's wife," Nicole told him. "Turns out, she and her kids were out of town the week before Memorial Day—including the night when Julia was killed. That corroborates their theory that the murder happened at Conklin's house."

The physical evidence supported this, too. Fingerprints recovered from the house belong to Julia, but Conklin's defense attorney might be able to explain those away by saying Julia and the councilman were having a consensual affair. The fingerprints alone didn't prove murder. And Conklin's pickup truck wasn't conclusive either. There were thousands like it that could account for the parking lot surveillance cam footage.

"So, the wife's statement, along with the forensic evidence, is making for a solid case."

Owen sighed. "I know."

"Add in what the dive team recovered, and it's a slam dunk," she said.

After analyzing Macey's video and using the embedded geolocation data, investigators had pinpointed the location of *Reel Magic* in the film. A team of divers had searched the area and recovered Julia Murphy's cell phone and purse half-buried in silt. The DNA evidence from Julia's fingernail wasn't back yet, but when it came in, it was sure to make the case even stronger.

Owen stood there, arms crossed, just looking at Nicole.

"Well, aren't you relieved?" she asked.

"Yes."

"Yeah, I can tell." She rolled her eyes. "I thought you'd be elated. This is your first major case to lead, and everything's coming together finally. If he pleads, then we won't have to have a trial." She stared at him, waiting for a reaction. "Macey won't have to testify," she continued, stating the obvious. "That's what you've been so worried about, isn't it?"

A knock sounded at the door, and Emmet poked his head in. He looked from Nicole to Owen. "Hey, did you talk to Brady?" he asked with a grin.

"No."

"What is it?" Nicole asked as he stepped into the room.

"It's done, man. He's toast."

"Who?" Nicole asked.

"Conklin. Word is his attorney got a look at Macey's video."

Owen tensed at the mention of Macey. "What happened?"

"All I know is they're talking about a plea deal now."

"What's on the table?" Nicole asked.

"No idea, but I'm sure he just wants to avoid death row," Emmet said. "I'm guessing life, no parole."

Owen frowned. "I'm surprised Conklin didn't push for a trial."

"I'm not. He's lucky to get a deal," Emmet said. "There's no way his attorney wants a jury to see a video of his client tossing a murder victim's phone into the bay. He'd get obliterated."

Owen checked his watch again and looked at Nicole. "Is that it? I've got to go."

"Sure. See you tomorrow."

Owen left, and she and Emmet stared after him.

"What's with him?" Emmet asked. "I thought he'd be happy."

"I don't know. He's been pissed off since lunch."

"Why?"

"No idea," she said, although that wasn't really true.

She would bet her badge that whatever was wrong had something to do with Macey.

MACEY'S HEART SANK as she reached the marina. She parked in front of Owen's building but didn't see his truck.

Disappointment needled her. He'd been working crazy

hours, including getting called out of bed early this morning. He'd told her he was off tonight, though, and she'd been hoping for some time alone with him. She had good news to share, and she'd been sitting on it for an entire day.

Macey grabbed her gym bag and got out of her car. Rick's was busy tonight, and steel drum music drifted down from the deck. She went to the back of the building and hurried upstairs. She was sweaty from her class and wanted a chance to clean up before Owen got home.

Macey let herself into the apartment and hung her bag on the hook near the door. She was careful not to leave her stuff all over the place. Owen didn't care, but she did. She was constantly aware of the fact that this was his space, not hers, although she'd fallen into the habit of spending almost every night here, only going back to her place to use the editing room and put cat food out for Possum.

Macey checked her phone. Still no word from Owen, although she'd texted him on her way over to get his ETA. It hadn't taken her long to learn that radio silence on his end usually meant he'd caught a new case and could be in for a long night.

Macey kicked off her flip-flops and walked into the bathroom. Tugging her ponytail loose, she stood before the mirror. She wasn't avoiding her reflection anymore. Her bruise had healed weeks ago. The dark circles under her eyes were gone, and her skin was looking better lately. She actually had color in her cheeks, and smiling came more easily to her—especially with Owen.

Just the other day, Josh had told her she looked like herself again—whatever that meant. Macey's perception of herself had changed this summer as she gradually began to process all that had happened.

Therapy hadn't worked for her. Macey had gone to two group sessions, and although she'd liked the people and listened intently, she hadn't been able to open up. She'd wanted to, but the words wouldn't come out of her, and the whole thing seemed pointless. Maybe she had too much of her taciturn father in her. The things she felt most deeply she couldn't express out loud.

What *had* helped her was tae kwon do. After a lifetime of being a nonathlete, she had finally found a sport. She'd been going three times a week for a solid month, and she loved it. When Siena had initially suggested the class, she'd been wary. But the first time her foot made impact, something inside her clicked. She couldn't quite figure it out because she'd never been a very physical person. She hadn't grown up with contact sports or siblings to wrestle. But with every kick and punch, she felt a surge of confidence.

Macey untied her white belt and set it on the counter as her phone chirped with a text from Owen.

RU home from TKD?

She smiled at the message. Maybe there was hope for tonight after all.

Yes about to shower, she responded.

Skip it. Put on something comfortable and come down to the picnic table.

She stared down at the message. Something comfortable? What was he up to? Whatever it was, it was sure to involve food. She threw on a T-shirt and shorts and freshened up quickly before heading downstairs.

Owen wasn't at the picnic table, but Macey recognized the smiling woman in a turquoise golf shirt. Macey scanned the lot for Owen's pickup as she walked over.

"Hey, Kirsten. Have you seen Owen around?"

"No, but he asked me to give you this." She grinned and held up a paper bag.

"He told you to give this to me?"

"It's from Rick's." She handed her the bag. "I think it's your dinner. And he asked me to bring you to the boat docks."

Macey's heart melted. "He did?"

"Yep."

"Okay, then."

They set off down the sidewalk, and Macey scanned the long piers. She spied a small white boat gliding through the water. A warm glow spread inside her at the sight of Owen at the helm, all tall and tan and windblown.

"There he is." Smiling, Kirsten tapped in the code and pushed the gate open. "You two have fun."

"We will." Macey stepped through the gate. "Thank you for helping with his plan, whatever it is."

"Well, he didn't explain, but I'm sure you'll enjoy it." She looked at Owen and gave a wistful sigh.

Macey knew exactly how she felt, and she hurried to the end of the pier to meet him. He wore a faded blue T-shirt and shorts, and it was a relief to see him without a badge and gun for a change.

"Hey, stranger."

"Hi." He smiled up at her, but he looked distracted as he tied the boat to a cleat. "You get the bag from Kirsten?"

"Yes, and it smells appetizing." She held it up.

"Here. Watch your step." He hopped onto the pier and held her arm as she stepped down into the boat.

"Is this the boat you keep at Joel's?" she asked.

"Yep. *Angeline*."

"Who's it named after?"

"Long story."

He stepped down to join her as she looked around. It was

a pristine white boat with six seats in back and a V-shaped bench in front.

She glanced up, and Owen was watching her with an expression she couldn't read. Something was bothering him. She could tell.

"What's wrong?" she asked.

"Nothing." He brushed a lock of hair from her face and kissed her. "You ready?"

"I don't know. Where are we going?"

"Sunset Cove."

She smiled. "Oh my gosh. Really?"

The corner of his mouth ticked up. "You've heard of it?"

"Sure. Why are you laughing?"

"It's a popular make-out spot."

"Oh. Well, I didn't know *that*, but now I'm even more excited."

"We need to hurry if we want to catch the sunset." He stepped behind the wheel. "You want to sit or stand with me?"

"I'll stand."

"Okay, hold on."

She braced her hand on the top of the windshield while he pushed the throttle forward and they got moving. The breeze wafted around them, and she looked out at the bay as they passed the orange buoy marking the no-wake zone.

Owen looked at her. "Hold on tight, now. You ready?"

She braced her legs apart and tucked her fingers into the waist of his shorts, and the warmth of his skin put a tingle inside her. "Ready."

He pressed the throttle forward, and they picked up speed. Soon they hit waves, and she gripped the top of the windshield for balance as they bumped over the choppy water. The air smelled briny, and water misted her skin. She closed her eyes and savored the wind on her cheeks and the vibration of the boat.

"Sure you don't want to sit?" he asked over the noise.

"I like it here."

He looked ahead, and she followed his gaze to a distant indentation in the shoreline. She watched the coast, taking in all the beach houses and boat docks and palm trees. She loved seeing the island from the water, and she'd been spending as much time as possible on research boats filming and interviewing the naturalists who worked on the bay. It was a unique place, and she felt lucky to be here.

She eyed the streaky pink clouds to the west. The sun was sinking fast.

"Will we make it?" she asked.

"Yes."

She wrapped her arm around his waist, absorbing his body heat as they cut through the waves. Finally, they neared the cove. He made a wide arc and slowed. Macey was surprised to see all the vessels already anchored, a combination of sailboats and ski boats, even a few kayaks.

"Popular spot," she said.

"Yep."

They went to the south side of the cove, away from the other boats.

"This okay?" he asked.

"You're the captain."

He idled the engine and stepped to the bow. With brisk efficiency, he took out the anchor and lowered it into the water. After securing the line to a cleat, he returned to the helm and gently reversed the boat to set the anchor.

"We made it." He glanced at the sun. "Just in time. Go sit up front before you miss it. I'll bartend."

"Need help?"

"Nope. There's a blanket under the seat cushion. Starboard side."

"Starboard. Check."

She opened the compartment beneath the cushion and found a navy fleece blanket. As she sat down, she realized it made the perfect pillow so she could lean back against the sloped windshield to watch the sunset.

Owen pulled a flask from a cooler and poured something into a red plastic cup filled with ice and juice. He handed her the drink.

"Wow, a bar on board, too. Why do I get the feeling I'm not the first woman to visit this make-out spot with one of the Breda brothers?"

He lifted an eyebrow. "No comment."

He grabbed a beer for himself and twisted the top off, then came to join her. "Scoot up."

She moved up and he sat down behind her. Then he pulled her back so she was settled against his chest.

She sipped her drink and tucked the cup into the cup holder near her feet. As she leaned back against Owen, a feeling of calm settled over her. She gazed up at the sky as a line of pelicans soared over and the boat bobbed gently on the waves.

"This feels good." She sighed. "How come we haven't done this before?"

"You've been working all the time."

"Uh, so have *you*."

"I know, I'm just teasing you." He kissed the top of her head. Quiet settled around them. Right before their eyes, the clouds were transforming from pink to fiery orange as the sun neared the horizon.

"Thank you," she said.

"For what?"

"Bringing me here."

He laced his fingers with hers and kissed her temple. "Are you happy, Macey?"

She felt a twinge in her chest, and she squeezed his hand. "Yes." She turned to look at him. "Are you?"

He nodded.

"I know I've been a little erratic lately," she said, thinking of the restless nights and the mood swings. She could go from snappish to weepy in a heartbeat, over nothing at all. He'd been understanding, but it had to be giving him whiplash.

She cleared her throat. "I know I'm moody. And hard to be around. You probably think I'm going to fall apart at any minute."

"I don't think you're going to fall apart. You're one of the toughest people I know."

Tough? Given that many of the people he knew were cops, she found that hard to believe.

"Well . . ." She didn't know what to say. "I know you've been worried about me. But I'm doing better." She squeezed his hand. "Things are good."

She turned to glance at him, and he was watching her again with a look she couldn't read. Now was the time to tell him. She shifted to face him.

"So, I have some news." She smiled. "You know that project we bid on with the state chamber of commerce? It came through. Can you believe it? I didn't think we had a chance."

He nodded. "Congratulations."

She searched his face. "You don't look surprised."

"To tell you the truth, I'm not." He paused. "I bumped into Josh today, and he told me about it."

She huffed out a breath. "When did you bump into Josh?"

"I picked up lunch at the Beanery, and he was there." He squeezed her hand. "Don't be mad at him. I think he assumed you'd already told me."

She shook her head and turned away, irritated that Josh had spilled her news before she was ready. She'd wanted to have this conversation on her terms, and she'd been waiting for just the right moment.

"Is there a reason you didn't?" Owen asked.

She caught the edge in his voice. Maybe now they were getting around to what was bothering him.

"I guess . . . I'm pretty overwhelmed by it," she said. "Making tourism ads for the state? It's a huge project, and I never thought we'd land it." She tried to put her feelings into words. "Ever since I started this business, I've been hoping for the best but bracing for the worst, you know? I don't think I ever dared to believe my little production company could actually succeed."

"Why not? You're really talented."

His words gave her a warm rush. He'd seen her work, and he'd been so supportive.

"I'll be traveling a lot, but it'll be worth it because the money's good," she said. "It'll keep us going strong while I finish my documentary. I couldn't ask for more than that." She looked at him.

"So, a lot of traveling?"

She nodded. "We'll need to scout locations. And of course filming. We can keep our base of operations here. Josh is really attached to Lost Beach, and he's been spending a lot of time with Rory." Her pulse was thrumming now as she got to the part that had been making her nervous. "I'm attached, too. When my lease ends next month, I'm thinking of staying."

She shifted to face him, and the look on his face made her heart squeeze. He closed his eyes, and she could feel his relief down to her bones.

"Owen . . . are you okay?"

"Now I am. I've been going crazy thinking you planned to leave."

"Why didn't you just ask me?"

"Because." He slid his hand over her thigh. "You've been dealing with a lot. I didn't want you to feel pressure from me on top of everything else." He leaned his forehead against hers. "People have been telling me to give you space and be patient. But patience isn't my thing."

"Who's been telling you?"

"Leyla. Nicole. Miranda."

She pulled back, surprised. "You talked to Miranda about it?"

"Yeah, I trust her." He paused. "Also, she had a violent incident last summer, so I thought she might know what I should do to help you. I feel like I'm flying blind here."

His words pierced her heart.

"You *have* helped me. You have no idea how much." She moved closer and slid her hand over his knee. "Spending time with you . . . I love it. You don't make me feel pressured at all. About anything."

He shifted to look her directly in the eye. "I want to spend more time with you. I've been wanting to ask you to move in with me."

She felt a flurry of nerves.

"You have?"

"Yes."

She smiled slightly, even though her heart was racing and she suddenly had a lump in her throat.

"What do you think?"

"I don't know." She swallowed. "What if I get all my gear over there and you change your mind?"

"I won't."

"How do you know?"

"Because." He lifted their joined hands and kissed her knuckles. "I know that I love you."

Macey's chest squeezed. She hadn't expected those

words from him. She searched his face for any hint that he was being lighthearted, but his blue eyes looked serious.

He kissed her, and everything melted away—the worries, the logistics, the perfect words she could never find to explain the rainbow of emotions she'd been feeling lately. None of it mattered except that he was *here*, and whenever she was with him, things simply felt right.

Owen touched her cheek as he eased away, and she wanted to freeze the moment. She never wanted to forget the sun on his face and the tender look in his eyes. She'd thought she'd been in love once before, but she'd been wrong. This felt different. Deeper. *More.* She wanted to tell him, but her throat felt tight, and the words wouldn't come.

"Hey." He slid his arm around her and pulled her gently against his chest. "I didn't tell you that to pressure you. You don't have to say it back." He kissed her mouth before she could respond. "But can I convince you to come live with me, and we can give this a chance?"

"You've already convinced me." She slid her arms around him. "There's nothing I want more."

Keep reading for an excerpt from
Laura Griffin's next standalone suspense novel,

VANISHING HOUR

Coming in fall 2022 from Berkley

M OLLY DIDN'T HAVE enough water.

It was a common mistake. But that didn't make it any less dangerous on a day when the air was like a hair dryer and the slightest trace of moisture vanished from her skin in seconds.

A horned lizard scampered across the creek bed and paused beside a rock, seeming to mock her with his natural adaptation to the environment. He darted behind a boulder, and Molly stepped into the meager strip of shade provided by the canyon wall.

The sun was almost directly overhead now, which definitely wasn't part of the plan. She pulled her water bottle from her pack, and her heart skittered.

Less than a third left.

How could that be?

She'd been careful, but not careful enough. The two-hour trek had taken twice as long as expected, and the sickening notion that she'd made a wrong turn was starting to take hold.

Trying not to panic, she set her pack at her feet and dug out the hand-drawn map. She'd pored over it by flashlight in her tent last night, memorizing every curve of the trail and every word of Camila's loopy script. Studying the landmarks, the conclusion was inescapable.

She should have reached it by now.

Molly tucked the map away. She twisted the top off the water bottle and took a tiny pull, barely enough to wet her throat. She was angry with herself. She hadn't prepped right—everything from her shoes to her water supply was all wrong. She couldn't afford to be so careless.

Anxiety bloomed in her chest as she dug out her cell phone. She stepped into the middle of the creek bed and powered up.

No bars, of course. She would have been shocked if she'd managed to get any. She tipped her head back and gazed at the cloudless sky. A swallow flew over and swooped into a mud nest beneath a ledge.

Molly's breath caught. *There.*

She took a few steps back and stared at the twisted juniper clinging to a rocky outcropping. The tree's tortured shape was unmistakable.

She tucked away the phone and water bottle and slung on her pack. Skimming the sloped canyon wall, she spied a faint trail.

Molly scrambled up the path, grabbing tree roots and warm rocks for balance. Thorny branches snagged her shirt, but she jerked it loose as she hurried up the trail. When she reached the top, she turned around, and there it was.

Panting, she stopped and took a moment to admire the axial twist, like the double helix of a DNA strand. But this life-form was even more mysterious.

Snap.

She turned and scanned the arid landscape. Green mesquite bushes fluttered in the sunlight, and a shadow shifted near a giant sotol. On instinct, she reached for the .22 in the pancake holster at the small of her back. She rested her hand on the pistol as she surveyed the brush. Mountain lions were rare in this area, but she had an irrational fear of predatory mammals. She didn't want to get between a mama and her kittens.

Snick.

"Hello?"

She listened closely, but the only sound was the faint whisper of wind through the scrub brush.

She turned to face the tree again. The Angel Tree. She didn't know who had named it or why. Heart thrumming now, she pulled out her water bottle again and took a sip to calm her nerves. The sip became a guzzle. Now that she'd reached her destination, she knew exactly how long it would take to get back. She slipped off her pack and set her gear on the ground. Then she took a deep breath and approached the tree.

It was taller than she'd expected. She studied the gnarled branches and peeling bark, noting the scattered rock piles from the hikers—pilgrims—who had come before her. Tentatively, she reached out to touch the trunk.

Nothing.

She stayed totally motionless, but nothing happened. She didn't feel a thing. A still, silent minute elapsed and then the wind gusted, kicking up a dust devil nearby. Delight zinged through her. Coincidence? Or something else? She didn't used to believe in "woo-woo nonsense," as her dad would have called it.

She didn't used to believe in a lot of things.

Once upon a time, she'd been practical. Logical. But desperation had a way of thwarting everything.

A warm tear slid down her cheek, and she brushed it away. Awe and reverence washed over her in a cooling wave. She took another deep breath. Now what? Should she say a prayer? Meditate? She'd never had the urge to build one of those damn rock piles, and now was no exception. But she had to do something to mark the moment.

Snap.

She whirled around.

"Hello?" she called, louder this time.

Molly squinted at the line of mesquite bushes. A man stepped out, and her heart jumped into her throat. He was tall and broad-shouldered. The brim of a baseball cap cast a shadow over his face. As he moved closer, she got a better look at him, and relief flooded her.

"Oh, it's you," she huffed. "What are you doing here?"

Not answering, he took another step. She caught a flare of something in his eyes. Her gaze dropped to the leather holster at his side, and she watched with disbelief as he slipped the pistol out.

She stepped back and looked at his eyes again. "What do you want?" she croaked.

His mouth spread into a bone-chilling smile. "I think you know."

AVA FOLLOWED THE curve of the dirt road to the string of emergency vehicles. She checked her watch and cursed. She was later than she'd thought.

"Not good, Huck."

The black Lab nudged her arm with his wet nose.

"We're going to have to redeem ourselves."

Ava passed a sheriff's SUV and squeezed her little red

car between a pair of dusty pickups from the parks department. Huck whimpered with impatience as she grabbed his lead off the seat and clipped it to his collar.

"Okay, let's do this."

Ava slid out. Huck hopped over the console and followed her. She felt dozens of eyes on her as she popped open the back hatch and retrieved her day pack. Hitching it onto her shoulder, Ava scanned the faces. None were familiar. All were skeptical. Several of the men wore the Henley County Sheriff's Office backcountry uniform of an HCSO ball cap, a navy T-shirt, and desert-brown tactical pants.

Ava spied some park rangers in olive green milling near a blue tarp that looked like operation headquarters. Beneath the makeshift tent, two rangers studied a map that had been spread out across a pair of tables.

"Help you?"

She turned around as a man sauntered over. Tall, sixty-ish, paunchy. He wore a sheriff's office cap and sweat-soaked golf shirt. He stopped in front of her.

Ava smiled. "Are you the incident commander?"

"I'm Sheriff Donovan."

"Oh." *Shit.* She thrust out her hand. "Ava Burch, West-Tex S and R."

He shook her hand and frowned down at Huck.

"We're here to help with the search," she added.

"They started five hours ago."

"Yes, I know. I was unavoidably delayed." She sensed a brush-off coming, and she glanced around. "Do you know who the IC is on this one?"

"That'd be Mel Tyndall," he said, nodding in the direction of the blue tent.

"Oh, good. I'll check in with him."

She led Huck away before the sheriff could think of any objections. She zeroed in on the park ranger who seemed to be giving orders—a wiry man with wraparound sunglasses perched atop his shaved head. Ava stepped under the tarp, and he glanced up.

"I'm Ava with WestTex Search and Rescue. Earl Dunn said you could use a hand today?"

Dropping the name of the chief ranger in nearby Big Bend seemed to do the trick. Tyndall stepped away from the table and looked her over.

"Are you trained up?" he asked.

"Yes."

He glanced at Huck, who wore his work vest. "Him, too?"

"Yep. He's logged more than a hundred wilderness searches."

She didn't mention that most of those had been with a different handler. But Tyndall seemed too distracted to nit-pick her credentials. He checked his sports watch and returned his attention to the table.

"The first teams deployed at oh nine hundred," he said. "We're just getting started on sector D."

Ava stepped closer to examine the map. It was a detailed topo of Silver Canyon State Park. A small red sticker near a campground marked what had to be the PLS, or point last seen. Sections bounded by natural barriers had been marked with letters.

"We just sent a team out to Lizard Creek Trail," Tyndall said, tapping the map.

Ava's stomach knotted as she studied the spot. Sector D was well outside the high-probability search area. They were getting desperate.

"You up for it?" Tyndall asked.

"Absolutely."

He handed her a clipboard. "Sign in, and I'll brief you on the way over."

Ava quickly jotted her info on a card and followed the ranger to one of the dusty white pickups. She stowed her pack on the floor and hopped into the passenger seat, signaling Huck to sit on her lap.

Tyndall wasted no time pulling out and maneuvering onto the pitted dirt road that Ava had just navigated. Huck pressed his head against the glass, squirming with excitement as they passed all the police vehicles.

Tyndall slid on his shades and glanced over. "You're new to the county?"

"Been here since November," she told him.

"Done any ops yet?"

"Three this spring in Big Bend."

They bumped along the narrow dirt road and hung a right onto an even narrower one. Ava visualized the state park in her head. She was familiar with it, but only from a few casual day hikes. She'd never been on a search team here.

"Silver Canyon is different," Tyndall said. "It's rugged country."

She turned to look at him. Big Bend wasn't exactly a golf resort. The sprawling national park consisted of more than eight hundred thousand untamed acres. But Ava understood what he was getting at. Silver Canyon was a new addition to the state park system, and it lacked even basic amenities.

"We've only got one paved road," the ranger continued. "It makes an outer loop. The interior roads are dirt, and they tend to wash out when we get a flash flood. The only cell service is near the entrance, so everything's by radio."

"Okay."

"Did Earl tell you about the op?"

"Just that it's a child missing."

Tyndall nodded. "A boy, three and a half."

Ava's heart sank.

"Noah Dumfries. He's been missing since oh eight hundred. Wandered off from his family's campsite after breakfast. His mom thinks he went down to the creek to brush his teeth."

"Have they—"

"We had a canine team there all morning. No sign of him."

Ava looked out the window at the limestone canyon baking in the midday sun.

"He's just over three feet tall, blond hair, brown eyes. He's wearing a red Spider-Man T-shirt with blue shorts and white sneakers."

She glanced at him. "What about the parents?"

"Mom is distraught, as you'd expect. She's at the campsite with her other son, who's five, in case Noah comes back. Dad is at the ranger station. He wanted to join the search, but we convinced him to stay back."

It was standard procedure. When a child went missing, there was always the depressing possibility that the parents could have something to do with it.

"Do they have any pets?" she asked.

"No idea. Why?"

"I want to understand if he's afraid of dogs."

"I don't know. I can find out, though."

He swung off the dirt road onto what looked to be a horse trail. He bumped across the feather grass and headed for the base of a tall cliff. A wooden sign came into view.

Tyndall skidded to a halt.

"Lizard Creek Trail," he said. "The other team deployed to the east about—" He checked his watch. "Fifteen minutes ago."

"Do they have a dog with them?"

"No. It's two of our seasonal rangers."

Ava's heart sank again as she looked out the window.

Seasonal was code for summer interns. And she knew what Tyndall was doing here. Inexperienced volunteers were being banished to the low-probability areas while law enforcement veterans conducted the real search. Ava got it—Tyndall didn't know her from anyone. And he didn't know Huck. All he knew was that she'd shown up five hours late and he'd never worked with her before. But with the clock ticking and only one other dog in the search party, it was a waste to give her a crap assignment. Especially with a missing child case. Under normal circumstances, a lost kid would have pulled in resources from all the neighboring counties. But a helicopter crash in Big Bend this morning had gotten a jump on everyone's attention, and the National Parks Service had no one to spare right now.

Tyndall reached into the back of his truck cab and grabbed a radio. "How much water you have there?" He nodded at her pack.

"A gallon."

"That for both of you?"

"Yeah."

"Better take more." He grabbed a bottle of water from the back and handed it to her.

"Thanks." Huck squirmed on her lap, anxious to get started. He'd been trembling with excitement since she put on his vest.

"You and your dog are Team Six," he said. "Check in every half hour, no exceptions."

"Okay."

"And it's hot out there. Don't forget to drink."

"Got it." She pushed open the door.

"You're headed west," he continued. "Cover as much ground as you can and meet back here in four hours." He checked his watch. "We'll have someone here to pick you up."

"Got it."

"If you see anything at all, call it in. Time is of the essence."

"I know."

He looked Huck over with a frown, and she knew what he was thinking. With his thick black fur, he was going to melt in this heat. But Huck was tougher than he looked. They both were.

"How old is he?" Tyndall asked.

"Four."

"And the medal on him?" He nodded at the silver medallion on his collar.

"St. Anthony, patron saint of the lost." She gave a self-conscious shrug. "It brings him luck."

"Luck, huh?" Tyndall squinted through the windshield at the sunbaked cliff. "Well, we're going on hour six here, so we need it."

Ready to find
your next great read?

Let us help.

Visit prh.com/nextread